Joanna Kavenna grew up in Suf............., ...d
has also lived in the USA, France, Germany, Scandinavia
and the Baltic States. Her first book *The Ice Museum* was
a poetic travelogue about northern lands, described by
Michael Holroyd as 'a most original book, both scholarly
and adventurous' and by Benedict Allen as 'an astound-
ingly self-assured debut'. She currently lives in the Duddon
Valley, Cumbria.

Further praise for *Inglorious*:

'Her stagnation is described with brilliant, paradoxical
energy and much last-ditch laughter . . . I loved it.'
Observer

'Rosa is like a female version of Withnail, and her failures
in the face of her peers' successes make her story a modern
spin on Gissing's New Grub Street.' *Daily Telegraph*

'Kavenna writes beautifully as she traverses the daydream,
dreamscape and nightmare . . . An elegant treatment of
the frequent unfamiliarity of modern life.'
Financial Times Magazine

'Smart, funny and warm.' *Elle*

'Kavenna has nailed Rosa precisely, imbuing her distress
with a dark, hopeless humour that surfaces in her undoable
to-do lists and caustic self-awareness. Her skewed world-
view casts a troubling, penetrating and often funny gaze
on middle-class values.' *Independent*

JOANNA KAVENNA

Inglorious

faber and faber

First published in 2007
by Faber and Faber Limited
3 Queen Square London WC1N 3AU
This paperback edition first published in 2008

Printed in England by CPI Bookmarque, Croydon

A CIP record for this book
is available from the British Library

ISBN 978-0-571-23261-1

2 4 6 8 10 9 7 5 3 1

For BM

But if he stood and watched the frigid wind
Tousling the clouds, lay on the fusty bed
Telling himself that this was home, and grinned,
And shivered, without shaking off the dread
That how we live measures our own nature,
And at his age having no more to show
Than one hired box should make him pretty sure
He warranted no better, I don't know.

Philip Larkin

Chi non può quel che vuol, quel che può voglia

Leonardo da Vinci

RETREAT

She began it on an ordinary summer's day when she found – quite in contravention of the orders of her boss – she was idling at the computer, kicking her heels and counting. Rosa Lane, thirty-five and several months, aware of an invisible stopwatch tolling her down, was counting the years, the hours spent sitting in offices, staring at the sky, at the flickering screen that was sending her blind. She had spent the previous ten years in a holding position, her legs locked under a table. She had typed a million emails and strained her wrists. She was no closer to understanding anything. Ahead she saw the future, draped in grey. Behind was the damp squib of her family's history. She was sitting in the present, with this past and future whirling around her. And outside the city was awash with daytime noise – the grind of traffic, blurred speech, elusive choirs. The noise was ebbing and rising again, and she heard the cries of birds in the eaves. She thought of the river moving and the flow of cars, smoke drifting across the shine and colour.

Sitting at her desk that day, sweating into her shirt, she thought, *If they told me I would never do anything more than this, would I want to live or die on the spot?* Then she thought, *What is the reason for it all, what is it for?* That really cut her up, so she wrote an email to her boss. It was terse and elegiac. It began with her youth, early career, thanked him for his patronage, communicated her deepest regrets and ended with the words 'I resign'. She was emphatic; she pressed Send and then she shut down her computer. She picked up her hat and coat and walked. She was having a fit of nerves by the time she passed the guardians of the gate, the two fat porters who sat there trading jokes. They sauntered towards her. If they had spent another second rattling the keys she would have crumbled and begged them to lock her in for ever. Then the gate swung open. 'Off home early,' they chorused, and released her. Rosa went out onto the street, where the cars were queuing to go forward. Then she went home.

It was a Monday in June when Rosa left her job. It was early afternoon, and she sat on the semi-empty train marvelling at the space, the available seats. She felt a gust of air as the doors swept shut. She stared at the adverts for phonecards and car insurance. Palliatives, she thought. She glanced at the passengers, barely noticing their distinctness. A less concentrated crowd but still part of the hordes. She laughed at an advert and picked her ear. A man caught her eye and she quickly dropped her gaze. She observed the dirt on the walls, she traced her fingers round the stains on the seats. She filed every detail of the carriage away.

She was at Dante's mid-point, the centre of life, when she was supposed to garner knowledge and become wise. This was assuming she had used her earlier years for study and application, like the poet, but she had measured them out in weekend binges and European holidays. For years she had been productive at work and as idle as anything in the evenings. Time coursed along and she earned money. She stayed firmly in her box. She had been a journalist for years, sliding her way upwards. She wrote on the arts. She understood – it was quite plain to her – that she was meant to be ruled, not to rule. She hardly had the mettle for power play and the tyrannical control of fiefdoms. Her life had been supported by a few buttresses: belief in her job, the love of her parents, her relationship with Liam. These had stopped her thinking about anything too deeply.

Yet recently she had been feeling dislocated. The death of her mother, in January, was the start of that. She understood it was natural process, inevitable and unquestionable, but it knocked her off course and she couldn't right herself again. She went into work and was congratulated on her perseverance, but at night she was troubled by bad dreams, grief sweats, fear of the void, internal chaos that she tried to keep well buried, aware that her experience was general not exceptional and she really ought to button up. She missed her mother, of course, she felt the lack of her like a deep soundless blackness, and she thought it was impossible that this should be the natural condition of life. She felt as if a seismic shift had occurred; the ground had fallen away, revealing depths below, shapes clad in shadow.

Her mind was casting out analogies, hints at a deeper complaint. She felt restless and she had vivid dreams. Her thoughts held her, stopped her being useful. She lacked a defining metaphor, a sense of coherence. She felt coerced to the social pattern, her instincts dulled. She needed a local mythology, some sense of a reason why. Instead, she was teeming with frenzy and obscenity. She could curse her way home, damning the street and condemning the innocent and guilty alike. And she noticed that her sense of things was changing, it bemused her to think about it. Instead of seeing herself as the centre of her own small world, with the city as the backdrop to her life, she began to see everything as a fractured mess, a wild confusion of competing atoms, millions of people struggling to live. She lacked a doctrine, a prevailing call. She was surrounded by monomaniacs, yet she was indecisive. All ways looked as impassable as the others. She was in a labyrinth, lacking a ball of twine! Disoriented as anything, and she couldn't kneel and pray, she was sure that wouldn't help at all.

In March, concerned about how detached she was feeling, she'd asked Liam to marry her. Liam said no, which shocked her profoundly. More than shocked, she was deeply offended. They flagged on for a few more months, but anyone could tell their relationship was holed below the waterline. There were days when she felt it all as dark comedy, bred of the absurd situation she found herself in. With the clock ticking, she was spending her indeterminate span of years on the Underground, holding on tight to a metal pole, sitting at her desk checking her emails, earning money and lining her belly. This sense of the ludicrous crept into her prose. In April she'd written an article on Swedish contemporary dance, which opened: 'Dark, dark, dark we all go into the dark. The dancers have all gone under the hill.' The editor had sauntered over to her desk, and demanded that she erase the offending lines on her computer. 'Never,' he said. 'Never quote that crap again.'

By May she was writing in fragments. It was unfortunate, as her job was to write and explain, to produce quantities of lucid prose. Instead, she stared at the computer, with the bare notes of a story in her hand. Embarrassed, she wrote: 'The Modernist Novel'. After another hour she wrote: 'Rosa Lane reports'. Then it was lunchtime and she wrote: 'If Lunch be the Lunch of Love, Lunch On.' Then later she wrote: 'Shuffle Off' and 'Mortal Coil' on two lines. Then she accidentally pressed Send, and emailed her few phrases to her editor, who ignored them. Her focus seemed to be slipping. Where once she had read the paper every day, noting the preoccupations of society and her colleagues, now she flicked through a few pages and tossed the thing away. She was left with odd words – 'BLAME', 'WORSENS', 'REPRIEVE', 'SILENCE' – and some images of a screaming mother, a model clad in satin, a bomb victim. None of it made any sense. Now she wrote: 'I want. We want.' And then she wrote: 'What is it?'

There was an evening in late May when she found herself standing on a street – she wasn't entirely sure where she was – and then it seemed to her that the street was widening and widening and the numbers of buses and cars multiplying indefinitely, and there were rows and rows of people stretching eternally, and the ghosts of the dead vivid and clear in the dusk. 'I had not thought,' she said out loud, attracting silent glances from the habitués around her. 'Bloody hell there's a lot of us,' she added. She reeled past the Albery eyeing the neon haze and the streetlights and the shadows seeping from the winding alleys. Then the crowds seemed to vanish altogether, and she thought of purse pinchers and long-gone hawkers, the flotsam of another era. She thought of them with their capes and cloaks and buckled shoes, and their hats and moustaches and the smell of the streets – dung and offal. They vanished too, and she imagined the city dead and gone, a fierce wind blasting across the earth. She shrugged that off, because it was making her worry. Because the buses looked teeming and drunk with weight she walked home. Three hours later, she arrived at her flat, grimy and sweating, talking quietly to herself.

Leaving her job had a few immediate consequences. Peter the editor called her up, which had never happened before. Gravelly and disappointed he said, 'What are you doing, Rosa? Are you ill?' Not ill, she had explained. She told him she was fine. She wanted a change of direction. 'Towards what?' he demanded. It was as if she had blasphemed in church. She thought of him, a holy confessor with a beard and a belly, sitting in his office with a view of the street. He never went home before 10 p.m. He had a wife and an assortment of children. A well-paid, powerful job. He lunched with politicians, artists, writers, contemporary sages and wide-eyed pundits; anyone he asked to lunch came along, talked to him with commitment. A Good Life, in his terms. 'You've worked so hard to get to this point,' he said. She thanked him, but she said she couldn't go back. 'Ridiculous,' he said. 'Give me a call if you change your mind. Don't leave it too long.'

She said, 'That's very kind.'

'Come on, Rosa, give it another go.' It sounded reasonable and she said she would think about it. She thanked him and then he was gone for ever. 'Do you really want to squander everything?' – that was Grace's version, two days later. Grace – compassionate, withholding evidence – hectored her over a bottle of wine. A hectoring from Grace was no ordinary hectoring. It had sound and fury, high drama. Grace was truly dazzling. She liked to smoke and blast out words. She was incessant in her talk, and that had first attracted Rosa to her. She was a comparatively new friend; it was hard to say if she was more Liam's friend than Rosa's. Rosa had found her at a party, and she swiftly became a fixture. She brought around takeaways and wine and spent long hours at their flat. She was good to be with: she was witty, hilarious, in a conspiratorial way. At parties, she whispered asides behind her hand. Like Liam, she was charming. She glistened with charisma.

'Do you really want to sink without trace?' Grace added. The phrase stuck in Rosa's brain. Sink without trace?

'I assumed I would,' she said. 'It's what we do.'

'Rubbish!' said Grace. 'Total rubbish!' Her hands were folded in her lap. She kept her gestures succinct and certain. She smiled as she spoke but she was steely all the same. When she smiled she showed dozens of shiny teeth. Her hair was blonde and she wore it round her shoulders like a vestal virgin. She looked elegant, as she always did, in a skirt that hugged her hips, an open-necked shirt that showed her verdant olive skin. Still, she was inquisitorial and there were certain things she stridently defended. Sitting with her legs crossed, brow furrowed over the matter at hand, Grace said, 'You owe it to yourself.'

'I have exerted my right to choose,' said Rosa.

'And you choose failure and ignominy,' said Grace, into her stride. Any moment, thought Rosa, she would raise a fist. She would stand and cry, 'To Arms!' 'What's your plan?'

Rosa had no plan. This caused Grace to release another tight smile. She looked briefly as if she pitied Rosa. Well, perhaps she did, because Rosa was in a sorry state, timorous and plaintive, picking at her nails with an empty glass before her. She had drunk too swiftly and now her head was clouded and her concentration was slipping. Still Grace had something to teach her. 'Always plan before you leave a job,' she was saying. 'Or the other way round, never leave a job without a plan. Are you hoping Liam will support you?' This she said leaning forward, face close to Rosa's, glass of wine in one hand, orb of justice in the other.

'No, not really.'

'Not really? Not really? Come on, Rosa, don't be ridiculous! You can't expect him to do that. You don't really expect him to do that, do you? What do you mean by not really?' Suddenly Grace seemed unhappy. Her mouth twisted and she looked pained. That was unusual for Grace, who conducted herself with compelling sangfroid, and it made Rosa stare at her. She thought it was something about her indecisiveness, her complete failure to act, which was distressing Grace.

'I mean probably I don't,' she said.

Now Grace became quite ferocious. She set down her glass and looked Rosa deep in the eyes. 'Rosa, you have to explain this. Probably? Please tell me what you're feeling,' said Grace.

And, nervous because Grace was so fixed on her, Rosa said, 'No, you're right. I have to stand alone. I was inert, idle, generally lazy. It's a shock when you hit the water, cold on your limbs, but now it's better. Now I am beginning to change.'

'Exactly, you said it,' said Grace. 'Don't just depend on Liam. That's a foolish thing to do.' She seemed to relax. She had been holding herself upright, looking angular, and now she curved again. Grace had a delicate slouch. She hunched her shoulders like a child. Her sudden tautness was perplexing at the time, then they moved on.

As for her father! Well, Rosa genuinely frightened her poor father. She understood the deal. He had worked hard, and now he expected a leisurely decline. His wife was dead and for a time he had been a wide-eyed embodiment of grief, quite crazy in the living room, later unkempt in the garden, given to sudden fits of weeping. He wept like he was dying, gasping and holding his head. Really, in the nineteenth century he would have died and they would have said it was from his broken heart. But the doctors had buoyed him with remedies. They cranked him up again and now he was running along well enough. He was not happy, certainly, and it bothered Rosa that she was making him anxious. Still, he had other matters to consider. Aside from the weight of grief,

9

heavy upon him, he was seventy, living on his pension, a recent convert to all sorts of homeopathic medicines, observing a waiting-room diet of fruit and vegetables. If he didn't make her his top priority she understood why. 'I don't expect any help,' she told him when he called to berate her. He held her up, pinned her so she couldn't struggle and told her off as if she was a child. On the counter-attack, Rosa began, 'I'll manage fine –'

'You always do,' he said, interrupting promptly. 'You always did, I mean, until now. I understand, Rosa. I feel desperately sorry. But this isn't the right thing to do.'

'No no, no,' she said. 'It's not a bad thing. I've decided to take stock,' she said.

'Take stock, what does that mean?'

'I've been feeling a little under the weather. As if I'm suffering from . . .'

Malaise. Intellectual disintegration. Epistemological meltdown. A strange rash on my arms that won't be treated. Hypochondria of the undistilled sort. An aversion to conversation. Acedia plain and simple.

'From what exactly? Really, Rosa, we must get to the bottom of this. You can't just run out of a good job for no reason. Whatever the circumstances, you can't do that.'

'I'm not running out for no reason. There's a compelling reason. Viz, I can't possibly do the job.'

'Why not?'

'It's reality, father,' she said, reluctantly. 'Reality is an empty abandoned town, as Musil said. Or was that imagination? Anyway, I don't see how I can sit at my desk presenting reality to people, tailoring it for view, commenting glibly on daily events, when I have no idea what is going on. Do you, really? Gamma rays, for example, I know nothing about them. Any of them. Invisible forces, belief systems, philosophies of the way, I know nothing.'

'Do you have the money saved to retrain?'

'No, I don't have any money saved.'

'Rosa, that was extremely irresponsible of you.'

'It's terrible, I agree. I've been duped.' *The best scramble to something they call affluence, hysterical borrowing and material clutter. The worst – well, who was she to talk about the worst?*

'You could have bought a flat, if you'd wanted to,' said her father. 'Then at least you would have something to show for yourself.'

'No, no, that doesn't matter. The property ladder!' And she thought, *The property ladder is a grand illusion – everything dangling out of reach, and the ladder running up and up higher and higher to a grand crash, the Götterdämmerung of wage slaves, in which the liveried masses will fight a final battle for a small house to call their own and be slain in droves and burnt to a crisp. From the ashes of the wage slave apocalypse will arise a better world.*

Meanwhile her father was saying, 'It's all so sudden, and extreme. Your mother wouldn't have wanted you to throw everything away.'

'Look, I'll be honest, Dad,' said Rosa. 'I'm never going back to that stinking pigpen. I'm not snuffling for scraps any more. I'm off to find the grail. *Il me semble que je serais bien, là òu je ne suis pas*, as Sartre said. To be plain, I am discarding the *Schweinerei*. I will have no more of it. Lie your own lies, Dad. I'm off to the temple of truth, wherever the hell it is.'

'Rosa, you should go and see a doctor,' said her father.

'That's not on my list.'

'Your response is disproportionate. Your grief is disproportionate, self-destructive. You refuse to accept that life is hard. Things are never perfect,' he said. He was always ready with a platitude. He was good at them, quite adept in their use. Some days he talked in fluent cliché. But so did she. It was a genetic trait. Her family had been unoriginal for generations.

'I understand. I'm one of the lucky ones' – this she told herself a thousand times a day.

'Well, now you'll find out,' said her father.

'Find out what?'

'If you are one of the lucky ones,' he said.

The other immediate consequence – aside from those that revealed themselves later, including debt, social ostracism, and a few other minor trials – was the end of her relationship with Liam. That was the storm-lashed bark, but really she would have stepped off long ago had the weather been better, the sea altogether calmer. She should have left months ago; that would have been the decent thing to do. But she was weak and a coward, clinging on. Liam, by contrast, and surprisingly, became clinical, like a surgeon. He assessed her chances and decided she was not going to come through. On the day she left her job he came to her with a thin smile. 'You did what?' he said. 'Really? You did that? Why did you do that?' That! Of all the things she could have done. For Liam, it was the last straw. He wanted to cast her out, denounce her. Then he shook his head. He gave her a profound look. It was an illusion, but Liam was a proper denizen, a firm believer in progress. 'Let's not discuss it,' he said. 'Let's eat.' He was terse that evening, and she wondered what he was about to say. He usually judged her harshly; he liked to tell her she was self-dramatising and, sometimes, obscene. He threw her a sortie of stern glances, pierced her with harsh looks, and turned to his food. Recently he had stopped finding her funny. They were both misbehaving at the time; neither of them was being reasonable. Rosa had an excuse, she had the stark fact of recent bereavement, loss of meaning, acedia and the rest, but really she hadn't been reasonable for years. Their life together looked impermanent. Things were definitely going down the pan. She didn't blame it on Liam. But she hadn't thought about it too hard. She had left her job, and now, she thought, she would get to grips with everything, all the things she hadn't been thinking clearly about. She had begun to mistrust herself. Her own self – that was a schizophrenic state, a piece of blatant nonsense. She needed to change her circumstances, but she was lazy and her habits were ingrained. Even so, she was sanguine as she sat there, casting glances across the table. She was upbeat, slightly restless. It was the summer, and she always liked the summer. She had walked out of the office, never to return, but she enjoyed the shifting of the seasons. Her plans were basic at the time, she was thinking of deep blue skies and how much she liked wearing shorts. She was planning evenings at the Windsor Castle pub, sitting in the garden with friends drinking wine. Saturday mornings, reading papers on Westbourne Grove. The season, she imagined, would run along as the seasons had been running along for years. No one really worked in the summer. They went to summer parties, drank wine from the ritual plastic goblet, and talked about sport. She would take up the guitar again. She would bake bread and cultivate window boxes. She would train rigorously and run every day. By the autumn she would be fit and lively again. She was only relieved she didn't have to go to work the next day.

Liam was quiet and watchful for a week, and then he said it all. It was a fine June evening when he spilled it. On that evening, like so many others, they were having a quiet meal. The only sound across the silence-shrouded table was the click of cutlery. They were like a pair of venerable cockroaches, dining together. She had cooked fish and vegetables with sauce from a packet. She hadn't taken too much time over the details. They were living in a high-rise block by Notting Hill tube. From their living room they could see the city, glowing and sparkling beneath, the cars weaving patterns of light, the buildings rising towards the centre. There was an orange glow hanging over it all, a dusty halo. The evening was crisp, the air was thin, and the noise of traffic filled the room.

Liam had no sense of occasion. He disliked high drama. He despised parties; he refused even to celebrate his own birthday. He was deeply uncomfortable at weddings. He thought it was all a fuss, a suspicious fuss. So he had hardly prepared a vio-

13

lent scene. He was dressed in his usual innocuous way: trousers in a cotton fabric, a long-sleeved blue T-shirt. He hated to be conspicuous. He never raised his voice and he disliked confrontations; it was why he struggled in his job. He could generally see the other side of an argument. He called it negative capability and referred proudly to Keats. She thought it was cowardice. They were all afraid, Rosa was afraid of a lot of things, most of them inchoate or unmentionable, but Liam was afraid of his boss and this enraged her. He mostly didn't try. He assumed that his opponents were benighted, but he lacked the will to convert them. He'd suffered a few minor hitches, the painful discrepancy between aspiration and realisation. Still, he was successful enough as a political lobbyist. He had a firm handshake; he looked good in a suit. He was plausible whatever he did.

Usually, they were measured with each other. He had thanked her for dinner, a solitary foray. 'Thanks so much. Delicious sauce.' 'Sainsbury's very own,' she said. 'Delicious.' 'Mmm, I know.' It was the sort of script that ended with a murder. Or death by mutual tedium. Someone had to crack! Now he was looking carefully at her, wiping his mouth. The dining room was untidy. They had a lava lamp in the corner, which had once seemed like the height of irony. The curtains were purple velvet and had been made by Rosa's mother years ago, when she was a seventies queen of home-baking and floral skirts. They had hung in the living room when Rosa was a child. They made the flat look like a stage, prepared for an amateur production, a village panto or a motley farce. In recent months she had found they pained her, brought it all back, her vanished mother, the very thoughts she was trying to evade. She had thrown out a lot of things, photos and letters, but she had left the purple curtains hanging there.

The floor of the dining room was covered with newspapers they somehow never managed to throw away, and the living room was just as littered with ephemera. They had a long black leather sofa and black leather armchairs, which matched nothing else but amused them both. Really, neither of them had any sense of style. Rosa had hung some pictures on the walls, West Country landscapes from her parents' house. The walls were white. Rosa distrusted colour and didn't like to use it. It made for an ascetic effect. Visitors often thought they had recently moved in. But they had been there for years.

Liam was rocking back on his chair. In this bland room, wearing bland clothes, Liam was a beautiful man. It was always a shock to Rosa to see how beautiful he was. Now, after ten years, they no longer spoke about the things that concerned them. It was another sort of quietness, like the quietness Rosa found enveloping her prose. He was beautiful, but Rosa wasn't whipping herself too hard. Rosa and Liam had certainly dropped out of the idyll. Their pocket utopia had decayed and a feeling of strain had developed between them. Familiarity made them slovenly with each other; they barely made an effort in their conversations. They gossiped in an easy way, about friends they had known for years, about their jobs. They liked to squabble about the washing up. Of course they loved each other. They had a shared past; they had been friends before they fell in love. Rosa had found Liam fascinating at the start: he was a handsome awkward man, her favourite type. Her love was a mixture of inevitable cliché and basic lust and a sense of shared sympathy and she liked his hurried way of speaking. It was easy to romanticise him, and she did for a few years, until they began to bore each other. They moved in together a few months after they began their relationship; they were inseparable, they couldn't bear to spend a night apart. When he went away for a few days she was bereft. Later they couldn't spend a night apart because the habit was so ingrained.

She had become insensitive and bullish, tardy in her praise. He had become obsessed with the minutiae of their living arrangements. It was impossible for her to explain it to anyone else, it sounded too much like an argument between people who have lived together for too long, but Liam picked at

15

everything she did, an amiable, almost affectionate picking, but it vexed her all the same. It made her reluctant to decide anything for herself, the colour of a cushion, the contents of the fridge, because Liam was likely to complain, gently, mildly, but complain all the same. It all got rancid, touched with fraudulence. When he was irritated his mouth sagged at the sides. He looked like a mangled piece of fruit. And Rosa was like a nought, her mouth constantly open in self-exoneration. She spent far too much time explaining why she put the towels where she put them, or the bread where she put that, or the rest. It was bad for them both. At work, Rosa was an efficient, sensible woman, or had been until she became inefficient and completely nonsensical. But at home she was ill at ease.

'Why do you bother?' she had asked. 'Why does it matter at all?'

He would seem to understand, but ten minutes later it would start again. 'Just leave that.' 'Why are there crumbs on the floor?' 'What is this doing here?' 'Where is my phone?' 'Don't move it again.' 'What is this?'

Initially she had rebelled, they had fought over trivia, and then she had compromised. She adhered to his customs, she obeyed the edicts of the kitchen, the rigid laws of the living room. Whatever she did, Liam was fussy; he developed an aversion to water, a loathing of open windows, a set of strange ideas about how you hung dishcloths. So they had piles of perfect dishrags and a committed silence about important things.

'Do you do it because you are trying to control me, or the environment?' she asked.

'You are the environment,' he replied. Beautiful Liam, so young-looking, with his muscular frame, his air of health, his smile, his ready charm. A handsome man. Women adored Liam. Men admired him. But she saw him as a nag, a man with his head in the dirt under the table.

When she had posed the question – trying to fix herself to a ritual, eager to get herself locked in to something permanent and unceasing, marriage, a romantic idea, good for morale, a ceremony, a party, her father would be pleased, fantastic, a wedding! and so on – and Liam had said no, of course they knew that was it. That precisely was it. Their own miniature Armageddon. The death of love! Completely trivial compared to the chaos around them, of course. It was hard to keep a sense of perspective. For herself she felt her miniature life was going badly. Her mother dead and burnt, and like a sap-headed coward Liam had stalled. He said he loved her, but it wasn't quite right. He had a few things to sort out. They could discuss it in a few months, he said. The rest – on he had gone, like a nervous actor given a difficult speech. Since then, she had been idle and uncertain but really she was waiting for the end. Unable to effect it, but expectant.

On that evening – the finale – Liam looked particularly beautiful. His brown, wavy hair, curling onto his collar. His small nose, which dipped towards his firm lips. The severity of his jawbone. His wide shoulders, his almost hairless chest. His long elegant legs, his small waist, his bony ankles. His white, crooked teeth, chipped at their ends. When she saw him curved into the chair she wanted to fall to the floor and beg for forgiveness. Instead she stood and began to clear the plates away. He was still silent, intent on his glass of wine. He looked fascinating. It was only when he opened his mouth that he betrayed himself. Then he poured it out, a steady stream, placatory words, words for falling asleep to. He didn't believe them anyway, he just poured them out. It was beauty-worship, she had diagnosed it long ago. She would hardly have loved him so long, had he not been so beautiful. Recently they had become more polite than ever. It had to be a bad sign. When Grace came round – which she had been doing constantly in recent months, as if she feared to leave them alone – she mocked them for their silences. She chain-smoked and explained that they had developed a fatal caesura. She sat there with her thin hands outstretched, refining her points.

Grace was a towering extrovert – 'fatal caesura' precisely the sort of showy phrase she would come up with – but she was considerate. When Rosa's mother died she had been formidable, relentless in her kindness. Though she had never met Rosa's mother, she said many things that even now Rosa remembered. Decent understatements, offers of help, quiet maxims. 'Don't ruin your life. Your mother gave her life up for you. Don't make her sacrifice worthless.' 'Don't sink. You owe it to yourself. You've tried so hard. And worse will come.' Really once Rosa wrote them down, they sounded hackneyed enough, but when Grace pattered them out she thought they were the sanest things anyone had said in a long time. Yet Grace wasn't always such a saint; she was fiercely critical and easily bored and when she found something dull she mocked it. She shifted jobs a lot: she had begun as an actress then she changed to TV production and retrained as a lawyer and most recently she had become a journalist, which was how Rosa met her. She lacked inhibitions, and she liked to talk about relationships, psychobabble much of it, but Rosa lapped it up, babbled it back and cited Grace like a friendly guru. For months, Grace had been coming round and saying, 'You two, you two are just so fine. You want to grind each other into the ground.' She called them pitted; their energies, apparently, were pitted against each other. 'It's like a World War One aerial battle,' she said. 'One of you has to bale out before you both crash. Someone must make the sacrifice, go down in flames.' When she said that, she raised her eyebrows and dared them to look uncomfortable. Still they sat there and took it, because they knew she was right.

She would never have been friends with Grace, had her mother not died. It was after the death – only a few weeks after – that she went to a party and got so drunk she started talking to Grace about extinction. Grace – always one for talk – lapped it all up and ordered them a taxi. Grace liked Liam from the start; she called him the beauty. Really she was a tonic, and Rosa soon found she was unburdening everything to Grace. She disgorged it all, and Grace smoked and made her salient comments, qua a lot of psychogurus and philosophers

18

Rosa hadn't read. While Rosa had lost all sense of myth and purpose, Grace was sure she had it cracked. 'Humanism, with dignity,' she said, Grace the oracle with long blonde hair. 'That's all we need. Compassion for fellow man.' And then she said, 'Bentham, Mill, utilitarianism, darker twist, Sartre and existentialism, Richard Rorty. Anti-Darwinism. No selfish gene. Dependent on others. The Beauty of Creation' – she said something like that, though it sounded pretty fluid when she said it.

On the evening when Liam spilled some of it out – not all, not all by a good way, a long shot short of the truth, but spilled out more than he had before – they were treading in matrimonial treacle, both of them well-stuck, struggling to lift a foot. That night the room was full of signs and portents. Liam had left his jacket on the floor – for him, a cataclysmic act. The kitchen was a serried shambles of pots and pans. The system had broken down. A dishcloth had dropped on the lino and no one had stooped to collect it. There were these small signs of ferment and then a few remnants of order, everything incommensurate. On the mantelpiece were some postcards, which had curled with the heat from the gas fire. The shelves were full of books they could hardly say one of them owned more than the other, the furniture belonged to both of them, tasteless though it was. The sofa, the inconsequential oak table with the matching chairs, the bookcases they had built together. The room felt like a museum, even as Liam started to speak.

'This can't continue,' he was saying. He was sounding very quiet and reasonable. That was a trick of his; it had nothing to do with what he was saying at all. There was a long pause, while Rosa wondered what couldn't continue, whether she had broken another of Liam's domestic codes, but there was something about his expression, the twitching of his brow, and the way he kept running his hands up and down on his arms, that made her think it might be the end. He was explaining that he had talked to her before about their problems. He wasn't sure they could carry on. Had he even said 'fight the same fight?' Or was it 'run the same race?' It was that sort of phrase-slinging, and then he said they had different goals. It was clear they had stultified. The marriage question had brought it all into relief. They had struggled on, but now they had to be sensible. He mentioned that you had to abandon a sinking ship. It was the best thing to do, for everyone.

'But the captain has to go down with it,' said Rosa. 'With the ship.' Though she realised that wasn't the point. So she stayed there on her chair and shifted around, bit her nails, picked a scab on her finger. He was talking about love and choice and other things she later found she couldn't really remember, and then he said, 'There's nothing else to do.' He mentioned the future, a future that would make them happy. He couldn't see it, he said, with his hand on the back of a chair. He couldn't imagine it at all. Then he said, 'I just don't feel I can offer you the love you need.'

That phrase, of all of the phrases he used, was the one that really stuck in her mind. Anyway, personal pyrotechnics aside, solipsistic whinging and so on, it was clear that he had an objective. Liam was rarely honest, he hated telling the truth, but he was decisive. He stood and walked to the window. The evening light was kind to him, faint and flattering. His face looked particularly high-boned and perfect; his eyes were cloaked in shadows. He cut a fine stoical figure.

'Things have shifted altogether,' he said. 'We have to let each other go.'

She put the plates back on the table, and sat down again. Already, he seemed more energetic. She realised he had been thinking this for months, perhaps years, and this caused her to reassess him. There was hardly even a chance to resist, so persuasive were Liam's pauses. Into the pauses, she understood, he was pouring the weight of his conviction. His brow was furrowed but he had stretched his legs out under the table. He looked settled and quite determined. He would stay there, stock still and patient, until she walked the plank, unstuck herself altogether.

'You know it too,' he said. 'We can't continue.' Rosa noted the shift. This can't continue, we can't continue; the transition from the impersonal to the specific was marked, almost literary in its contrivance. His speech had definitely been rehearsed. There was even a suggestion he had been coached. She wondered briefly which two-bit swine had helped him, but really it didn't matter. He said, 'Rosa, you know I love you. I'm really sorry about the death of your mother. But we can't lie endlessly.' His face was flushed and he slapped his hand on the windowsill. He sounded angry.

'I know things have been bad. But why now, precisely? Is it because I've left my job?' asked Rosa, weakly.

'Of course not,' he snapped. 'That's just another disaster. I wanted us to split and then your mother died, and so I couldn't. Now, I suppose, I ought to think that we can't split because you've left your job. But I can't think that any more. Fundamentally I'm not the right person for you. I feel this now, more than ever before. You must feel it too. There's a danger because of recent events that you might just cling to me, and that's a bad idea. That will make things worse, and we'll be even more trapped. We would have had this conversation ages ago, if it weren't for your mother.' His use of the subjunctive was needlessly baroque. It didn't suit him. He was standing at the window, silhouetted against the haze, looking quite composed. It seemed that he had decided everything. She suddenly understood that there were plans built around this speech, a whole structure of necessary changes. He was far ahead of her.

He was lucid and, she later understood, dishonest. He told her he loved her. There was a lot of sad talk, and he mustered some tears. It went on for hours. At one stage she even thought he was enjoying it. He said, 'Rosa, will you be OK?' and tried to touch her. She brushed him off, angrily, and said, 'Yes, yes of course.'

'Of course I will move out,' said Liam. 'I'll go as soon as you want me to.'

'Or I can,' said Rosa.

'No, Rosa, definitely not,' he said, shaking his head. Again he tried to move towards her and she stepped back. He said, 'I won't hear of it. I'll go and stay with Lorne.'

At that, she nodded. She had a few ideas in her head, mingling with the glutinous stock of her earlier thoughts. She realised that he was her home, that he had been for years, and so wherever he was not was not her home anyway. *Makes this room an everywhere*, she thought of saying, but realised it was hardly relevant. For a long time, she had relied on love – her patched up version – to keep her sane. Later, she decided she would be the one to go. They parted at the door of the bedroom, and he hugged her to him. They held each other for a while, though in retrospect it seemed a beggarly amount, after all those years. She was startled and she couldn't cry. She was waiting for a final confession, but he stepped back, red-faced, and said, 'I'm just going to sort out a few things. Goodnight.'

And this time goodnight was absolute, a categorical goodbye, she thought as she undressed and got into bed. She lay there for an hour, listening to his careful motions outside, her stomach making little flutters that stopped her from going to sleep. Rosa – staring at the electronic alarm clock, the pile of books on the bedside table, his and hers, the trappings of their life together – waited while Liam turned the handle of the door. He came quietly into the room. He reached the bed and paused. He was fumbling under the pillow, and she realised he had come in, not to caress her one last time, or to weep for the death of love, but to find his pyjamas. Submerged in bathos, she turned her head to the wall. Liam moved softly to the door, and walked out.

When morning came, she pushed the curtains apart and watched a low mist tumbling along the tops of the houses. She saw it was a tranquil day, beautiful in the soft shifts of light and the tender moan of planes and cars. She drew the curtains again and waited with her head down until Liam went to work. She hid under the covers when he came to get his clothes. She heard him slide the wardrobe open, and feigned sleep while he rustled through his suits. He was stepping quietly, trying not to wake her. The sheets were clammy with her sweat. When Liam had gone, she walked through the flat touching their stuff. She sifted through the shirts hanging in the wardrobe. She handled the photos scattered on the desk, their books, their CDs. She admired their taste in art. In their years together the boundaries between them had become permeable. Their personalities had combined in some things. In others they were distinct and mutually unintelligible. As she walked through the kitchen she thought there was nothing she wanted to complain about. She smiled as she ate breakfast and watched the sunlight flickering on the floor. She wondered if she should take the milk with her. 'Now your ties are really cut,' she said. 'Quite right too.' *I do not fear to be alone*, she thought. *And I am not afraid to make a mistake, even a great mistake, a lifelong mistake.* But that was hardly true. She was afraid, trembling with a sense of foreboding. So she occupied herself with practicalities. She always enjoyed packing. She spent the morning throwing out her papers, superfluous clothes and books, aged detritus. She took a large suitcase and filled it with things. She bundled the rest into boxes and stuck notes on the top. 'ROSA'S BOX' they read. Then she called Sandra Whitchurch and asked if she could stay.

QUEST

Then it was October, four months had passed, and she was really out on a limb. Things had followed a clear course. She was persistent and she stripped herself down. It was amazing how quickly it happened. All those years on the train, rushing in and out of the city, and before long much had changed. Once you cut a thread, the tapestry unravelled. They waved you off – no one minded at all. Sure, they were saying, laughing into their hands, go off and find yourself. Whatever, excavate that navel of yours. Delve deeply into your inner being. Try to grasp the secret of the universe, find a reason for all this perversity and violence and chaos. Oh yes, you take as long as you like! We're sure you'll crack it! You were free, of course, free to sink. She had a few fathoms to go; she hadn't plunged the furthest depths. Still, she had not quite managed to float. Revelations had been withheld, yet she was still ambitious. Meanwhile she had drifted into a state of insolvency, and that had become the most pressing element of her life and a burden on her thoughts.

She was out on the street because she was going to the bank. It was early and she was walking slowly with her hands in her pockets. In the half-light of a misty morning, she saw the concrete buttresses of the Westway and the shining hides of successive cars. Beneath it she saw – at first indeterminate and then coming closer – the shape of Sandra Whitchurch. Whitchurch was walking towards her, blameless in a grey suit. She was walking with her feet turned outwards, it lent a waddle to her motions, and she still had her hunted look. It was strange she was there, on the wrong side of town, clearly late for something. She was moving steadily, looking at her watch as she walked. She looked nervous, it was something in the motion of her head. Rosa had always liked Whitchurch's nerves. Whitchurch was the sort who trembled when she smiled. She poured you coffee, her hands shaking. If you looked at her too long, preserved a pause, she shivered. At the sight of her, Rosa tried to run. It was poor behaviour, but she couldn't help it. Certainly it was futile, she got stranded in the middle of the road and knew immediately the game was up. She was preparing an innocent phrase as Whitchurch raised her head and saw her. It crossed her body, a spasm of fear. It was clearly ironic to think about Whitchurch's nerves when she was trembling at the prospect of a conversation. It was an overreaction. Irrational, of course.

Whitchurch had only been kind to her. After she crept out of her office and crawled out of her flat, she spent some time on the sofa in Whitchurch's flat, in a sliced-up house in Angel. The sofa was clearly the *axis mundi*, Rosa realised, as she lay there day after day with her eyes on the ceiling. She found she was nervous and excited, and in the mornings she was so tired she could hardly stand. This made her think she might have something, some explicable disease that could be treated with drugs, but after a few days she felt OK again. Then she tried to sell her possessions, putting adverts in shop windows. No one really wanted used clothes and books and CDs, unless they were antique or collectible. In the area she lived in, people gave things away, offered them out like indulgences, so she did that too, taking stuff in big black bags to Oxfam. She didn't mind losing some of the clutter she had been dragging around. She had given away all of her books, except Wollstonecraft's *A Vindication of the Rights of Women* and the complete works of Shakespeare. When she wasn't reading these, she sat in the library using the Internet, typing in web addresses. This didn't do much, but it made her feel industrious. Before it got so cold she had spent the summer sitting in parks, and that had been much better. Really it had been like a holiday; it had lulled her into a false sense of security. She had thought she could do it for ever, passing days in Regent's Park, watching people pushing prams and rabbits scuffling on the grass and squirrels moving along the branches. She was all for aping Rousseau, marshalling her thoughts in a series of walks. The marshalling hadn't happened, but she had at least walked. It had been a proper summer Eden, but the autumn cast her out.

It was Whitchurch's honesty that had done for her. Better had she lied like the others. Poor Whitchurch, blushing and talking very fast, had told her just what Liam and Grace were doing. It was the greatest revelation Rosa had so far experienced, this jangling echo from the life she had left. In August, good kind Whitchurch had spilled it all, supplied some surprising details, and then she had walked with Rosa to Tottenham Court Road asking her if she was going to be OK, apologising so sweetly and sadly for being the one to bring her the news. Liam and Grace were in love. Better still, they were getting married, in a public ceremony. No one had condemned them! Rosa was naturally surprised, and then she was incoherent and eventually silent. She knew that she had been deceived, but she was dull-witted and she couldn't remember much. She restrained herself in Whitchurch's presence, and this sterling repression left her spitting choler after Whitchurch had shot her a final look of compassion and gone back to the office. For a week Whitchurch's compassion was so mighty and terrible that Rosa thought she might be crushed by the weight of it. Then she heard that Jess had a spare room, so she offered Whitchurch thanks, and moved to Kensal Rise.

Now Rosa felt a brief pang, thinking of how her life had thinned out, how she had whittled it down to the basics. She had lost sight of Whitchurch and so many others. For a while she had missed her, and yet now she fled when she saw her. Would it be so terrible, to meet a Whitchurch, she wondered? The woman looked benign, moving purposefully, checking her watch. She was carrying a heavy bag, leaning slightly to one side. Here she came, lugubrious with her heavy limbs. Moving to her own personal pace, in her own decelerated version of a hurry, Whitchurch walked on. She nodded to Rosa and Rosa nodded back. Then they were a foot away from each other, and someone had to speak. So Rosa said 'Hi, Sandra' thinking it was best to start.

'Rosa, how are you?' Whitchurch wasn't sure whether to kiss her or clasp her hand, so in the end she did neither and they stood with their arms at their sides.

'Very well, how are you?' said Rosa. She was determined to be jovial, and so she managed a smile and stood there, quite lock-jawed with the strain of holding it. Whitchurch was equally determined, her eyes wide open, nodding vividly.

'Very well,' she said. 'Just off to a meeting. Somewhere around here. At Westbourne Studios, is it far?'

'No,' said Rosa. 'You're very close. Just a few streets further and then cross a footbridge.'

'That's a relief,' said Whitchurch. 'I'd begun to wonder if I'd be wandering around all day.'

Rosa laughed too loudly, lifting her head and catching an observant glimmer in Whitchurch's eyes. Indeed, as she laughed, she noticed Whitchurch looking her up and down, aiming to assess her. 'So, what are you up to?' said Whitchurch.

With unconvincing nonchalance, she rubbed her eye with a finger. That smudged her mascara, and Rosa wasn't sure if she should tell her.

'Oh, you know, looking for work.'

'Are you still living up in Kensal Rise?'

She meant it well enough, so Rosa smiled and said, 'Yes, still with Jess. She's been very kind. Her boyfriend is great too, very welcoming. They seem a happy couple.' That was flannel, superfluous to requirements. She was trying to emit bonhomie, but something wasn't right.

'Good,' said Whitchurch.

She screwed up her face so it cratered like the moon. She was sweating at the collar. Whitchurch was like a beast, come out to graze in the morning light. She had the thick thighs of a venerable woman, the sort of woman who does a lot of work and never has time for the gym. Rosa appreciated the ample curves of Whitchurch, and then, aware that they had both paused, silence had slung a lasso around them, she said, 'And how are you, Sandra? How's work?'

Whitchurch moved towards her. Now her large, friendly face was close to Rosa's. She had healthy red skin, freckles on her nose, and a few white blotches on her neck. Her brows had been plucked into oblivion, her follicles had been purged. Her skin was lined, but the lines were soft, quite pretty, and they bracketed her mouth and set off her eyes. She was a handsome woman, but the sight of her waggling her pruned brows, smiling urgently, unnerved Rosa and she stepped back.

'Work is great,' said Whitchurch.

'Why great?'

Whitchurch shrugged her shoulders. This she did with some effort, because her bag looked heavy. Rosa thought she wouldn't stop for long.

'Oh, everything's going well, as ever. Lots of big clients in town this week, so it's very busy.'

'I should let you go,' said Rosa.

Whitchurch glanced at her watch. 'Oh, well, a couple of minutes will be all right,' she said. She licked her lips, her malleable mouth. *A couple of minutes – time for what?* A bus moaned past, causing Whitchurch to raise her voice. That tightened her consonants, made them sibilant. *Time for a quiet confession.* 'I haven't seen you for a while, since you moved out. I felt like the messenger who got shot,' said Whitchurch.

Well, it was true. 'No, no, Sandra, not at all,' said Rosa, trying to smile. 'I'm glad you told me. At first I was surprised, but now I'm well on the way to understanding.' Quite en route to something like acceptance, though her hands bled sweat as she talked. She understood that Grace had merely been a purgative. She had forced the issue. That was the best way to think of it, and, in her finer moments, Rosa did. There was something about it that concerned her, all the same. It was a sense of coincidence, the curious chances of their meeting, that if

31

Rosa's mother had never died then Rosa would never have talked drunkenly to Grace and embarked upon such an intense friendship with her, and Grace would never have come round to the flat all the time and Liam would never have fallen in love with her. It was a shocking run of coincidences, as if the fates had been conspiring. But Rosa, unsure if there were fates anyway, couldn't unearth it, and this was what perplexed her. There were days when she thought that Liam must have been looking for a way out, to fall so deeply in love with the first new friend who came to their flat. She couldn't work it out, though undoubtedly it lent another layer of significance to those evenings when Grace sat in their flat, telling them they were 'fatally stuck', that they needed a 'swift transition, a mutual release'. Grace with her legs curled up, toying with her food, because Grace was so full of ideas that she hardly ever ate. Rosa had believed it all. She wanted Grace to tell her what she was. And Liam was just a sucker for a beautiful woman who spoke in whirling subordinate clauses.

Whitchurch was waiting, and Rosa said, 'I've just been hiding out from everyone. I set myself some ambitious targets. Initially I was whipping through them, but recently I've had to focus on work, jobs, you know. My money ran out. The rest is ignominious.'

That made Whitchurch nod in a distracted way.

'Good, good,' she said. 'Because I wouldn't want to think you blamed me for anything.'

'No, no, I only blame myself.' *And Liam, Grace, my parents dead and alive, Yabalon and the laws of the universe. But mostly myself.* 'Really, I'm sorting things out. Perhaps we could meet up, when everything's less chaotic. I can explain it all in tedious detail.'

Whitchurch nodded again, and scrutinised her watch.

'Same numbers, you know how to reach me. Are you – perhaps you aren't – are you going to their wedding?'

'Their wedding,' said Rosa, aware of her voice rising, tightening, for all her efforts to suppress the signs. Shrilly, squawking like an exotic bird, she said, 'No no, I won't be going. They did invite me. But I have to go away on Friday. It is this Friday, isn't it?' she added, wanting to sound uncertain. Whitchurch nodded. 'Well, other things to do. You know, send them my best. I have already, but you know, never hurts.' And she laughed. She laughed as if she might be about to choke.

'OK, of course,' said Whitchurch. Now she was turning to leave. Whither Whitchurch, thought Rosa, and then she thought hwaer cwom Whitchurch. She had treated Whitchurch badly. It would be impossible to reignite that friendship. For death, people made allowances. But only for so long. And for the rest, the rest was chaff. Rosa's crustacean mores hadn't impressed them at all. She had kept herself under a rock and now they had stopped trying to prise her out.

'You know, everyone misses you,' said Whitchurch.

'I miss them,' said Rosa.

'They feel awkward, of course.' That was because of Liam, she thought. Really he had made the whole thing like a gladiatorial contest. She had been preoccupied and she hadn't bothered to state her case. Meanwhile, he had conducted a briefing campaign against her. He was guilty, or angry she had wasted so many years of his life, anyway he had been telling everyone she was crazy and sad. It made them reluctant to see her. And if by chance they did see her, it made them look holy, which was what Whitchurch was doing now. Whitchurch was a font of holy-watered concern. 'I've been useless, I know,' said Rosa. 'I've been out of touch with everyone.'

'Well, they're still around,' said Whitchurch. 'You could go and see them sometime.'

Rosa said, 'Oh yes, that. I see,' and smiled faintly. 'Yep, I'll go round and see them sometime.' The conversation was fading fast and she let it fade.

'Anyway, in the interim, tell them I said hi,' she said.

'Who?'

'Liam and Grace, when you see them. And anyone else who . . . you know, you'd like to tell I said hi,' she said.

'That's confusing,' said Whitchurch, smiling. 'But I'll try my best. Now I really have to go.'

'Yes, of course. Oh, and, Sandra,' she said, urgently, as Whitchurch turned away.

But Whitchurch was glancing at her watch. 'Yes?'

And she wondered what she wanted to say. *I'm sorry? Thank you?* Or perhaps she really did have a message to give her, something to tell Liam and Grace as they walked down the aisle to the altar. *I wish you all the luck in the world. I love you both, in an eternal and profound sense. I forgive everything. I hope you forgive me.* Unlikely, she thought. Highly unlikely. *I damn you to hell! The pair of you! Cowards and traitors!* Unlikely she would say that either. So she stopped and wheezed gently for a moment. Instead she said, vaguely, 'Good to see you. Hope your meeting goes well.'

'Of course, Rosa.'

And Whitchurch walked slowly onwards. Still, the sight of Whitchurch had summoned the lot of them. Liam and Grace and the rest. Liam and Grace, those servants of Cupid, kept occurring to her as she went along the road. She moved quickly to avoid an oncoming rush of people, recent fugitives from a commuter train. They seeped along the streets, towards the maze of their working lives. A man tripped her and she stumbled and stretched out her hands. That made her collide with a boy wearing headphones who slurred something she didn't hear. And he didn't hear her when she asked him what he meant, so they both dropped their eyes and walked on.

She had found in recent months that her thoughts were undisciplined, and tended to swirl towards the things that pained her – unless she kept her mind on practicalities and trivia. So she was thinking of that pair of beauties, Liam and Grace in the back of a mini cab, sitting very close to each other, while Rosa argued with the driver and smirked at them. She raised her eyebrows at them and they smiled back. They were all tired, coming home from a party. It was almost light, the stars were fad-

34

ing in the sky. Perhaps the birds were already singing. She couldn't remember, but there they were – legs touching? hands? – with Rosa in the front, drunk and even happy! She was oblivious to nuance. Grace was staying the night, because she lived in Tulse Hill and it was too far to go. She had stayed a few times, sleeping in their living room on the sofa bed. Really Rosa had no idea how long it had been going on for. She didn't care to think. Still, when she remembered Grace in the living room with her hair in plaits and her lovely head on a borrowed pillow she wondered whether Liam had left their bed that night, and crept in to see Grace? She imagined their efforts to be quiet, their nerves, their excitement. They were a fine pair, physically; she had seen them both naked many times. Liam more, of course. But she knew the contours of Grace's body too. Once their friendship flourished, they swam together a few times a week. Grace had small thighs, long arms, an elegant back. Her skin was tanned. She had a tiny, beautiful body and delightful breasts. All the right curves and shadows. She was definitely in her prime. She was a little short for some, but people admired her. Even with all of this, even with her fully realised sense of their bodies, Rosa couldn't quite summon the vision, the final – my eyes! my eyes! – image of them in the living room, passionate and entwined. They had officially announced themselves a few weeks after she left. That left two plausible interpretations – unfaithfulness or a rebound so spectacular that it was surprising Liam hadn't cracked his skull. Either way she had been a fool. She had noticed nothing at the time; she was preoccupied. Grace dropping round, bringing her bread and bottles of wine, had seemed like simple kindness. The suddenness of their friendship had seemed part of the bizarre pattern of events after her mother's death. She hadn't thought it through; her mind wasn't clear at the time. Still, Liam's anger and frustration suggested he had been eager for the next stage. He was tired out, perhaps bored. And Grace was waiting there, beautiful, courageous, full of vitality.

*

The wedding was close now, only days away. She had received an invitation a few weeks ago, an impressive gold-embossed piece of luxury card, 'Mr and Mrs Bosworth would like to invite you to celebrate the marriage of their daughter Grace Maria to Liam Robert Peters.' *Mr and Mrs Bosworth would like to invite you to celebrate the triumph of their conniving offspring Grace Maria misnamed for holiness by optimistic parents to Liam Lothario Peters.* She never liked it when the parents invited you along. It was plain tacky. All that conspicuous bumf and litter came with a set of directions to the church and some friendly suggestions for hotels in London which began 'London, as most of you will know, is a very expensive city!' There was even a note about presents. 'If you would like to buy Grace and Liam a present . . .' She thought she wouldn't like to. Not really at all. Later Liam wrote her a letter. 'Rosa, I know you are hurt. But I would really like you to be there. It's of course up to you. Whatever you feel able to do.' Able to do! The scandal of his lazy prose! Raging and trying to conceal it, she sent him a short email. 'Will think about it – R.' He wrote back with an email gush, the sort of disposable rubbish people pound out between one meeting and the next. 'I'm so glad to hear you will. We can hardly wait to see you there. With love, as always, Liam.' He sounded like a parody, as if he had entered a competition to sound as plastic and inanimate as he could, like a replicant pretending to be a human, but that was ages ago anyway. It had been weakness to write anything at all. At least she had pared it down, from a letter eloquent with rage. *Dear Liam, You write to me as if I am an invalid, recovering from an unfortunate ailment. Perhaps my belief in your steadfastness was my sickness, from which I am mercifully cured.* It went on, a violent torrent, and if Liam was a replicant she was a failed nineteenth-century novelist, spilling out melodrama for thruppence a volume. *I condemn you! I anticipate your doom! You are the anti-Christ! On the day of Judgement you will be ravaged by devils!* She threw away the letter. Later she threw away the invitation.

Still, the date and time were scored into her memory.

Liam and Grace, she had written a while back, *I won't be coming to your wedding. It's not that I don't wish you well. I hope you'll be happy together. Really, it doesn't matter much. I could come along, smile and nod, wearing a hat, but I think it would be unseemly. Frankly, I would become part of the spectacle. They would call me 'the ex' and stare at me! They would await a scene. They would expect me to cry, and whatever I did they would say I had been crabbed and furious as you went up the aisle. Bent-backed with rage. But you know, I'm not angry at all. Yours, Rosa.* Grace had called her up a few times, after it all came out. Someone must have told her – perhaps it was even Whitchurch who spilled the truth – that Rosa knew. Rosa knew! Cue for thunder and lightning! Or, in Rosa's case, because the epic was hardly available to her, slight drizzle. Grace left messages of great pertinence, pert little messages which made Rosa bite her lip. When Rosa picked up the phone – thinking it might be someone else entirely – she heard Grace saying, 'Rosa, now, don't hang up, can we talk? I want you to know I understand your position.' Grace wasn't penitent, exactly. She wasn't nervous at all. She fundamentally believed that Rosa was suppressing her emotions. She explained this, briskly but with sympathy, as if she understood that Rosa was having trouble understanding the irrefutable truth of it all and she was trying to help her get on board. 'I understand your position, but I am hoping you will understand mine,' she said. Her position – it was one more piece of Gracean Ur-babble.

'I understand you are sated with turmoil. You have run the gamut. Your spirit is almost dead. And you were clinging to something that had died a long time ago,' Grace said. 'You were shattered, mourning your mother. You weren't in a state to be courageous. You still aren't. But your relationship was dead. You knew that. I could see it, as soon as I saw you and Liam together. And I know you want Liam to be happy. He is, he really is happy. He suffered for so long, living with you.'

37

'I don't care,' said Rosa. 'That's fine. Vade in Pace.'

'What do you mean?' said Grace.

'Enjoy yourselves. Why not?'

'We have to meet and talk this through.'

'Ughghu?' said Rosa.

'By the end he was a counsellor for you, not a lover,' said Grace. 'And he's a young, beautiful man. You wouldn't want him to imprison himself in a moribund relationship?'

'Dear Grace, we are all in a moribund relationship with something.'

'Well, that's precisely the sort of remark which makes me understand what Liam means.'

'Means about what?'

As a concession, Grace pretended to stutter. That was a feint; she was so far from being awkward that it was a holiday humour for her. 'Say what you like now, I understand it's hard for you,' said Grace. 'But you must keep articulating. We must keep the lines of communication open.'

That made Rosa flush with a renewed sense of humiliation, and then she said, 'Shugugug', and put down the phone. Unplugged the phone, ripped out the cord, and explained it to Jess later.

Things to do, Monday

Get a job
Wash your clothes
Clean the kitchen
Phone Liam and ask about the furniture.
Buy some tuna and spaghetti
Go to the bank and beg them for an extension – more money, more time to pay back the rest of your debt
Read the comedies of Shakespeare, the works of Proust, the plays of Racine and Corneille and The Man Without Qualities

Read The Golden Bough, The Nag-Hammadi Gospels, The
Upanishads, The Koran, The Bible, The Tao, *the complete*
works of E. A. Wallis Budge
Read Plato, Aristotle, Confucius, Bacon, Locke, Rousseau,
Wollstonecraft, Kant, Hegel, Schopenhauer, Kierkegaard,
Nietzsche, and the rest
Hoover the living room
Clean the toilet
Distinguish the various philosophies of the way
Clean the bath

Now she stirred and walked along again. Rosa, a handsome
woman, if thinner of late and a little pale, was turning the corner, heading for the bank. Still she heard the sounds of the
street. She was thinking, as she always tried to, about the day
ahead. It was clear to her that she had to be more dynamic.
Action was required to scoop herself up, avert the slough. She
had a list in her head of things to do. She was telling herself
there was a lot to be cheerful about. This was a positive thinking exercise someone had told her to do, one of those benevolent quacks she had been seeing. She was thinking how good it
was that the sun might shine and how lucky she was that she
was still fit, though she had been dizzy recently and suffered
from headaches. Stress, she assumed. The decline of her faculties, the clash of warring theories eroding at her cortex, the
human condition! Yet even now, she wasn't down and out, not
destitute at all. There was no reason to cave in yet. The earth
hadn't yet exploded in a ball of plasma. There had been no
catastrophes, no meteorite showers, nothing that immediately
threatened the existence of the species. She had not been productive recently, but she was sure the dam would burst. It was
late in the day, but not too late. She still had a bed to sleep in,
though Jess had recently stopped talking to her. That was a
shame, but she was sure she could claw it all back.

She was moving through the furtive morning of the city, saturated clouds hanging over the high-rise buildings, human

currents coursing along the streets. It was winter and dawn came later by the day. She was outside a burger bar, chrome seats housed in an art deco building. She noticed bricks and fluting; at her side she found a row of shops – a jewellers, an Indian Fusion shop, a Chinese medicine shop, Middle Eastern restaurants, a Plant Essences House, whatever that was, a shop advertising BIG BIG SAVINGS! She stamped her feet as she walked and kicked up dust. The pavement was spotted with litter. The post office had been closed down, said a sign. It was being turned into luxury flats. She nodded and passed under a red canopy which was fluttering in the wind. *Very deep is the well of the past. Shall we not call it bottomless?* and then she thought, That hardly helps. She had been living in untruth, that much was true. *Yes, yes, elegant as anything, your thoughts.* The untruth of the true. The truth of the untrue, discuss, with reference to some philosophers you have been taught to trust! She was one of those that can bear no grief and desire but to bathe in bliss. That was a quote, though she couldn't remember the source. She sniffed, wiped her nose on her sleeve, said to herself, *One who has no god, as they walk along the street headache envelops them like a garment.* Did it have to be so melancholy? Since sadness had got such purchase on her, how could she bash it away without developing her illusions again? To live free from illusions, but content. Impossible! she said, aloud. Insane! Now a shop grill rattled up behind her. A man passed her, with a dog at his side. Then there was an early morning pensioner, dragging a bag on wheels. She passed a renovated church, sandblasted, and in a garden she saw a forest of miniature trees. A line of cars crept past her and she stood at a crossing, wondering whether she should walk or wait for the lights to change.

She saw spray-painted letters spelling *TEMP* – she had been seeing this around for months. A lonely word, splashed on bridges; she had once seen it on the side of a train, blurred by speed. *TEMP* – a cry from the secretarial classes, or those who worked in the constant peril of a short-term contract, she thought, passing it by. Or an unfinished word: *Tempo, Tempus fugit*, like a warning, or an elegy, *temps perdu*. It seemed to be important, but she wasn't sure. She felt it was a hint, something she should try to follow. She saw the trains snorting towards Paddington, their noses on the tracks. She understood that everything was accelerating. She had thought that diving out of the office would make the days go slower, but it seemed like they were speeding up, racing towards a conclusion she couldn't anticipate. She saw things in quick-step, like an old-fashioned film played on modern equipment. Quick march Rosa went, along the street, as if there was a prize for getting to the bank first. She skirted round the news-stand and started running under the bridge. The cars pounded above her. A car honked and she crossed and waved a hand.

As she walked she thought that she must definitely wash her clothes. And clean the kitchen. She should certainly – today, having failed to do so yesterday – call up Liam and ask about the furniture. It would help if he sold it, or gave her the money. She should call Kersti – though Kersti was sometimes frosty, if you caught her at the wrong time. But before, Kersti had offered to help; Kersti who was a lawyer had said she would write a legal-sounding letter to Liam. *Dear Mr Peters, Our client Rosa Lane expects the return of her furniture or a financial agreement. Failure to comply will result in another such letter, phrased in a more baroque dialect. Then we will whirl you into the abyss of legalese.* As well as that she should really get a job. That was clearly a priority. Reading *History of Western Philosophy* was not immediately necessary, but it might help her with the basics. There was much she had to read, but she also had to *buy some tuna and spaghetti. Sit down with Jess. The bank* – she had been putting that off for days, but a quick personal appearance might still win them round. *Shakespeare, Kierkegaard, Nietzsche and sundry others* – if she had time. *Hoover the living room* and most important of all – *clean the bath and toilet.* And now she really had to write to Whitchurch. She felt bad now, that she hadn't apologised. She should have thanked her. Though for what, precisely? The beer, the consolatory shandy? That had been kind, the carrion hunting vulture. She thought of calling her up. *Hi, Sandra, sorry to bother you at work. How are you? I wanted to call to say I'm very grateful for all your kindness. Let's meet again soon.* She thought of Whitchurch in her office, biting her pencil, totting up accounts. Truly, she was blameless. *Dear Sandra. Great to see you. Thanks so much. Thanks so very much. Soon you'll be ashes, or bones. Yours, Rosa.* If she had an hour before bedtime she could consider the lilies, sort through her papers and phone her father. Now she could hear the sound of birds singing. They were perched on the branches of the trees, and for a moment she thought how beautiful. The colours were pristine in the morning – the cold white sky, the white buildings dappled with sunshine. Everything was scrubbed and pure, the streets were clean.

In the bank there was a low sound like the sifting of envelopes and a mechanical whir. Machines beeped and gave out money. There was a long line of people, receiving cash. She had once seen a sci-fi film about a lottery. Each week you bought a ticket and entered into a draw. There were two prizes: one was 50 million dollars, the other was public execution. The chances of either were equally slim. Yet people entered, bought their tickets and waited. She had waited with her hand out at a million cash machines. Part of the cycle, taking and giving money. Now her own personal supply had dried up. She had a small segment left of her debt, a tiny pile of remaining slosh, and then even her borrowing would be stopped. This had caused her to question her assumptions. She had thought they let you pile up debt indefinitely, but that wasn't true. They let you pile it up while they thought you could pay. When they realised you really couldn't pay, they stopped the flow. They dammed up everything and told you to come in and talk about a repayment plan. They sent you tactless requests for money. They left messages on the answer machine. It was nice of them to call, but it didn't make things better. She had to tell them that it wasn't a lack of concern for her place in the international system of debit and credit, she was fantastically concerned about it, but she had been prioritising other things, and she had lost her sense of financial basics. She had ignored the rules of supply and demand, and her supply had simply vanished.

Therefore, she waited patiently while the clerks talked to each other and then she asked if she could see the manager. Of course he was busy, this moneysmith, and they told her to come back later. Better still, she could ring in for an appointment, said a brusque woman with a face like a piano. 'Just a minute or so?' said Rosa. 'I'd be very brief. Just a question or two really, simple questions, requiring simple answers.' *Can you give me more? More time to pay off my debt, or more debt?* She knew the answer anyway. But the heel-clicking woman didn't want to help her. She didn't even want to talk to her. Perhaps she looked unkempt, or maybe it was her unstudied air of desperation. 'I'm sorry, but Mr Rivers is very busy. We can do you an appointment for Thursday,' she said, this zipper-mouthed woman. *Do me?* thought Rosa. *Do me an appointment?* Thursday was three days away. 'Perhaps tomorrow?' said Rosa. 'Tomorrow morning, first thing?'

'Why not leave your number,' said the woman.

'Mr Rivers has my number.' That old Sharkbreath knew everything about her. He had been patient for a while, but now he was getting sterner by the hour. 'I'm sure he would like to see me,' she said. 'Please could you at least ask?'

Thus conjoined, Mandy clipped off. She vanished into another part of the bank and Rosa waited. She was too nervous to sit, so she stalked along the banks of machines and watched people taking money from them. *We can do you an eviction on Tuesday*, she thought. *We can do you a spell in a reform centre for the fiscally incontinent on Wednesday.* She edged around posters of perfect people with mortgages and TESSAs, smiling broadly because their mortgages made them so very happy. Whatever they might all say, she had really been

43

trying to get a job. She knew money was an illusion, but she also knew that she needed food in her hardly illusory belly. It gave her something to aim for, and in recent weeks, she had tried a teeming array of things. Her terms were vague enough. She had to find a way to make money without being required to lie, to feign a certainty she didn't possess. She thought that was broad enough. So she had tried to become a gardener. For a week she sat in the local library reading books about botany. The supply was patchy, but she learnt some definitions, tallied words with pictures. She pushed flyers through letterboxes and had a few calls. She went round to the house of a Mr Lewis, and they were getting on fine until she dug up a sunflower and he sent her away again. She had been applying for a variety of things, writing letters.

Dear Sir, I would like a job. Actually that's not true. Without wanting to trouble you with my ambivalence, a job is what I need. Sheer bloody debt has forced me back. I am quite free of many of the more fashionable varieties of hypocrisy, though I suffer from many unfashionable varieties of my own. I have many strengths, most of which I seem for the moment to have forgotten. However, I am a goal-oriented person and so on, und so weiter . . . Yours ever, Rosa Lane.

Dear Madam, I am a person of inconstant aims and mild destitution. I find this combination of qualities excludes me from many jobs. But working together, I'm sure we can exploit my talents successfully. I still have a cream suit, a relic from a former life. I am unexceptional in every way, and eager to serve. You can find me in a borrowed room, in west London. Yours faithfully, Rosa Lane.

More recently, she had written to landlords and restaurateurs.

Dear Sir/Madam, I would like to be considered for the post of barmaid. I have no experience at all, but I have an abiding interest in bars. I like a nice glass of beer, from time to time. Some of my most memorable moments have occurred in bars, some of my most desperate humiliations and fleeting patches of pure claritas. So far she had been dismissed by every barman she met. Kindly, politely, but dismissed all the same.

A week ago – her finest hour – she had signed up for temping and gone along to a place where alcoholics rang to ask for help. She was put in reception and told to type letters. For the first day she was productive, working steadily through her in-tray, enjoying the flick of her fingers and her downright efficiency. She powered through a load of letters and cast them into her out-tray. By the next day, the novelty had worn off. Then she found the office air was stale and on the third day she was bothered by the conversations of the people to her left. It wasn't fair, they were nice enough, friendly and clearly sane, but they did keep spilling out words. While she was typing up letters . . . *Dear Sir, On July 21st we made an application for 20 purple box files with interior clips. These have as yet not arrived* . . . they were pouring forth. Perhaps it was unkind to hate them by the end of the day. She knew it was. The following morning she realised they hated her. That hurt her feelings; she always preferred her hatred to be unreciprocated. They blanked her at lunch as she sat there with a plastic fork in her hand and a takeaway salad in a plastic box. Later she saw them queuing in the café, and it was hard not to feel sorry for them all, Rosa too, standing in their cheap clothes, waiting for a cup of coffee. When she got back to her desk her mood had darkened. She typed a few last letters . . . *Dear Sir, On July 24th we ordered 504 brown envelopes and 10 million pencils and 30 trillion stamps and yet you have sent us 304 envelopes and only seven million pencils and only three trillion stamps please rectify this appalling oversight immediately before something terrible happens some unfathomable doom* . . . and then she went home. The next morning she phoned to say she was ill. Her father called it lassitude. 'You have to be able to get up in the morning,' he said.

'And I do,' said his daughter, who was sitting in bed at the time with a cold compress on her head.

'No one likes their job that much,' said her father.

'You liked yours. Mother liked hers,' said Rosa.

'Well, find something you like.'

'Yes, yes, yes,' she said. She still hadn't found a way to resolve it all. 'It's ridiculous. You think, would the knights on their grail quest, would they have been able to do it, find the grail and the rest, if the bank had been constantly telling them about their overdraft and how they weren't getting any more money when they finished the hunt? Would Jesus have done so well, had he had Mr Sharkbreath ringing him up and asking him to discuss a debt repayment plan?'

'Rosa,' said her father. 'Please don't add a Messiah complex to your list of woes.'

'That's not what I mean.'

'If you don't like the office, then do something else.'

'I mean, there's so little time, and how are you meant to consider anything at all, when there's this constant thing at your back – not even time's winged chariot, I mean that's there too, but the imperative – the imperative to earn money. And for that you have to adopt a mask. Dress up. Mark time. Squander days.'

'It's a basic,' he said. 'There's no escaping it.'

Successive nights like rolling waves convey them quickly who are bound for death, she quoted, whenever anyone would listen. 'Melodrama,' said Grace, when Rosa said this to Grace in July when she had been ignorant and they had still been friends. 'Plain melodrama! Get a grip, Rosa! You're acting like a child!'

'But a child doesn't know the horror! The horror!' said Rosa.

'Don't try to quote your way out of it,' said Grace. 'Don't drag literature into it. You've had a terrible time. But we have to work. We all have to work. You just have to grow up!'

With her back against the wall (and on the wall was a poster saying ARE YOU MAKING THE MOST OF YOUR

SAVINGS?) Rosa knew they were right. All of them: Grace, her father, the Grail Knights, the whole lot of them. (And now she thought *TEMP* might mean the Knights Templar, that seemed quite probable as she sat there with her hand on her heart and a feeling as if her blood was fizzing through her veins. A local branch. A modern version. Galloping towards truth.) They were joined together in a rousing chorus, the refrain something about getting on with it, not festering. Sharkbreath was in there too, telling her she couldn't borrow any more. We all have to work, they were singing, moving crabwise along the stage. We all have to work! Life was short, and indeterminate, the mysteries of the universe quite out of reach, but action was required. You had to play a part. Simply, you might as well join in! You couldn't just fall off the horse at the first hedge! Your mother has died, but worse things would happen. Your father will die, your lover, your friends, everyone will die, you included! Still, whenever she saw something that suggested a return to the office she found she couldn't tick it. So she had gone along to the local library and asked if they needed any help. There at least she could read, she thought. She could brush her hands over the soft spines of books, stack them on shelves and she could sit at a desk and direct people to the large-print novels. She was mobile and fairly bright, she explained. She knew a few jokes and she had once been a decent raconteur. She could definitely manage a stamping thing, she said, a book stamper, a stampe de livres, whatever it was called, and she knew how to talk about books. A woman with bright red lipstick had asked her for references. Rosa said she would supply some soon, and offered to show just how she could stack. She had read a lot of books, she said. Mostly modern classics, though she had recently begun a course of reading, from the Ancients to the present day. Meanwhile she had read a lot of Dickens and much of Dostoevsky. Some of Gogol. Most of the Eliots, George and T.S. . . . Ask me about a book, she said, any book, I'll pretend I've read it. She was trying to look practical and efficient, like a woman with better things to do who happened to feel like working in a library. But the red-lipped woman turned Rosa down. Apparently she didn't present the right qualifications. Then she applied for jobs as a farm worker. She had a soothing image of herself living it up on a Welsh farm, drinking cider in the evenings and falling in love with a boy called Glynn. But so far no one had written back to her.

Another waste of time had been her interview with Pennington, the other day. She had really thought that job might be the one, a thing she could commit to, but Pennington had sorely disappointed her. The auguries were bad, and when she saw Pennington's house she knew they were doomed, both of them. She was up in Kensal Green, at a forgotten line of houses far from the tube, and she looked at the snagged gate and the paint-peeling walls and the dirt-flecked windows and she stopped on the pavement, her hand poised above the gate. She was irresolute for a few minutes, perhaps it was longer, and then she found she was knocking on the door. She regretted it when she saw Pennington standing there, a man with a thatch of grey hair and a booming voice. He was smiling at her, rubbing his hands. His glasses, which were smeared with grime, had been mended with sellotape. He was looking for a proofreader, his advert had explained. 'I have been working for twenty years on a definitive history,' he said, as he led her through the hall to the living room of his small, shabby house. 'I have various theories to prove. I need someone who can work with me on it. I can't pay much. You'll find it adequate, as long as your expenses aren't great. Your main motive would be the experience. You would be dedicated to the research itself.'

No good, then, thought Rosa. *I am dedicated only to my debt.* But Pennington was saying, 'I am very fastidious. I like people to work hard. I strongly believe the book will make me very famous. Possibly rich, in which case I would pay you a bonus. Of course if you found me a bear or if I found you a slouch' – and he fixed her sternly, all of a sudden – 'we could of course agree to part. I have been through a couple of assistants already. Since I began, a dozen or so. Good ones are hard to come by. Do you know anything about Ancient Egypt?'

'A little,' she said. 'I have spent a lot of time in the British Museum.' He was staring at her, screwing his face into a thousand tucks and creases, mapping himself.

'Well, we have all been to the British Museum,' he said. 'Anyone from your schoolboy to your young Turk' – my young Turk? What was the man saying, she wondered briefly? – 'has managed to go to the British Museum.' He said this with disdain. He definitely had her down as one of them, a vulgar day-tripper, lagging on the steps with an ice cream.

'If I held up this,' and he held up a hieroglyph of a figure holding a quill. 'What would it mean?'

'To write?' said Rosa.

'Good! Good! And this?' And he held up a hieroglyph of a figure with its arms raised.

'To praise?' guessed Rosa.

'Excellent. And this?' And he held up a picture of a man tied to a stake.

'Prisoner?'

'Wonderful. And this one?' And he held up a picture of a figure sitting in an arch.

'I don't know,' said Rosa.

'That's a god wearing the sun's disk and grasping a palm branch in each hand,' he said. 'But that one was difficult.'

Idly, Rosa wondered how long the game went on. And she discovered it went on for quite some time, as Pennington asked her to guess the meanings of another batch of hieroglyphs and to translate a line of them. 'See how you do!' he said.

Pen in hand, she went to it. She still wasn't sure what he was paying. He had a fixed stare. He smiled a lot, but she couldn't tell how deep the charm went. Unmarried, she assumed. Simple and terrible in his way, with his staring eyes, his shocking refusal to break eye contact. He dropped this stare only when he was reading through her translation, laughing richly at her foolishness, then he lifted his eyes again and looked long and hard at her. Eventually he said, 'Brilliant!' He was laughing at her. 'Complete nonsense! But they often are! How were you to know? How could you possibly do it? Impossible! You were bound to get it all wrong. And you did! But you tried, nonetheless, you tried. And that is very important.'

She thanked him while he snorted and told her not to worry, it was quite all right, he often – now that Egyptology had become so popular, something to do with Hollywood perhaps, and he said this with distaste – got applicants who were unsuitable. She apologised to Pennington for wasting his time. He nodded with a steely little smile. 'Thanks so much, good-bye, dear, goodbye.' Goodbye for ever, he meant, and Rosa thought, *Well, that's that.* Once he had shut her out she went back out through the little gate. She side-stepped round a yellow digger, which was sitting on the kerb like an industrial scorpion. Pennington was nothing but a diversion. He was a wrong turn, if anything, and for a moment she wanted to go back and tell him. She had a few urgent questions to answer, and none of them, but none of them, had anything to do with Osiris. Except, it was Osiris who weighed you in the balance after death. It was Osiris who put a feather on one of the scales and your heart – or soul – on the other, and if your heart sank lower on the scales than the feather, then you were doomed. Well, we must all be doomed, she thought. Every last one of us! For who, in this day and age, can make any claim to having a heart lighter than a feather!

'Mr Rivers is in a meeting,' said the woman. Mandy had come back from the store cupboard with this news. 'Really, are you sure?' said Rosa. She tried to sound incredulous. Had Sharkbreath really not wanted to see her? 'Can't you try again?' said Rosa.

'He is too busy to see you,' said Mandy. She said that with

an officious twang, rustling her papers.

'But I really do need to see him,' said Rosa. 'I've been a good client, a client of many years. It's true, my debt is quite bad. I'm not pretending there's no debt. But I am actively seeking work. I am busy about it. And I just need some flexibility on my debt.'

Mandy bridled. She was definitely becoming sanctimonious. 'If you're in debt, then there's nothing I can do about that. Mr Rivers can't see you. I can't help you any more,' she said.

'Perhaps you *can* help me,' said Rosa, in a tone of ill-advised optimism. Mandy shrugged and looked as if she thought it was unlikely. When Rosa said a couple more things Mandy told her she had to talk to Rivers. Shaking her head brusquely, Mandy walked away.

Eager and ready, awaiting enlightenment, Rosa sat on the top deck of a bus as it rounded the corner and moved on to Kensington Park Road. There was still much to anticipate. Today she had an interview and she hoped she would get the job. She had to go back to Jess's flat, pass the day writing applications, and prepare herself. She had to prime herself for her interview at 4 p.m. It seemed a real possibility, this job she was going to win. Her deviation would be corrected; she would climb out of her fiscal pit. After that, when that was settled, she would really get to grips with the basics, with the essential mysteries and underlying causes. She inhaled sharply as a woman elbowed her in the face. She heard Arabic behind her and German to her left. *Auch wenn wir nicht wollen: Gott reisst.* Then she heard the tinny sound of an iPod, whispering a tune she couldn't remember. The bus scraped past the parked cars and people. A scaffold and the sound of drills. The yellow-fronted self-service laundry, always for let. Shops with their windows full. Pale slabs. Enfeoffed, she thought. My kingdom for an epiphany. The sun ascending. The sky a lustrous pale blue. Soon it would be mid-morning. The morning was half-finished, half-begun. And onward the day went, unstoppable, quite incessant in its vigour.

Ahead she saw the blue bridge hanging over the road, cars filing across it. It was a slung construction of steel and on its curved belly were signs and shapes, cryptic clues, left there by the taggers. *TEMP*. She had a fine view of a high-rise block, faded turquoise trim on the windows. On a balcony she saw two eagles, painted in gilt. Then there was the pebble-dashed side of another bank. Another bank, she thought, with bars on the doors. But there was no point trying to get symbolic about the fact that she had ripped through her overdraft and failed to supply a payment plan. The glass shivered as the bus turned abruptly and everyone swayed, rubbing shoulders in a friendly way. For all of this, despite the deep sense of community, the Blitz spirit of the upper deck, Rosa found she had her head in her hands. Suddenly she wanted to get out, she was racked with a sense of unease, and when the bus came to a halt under the Westway she ran down the steps. At the side of the road, she wondered if she should wait for another bus or walk home. Indecision stopped her for a second, then she walked up the hill and along the street thinking that here was another Georgian terrace and here a window with the curtains gusting in the breeze. She picked her way past the station where an old man was chanting a mantra, begging for change. A man with a grey face was selling papers, his hands in fingerless gloves. He mouthed an 'A' at Rosa, and then she heard the rest: 'ARSENAL WIN CUP' he was saying, and then his voice faded again. Pressing her feet carefully on the pavement she walked up the hill, passing the stalls selling falafels, the late night shops, the all-night chemist. She noticed the taggers had scrawled new words along the walls. EASY I, she read. THAT and what? she thought. She couldn't read it.

She reached the funeral parlour on the corner with the growl of the Westway at her back. The houses were yellow and blue and some of their lintels were crumbling. The traffic lined up in queues, and she heard the low moan of brakes. But really, she added, we're nearly in the suburbs. She stared intently at the rooms she passed, seeing an African woman with her hair scraped into a bun, spreading out sheets on a bed, and a Middle Eastern man tying back the curtains of a bedsit – she could see the bed behind him and beyond that the shabby frame of an ancient cooker. He caught her staring and she looked away.

Everything was named for outmoded pastoralism – Oxford Gardens, St Michael's Gardens, Ladbroke Grove. There was a sign pointing left, saying EQUAL PEOPLE. So that's where they live, she thought, moving past. The houses on this road were Victorian, with pillars and grand windows. They were haughty in the cold sunlight. There was a mural on the side of one row, an image of stairs ascending to a celestial place. Even here they were bugging her with thoughts of eternity. Meanwhile she nodded at the blue plaque which said 'Phiz lived here', nailed to a house with yellowing curtains, a neon light by the door. Now she could see the Trellick Tower with washing on the balconies like semaphore flags. A pair of men who were covered in paint and a kid with a hood slung over his eyes. There was a blue sign saying offices to let, and a man saying 'Fuck shit' to the open air, and the number 52 was shuddering past. Beyond the prophet on the corner was the roundabout where everything looked ruined, patched in pinks and blues. There was the cheap call centre, the takeaway with its plastic pictures of faded food in the windows, a set of banished office blocks, and on a low wall running up to the red steel bridge she saw *TEMP* again, and a billboard saying HERE COME THE TEARS. Her mouth filled with fumes; the air was thick with the smell of petrol. Rosa always turned the corner wheezing, vowing to get out of the city. Her street had a few Victorian houses, stranded amid rubble and nothing, as if the row had been bombed and never rebuilt. On the other side of the street was a high-rise block. There was a hoarding further away, decorated with leftover scraps of former posters. One day they had pasted a sign up saying ARMAGEDDON.

It was a huge hint from God. The back windows of Jess's flat had a view of the receding parallels of train tracks, coated with moss, and a red steel bridge. To the west was a gas tower like an abandoned shrine and a burial mound of rubble.

Her mouth was dry and she could smell her own breath. Somehow the door came closer and closer until she could see the peeling paint and the small bare garden and then she dropped her keys. She scrabbled in the earth thinking it is today and I am the mother god. When the door opened she felt faint for a moment and stumbled in the hall. At the door to the flat she paused and wondered if she heard a movement within. That made her heart thump madly in her breast. She had avoided Jess for days, but it was never certain when she would be at home. She was holding the handle, but she couldn't twist it. Then she heard a noise and the door swung open.

When she regained her focus, she saw Jess had a steely gaze and a resolute air. She was by the table, a Marlboro Light in one hand. Jess was dressed in pristine cream, she had a first-rate brain, and she commanded a decent salary that she had used to buy a flat in no-man's-land. Jess was a guardian, tending her own personal shrine to normality. She was standing straight-backed, making herself as tall as she could. She stood with her cigarette in one hand, the other hand in her pocket, eyeing Rosa calmly. Then she tossed back her glossy hair; Jess was defined completely by her brown mane. Rosa had never seen her naked face; it was always half-concealed by hair. Jess lined herself up with the window, and cast a reluctant glance towards her. *By God, you are a redoubtable foe, and I concede before the contest*, thought Rosa. She had nothing in her armoury at all, nothing to say, and no way to defend herself. Besides, her head hurt. She knocked something off the table, a bottle of something, and it rolled away, under the sofa. *Something to sort out later.*

'Rosa, now we've coincided, let's go and have brunch,' said

Jess in a flinty tone. 'I've been working from home this morning. Now I have to go into work. Let's grab a bite to eat while I'm on my way. We need to talk about a couple of things. Have you got time now?'

That was clearly ironic, and Rosa rose with a sense of foreboding, staggering under it, or under the weight of something else she couldn't identify. 'Of course. Just have to wash my face,' she said, her throat tight. Jess nodded, as if she understood Rosa's reluctance, commended it as a fair assessment of the situation. 'I have to drop off some dry cleaning. I'll meet you at Café 204 in twenty minutes,' she said tersely, and stalked out of the door.

In the bathroom Rosa put her head under the tap and washed her face. She rubbed the condensation from the mirror and looked at herself – mostly unchanged – wry smile, deliberately cultivated at fourteen, thin face, pale cheeks, dark eyes, nothing unattractive about her, older of course, but her family aged well, their cheekbones grew more chiselled and their jaws kept their lines, and their fat turned to scrag. Recently she had noticed deep lines across her brow, a sceptical puckering of the skin. A vein had burst on her cheek, but there was nothing else that singled her out. She looked well enough. Slightly anaemic, but she had always looked bloodless. The bags under her eyes were swarter by the day, but that was to be expected. Anyway, swart was just her colour. '*Amor fati*,' she said to the mirror, the steamed up smear in front of her. 'There's no happy ending anyway.' Through the narrow window of the bathroom she saw the feathery texture of the sky. Later the sun might shine on the city, brightening the grey fronts of the Georgian houses and the dusty terraces. There would be a smell of the approach of winter and dried out petrol and she would walk in Kensington Gardens and watch sunlight skimming on the surface of the water and people playing football in the grass. If she went to the interview and did well, she thought, then she would take a book to a quiet corner of the park and read for a while.

Now she turned off the taps. The pipes made a low groan. She took a towel from the rack and smelt it. She used it sparingly on her skin. Because Jess had already gone out, she drew the curtains and dressed quickly in the living room, looking round at the familiar objects, silhouettes in the half-light. In the corner she saw the diodes of a stereo, glinting like rubies. She could see Jess's coat hanging on the half-open door like a timid man too nervous to approach. Then, prepared to beg, she walked out onto the street.

She caught up with Jess at a café on Portobello Road, a place where they sold designer clothes and food at the same time. The waiters passed their time sniffing down the menus, styling themselves on Satan and his minions. In the designer kitchens of Beelzebub they were dishing up much-adorned plates. Everyone in there was well clad, loaded with the latest styles. Even the brunch was as elegant as anything. Rosa didn't care about the contrasts. It was only when she had eaten half her salmon and eggs that she understood she was there to receive advice. Jess was a small, precise person, who always thought before she spoke. She had been generous for months. Now Rosa's whole *Weltanschauung*, to give it a name it hardly merited, was wearing thin. They ate toast and failed to talk seriously until a second round of coffees came. Then Jess – who was a kindly person and really quite hated to kick people in the teeth – said, 'Rosa, I brought you here to suggest that you take a break. Why not go away for a while? A change of scene. How about it?' She was twirling a napkin round her neat little fingers.

'No need,' said Rosa, her mouth full of toast.

'Now, Rosa,' said Jess. 'I mean it. Have a holiday. Take a break. Go on, go and see Will and Judy. You said they invited you the other week. Go for some brisk walks, get some country air. I'll lend you some money, if you need it' – and Rosa said, 'No thanks' – and Jess made a pishing noise as if to say that they would argue about this later. 'So why not go off for a while and then we'll see if you don't come back full of gusto. Give them a call later.'

'I'm fine,' said Rosa. 'Quite enough gusto. Thanks for the suggestion.'

'Why not consider it at least. It's easy to get trapped in a way of thinking about things. You'd find it'd give you some distance. Look, I'll square it.'

Rosa was about to say *no thanks*, but then she realised she wasn't sure if Jess meant her holiday or her brunch. The holiday she could turn down with dignity, but she was hoping Jess might expense brunch. Playing for time, she said, 'Jess, you've been really saintly. As soon as I regain my poise' – at this Jess kept a straight face and said nothing – 'I will definitely take your advice. But for the moment, I don't want to leave the city when everything is so indeterminate. I have to get a job. I can't just borrow money from you.'

Jess greased her lips with spittle. She said, 'As long as you know the offer stands. The other thing is, well, I think it might be time for you to move on.'

'Move on from what?' said Rosa, with a heightened sense of foreboding. There was a pregnant pause while Jess seized her coffee and drank it down. When she had finished she said, quite calmly, 'From my flat.'

'You want me to move out?'

'In short, yes.'

That was a blow, though far from surprising. Really, Rosa agreed. She was an imposition. However penitent she was, she was still there in Jess's flat all day, scattering books and scraps of paper across her stripped pine floorboards, violating the sanctity of the bathroom, leaving stains on the coffee cups. She was intrusive and the offer had originally only been for a few weeks. Besides, Jess and Neil were settling down. They wanted to start a family, Jess was explaining. 'At thirty-four,' she said, 'we think it's high time. We just want a bit more space. You know, so we can sort things out and really get on to the next stage.'

The logic was irrefutable. The next stage was beckoning and who was Rosa to stand in the way? Jess was eager for her next part, ready and willing to play it. The argument was done and dusted by the time Jess had unfurled a few reasonable sentences. It was a pedestrian moment but it left Rosa with the awkward question of where she would go. 'Sure,' she said. 'I understand.' She squinted at the table. 'I can go as soon as you want.'

'No no, just as soon as you can,' said Jess, suggesting that it would be physically impossible for Rosa to go as soon as she wanted. 'I don't want to sling you out completely. Let's just work towards you going as soon as possible. Think about it today and tell me how soon you think that will be, and then I'll make plans around that.'

That was pretty brutal, and Rosa thought about launching a protest. *Jess, if I may beg you?! I understand, you have been generous, toweringly generous, far more than you needed to be. In honesty, we were never close friends, you and I. Cordial with each other, part of a bonded group, but there was no particular tie between us. Which makes your patience still more commendable. But perhaps you are being hasty? After all, I've been here only two months and in that time I have made good progress. I have read some of Euripides, a bit of Seneca, a few poems by Catullus, a little (though tentatively and in some confusion) of Plotinus, and, in my leisure hours, some Wordsworth, a lot of Blake, a number of sonnets by Donne. I have really cracked on with ancient philosophy. While doing this, I have managed nonetheless to pay rent every month. I understand, you gave me a good rate on the room, minimal compared to the market rate, I can hardly complain. Nonetheless, Sharkbreath will tell you, that money was sucked out of my account each month. Eventually it was sucked from my debt. I have not been tidy, I know, but I have never been late with a payment!* And she thought of the hours she had spent pacing the streets, or sitting in cinemas and bars, trying to avoid going back to Jess's flat, giving her evenings on her own and evenings with Neil and disappearing when Jess had guests over – as if she was merely a sponging interloper, the recipient of charity. Still it was hard to construct a case. There was no way she could justify herself. Instead she said 'Of course' in a weak voice. 'Thanks so much for letting me stay for so long. I know it hasn't been ideal for you.' She sipped her coffee and thought, *Now what will you do?* There was a pause, while Rosa considered the question and Jess looked eagerly for the waiter.

'I still think you should just get away,' said Jess. 'I'm really happy to lend you the money. Let me know. And if I can help you in any other way.'

'Oh no, that's fine. You've really helped already,' said Rosa. 'It's not your fault at all. I'm sorry if I've been inconsiderate.'

Jess shook her head, impatiently.

'In truth, Jess,' said Rosa, 'these months have been a trifle hard.' A trifle trying, she thought, these last few months. 'I feel – well, frankly, I feel as if I am presiding over a small tranche of chaos, my own, but completely beyond my control. It's a sort of self-consciousness I feel. I'm watching the descent. Like a novice skier, I am flying down the slope, without a sense of direction.' Jess looked unimpressed. *The wind is whipping at my ears. Someone! Slow me down! The wind is really chasing me along. I can see a few faces, a few spectators, but they can't stop me. It's a following wind, following me along, gusting me into what can only be a crevasse. A great gaping chasm. I don't want to plunge in, I want to turn the skis around, or at least fall to the side into an accommodating snowdrift, but the snow is too pacey and slithery and I'm gathering speed, hurtling faster and faster and now I can see the blackness opening up before me, do you understand? I should be screaming at these people standing around on the slopes. I should be screaming HELP ME! SAVE ME! But I'm worried they might have other things to do, better things to do, so I'm skiing along, smiling at them, trying to look like I know what I'm doing. It's trenchant, the darkness. Black and compelling. Here we are, faster and faster and here's the hole! Here's the damn dark hole! Ahead! Ahead!*

Jess asked for the bill. When it came she said, 'I'll get it', and slapped her credit card on the table. Rosa let her pay.

*

Later she and Jess went their separate ways: Jess to the tube with a spring of plain relief in her step and Rosa back to the flat, her own personal sword of Damocles dangling above. At the flat, she checked the post and wrote a few petitions, attempts to placate the fates. She wrote a letter to the Flower Shop, applying for a job tying bows round bouquets. *Dear Sir or Madam, I would be delighted to be considered for this position. As a child, I was quite good at playing the piano and the violin. I have always enjoyed using my fingers. Really, though my training was in journalism I have long felt that flowers were my true metier.* She could imagine herself there, tying up a bouquet, one hand to her temple, the other struggling with a piece of ribbon. 'Fancy a batch of lilies, sir, quite your nicest funeral flower?' 'There's Rosemary, that's for remembrance. And there are pansies, that's for thoughts. There's rue for you. There's a daisy. Thanks so much. Come again soon. For bonny sweet Robin is all my joy.' She wrote,

Dear Mr Pennington, Thanks for your time the other day. Just to emphasise, I really am very interested in the culture of Ancient Egypt. I know we didn't get on so well, but I'm never at my best under pressure. And you were a funny old man, not my kind of person at all. But Ancient Egypt – it's been a fascination of mine ever since I saw the sarcophagi at the British Museum as a child. We went on a school trip, all the way from Bristol. We were eleven or twelve. The tube train stopped in a tunnel and we all screamed. Then we saw the gold cases with their inscriptions – I remember wondering if there were still bodies inside.

She had wandered around with her mouth open. She had often imagined going to Egypt, sitting at the edge of the pyramids watching the sun set across the sands, with the age-blasted head of the Sphinx above her. *I would be so honoured to help you with such a fascinating project. Yours ever, Rosa Lane.*

Dear Mr Sharkbreath, Thank you for your letter dated when-
ever of whenever threatening to send bailiffs round to my
address if I don't pay the interest on the loan you gave me in
August. You are of course welcome to drop round, but Jess
might be angry. Jess owns the flat I live in, and all the furniture.
I am afraid that in recent months I have given most of my
things away, or sold them. There are a few things I could offer
you: one smart suit in cream (more like oyster, really), a pair of
jeans and a jumper, two shirts, my small collection of under-
garments, four pairs of socks, a very warm grey coat, and a
couple of second-hand books. If you feel any of this would
help then do come and get it. Yours ever, Rosa Lane.

Dear Viracocha, Buddha, Osiris, Isis, Zeus, Allah, Jehovah,
Shiva, Humbaba, Yabalon and the rest,
What is it that you want me to do? Just what is it? Yours
expectantly, Rosa.

She tore that out. 'Impractical,' she said aloud. She was still
racking her brains.

She took the paper and circled jobs. She smiled as she went.
Here she was, rushing towards a blank wall with little in her
pockets, and there were thousands of opportunities out there,
marvellous jobs, well paid and with associated perks, company cars and the rest, presenting the perfect prospect of fulfil-
ment. She only had to tick the boxes, marshal herself.

Wanted, she read. *European Sales and Marketing manager.*
London-based Design and Product Distribution company
seeks an experienced Sales and Marketing manager for
Europe.

Can you focus on the detail while keeping sight of the big
picture? No, thought Rosa. No, she wasn't sure she could.

Leading London-based media measurement agency seeks
go-getting grads with excellent writing and analytical skills.

She shook her head. *Communications Coordinator,* she read.
Excellent opportunity! Depending on how you look at it.

Marketing office administrator. This could be the job for you!
Do you want to be part of the fastest growing Communications
agency in the UK?

No, thought Rosa. No, she didn't. *Wanted, a secretary for a*
busy London company. She or he will be stylish and efficient,
ready for the thrust and parry of office life, and great at deal-
ing with people. Starting salary of – but Rosa had flicked over
the page. *Do you long for opportunities to travel? If so, this*
job is for you! Personal assistant to head of company, always
on the move, needs efficient person to manage his meetings
and schedules. Degree preferred. Apply to . . .

Do you long for the peace that passes understanding.
Apply to . . . – but she couldn't find an advert that said that.
Instead, she began scribbling words. *Wanted Customer*
Manager for bright bubbly company in Vauxhall. Wanted
Director of communications for a small dynamic company in
Angel. Wanted spawn of Satan for a saucy company in
Stockwell. Wanted brethren of Beelzebub for a blazing bub-
bling cauldron in Bow.

Her lists were creative acts in themselves. Initially she had
written with the bold idea that she would actually achieve the
things set out on them, but after a few days she realised that
wasn't going to happen. They represented what was required
of her, with a few extras thrown in that were plain unlikely.
But she couldn't get through the entries, unlikely or otherwise.
It was pure catharsis, writing them out.

Now you are home, it's definitely time to:
Get a job.
Wash your clothes
Clean the kitchen.
Phone Liam and ask about the furniture.
Phone Kersti
Find a place to stay
Buy some tuna and spaghetti
Go to the bank and beg them for an extension – more money,

more time to pay back the rest of your debt.
Read the comedies of Shakespeare, the works of Proust, the
plays of Racine and Corneille and The Man Without
Qualities.
Read The Golden Bough, The Nag-Hammadi Gospels, The
Upanishads, The Koran, The Bible, The Tao, *the complete*
works of E. A. Wallis Budge
Read Plato, Aristotle, Confucius, Bacon, Locke, Rousseau,
Wollstonecraft, Kant, Hegel, Schopenhauer, Kierkegaard,
Nietzsche, and the rest
Hoover the living room
Clean the toilet
Unearth the TEMP

She drank her tea. She took a slice of bread and put it in the
toaster. 'But come now,' she said to herself, standing with the
lemon walls around her staring at the kettle and thinking she
might pilfer some more tea. Really, she was reminding herself,
things weren't that bad! If she could just get the furniture sold
then she would feel much better. If Liam would only sell it, she
would have money for a month or two. But he was clinging
onto it, the hankering hand-me-down swine. Why he wanted
to guard the shiny black sofa and the stained dining table, she
didn't know. A month or two seemed like a long time, the way
things were. It would tide her over. Though to what? And
where would it wash her up? She wasn't taking any chances.
At 4 p.m., she would go and see Mrs Brazier about the job. A
few weeks ago, she had written a little advert and walked
around putting it up in shops. *Intelligent* – in theory – *and*
qualified. Can teach English and History to children up to the
age of twelve. Also the piano up to grade five. Flexible hours.
Good references on request. No one had answered for weeks,
and the advert started to droop and fade and generally look
like a symbol of her inner blah, until Mrs Brazier rang her the
other day.

   She set down her pen. She folded up the list and put it in her pocket. Then she turned to the room. Jess's flat was at the junction of several fields of noise; always you heard cars skimming past the front and trains hammering along at the back. Jess lived in denial of hostile elements. She didn't care that a gas tower squatted at the windows and a nearby billboard said *Abandon Hope*. She had furnished the place with care. First she had bought up a stock of self-assembly furniture. She had fitted in a long beige sofa and some shelves. The chairs were fold-away, because the living room was so small. Jess had built-in cupboards like stowage on a boat, with novelty portholes. On the wall she had put up framed posters from exhibitions she had seen at the Tate. She had painted everything pale pink. The furniture – such as it was – had been angled carefully round the TV. The kitchen Jess had painted yellow. Everything in the kitchen was yellow: the crockery, the kettle, the washing-up bowl, the cupboards and even the fridge stood behind a yellow door. It was moving, how colour-coordinated Jess had made her flat. A Roman blind obscured the graffiti-laden tracks behind, the names of taggers and the word *TEMP*. Rosa, who slept in a room at the back, woke with the early trains. She liked that, though now it was nearly winter it meant she opened her eyes before the sun rose, and lay in the darkness wondering what time it was and if she should sleep some more. *No need to complain now*, she thought, *when you are leaving anyway. So, the cheap accommodation hasn't suited you! Well, now you can find some more!*

TEMP, she thought. *Temper. Temperature.* The tempo of the times. Time's grasping temper. The temperature of the city. Was that what it meant? She couldn't be sure. *Temptation.* The temptation to do nothing. It was heavy upon her. A few months ago she had still been industrious. She went out seeking advice from anointed experts. She had been to see Dr Kamen in September because she was concerned her mood had dipped. She wasn't ill, she explained. She just needed something to steady her, calm her nerves. *I have undertaken a labour.* If she was honest, she was sometimes disturbed by the intensity of her thoughts, the way they held her. She couldn't control her obsessions. Months after leaving her job, she was still undisciplined, still quite out of sorts. *I feel myself driven towards an end that I do not know. I have been panicked. I am seized by the play of opposites*, she had suggested to Dr Kamen, as they sat in the small room where he worked, a room like a throat lozenge – purple walls, tapered sides. 'You know, the usual ones, being and not being, life and death, beauty and ugliness, good and evil, the rest.' It was nothing serious, she said, smiling in embarrassment. 'It just stops me using my time properly. Getting on with things. Work, that sort of thing. I just walk around and read and run my over-draft closer to the limit. I make long lists of things I have to do. It's hardly the way to use a life. Time is so short, and there I am drifting quietly, lagging out the days.' Perhaps it wasn't her thoughts that were the main problem. A few thoughts never harmed anyone, she added. The thing was she would try to get back to earning money and there she would be, dropped back, inert, prone, quite incapable of action. To earn was not to think, she explained. Work – the sort of work she was fitted for – and thought were, though ideally allied, not necessarily – when thought was excessive – best friends, not strictly speaking teeming with mutual amity. 'Do you understand?' she said to Dr Kamen. Dr Kamen said, 'Not quite yet, but we'll soon get to the bottom of it.' Dr Kamen was a good doctor; Rosa had always liked him. He took her temperature, peered in her ears, made her stick out her tongue. He asked her if she had any aches or pains. He did some blood tests and said he would send them away to a lab. Then he wrote something in his notes.

Kamen told her to explain her problems as she saw them. Rosa saw them in lots of ways which never quite formed a cogent pattern, but she talked quickly, qualified herself, decid-ed that wasn't what she meant, began again, lost herself in tan-gents, dried up and stared at the rug. She thought her symp-toms might be psychosomatic, she added.

'I can't be sure until the tests come back, but I would say you are not physically unwell,' he said, a man with a brown beard and greying hair. He had an avuncular air, it made her submit to what he said. 'You are young, fit, you say you exercise. You are thin and should try to eat a bit more. But the skin is healthy. The eyes are healthy. You might be a bit worn out, or agitated. Do you sleep well?'

The room they were in was tight and cramped, with a low door which you had to stoop to get through. You entered bowing and Dr Kamen bowed too. Despite his cramped quarters, Dr Kamen kept up the gravitas. He was a neat man; his beard was trimmed and his clothes were freshly ironed. He was certainly reassuring. Through the window there was a view of bricks and grey sky. They were in Kilburn, on a street of bay windows. The area was suburban without being friendly, full of the disenfranchised and uncertain. She had seen them walking outside, the minorities left to stew, piled in together, and the single mothers pushing prams in high heels, bellies out, and the truant gangs on the corners. She wondered briefly about Dr Kamen. What did he do on Sundays? Did he play cricket? Go to the pub? Not, she thought, to the church. She imagined he liked a pint. She saw him with a beer and a bag of crisps, reading the papers by a fire. She was sure he had a well-organised life. Time management, the relegation of certain things to certain parts of the day – he looked the sort. He didn't seem troubled by global war or the rule of violence. He had crinkled eyes; his face was neither young nor old. He was easy with his gestures, self-confident but not flashy. He was a measured, contemplative man. Alert to the frailties of the human frame, of course. Quite aware of the skull beneath the skin and the rest. As a doctor you could hardly ignore it, you could hardly bury your head in myth and hope it wasn't happening. But it didn't stop him getting up in the mornings. He must be pragmatic, she thought, as he said, again, 'Are you finding it hard to sleep?'

'I don't sleep especially well,' she said. 'But I never have. I

66

have always been a light sleeper, I mean. But I don't have insomnia, no.'

'Do you wake early?' Dr Kamen was saying.

'Yes, quite early.'

'Do you have panic attacks, anxiety attacks, difficulty breathing?' he said. In his hand he held a pen. He had her notes on a computer screen, her small ailments of the last decade. Sometimes she was troubled by flu and once she had turned up with bronchitis. Then he had told her to stay off work for two weeks. On his desk there was a photo of his family – a wife, three children, it looked like, but Rosa couldn't quite make them out. Young children, she imagined, looking at the crayon drawings pinned to the wall behind his desk. A tractor. Signed Oliver.

'No no, nothing like that,' said Rosa. 'I just feel a bit withdrawn.'

'Withdrawn, you say?' Dr Kamen looked slightly concerned.

'There's just something, like an unseen impediment.'

'An impediment?'

'A temporary something, you know, I can't see. Some basic fact. Or a conjunction of facts. Perhaps not even facts, just things. And then some days I think that maybe this is what I'm trying to get to, this fact – or facts, this thing – or things – that would explain everything.'

'And why do you feel that?' said the doctor with an eyebrow raised.

'Because . . .'

She stopped short, reluctant to dwell on things she didn't understand. She was aware she seemed recalcitrant. Now they were staring at each other, and then she felt awkward and dropped her gaze. She fiddled with her nails, bit one, scratched her ear. Still Dr Kamen was waiting patiently, glancing at the screen, at his watch, clicking a pen in his hand.

'Because, you say?' he said finally, after the clock had scraped round a few more minutes. He wasn't going to sit there in silence for ever.

'I was aware I was stuck in the – you know – the rut people mention, when they're on this subject. Eyes down. Head to the desk. Nose to the grindstone, you know. And I was angry with other people. Bystanders, all of them. Then I realised how comic it was. Quite impossible, the whole thing. But I haven't progressed. I was trying to focus my thoughts, but I've found the last few months have been as confused as those that went before.'

'Well, we all feel that,' said Kamen, smiling. 'Particularly after a bereavement. You are bound to feel confused, knocked back, depressed.'

He meant it was hardly a pathology, hardly deviant at all.

'Now I feel as if everyone speaks something else, some other language,' said Rosa. 'I really find I can't raise myself to the challenge. There is something I am still failing to understand. A gap. Truth.' Kamen nodded, perhaps impatiently. It didn't sound any better the second time. 'Perhaps beauty,' she said, but that didn't go so well. Kamen wasn't interested in Rosa's under-cooked theories of truth and beauty, her mixture of other people's ideas and prevailing cliché.

'Yes?' said the doctor, expectantly.

'I feel as if the real world, with its laws of time and space, its economics, politics, and even morality, has dissolved. Or I have been detached from it, and have emerged somewhere – I'm not quite sure where. But really it's much better here, on the edge. It affords quite the best view. The only problem is debt, of course. And that's why I need to change a little, sort things out.'

He smiled. She thought it was simple enough. There must be a reason behind it all. What did she and Dr Kamen know about the order of the universe? What could they know? Everything might be preordained. It might be part of an immaculate order, impossible for them to understand. Of course as Stoicism would have it no action that befell the individual – death included – could be bad, because everything that was part of *logos* was fundamentally good. In that case, her mother's death was part of *logos*, and her current state must also be, and who was she to resist? If it left her quite shattered that was simply her impoverished perspective. She lacked *pneuma* perhaps, she was deficient in life force, but she was sure that things occurred for a reason. She was, she said to Dr Kamen, no Epicurean. 'My mother disagreed,' she added. She was explaining this to Dr Kamen, adding that they were a very primitive species, with very little to be proud of, while he nodded slightly. He wrote something down on a piece of paper.

'I think,' said Dr Kamen, straightening his tie, 'you're depressed. You should have a holiday. Go to see some friends, some good friends who cheer you up. I'm going to prescribe you some antidepressants and see if they might help you. At this stage of things you really just have to manage. If things get worse I could refer you to a psychiatrist. At present, try this course of tablets, and we'll make another appointment soon to see how you're getting on.'

'Thank you very much. Very kind,' said Rosa. He had her wrong, she was thinking. She wasn't depressed at all. Earlier, she had been depressed. Now she woke each day at dawn; it was her excitement that was making her rise so early. That and the grinding of the trains. It was just her thoughts, she wanted to say. But Kamen had his eye on his watch, so she stood up. As she walked away, he said, 'Don't worry, your prince will come.' It made her stop with her hand on the door.

'My prince?' she said. She thought she had heard him wrong, but he was smiling back at her.

'Yes, your prince,' he said. His face had wrinkled up and he meant to be kind. Like so much these days, it made her quite confused. She couldn't think how to reply. Well, perhaps she appeared solitary to him – was it the deep lines in the centre of her brow, or something else about her all-over aspect, that made him think she was questing for love? She wanted to say 'No, no, you've got me wrong, all wrong, that's not the point at all' but it got tangled up. She ended up blushing and backing out of the door.

*

69

Now she heard the distant chimes of a church clock. 1 p.m., and she really had to deal with the day's events, rather than wallowing in thoughts of the past. She had three hours until her interview. She was considering the importance of living in the present when the phone rang. That made her jump and then she edged towards it. Nervously, she held her hand above the receiver. She meant to let it ring, knowing it was likely to be someone either threatening her with dissolution or offering her advice. Yet she lacked willpower. She was too lonely and eager to leave a ringing phone. There was a pause after she answered. 'Rosa,' said her father. 'Rosa, how are you?' The old rasper, on the phone again. *Good God*, thought Rosa. He wanted to mend her, with his rasping voice. It was with a thick throat that she answered.

'Dad, hi. I was just about to call you. I did get your messages. Thanks so much. I wanted to call you when I had some news, but nothing so far has happened.'

'Yes, yes. So what's happening?'

'I'm going for an interview later, then I'll call you and let you know,' said Rosa. Her father sniffed and paused. He was about to challenge her outright, and then he decided that being wry was best, so he said, 'Excellent, Rosa, what is it for this time?'

'Oh, something I'd like to do,' she said. That wasn't true, but she didn't want the inevitable row. She didn't like lying to her father. But the other option – being honest with him – was out of the question.

'Well, you really do need to get a move on with it. Speed up a bit. So silly! Such a silly waste of your talents.' He was still angry. But mostly he was confused.

'Dad, the last thing I need is more speed. Everything's fast enough already. Even today – the morning has just vanished.'

'Vanished has it? Another day! Of course – because you don't have a plan. Look at me. I'm retired. I woke at 7 a.m., learnt some Spanish, read an account of the fall of Berlin in 1945, took the dog for a walk, went for a Spanish lesson, and later I'm meeting my friend Adam for lunch, playing a round of bridge with Sarah and two of my neighbours, and finishing that account of the fall of Berlin this evening. And then my doctor tells me to take it easy!'

'Gosh, Daddy,' said Rosa. 'Are you sure you shouldn't take it easy?'

'Yes, I'm quite sure. I feel better by the day,' said her father. 'Now, let's see, I have to come to London tomorrow, to see a friend who is emigrating to America. You know, at my age, you have to mark these partings. So why don't we have lunch? You can tell me all about the job.'

'Let's,' said Rosa. 'Thanks for the invitation.'

'If you want to come for the weekend some time, do come down and stay with us,' he said.

She said, 'Thanks, thanks so much.' Us meant him and Sarah. Sarah was new, improbable, but there was no point getting into a funeral-baked-meats frenzy about it all. She didn't want to think about Sarah, she didn't want to stand on the parapet mouthing *Oh that this too too solid flesh would melt* so she had been avoiding her father. That was unkind, when the man was like a mummy, dried out and shrivelled and really not looking his best. She ought to have been glad he had Sarah. When you were seventy you had to get along as best you could. Really, Rosa understood that. She didn't judge him. She just found it hard to talk to him. She understood what he was doing. If he could sling it all off, mourn and then displace his wife, then she admired him. It was just Sarah's lisp and her wide-eyed benevolence that made Rosa want to wander away yelping like an injured dog.

But now she wondered if she should just go home after all. Get a job in Bristol, and live with her father. She thought of going back to that tall cold house and imposing on his privacy, disrupting the delicate balance he had established for himself. He and Sarah in their last-stop love nest – it would hardly improve her mood. Rosa wandering down to breakfast, into their cloud of amiable grey. It was regression, or worse, but she was tempted by it nonetheless. They fixed a time and Rosa's father said, 'Don't forget like last time and don't be late,' and then they said goodbye.

Things to do, Monday

Get a job.
Wash your clothes
Clean the kitchen.
Phone Liam. Furniture. Ask him.
Phone Kersti. Entreat.
Find a place to stay. WHO? Whitchurch? Impossible! Kersti? Too flinty by half. Then WHO? Andreas? Could you? Absurd!
Buy some tuna and spaghetti
Go to the bank and tell them you need more time – more time to pay back the rest of your debt.
Read the comedies of Shakespeare, the works of Proust, the plays of Racine and Corneille and The Man Without Qualities.
Read The Golden Bough, The Nag-Hammadi Gospels, The Upanishads, The Koran, The Bible, The Tao, *the complete works of E. A. Wallis Budge*
Read Plato, Aristotle, Confucius, Bacon, Locke, Rousseau, Wollstonecraft, Kant, Hegel, Schopenhauer, Kierkegaard, Nietzsche, and the rest
Hoover the living room
Clean the toilet
Distinguish the various philosophies of the way – read History of Western Philosophy
Sort through your papers and see if there is anything you can send to anyone who might plausibly pay you some money for it
Clean the bath
Unearth the TEMP
Go to see Andreas and ask him for somewhere to stay for a few days until you find somewhere else.

The last she could do, or at least she could certainly go to see Andreas. It was a quick walk to the corner, and at the corner she saw pink and blue walls and signs on the guttering and she heard the planes whining their descent and the trilling choirs of birds. An immaculate day stretched out before her, around her, and Rosa was walking past the lines of cars and the ragged thin-stripped trees, laughing quietly to herself. 'Ridiculous,' she said. She was leaning back now, finding that her head was sore. She was aware of a vague smell of sweat and dust. Her mouth was dry and she wanted something to drink. She saw the roads winding along the canal, and the concrete skeleton of a new block of flats. There was a church and a matted line of old hous-es. She saw everything in monochrome, because she had screwed up her eyes. The light made her head pound, but really, the doctor had misdiagnosed her. It was perhaps not significant, but she had a prince. It was uncertain what they were to each other, but he was called Andreas and he was a fine man, presid-ing over a few feet of space by another stretch of railway tracks. Had she been less distracted she might have fallen in love with him. But love was quite impossible, given the conditions. With things as fleeting as they were you couldn't risk it. Instead she turned up at his flat and they slithered in the darkness. He was young – perhaps too young, at twenty five – but he was beauti-ful, with his brown hair, brown eyes, long limbs. He was German and he wanted to be an actor. Beauty hadn't yet pro-pelled him onwards, so he waited on tables and taught German. They had little in common, and they couldn't express them-selves together. Nonetheless she liked talking to him.

She could see a slanted forest of cranes in the distance. They were angled over a building site on the horizon, suspending cables. She turned left and saw a pub. Thin black doors, a big Victorian advertisement on the upper wall: *The PARROT. A Fine Victorian Pub. Original features. Fine Ales. Good food.* She had always liked the atmosphere of pubs. That was because her parents often ate in pubs: at the weekends, on holidays, they went for pub lunches, and so, perversely enough, she associated pubs with her childhood. She had played in the gardens of a hundred pubs, pawing the grass with other infants, as if the grass was a lost continent a thousand miles wide. She remembered the pub they went to on Sundays – a big Georgian hotel on a long winding street – had a donkey in the garden. It was roped to a fence, and it groaned and shrieked as she played. And there was another pub her father liked, with a view of the Avon Gorge. She remembered playing on the patio there, the paving stones stern in the dusk. At the edge was a deep drop to the muddy estuary beneath, and upstream was the inverted arch of the Suspension Bridge. In the summer months she liked to stand by the wall watching the light shining on the muddy water, though her mother always summoned her back from the edge. The gorge was vast and green, its slopes full of slanted trees.

As she walked, hands in her pockets, chin lifted, quite alert and aware of the seeping colours of the sky and the progress of the cars, she was thinking that Andreas had appeared to her one night in a bar. That was a few weeks ago, when she had been sitting on her own drinking wine. She had taken herself out because Jess had told her she was having a dinner party. 'Friends for supper. Will you be here?' which meant 'Can you not be here?' She had been in the bar for a while, picking at the complimentary nuts and writing in her notebook, when Andreas came over and asked if she was waiting for someone. She wasn't sure what to say, and then she held up her hands and confessed, 'No no, I'm not. No I always come here and drink alone. Pretty much every night.' She thought she might have blushed.

'That's not true,' he laughed. 'I work here pretty much every night.'

She was apprehensive, monosyllabic at first, but they drank a glass of wine together. They could hardly hear each other, and he kept putting his lips close to her ear, and she discovered he told plausible jokes. At one point she laughed, genuinely and without strain. When they had shouted for a while, he said: 'Shall we get out of here?' and she said 'Yes.' Her friends would have told her not to bother, had they been there. But they weren't. Rosa was really alone and the thought of walking back to Jess's flat and twisting the key in the door, nodding her way through the living room and retreating to her bed, made her take his hand on the corner. This was how she got to know him, through lust and a fear of solitude. Still, they scuffed along the streets, suddenly self-conscious, and he said, 'Do you like jazz?' and Rosa said, 'No, I detest jazz.' And he laughed. 'I was about to say,' he said, 'that there's a fantastic jazz club which I go to. But I suppose that's not of interest any more.'

'Is there another sort of music you enjoy?' asked Rosa.

'No, only jazz,' he said. They were standing outside a large church, a grey spire behind them. The sky was thick with clouds and she could hear the leaves swirling along the pavement. It was quite cold.

'Well, that's a shame,' she said. 'For you, anyway.'

'I feel a great sense of sorrow,' he said.

They stood stock still, and he seemed embarrassed. They were smiling at each other. He was tall, statuesque, and when he turned his head to look at the street she saw he had a stark profile, a long nose, an overhanging brow. His features were unsubtle in their handsomeness; it was hard to tell what age would do to them, whether it would refine them or blunt them altogether. She caught herself looking at his lips, which were bright red against a surrounding shadow of stubble.

'Well,' he said. 'Here we are.'

'Here we are,' she said. Inevitably, they kissed. He smelt strongly of aftershave and more remotely of smoke. It was curious but far from seedy; she was surprised how glad she was to kiss him.

They spent a weekend in his flat on Tavistock Crescent. It

was part of a modern development, handy for the shops of Portobello Road, set back from the terrorist safe house nearby. After that weekend she had seen him a dozen times perhaps. She found him relaxing company. He expected very little of her. He seemed to understand that she was not quite herself. He told her that she was a beautiful woman, but sad and grave. He explained to her that they transcended the boundaries of youth and age. In this equation, she suspected she was age. He enjoyed being naked, he explained. He wanted to worship her body, and he announced that he loved her thighs. 'And the curve of your back, and the muscles on your arms, long thin muscles,' he said. 'You're very graceful.' That should have been a sop for her ego, but she couldn't absorb it. When they lay in bed listening to the trains hammering past and the usual grinding of the Westway, he said, 'I would like to take you on holiday. You seem tired.'

'No, no, I couldn't possibly be tired,' said Rosa, reclining into a pile of pillows. He had dark hair and alabaster skin. It was a good contrast, and she admired his youth. It gave her an illusion that she might also be twenty-five, poised on the brink of everything. At twenty-five she had been naive and driven. More naive, less driven than him. She had been resolutely, devoutly fashionable; it amused her to remember her faithful adherence to fleeting trends. She had spent so much time trying to enjoy herself in the usual ways – clubbing, drinking, dying her hair. Her bathroom had been full of balms and ointments. Now, at the stage when she was meant to be plastering herself in unguents, she had thrown that stuff away. At twenty-five she had felt that there was time, that life was long. Now, the years since then had been soft sift in an hourglass, they had poured through so quickly. She wanted to tell this to Andreas, but there was little she could offer him. Compared with Rosa at twenty-five, Andreas was distinct and resolute. He told her she was going through a bad patch. It sounded reassuring that way, as if it was all just as fleeting as a fever. He understood, but he wanted her to

76

know that he found her fascinating, he said. 'Your eyes, your dark wit, some days you are pained, others quite childlike and funny. I like your range. I think you must always have been like this. I have no depth at all, but I admire it in others,' he said. When he talked like that she lapped it up, her with her dented self. She enjoyed it, and didn't care if he was filling time. He had that sort of carelessness. Sometimes she knew he was talking for the hell of it, to stop a gap, stuff a bung in a silence.

He had photographs of his parents on the table by his bed. His mother looked beautiful in a high-cheekboned way. His father was tall and thin, bent slightly. Andreas polished the frames, laughing at his reverence. He slung his legs out of the bed and offered to bring her coffee.

'My mother', he said, when he came back with a tray, 'always told me I should learn how to wait on women. She says it is an important skill, perhaps the most important.'

'It is a skill,' said Rosa. 'Knowing when to serve and when to command.'

'I can do either,' he said. Their repartee was a little forced. But his eyes shone when she kissed him. He listened well, laughed in the right places, generously plied her with questions. Still, the balance between them kept slipping. Within a few days, he was offering her advice.

'You need to get a sense of what you want to do,' he kept saying. 'You have to do something. We all, we all have to do something. I feel I can help, at least with this.'

'I just need to get back into the Polis,' she said.

'The Polis,' he said. He sounded tired. They were wrapped in sheets. Theirs was a bed-bound romance. It did best at night. But now it was early morning, and they were both hung-over.

'It's hard to get back in,' she said. 'Once you fall out.'

He stayed silent, looking at her. Then he rolled over and folded his arms around her. She was pressed into his wide chest. He seemed to be smiling. He kissed the back of her neck.

I just wonder what it means, she wanted to say. Us, here, in this tentative version of romance, and before, Liam and I. These entanglements. All of us with our bare bones of knowledge. Not knowing what we are. The birth of tragedy. This smallness I feel deep inside myself. The Birth of Smallness. Yes, yes, after the Egyptians, the Greeks with their fetish for dying beauty, doomed greatness, comes the birth of smallness, the soaring rise of the insignificant. *Here I am*, thought Rosa, *the living embodiment of the new age of minutiae*. She understood it clearly. Gradually everything had been taken over by people like Rosa. In general, her kind were doing very well. She had been given a generous slice of the pie; it was just that she couldn't quite eat it.

Andreas was explaining that he was naturally idle. It was only by an effort of will that he made himself do things. The key was to set yourself small goals, he said.

'So there's one thing we must establish – what are your small goals?' he asked.

'Oh, nothing much. Avoid the onslaught. Stay out of trouble.'

'Well, that's not quite what I meant. As goals, I am not sure they work. Because eventually something will come to you, debt or death, or something anyway. This onslaught, you can't really avoid it.'

'Why?' she said.

'Why can't you avoid death? I don't know, for pity's sake,' he said. He raised a long, thick arm and slapped his hand on his forehead.

'No, I mean the everlasting why,' said Rosa. He yawned, and turned onto his front. He crossed his hands above his head, defensively.

'I thought it was an everlasting yes,' he said into the pillow.

'No, that must be something else.'

'Anyway it's not a goal.' He scratched his arm. He had a

hand on her back, she could feel the warmth and pressure of his hand.

'Why?'

'Let's not go round again.'

'No, I mean why is "why" not a goal?'

Now his head was buried in the pillow. His voice was muffled. 'In the name of God,' he said, 'in the name of God in Heaven, "why" is a question, not a goal. It's a goddamn question!'

'Huh, profound,' she said, but it wasn't fair to mock him. Now he sat up and took her hand.

'You say you are tired. Well, give yourself a few weeks, and then really get cracking.'

'Get cracking?' she said.

'Is it not a contemporary phrase?'

'No, it's perfect,' said Rosa. 'It's just the right phrase.' And she kissed him, though she knew she was wasting his time.

He was vain, and his motions were sometimes contrived, the studied flick of his head, the way he moved his hands. She could see his health was immanent. She was sure any woman would like him. Because they saw each other so seldom, she was convinced he must have another lover, a batch of them. This made her distant and sometimes preoccupied. It wasn't jealousy she felt. It was a relief, if anything, that he wasn't hanging around expecting love. Still, in a few weeks she knew a lot about him. He filled her in on the basics, meticulously, sparing her none of the details. He came from Berlin. His father had been a diplomat, and had been posted to China and Morocco when Andreas was a child. So by the age of seven he spoke German, English, French and a little Mandarin Chinese. His English was grammatically impeccable, but his idiom was inconsistent. It was a sort of cinema slang, derived from English-language films. He was tall and pale, with a smooth, line-free face. His hair was slightly curly and he wore it long. He had fine muscular legs; he liked to run. He walked with great confidence; he stood upright with his hands resting in his pockets. He was rarely pensive or demoralised, as far as Rosa could see. In fact he seemed to possess a blissful sense of optimism that Rosa dimly remembered, and felt was bound up with youth. He always dressed well, in smart, freshly ironed clothes, and his underwear was striped. He had a slight accent, but it was not immediately possible to place him. Initially she had thought he might be American.

For all this, she wasn't quite sure what he wanted from her. What meaning did he attack to their liaison? She hadn't got round to asking him the question, but she was sure she should. He was far too robust to lie around droning on about the self. He was too young, too optimistic, too fixed on his as yet non-existent career as an actor. He was reasonably interested in the contemporary novel, he said. He was good at entertaining himself. Other than jazz he liked Wagner and The Pixies. That seemed a contrivance to Rosa, but she didn't mind. He moved with the grace of someone whose gestures have not yet become habitual, as if he would be quite capable of casting off his ways of speaking and moving, switching them suddenly for another mode.

Now she was at the peeling door of his flat. There was a Moroccan sitting on the balcony above, smoking a cigarette. She nodded at him, and he bowed his head. A mother and child were playing in a multicoloured playground behind her. She heard childish squeals, adult congratulations. 'Very good!' 'Very very good sweetie!' A TV was on in the flat next door, and she saw the colours shifting in the glass. She waited while the day continued, and when Andreas answered the door he said, 'ROSA!!' and weighted the word with exclamation marks. 'It's so nice when you come round,' he said, smiling and kissing her cheek. 'How are you? And what, what has been happening?'

'Nothing at all. And to you?' That was their chaste opening, and they stood in the hall with their hands in their pockets. He was wearing the whitest shirt she had ever seen. His body felt warm, and she grasped his hands. There was the cuckoo clock behind him and she saw her face was red in the distorting mirror.

'It's so boring, but I have to go out any minute,' he said. 'So boring. Just to the dentist, but I have to go. I've waited a month for the appointment and I'm in agony. My mouth is disgusting, I'm ashamed.' He gestured at a tooth, and made a grimace. 'But can I walk you some of the way home? The dentist is just by Ladbroke Grove. So you see, it's perfect, if you don't mind going back that way? Did you have something else to do over here? Are you on your way somewhere?' A few stories came to mind, but she said, 'No, I just did some shopping on Portobello Road, and thought I'd drop by.'

'What did you buy?' Her hands were empty.

'Oh, window shopping, nothing.'

'So you'll walk back with me? As an unexpected treat before I go to my torture.'

'OK, that would be nice.'

'Just wait here, wait here just a second.'

He vanished along the corridor, and she heard him switching off a radio.

Hand in hand for a while, and then walking apart, they passed along the crescent of balconies, satellite dishes hammered up on the walls and washing floating on invisible currents of air. They neared the metal haunches of Westbourne Studios. She thought of Whitchurch at her meeting, speaking in a soft voice. She would be poised, convincing. Then she would leave, safe in the knowledge of her continued relevance.

She said, 'How are you?' and he said, 'Good, good. I've been thinking about you this week.'

'That's kind of you,' she said. 'Depending on the way in which you have thought of me, of course.' They arrived under the concrete slur of the Westway. She saw the sign scrawled on the bricks. *TEMP* – it ran over and over again – *TEMP TEMP*

TEMP TEMP – in red spray paint. Next to it were some stencils of a man walking backwards. *What the TEMP*, she thought. She saw the day spread out, the trees and the sky.

'Oh, mostly about the curves of your ass, I'm joking,' he said. 'But how are you? Are you tired? You look a bit tired.'

'No no I'm fine.'

He kissed her nonchalantly. He had a hand on her back, and she could feel his breath on her skin.

'I was thinking that when I have more money, we should go away,' he said. 'You'd love it. A weekend in Berlin. We should go when my parents are away and we can have the run of their flat. It's a gross place, in many ways, terrible furnishings, but you'd probably enjoy it. We have a few really dreadful family portraits, painted by my sister, who has no artistic talent at all.'

'Of course,' said Rosa. But that made her laugh. 'Well, that sounds good.'

'Would you really like to come?'

'Oh yes, that sounds great.' And she thought she would.

'When?'

'Well, soon. Soon would be great,' she said.

'Soon, well, I'll check my diary and see what I'm doing. Anything more specific?'

'You know, I'm between jobs, I can fit in almost any time. You're the one with the packed schedule,' said Rosa.

'Yes, I'm pretty in demand. An audition here, a phone call here, another rejection here. Though I do have a job – I'll tell you about it later. Not now though, it's a real yarn.'

'Congratulations,' she said. 'A job, that's great!'

'Great!' he said, mocking her. 'Great!' and now he seized her arm again. Here they were trimming the trees, and their conversation was drowned by the sound of a chainsaw. Anyway it was a very short walk, hardly supplying enough time to pose the question. She was wondering if she could slip it in. It would change something, if she said it. She wasn't even sure how she could phrase it. *Andreas, funny thing to ask. Bit of an embarrassment. Row with my flatmate. Just need a place for a few days, until I sort myself out. You can say no.* But that would involve a full-on confession, revealing much that she had not yet told him, the fact that she was debt-laden and generally adrift, more adrift than he thought she was.

'I really don't think you're being entirely honest,' he was saying, which made her snap her head towards him. Now the sound of the saw had died away.

'Why?' she said, caught out.

'I think you're just fobbing me off, and thinking you'll find an excuse another time. Is it my sister's art that's putting you off? We don't have to look at her portraits, I promise. I know I haven't really made the flat sound so nice. But it's fine really.' She realised he was joking, and smiled.

'Really, it sounds fantastic. I can't wait,' she said.

'Still not convincing. Perhaps it's me? You'd like someone older and fatter, some ancient relic, really yellow in the gills?'

'Green about the gills,' she said, automatically.

'Thanks, thanks so much.'

So she laughed like a drain and turned away. She stared out at the patchy, greying branches of the trees, the pale washed sky.

'Do you really mean it?' he asked. 'Would you like to go away?'

'Yes, I always mean what I say,' said Rosa. That really was a lie. With Andreas, she almost never meant what she said. It was a shame, but she had discovered that when she spoke to him she was usually incapable of telling the truth. She saw the word again, *TEMP*, sprayed on the stone rafters. And she saw billboards with words on them – THE KILLS: LOVE IS A DESERTER. HEY LYLA – A STAR'S ABOUT TO FALL. Vowing readily, she followed him along. *Ask Andreas. Clean the kitchen. Explain to Jess. But ask Andreas. Ask him for somewhere to stay. Get a job. Read* History of Western Philosophy. *Read the later plays of Shakespeare. Clean the bathroom and scrub the toilet. Really, explain everything to Andreas.*

*

83

At Ladbroke Grove station she felt a low sense of disappointment because she had failed to ask. Something in his cordiality prevented her. He kept it all humorous, and she was forced to play along. He made jokes and laughed loudly and she thought, *A BED!* Still she couldn't summon it, and he pushed his hair out of his eyes, wrapped his arms around her and said, 'So I'll see you later?'

'Later?' she said. 'Why?'

'Is that why, or the everlasting why?' he said. He had been making this joke for a few weeks, ever since she had mentioned it. Still, she laughed politely. 'I'm proposing that we meet again later. Because I haven't enjoyed enough of your company just now. How about it? Dinner? Something? Drink?' He shrugged his shoulders at her.

A place to stay? she thought. Anyway it was a reprieve. She could go round and ask him over a bottle of wine. Casually, not urgently and in the harsh daylight. So she nodded. 'That would be great,' she said.

'Always great, this word, great.'

'It is all great,' she said, and he smiled a thin determined smile and said, 'See you later. Any time. Drop by. I'm just learning lines,' he said. 'Any old time.'

'OK,' she said.

'*Ciao bella*,' he said.

They kissed at the entrance of the tube, surrounded by the milling floods of people and then she turned and, like a villain thwarted, walked home again.

Things to do, Monday

Get a job.
Wash your clothes
Clean the kitchen.
Phone Liam.
Ask Andreas if you can stay
Read widely in world religions

Buy some tuna and spaghetti
Call Jess and apologise.
Go to the bank and beg them for an extension – more money,
more time to pay back the rest of your debt.
Read the comedies of Shakespeare, the works of Proust, the
plays of Racine and Corneille and The Man Without
Qualities.
Read The Golden Bough, The Nag-Hammadi Gospels, The
Upanishads, The Koran, The Bible, The Tao, *the complete*
works of E. A. Wallis Budge
Read Plato, Aristotle, Confucius, Bacon, Locke, Rousseau,
Wollstonecraft, Kant, Hegel, Schopenhauer, Kierkegaard,
Nietzsche, and the rest
Hoover the living room
Clean the toilet
Distinguish the various philosophies of the way
Unearth the TEMP
Collate, sort, discard your so-called papers
Clean the bath
Before Jess gets home – clean!

When she got back she saw the answer-machine light was
flashing, and in the hope that one of the messages might be for
her, she pressed the button. Eternally optimistic, she was
thinking the flashing light might save her. If she had been
offered a celestial helping hand, she would have grasped it. But
instead there was a computer pretending to be a man:
'HELLO, THIS IS DAVE CALLING TO TELL YOU THAT
YOU HAVE WON AT LEAST A THOUSAND POUNDS' it
said. 'CALL THIS NUMBER TO CLAIM YOUR PRIZE.
MANY CONGRATULATIONS!' The computer pretending to
be a woman said 'To listen to the message again, press one',
and Rosa pressed two instead.

'This message has been deleted.'

'Hello, this is Jackie from the bank calling for Miss Lane.
Can you give me a call when you have time.'

An emissary of Sharkbreath, so Delete! DELETE! Rosa instructed the friendly computerised voice, and the message vanished for ever.

She thought she might clean the kitchen, but instead she made another call. After a few rings Kersti answered. Kersti was definitely becoming waspish. Here they were, this afternoon, this day fleeting softly towards evening, and Rosa said, 'Hello, Kersti, it's Rosa' and there was no reply. No trace of friendly recognition at all! That sounded bad, so Rosa, nervous and picking up speed, said, 'Hi, Kersti, sorry to bother you, it's Rosa.'

'Yes, Rosa, what?'

'Hoping you have worked a miracle of legalese.'

'Don't you know it's Monday?'

'Monday? What happens on Monday?'

'Monday is my worst day.'

'Should I perhaps call later?'

'I haven't been in touch with Liam,' said Kersti. 'I'll let you know when I do.'

'Look, Kersti, I know you're very busy. It's very kind of you to help. I know it seems stupid, trivial, to be quibbling about a tacky sofa and some chairs, a second-hand bed, the rest. But my credit card is about to explode in a ball of fire, so satanic is the interest. And then there's the overdraft, you know, it's dull but it would really help,' she said. 'The furniture would help. If Liam would only do the decent thing, sell it, give me my half.'

'You see, Rosa, the rest of us prefer to have a JOB,' Kersti said, repeating the refrain. Everyone hymned it in a different way, but they all hymned it the same. It reminded her of a song someone sang when she was young. *You got to have a J O B if you wanna be with me.* Anything would be better, Kersti was saying, than ringing around begging her ex-boyfriend to sell her furniture. Almost anything would be more dignified.

'A lot isn't,' said Rosa. 'Believe me, I've had a look. A lot out there isn't dignified at all.' And after dignity, there was the getting up, getting there on time, sitting yourself down, the rest.

'Rosa, I have to go,' sighed Kersti.

'It's not lassitude that stops me.'

'Rosa, I'm going now. Talk to the bank.'

'The bank is proving intractable.'

Kersti said, 'Yes, tell him to come in. OK, Rosa, time's up. I'll have another go soon, OK. Now Mr Wharton is waiting.'

'I do understand, absolutely. I agree, you must get on. If you could call Liam, that would be great. But I'll understand if you're too busy.'

'Yes, thanks for your call. I'll get back to you soon,' said Kersti, because Mr Wharton had just come in.

'Well, it's very kind of you. I am very grateful,' said Rosa.

She had phoned a few too many times already. Really, it was sketchy of Liam. He was holding onto the stuff, waiting for her to succumb to madness or to marry rich. She couldn't think why else he was delaying. Negotiations had stalled. The furniture was still in his flat. The bank sharks were getting vicious, showing a distinct sense of purpose. They really wanted the money back. Or her head on a platter. Now it was just Rosa and Kersti, trading barbs. Kersti smiling through her deep sense of frustration.

'OK, Mrs Middleton, I'll speak to you soon,' said Kersti.

Then the line went dead, leaving her standing with a rictus grin and a receiver pressed superfluously to her face. *Tabula rasa*, she thought. *Hardly possible at all.*

Now she heard the dry speech of the commentator, releasing the latest. *Today the war continued. The police caught a man trying to board a train with a bomb. The prime minister announced that global warming is a serious threat, perhaps the most serious our civilisation has faced. Interest rates went up. The archbishop said that abortion laws should be revised. England lost at sport. And, breaking news, Rosa Lane distinctly failed to pass the guardians of the gate and unearth the thing that lies within. Yes, that's right, initial reports are confirming that Rosa Lane – thirty-five and quite a lot, creeping towards the end that awaits us all – is still steadfastly failing to cast off the manacles, mind-forged or otherwise – and gain the pearl beyond price! We'll be following that story through the evening but now let's go back to the war.* The clock in the corner was like a metronome. It steadied her nerves. She found some pieces of paper on Jess's desk, and a black fountain pen in a silver box. She sat down to write. She wrote to her father, telling him not to worry. Things were fine. The furniture was well in hand. *The furniture is definitely going to come good. The cash is mine, daddy, all mine.*

She wrote to Liam. *Dear Liam, Please can you sell the furniture. I need my half. Or could you buy your half from me? It is quite urgent. Thanks, Rosa.*

She wrote: *Dear Mr Martin White, I have never written for your publication. I wrote for years for the Daily Rag. I was a mediocre but fairly successful journalist. I wondered if you might be interested in a few ideas I have. An article perhaps about graffiti and its significance, the mythic suggestiveness it contains? I promise you, there is ancient lore being spelt out on the streets, prophecies of the future. I can't unravel them, but I can see they are there. Or, perhaps, a piece about elective destitution – an inexcusable squandering of one's job and training, a burgeoning refusenik cultural movement?* That was Rosa, she knew no others. *Devastating to those who have struggled to support you. Clearly ungrateful. Prompted by something difficult to treat, apparently, some lurking sense of WHY BOTHER? I have many more ideas, and look forward to talking to you. Yours ever, Rosa Lane.*

Then she wrote: *Plot scenario. Rosa Lane is saved. Flights of angels sing her to her supper. She is carted away from the weariness, the fever and the fret. Ahem.*
She meant Amen, but it was so long since she had written the word she had forgotten how to spell it.

'Oh God,' she said to the room. She tore up the piece of paper and dropped it on the floor. Then she wrote: *We live in the conviction that we are masters of our lives, that life is given to us for our enjoyment. But this is obviously absurd. Surely we can be happy in the knowledge of our mortality? Surely we must be? There is no eternal substance in the universe. Even the stars are subject to flux. Even the sun must fade. If we look around we understand that mutability is the inevitable state. So why not a religion of the mutable, rather than the eternal? Worshipping the ceaseless tendency of things to alter? This is my philosophy . . .* She tore up that as well and threw the pieces away. She whistled guiltily and thought about giving Liam a friendly call. At least then she could wish him luck and check on the furniture. It seemed odd that he would marry so soon, but there was nothing she could do and she wanted him to know that she was glad, really, ultimately she was happy he was so well. He had jumped, head first, into the consoling barrel, the malmsey marriage butt. And here she was in the great loneliness, trying to keep her nose in the air. She aimed to smile, but found she couldn't summon it. She was confused, thinking about food and money and the death of love. She found she remembered so many small things. Things of life. The almost invisible backdrop. Years flooding past her. Only a few years ago she had been young and it seemed like there was a lot of time. Doubtless she had wasted far too many days. Of course she had always surrendered hours to the simple business of stuffing her belly. But that was inevitable. *Eros agape and amor*, she thought. Now she remembered an evening when she and Liam had sat together in a restaurant. She had it clear in her mind – both of them tired, in smart clothes, having come there straight from work. It seemed an age ago, an eon back, in a misty past when she was the suave owner of an array of A-lined skirts and smart jackets, and wore them elegantly, with a scarf around her neck. She tied her hair up, clipped it into a chignon. Then she and Liam looked well together, her clicking in high heels, and Liam in a sensible suit and a pastel-blue tie. Each of them with a glass, sure of themselves.

On their table was a flower standing in a slender vase. There were photos on the walls, patched pictures of forgotten celebrities. The place was subdued, a little seedy, but the pasta was edible, caked in cream. They were both labouring over their plates. When they were no longer hungry, they fought half-heartedly about a crisis Liam was having at work. Liam was fighting a rearguard action against Rosa's insistence, her pointed questions. She was asking him to try harder. 'Go back and renegotiate,' she was saying. 'Tell them you won't take it. Threaten to walk out.'

'Impossible,' he said. 'I just don't do things that way.'

'Well, you have to. Otherwise you'll never get anywhere. They'll ignore you. The reason they treat you this way is because you never stand up for yourself. In this, you're hopeless.'

'Hopeless?' He looked hurt.

'Only in this. In this you are spineless. What would be so wrong about saying what you think?'

'It's more complicated than that,' he said.

'Well, what does that mean?'

It was ironic, how ambitious she had been for him. She jostled at him; she hardly ever praised him. That was her fault. Those evenings when she picked at him, explained what he was doing wrong, standing on the pedestal of her so-called career, she had slowly forced him into action. Liam was tortoise-brained, he liked to move to the slowest available timescale, but eventually she made him resolute. Bedding Grace was a *coup de théâtre*. Perhaps it was an act of revenge. That evening, she recalled, they had passed some hours discussing his latest small failure. Rosa was steely and certain of herself. At the end of the beating he picked up the bill. It didn't help to pity him. Still, the hours they had passed discussing his job! Tearing him apart, mostly. Why did she care so much? She had been too engaged with it all; she had been too frantic. Evening after evening they had debated their small lives, writ them large together. And though she saw her enthusiasm – her concern for these elements – as incomprehensible, quite inscrutable from her present state, it remained strange to her that it should be impossible to return to these evenings, that she would never sit again in a small Italian restaurant with Liam. At the time it had seemed ongoing, each evening part of a limitless series. Her relationship with Liam, because it had endured for so long, allowed her to develop an illusion that they – alone of everyone – might transcend the absolutes of space and time. Because they returned daily to the same point – the two of them, waking in bed together, in their familiar bedroom with the same sounds for each morning – it seemed as if this pattern would recur for ever, an eternal recurrence. Eventually she found this stifling, but for years it allowed her to evade reality, delude herself about the incessant passage of days. Because of this she had failed to notice many signs. In the last months they stopped eating out. It was all too pursed and formal. In public they were uneasy, suddenly aware of themselves, of the lies they were spinning.

There were days when she wondered if she had been profligate. If she had been idle, and inert, sluggish in love and then in saving herself. Perhaps she should have fought for him, challenged Grace to a duel. And that wasn't such a bad idea, she thought. She would have liked the chance to blast a shot at Grace. *Pistols out. The foes, cold-blooded and unspeaking each took four steps. The clock of destiny chimed, and the poet, without a sound, dropped his pistol onto the earth.* Better to be Lensky, or Pushkin, blasted and shot to shreds, than no one at all. She always liked the absolute insanity of the duel, the loss of a sense of proportion inherent to the ritual. Grace would have tried to talk her way out of it. Laconically, she would have said, 'Essentially, Rosa you are succumbing to an atavistic – and unfeminine – urge for violence. Why? Why suppress centuries of progress, because you are feeling upset?' – but Rosa would have her pistol cocked already.

Sitting in the present, a cold wind swirling at the windows, Rosa wrote: *tat tvam asi. In another we recognise our true being.* She screwed up the piece of paper and held it in her hand. *Bodhi*, or something like, the pure beauty of the bed, the origin of the world. The love grotto! The enchantment of the heart, a moment of perfect suspension, above the clashing forces of desire and loathing, a moment of beauty. Love as a casting off of the bonds of the ego. Supplying an instant of perfection, ecstasy in beholding the object of this pure and selfless love! A condition remote from the sneering final stages of her relationship with Liam, it had to be acknowledged. *Yet for a few years, Liam was your god.* Now she heard the thrum of the rain. A sudden storm had begun. The sash windows rattled and she heard the softened sounds of tyres on the road. The clouds swirled. *Later there might be thunder*, she thought. Later there might be thunder, she wrote, and tore up the paper and threw the pieces into the toilet.

She felt sick, but that was because she had drunk too much tea. It was clear she had to get away, out of her head. Out of the city which had a dark cloud hanging above it, apprehension, fear perhaps. She perceived that the flat was small and the house was whirling in space. *We are all*, thought Rosa, *speeding through space, a velocity too wild to contemplate.* Of course her surroundings were significant, but they changed so quickly. Time's winged whatsit, flapping at her back. These feuds, wars, everything spinning in emptiness. And Rosa as her own fleeting vantage point. Changing all the time, even as she tried to think of herself as the still centre. Even Whitchurch was spinning, turning swift circles. She could move as slowly as she liked, and she couldn't change a thing. The earth wobbles on its axis and turns through the days and wanders round the sun. Everything is speed and light, and will be until the galaxy becomes static and dark. The Vedas talked of a pattern of dreams. Brahma dreamt of a serpent on a river, and on the serpent's back was a tree, and each leaf of the tree was a dreamer, dreaming their own dream. Every few thousand years Brahma would awake, and a flower would appear from his navel and drift downstream. Or something like that.

Definitely a flower and a navel involved. She remembered a song her grandfather had sung her when she was a child. *Row row row the boat gently down the stream, Merrily merrily merrily merrily, life is but a dream*. It was a neat little Heraclitan ditty, and he had sung it as a lullaby. Hardly consoling, she thought. Even worse, life is but a dream of a dream, said the Vedas, a dreamer dreaming of others dreaming, more perplexing still. Indra's net. You were netted at birth, confined and quite entangled. She didn't trust much, except experience, her own small sense of things. In this she called herself Jamesian, though really she knew little of William James. Any number of labels would fit this feeling, she was sure. And her experience, though she perceived it as her own, her unique perspective on the world, was most likely collective; it seemed unlikely she was privy to any secrets.

Wiping her hands, she walked to the bathroom. *Clean the bathroom!* she thought. She ran the tap, and watched the water whirl into the plughole. She touched the plastic of the shower curtain and saw light sliding down it. The universe was riddled with impossible elements, she thought, absurd symmetries. It was curious to her that she was presented daily with irrefutable evidence, these traces of vastness, a galaxy of stars and lights spiralling into infinity, unknown space. Faced with the moon and the stars, now visible in the rising dusk, she was briefly aware of the absurdity of considering anything at all. Reality became a meaningless piece of fabric, tugged around this cluster of humans, as they waited on their fertile rock. And yet people lived with passion, conviction. Even though they saw the stars and accepted the passage of millions of years, antiquity stamped on the surface of the planet. They lived and died for manufactured causes. She understood almost nothing of the materials of her universe. She knew of gases and solar flares, of intense variations in the brightness of the sun. When she thought of the sun she thought in lists of words, of gamma rays and optical emissions. She understood that the sun was a collective term, that the light she saw derived from the photosphere, where gaseous layers became transparent. She dimly apprehended that the sun's corona, alone, burned at a temperature greater than one million degrees Kelvin, she had once been told. That was the sort of fact she couldn't process at all. They might as well tell her the earth was shaped like a dinner plate and floated on a pool of eternal water. She had her five senses, concerned as they were with basic survival, and her brain was busy with the functions of her body and something she had been taught to refer to as thought. Then she had this intimation of something else – a knowledge that if she only could – if she only could! – she would break away, break out of bondage, and stand free of it all, transcend it somehow, find the World Will, sink into the *Geist*, whatever the hell it was that she was trying to unearth – and when she read Schopenhauer she thought it was that, but she was impressionable and another book would cast her thoughts in a different light, shade them in differently. She had all of this to struggle with, and instead she thought about Grace and Liam! It was a travesty, when she could be trying to understand the sun.

She splashed water on her face. She wore her last suit and forced her hair to settle. Because her shoes were grey and weathered she borrowed a clean pair from Jess's cupboard and forced them on. When she was dressed and ready, she took a Hoover to the living room carpet. It was goodwill cleaning, an attempt to make things up to Jess. She marshalled objects in the kitchen and hoped that made a difference. She ran a cloth round the kettle. She aimed the showerhead at the bathroom and left it like a banya. Then she took all her papers and her pen and her coat and thrust them into her bedroom. Pausing only to take an apple from the kitchen, she ran out of the flat and vaulted down the steps.

TRIALS

Now she was brisk and urgent. It was important not to be late, or she would lose this job, like all the others. Then Mr Sharkbreath would be angry, and her father would sound disappointed again. These were immediate concerns; the rest was indeterminate. Umbrella in hand, she walked back to the station, passing along the queue of cars. IT'S NOT ENOUGH said a billboard. TEARS ARE GOING TO FALL said the next. *TEMP TEMP TEMP TEMP* said the writing on the red steel of the bridge. She nodded and walked on. The air was damp. It had been raining earlier, and there were puddles where the roads dipped to meet the pavements. She heard fragmented conversations, and the dulled sound of music inside cars. She breathed deeply. She could walk all day, except it made her hungry. She passed a bank of adverts by the tube. Bras, beer and butter. We are meant to be cheerful. She nodded and walked on. A man was leaning against a wall, whistling. He was a tall African, his arms folded across his chest. He ignored Rosa as she passed. A gang of kids cycled past, a few of them spitting into the gutter. 'Fucking slag!' one of them yelled and Rosa thought, *Do they mean me?* There was a poster outside the tube, a decorative frau, legs hairless and shining. Now she carried on walking, avoiding a glittering puddle like a stranded mirror and stepping round a woman with a child strapped to her body. Everything was fine when Rosa walked. She made a steady progress along the road, threading a path from streetlight to streetlight.

Despite her sense that she was quite out of synch, she was still acutely aware of the things around her. The people filing along, forming impromptu patterns then dispersing. A man in a black leather coat who was dragging a white dog along on a

97

lead. A woman in a burkha. Then a woman walked past, pushing a pram. She was wearing knee boots and a fur coat. Further along a man was sitting outside a second-hand clothes shop, whistling a tune. He was dressed in a smart red suit. In his gloved hands he held a cane. He had a carnation pinned to his lapel and Rosa thought of him standing in front of the mirror, fixing it there with trembling hands. All to sit on a folding chair outside his shop! It was raining softly now. But the man stayed there, stroking his cane. His eyes were turned towards the street, and she wondered what he saw. The cars slipped by. The lights changed and changed again. There was the flower shop, bouquets stacked in buckets. It always lifted her mood when she saw their forms and colours.

Suddenly the clouds moved and there was a cold bright sun shining on the street. The dog-touting man moved slowly behind her. She could hear the lead jangling. The dog was straining towards a tree. A woman was running towards her, in shorts and trainers. On a pedestrian crossing a man moved slowly. Music was coming from an open window, a radio playing a contemporary tune, something with guitars and a kid singing falsetto. At the gym she saw people sitting outside, drinking coffee. It had once been a hospital, or a lunatic asylum, she thought. She wasn't sure which. Inside she could see people running on treadmills. There was a sign saying 'HazChem' on the wall.

Now she passed an ancient woman who looked like a sage, quite decayed and withered, moving slowly on her stumpy legs. Propelled by something, some inexplicable urge to go forward. Meanwhile Rosa was solid and vital, not exactly youthful but passably fit, walking towards Holland Park. The old woman was moving along, trembling with each movement, and if she was still standing then Rosa had no excuse. If she had thus far failed to release her cognition from the services of the Will, and the rest, then she really had to try harder. If there were mornings when the street appeared as an endless tunnel, drawing her into a pool of darkness, that was clearly her own small problem. On St Mark's Road, things were mostly seedy: a group of boys yelling and kicking skateboards off the pavements, laughing as they tripped, cars speeding through the narrow streets, crumbled bricks ornamented by graffiti. DEATH TO YOU ALL. FIGHT THE STATE. Slogans, the occasional *cri de coeur*, scrawled machismo. FUCK YOU ALL. Maxims: WE CAN DO IT IF WE TRY. Pleas: DON'T LET THE LIGHTS GO OUT. Do not go gentle into that good night. She turned away and went into a corner shop to buy some chocolate. The shop was full of faded adverts for long-vanished brands. She took the chocolate from a grinning man, and fled onto the street. She saw a man in a suit walking swiftly up the hill, so she followed him along for a while, watching the regular movements of his limbs. She stalked along behind him, matching his stride. He had soft blond hair, which curled onto his collar. She couldn't see his face, until he turned to pull his phone from his pocket. On the corner of Clarendon Road, he stopped and said a few words to someone. She craned her neck greedily towards him, but she couldn't hear what he was saying. Then he sped up, and waved his arm for a taxi. With a slam of the door, he disappeared.

Still you must get a job. Find somewhere to live. Talk to Jess – perhaps you can beg her! Talk to Liam. Beg the bank. Collate your papers. Read the comedies of Shakespeare, the works of Proust, the plays of Racine and Corneille and The Man Without Qualities. *Read* The Golden Bough, *the Nag-Hammadi Gospels, the Upanishads, the Koran, the Bible, the Tao, the complete works of E. A. Wallis Budge. Read Plato, Aristotle, Confucius, Bacon, Locke, Rousseau, Wollstonecraft, Kant, Hegel, Schopenhauer, Kierkegaard, Nietzsche, and the rest. Get to the bottom of this TEMP.* She ducked into Holland Park tube and stayed quiet and thoughtful on the platform. She heard voices from the tannoy, injunctions, exhortations. *Do not travel without a ticket. Buy a Season Saver. Do not stand at the edge. Do not hurl yourself on the tracks. Do not take the tunnels as a metaphor. Do not despise your fellow commuter. We are all human, only human. Each separate thing, regarded in and for itself, dissociated from the temporal flow of casual laws becomes, when so regarded, an epiphany of the whole, equivalent to the entire unending manifold of time. Mind the doors.* There was a busker playing Bach on a flute, the music cracked and beautiful. The platform was grey and stain-daubed. The walls were spotted with mould. Above she saw lines of neon lights, and everywhere she was surrounded by useful objects, fire alarms, signs telling her the way out, should the platform burst into flames. *You cannot take the tunnel as a metaphor. Because there are no fire alarms and hammers encased in glass to help you through your own private tunnel, this metaphysical corridor you think you're in. Not a single miniature mallet to smash a way out. Not a single mallet!* Now a train rocked along, scattering the mice and rats to their tubeside hideouts and Rosa positioned herself by a man with a T-shirt saying 'THE REAL THING' and read a poem on the wall (poetry on the Underground), which said 'I am trapped in time/ Living without a purpose/ Waiting for the end' – Of course not! As if they would put that sort of rubbish on the walls, thought Rosa. That would certainly demoralise commuters, as they stood crushed together, sweating onto each other. Instead, the poem said, 'We are feverish and then we fly/ All is gracious in the sky/ Like angels blazing higher and higher/ Into a celestial fire/ Oh God – my God, your Allah, your Buddha – you understand our prayers/ They are for peace and for celestial stairs/ To reach the place beyond all cares.' *Beyond all cares.* It sounded like the perfect destination. Caring was precisely the problem. She shivered and stared round at the passengers. All of them innocuous enough. *Beyond all cares,* she thought. She wanted to imagine her mother in a transcendent state, lyre in hand, or somewhere, in some sentient shape, but instead she thought of her mother as scattered dust, wafted across the Mendips on a windy day, having been shaken from an urn by her daughter – tight-lipped, quite unaccepting – and her husband – shuddering with horror and in tears. It wasn't too bad, to be scattered dust in the wind. That really wasn't so terrible at all. Better than a lot of options, the circles of hell, eternal torment, reincarnation at the bottom of the wheel and the rest. *Feel Your Inner Purity* said an advert for Japanese beer.

As the train went through the tunnel Rosa saw the headline on a paper. MODEL, 17, FOUND MURDERED. The platform vanished and she saw blackness and her own reflection, mingled. A poster above her head saying 'Millions are happy with our insurance!' Another said 'Simply inspired'. The heating was on too high in the carriage, and Rosa's hands were sweating. If the train stopped she would be late, but the train kept running steadily along the tracks. For this she gave thanks to the driver and all the functionaries of the Underground. At Shepherd's Bush she saw the platform sliding towards her as the train uncoiled itself from a tight corner and came to a sudden halt. The platform had been ornamented with green and red pillars. In the tunnel she heard three men talking about football, and she passed a crowd of women in burkhas holding bags from Harrods. A sign said *MILLIONS*. They kept on with the bombardment, until you capitulated. They wanted you with your hands up, saying 'Yes, yes, I'll buy it! Whatever it is!' As she stood on the escalator going upwards she saw the face of a celebrity, she couldn't remember her name. *If You Can Imagine It You Can Achieve It* said a poster for a motivational agency. But that was clearly untrue, thought Rosa. It was precisely the problem; there was much she could imagine but couldn't achieve. *Dream the dream the dream the dream* . . .

When she came up into the sunshine she waited for the lights to change. There was a sign in a shop saying MORE FOR SALE. More and more and more. The water tower stood like a totem. Ritualistically, the cars circled it, lucid strings of red and blue and silver. A man was running quickly towards her, followed by a man with a broom. She stepped aside and let them pass. The lights changed and she crossed in a group, losing the others at the other side. Now she was walking swiftly, realising she was late. There was a brown high-rise block and an immaculate white shopping centre. She passed a jeweller's and a shop selling Aussie Pies. There was a queue at the bus stop, and a formidable block of banks. *Still you haven't managed to see Sharkbreath*, she thought. *Plain reprehensible. They have certainly tried to help you.* The bank had been sending her sympathetic offers, suggestions for repayment plans, and really it was only recently they had brought on Sharkbreath. It was unfair to demonise them, those legions of lenders and their zipper-mouthed minions. So they had taken an axe to her credit cards? What did she expect? Why would they entrust them to her any more, when she was so clearly incapable of paying them off? She understood the rules, they had been explained clearly to her, and if she was incapable of abiding by them – 'Well, then you get Sharkbreath,' she said aloud.

The green was clad in trees, branches defined against thick clouds. She walked down Shepherd's Bush Road, where every shop was selling cut-cost bargains, and picked a path through slow-moving children and men like Elde and the disconnected variety of the crowds. A man was shouting at an intercom. She turned left and found herself in quieter streets, so idyllic that the houses had a sense of smugness to them. There were geraniums in the gardens and ivy on the walls. There was a penguin statue on the steps of a cottage. That was a tidy gimmick, she thought. Her footsteps rang out as she picked up speed. She saw a car sticker saying 'Experience the Meaning of Life'. She turned at a corner where a man with a white beard was brushing the pavement, and a woman was saying '*C'est catastrophique*' to her friend as they stood in the garden of a cottage.

At Brook Green she was late and trying to run. Hindered by her stacked-up shoes, shoes made for self-mutilation, she hopped and skipped along the street. There were people playing tennis though the day was cold. She passed them quickly, and ran up Bute Gardens. To the sound of dogs barking she rounded another corner, nearly collided with a group of kids singing, saw the blank glass of an office block and stepped onto the main road. Hammersmith was a woven mass of cars, steady at the lights. Trees, glass, marble and old white stones. A pattern of materials, she picked them out against the cold sky. Behind stood the old shopping centre and the sign of the Underground.

Now she was cursing as she ran, staring down the lights while they ambled on red, slalom-racing along the road, twisting out of the way of other people. Her hips ached, and she found herself panting along the river, past the backs of quiet pubs. Her head was still sore and she wondered what was ague and could she have it? She thought she might. At the prospect of an interview she felt a mingled sense of joy and death come quickly. She wanted to be saved but the taste was bitter. Acrid air around her and a swelling on her heels. She should stop borrowing Jess's shoes, she thought, they didn't fit at all. Then she found she was lost. She was frantic for a few moments, scrambling around dirty streets, finding herself in a housing estate which had a map like hermetic code and she was spitting mad when she found the path again. But other than that it was a fine day. Her suit was tight and she had sweated liberally, but the water glinted in the sunshine. The big old muddy river was tranquil in the afternoon and the sky was clear above it. So she walked more slowly, trying to catch her breath. On the iron bridge a dozen cars coursed along, crossing into the south.

There were lions by the gates, grim-faced, chipped by age. She stepped past them, her heart thumping. She saw pebble borders containing sumptuous flowerbeds and a big wooden door. She adjusted her shirt, tucked it into her belt, noticed she had scuffed Jess's shoes, blew her nose on her hand and wiped her hand on a hedge. She saw a gargoyle doorknocker and used it. There was a pause, and then Rosa found she was being drawn inside by a woman with long thin hands and a bony face. She was admitted to a long grey corridor where the walls were decked with portraits. It was clear that Mrs Brazier had been a handsome woman until she had her skin tightened. She had shining auburn hair, in abundance, and her face had been stretched behind her ears. Her breasts were made of marble, or some modern equivalent. She looked pretty surprised about all of this, but that didn't help her much. She had an ironical voice to match her ironical face, and she never smiled. Insistently thin, she had made herself still more angular by squeezing everything into jodhpurs and stiletto boots. Her hair was curly and she looked like a Corinthian column. This unnerved Rosa, and she stumbled as she went to shake hands. Rosa said, 'Hello', and Brazier said, 'You must be Rosa.' She had a cool, manicured hand. Anointed with expensive oils. 'Pleased to meet you,' said Rosa, smudging sweat onto la Braze's pearly hand. Further platitudes followed, which Rosa failed to commit to memory. Mrs Brazier wanted a tutor for her children, who were small and apparently gifted. Rosa wanted a shot of adrenalin and a large gin and tonic, but she sat there nodding politely, raising her accent with every syllable.

She noted that the doors were arched, and found bouquets arranged on the tables. The house was clad in lustrous flora, and every piece of wood was recently polished. The floors shone. Paintings were hung in hammered silver. The chair Rosa sat in, like a tarnished throne, was – said Madame Braze – a family heirloom, which went back to the Tudors. She stroked the arms and felt the shock of the old.

There was some talk of pay. It sounded good enough for Rosa. She quickly came to understand that Mrs Brazier was a flinthead who despised the younger frau. She emanated an air of refined selfishness. She offered Rosa tea in so reluctant a way that Rosa knew she had to say no. So she said no, though her mouth was dry after running from Shepherd's Bush station. She kept her lips pursed and hoped she didn't smell too foul. Brazier explained in detail what she wanted, and said that Rosa would have to start on Monday. Rosa said that would be fine and clamped her mouth shut. The children came in, Tabitha and Harry, and they were spoilt little darlings kitted out for luxury. At forty-five or so, which Rosa thought la Braze must be behind her face, she had two children of five and seven. Must be tiring, thought Rosa, but la Braze treated her infants like members of her retinue. Little Tabitha ran for mummy's pashmina and little Harry was told to take the dog to Nanny. So the dog and Harry trotted off, leaving Rosa and Madame Braze looking at each other across a luxurious room. Cream cotton and rouge silk, thought Rosa. Taffeta, a word she hadn't thought for years. The table was crystal. The fireplace was original. There was a Regency mirror which reflected Rosa half her girth. Madame la Braze said she felt the secret of good parenting was discipline. This was Rosa's cue to agree slavishly, so she did. She nodded like a nodding dog, and said she couldn't wait. They talked about qualifications, Rosa had few, but she held out her degree like a votive offering, and la Braze nodded curtly. Rosa said she loved children, loved them passionately. 'They are the future,' she said, with what she thought was an eager smile. La Braze didn't respond. 'It's very important to educate them well,' said Rosa, pushing on, and Brazier snapped out, 'Of course it is. They have to be taught how to think.' Interesting, thought Rosa. Very interesting. Then Rosa took the hand that was extended to her, received a still more stony nod, and turned to leave. She tripped again on a Persian rug, steadied herself on a plinth, and skirted round a statue of Athena. By then old Braze had gone off to slap another layer of acid on her face. Smiling at the retreating form of the nanny, Rosa walked out onto the river path.

Well, la Braze was truly spoilt, she thought. So terribly spoilt. What the hell did Brazier ever do for her cash? She hadn't met Mr Brazier, but she imagined him louche and resilient, big-boned, with deep pockets. They were both rich, both steeped in wealth. She envied them their house, their fine little kids, and their view of the river. They woke to the sound of cars and planes all the same, but they walked into the sun-striped beauty of their living room, sat on the ancestral furniture, everything dusted by the cleaner, gazed out over the garden as the nanny made them coffee. She imagined Herr Braze coming home from his office, finding his wife had been under the knife again. 'Darling, new face?' he would ask, as he picked up the newspaper and rustled it open. 'How do you like my eyes?' la Braze would ask, as if she had just bought a new dress. 'Love your eyes,' il Braze would reply, scanning the stocks and shares. There would come a day when Lady Braze would stop talking for fear of sagging back the latest stretch. She would stand, immaculate and eternal, nodding imperiously at her children. Did it frighten them, thought Rosa, to see mummy in so many guises? But she was being cruel. She could hardly judge others. They were all scrambling away, filling time, and if la Braze wanted to tighten her face who was Rosa to tell her not? She walked slowly back to Hammersmith, because Jess's shoes were too small and had carved off the skin on her ankles. She was hobbling along, breathing deeply, enjoying the distilled smell of city breath, and she heard a low humming in the air. The light was fading behind the houses. *And then the lighting of the lamps*, she thought, and wanted to laugh. *His soul stretched out against the sky.* Anything but that! she thought. It was a bad business when you thought Modernism could help you. *I am a bat that wheels through the air of Fate*, she thought. *I am a worm that wriggles in a swamp of Disillusionment. I am a despairing toad. I have got dyspepsia.* Now she smiled. That wasn't what she meant at all. There was much she couldn't remember and her efforts kept her stationary on the corner of Brook Green for a few minutes, as she rocked backwards and forwards, trying to summon whatever it was she had forgotten. She stared at the sky. Clouds scudding. Later it might be fine. Then she abandoned the attempt, and retraced her steps past the green, noticing the tennis players had gone. The last ball had been thwacked, and now they were heading home for tea and buns. She knew full well there were places in London where people did just that, sustaining their perfect rituals, bestowing gifts upon themselves. She passed a crowd of kids, hissing on a corner, eyeing her with practised stares of contention. She smiled weakly and shuffled on.

She thought of her childhood and her parents who taught her to read themselves, of course, without any hired help. The idea would have been inconceivable to them, to invite someone in and pay them to take their child in hand. She remembered her parents reading to her in the evenings and she remembered a few early books they had read. Susan Cooper, C.S. Lewis, J.R.R. Tolkien – who taught her about death – Joan Aiken, the rest. She remembered being taken to a mobile library by her mother, and told to choose some books. Then there was the city library, a place with a bright inflatable caterpillar and rows of splashy children's books, and she remembered her mother guiding her through the shelves, suggesting books she might enjoy. Her parents liked to read, and their house was full of books. Rosa tried to climb up the bookshelves as a toddler, and was grabbed and rebuked by her mother. Always in these scenes it was her mother in the background, teaching her, telling her how to do things. With Liam she had considered the question of motherhood, and was never sure how to weigh it against her career. That had caused her to delay matters, though she knew that Liam had been urgently waiting for fatherhood – the next stage. It was curious to Rosa that she was the last of her line – her parents both only children – and yet she had postponed and postponed for a job she now realised she couldn't do. And if she couldn't do that job, tot up alleged facts and feign them into coherence, then she could hardly presume to bring up the young! And now she wondered if she was merely a coward, afraid of the pure biology represented by pregnancy, the immersion in the body it required. Or that was blather, and she was only trying to step aside from adult responsibility, the subjection of her own desires. Trapped in analysis, Rosa stared around, saw the street as a succession of indistinct shapes, colours shifted by sun and shadow. Her mother had never said a word, but Rosa knew she was expectant. Well, there was another thing, that if she ever came to terms with procreation, and found a partner in the act, her child would never know her grandmother, and that was the sort of thing Rosa would have cried about, had she not been gritting her teeth and trying to quash another sort of feeling, a plaintive cry, the cry of an abandoned child, Mother! Mother! Entirely impotent, and she started to move onwards again, feeling the pain in her feet like a slap in the face, bringing her round.

She wouldn't suffer the scrutiny of the tube, so she walked home. Because her heels were raw and bleeding she took off Jess's shoes and trod on tiptoe along the streets, stepping from light to shadow. Her hands were pearled by the sunlight. It was a hazy, gauzy afternoon; the sunshine was grated by the shadows of the trees, falling in flakes on the grass. She whistled 'Ode to Joy'. She was impressed by her composure. She had out-brazened the Brazier. She had spoken through her teeth, keeping her face in a constant smile. She had managed to look thin by luxury gym not thin by nerves and overdraft. She was now within grasping distance of a job. It was a spitting mockery of a job, but it might be hers. It was better than some of the rest. *Today*, she thought, *you may have won the chance to sell yourself again!!* Sold in a better way than before! Perhaps this was it – pure compromise, the thing they had all been telling her to do. She was sure Brazier had wanted her! La Braze had praised her, high praise indeed, from a taut-skinned millionaire with a palace by the river. And suddenly she felt sick and found she was clutching at a wall, her eyes swimming and a cold fog closing around her. The noise receded, all the intertwined sounds of the street, and she put her hands out, holding onto the wall behind her, quite sick and bemused by it all. Now she looked she saw her ankles were stained with blood. *Yes*, she said, *that must have worked in my favour!*

'Second candidate, the one with the bloodied leg, like a girl who shows a bit of gore, let's have her.' She saw herself, here, a dozen years ago, working as an amanuensis for an old journalist – he had lived just round the corner, on Milson Road, in a tall, narrow house with a grand piano. He sat at a desk layered with papers. He went out early and bought all the newspapers, sifted through them for material for his columns. He liked to drink wine at lunchtime, and he had taken her to the local pub and paid for her to eat. He had been kind, she thought, but she had barely noticed it. Then she had really thought she was an aesthete. She had been reading Oscar Wilde and hadn't had a chance to adjust to the real world. It took her years to understand that there was no bohemia to find and anything she did would be assessed for its financial worth. She sat in the journalist's basement struggling under the weight of her ambition and she stared at the walls, the rust on the drainpipes, the paving stones, the pale bricks and the low green hedges. There was a ladder with broken rungs, and a set of shattered plant pots, like broken relics. The journalist was always at his desk, peering at the screen of his computer. She had sat in the basement of his house, with ivy at the window, and a view of a long garden, running towards a pond. He was a kind man.

So she walked on slowly, Jess's shoes pressed to her chest. She rounded a corner and saw a church silhouetted against the sky. There was a faint smell of carbon lingering in the air, but the square was quiet. The sports cars, Volvos, 4WDs and Rovers were parked, each next to their respective mansion. Everything was quieter for a few streets, as Rosa passed boutiques selling brightly coloured children's clothes and a restaurant with its tables full. The evening rush was beginning, and the hum of cars from Holland Park was constant. Rosa trotted down a few more mews streets, past neatly painted houses. On Holland Park Avenue everything was blurred. She walked faster, hoping to tire herself out. She turned uphill to take a look at the park. The winter was sitting hard on it, and the fronds had withered. She stood at the edge, watching squirrels. So much bounce, she thought, in your average squirrel! But that was plainly irrelevant, so she turned to the pond and watched ducks paddling around a small lake. A few geese stood on the side, emitting sporadic honks. It was almost the end of the day, and the park was emptying out. The benches were empty now. On the surface of the lake she saw the reflected forms of the buildings, the abandoned tearoom, the ice-cream shop which was closed for the winter. She stood at the gates for a while, passed by successive mothers with pushchairs, and then she turned away.

She crossed the main road and saw everything the same as she had left it. At St James's Place the houses were immaculate, still in their undivided forms. Each mansion was supplied with its own single buzzer, the badge of the millionaire. The windows were lit up, a halogen glow, showing rooms clad in books, everything plush. Rosa liked a spot of *lecher les fenêtres*, it was *modus vivendi* for those who could never buy. London spun you out like that, made you envy wealth. You envied it because it seemed like freedom – the freedom to choose where you lived, to travel as you liked, to conduct research and leave London, if you wanted. This hyper-wealth was everywhere, impossible to ignore. In one room, a man sat at a fine oak desk, leafing through his papers. In another, a woman read by a fire. She caught a glimpse of flames and a lustrous hearth. *Still you must get a job. Get a place to live. Ask Andreas. Talk to Jess. Talk to Liam. Beg the bank. Collate your papers. Read Shakespeare, the works of Proust, the plays of Racine and Corneille and* The Man Without Qualities. *Read* The Golden Bough, The Nag-Hammadi Gospels, The Upanishads, The Koran, The Bible, The Tao, *the complete works of E. A. Wallis Budge. Read Plato, Aristotle, Confucius, Bacon, Locke, Rousseau, Wollstonecraft, Kant, Hegel, Schopenhauer, Kierkegaard, Nietzsche, and the rest. The TEMP. A JOB! Really! NOW!* Soon she discovered she was walking swiftly; she was hastening along with her chin into her collar. And then she thought, *If you don't get this job then what will you do?*

She arrived panting at Ladbroke Grove, gulping down lungfuls of Westway smoke. She stood on the edge of the pavement, watching the lights change and the day grow darker. The Arabs were standing behind her, laughing together. Now a man threw a cigarette in the gutter, and checked his phone. She counted the number of people holding phones to their ears. Dozens, and then she stopped. She counted hats and colours. With a grimace she forced Jess's shoes back onto her feet. The tube was beginning to pour out commuters. She heard the trains clattering overhead. Nice to have the tracks above the road, she thought. Gave you a view when you went home. The westbound trains were heading out to Shepherd's Bush and Hammersmith, edging towards the curve of the river. The shores would be dim in the dusk. Beyond was the smog of the motorway, the exit routes. This time of day there were no short cuts. The cars nestled bumper to bumper. The air was warmed by car exhausts, and the streetlights had just come on, each with its surrounding circle of light. *Consider the meaning of TEMP* – she thought this as she passed below the bridge and saw the word, still up there, repeated across an iron buttress. *TEMP* the rest, she thought. What the *TEMP*! The light was fading across the grey-fronted grime-dusted houses. But today the sky had dazzled her. Now the evening was crisp, the wind was swift and cold.

In the shop on the corner they never greeted her, and she appreciated their discretion. She asked mildly if there was any semi-skimmed milk and was gestured towards a sour-smelling fridge. A radio was playing a tinny tune, something from the eighties, remixed for the present. The shop door was banging in the breeze. She scattered a few packets of biscuits in her basket, then she bought an apple and a banana and a tin of tuna and a tin of tomato soup. She saw a man with a wart on his forehead, like the eye of the Cyclops. That disturbed her, and she stood by him for a moment, watching as he dropped mushrooms into a paper bag. When he had gone she moved towards a pile of tins, each tin with a miniature portrait of peas or carrots. It was hard to know which one to choose. The fridge was full of creams and fats, and now she found there was nothing else she wanted to eat. So she stood in a queue marking time and then a bag was slung towards her. 'Thanks,' she said, and received a returning silence. 'Goodbye,' she added. The silence was rich and thick, so she took the plastic bag and walked round the corner, casting casual glances at the things of the street – the paving slabs that were chipped and cracked, the trees rooted in their small patches of earth, the shut up windows, the bolted doors.

Now she was outside Jess's flat. Pausing to note that the bins were still overflowing, she opened the door. Inside she kicked off her shoes and undid her coat. The bag rustled when she set it down on the kitchen table. In the flat she took off her smart clothes and exchanged them for jeans and a sweater. She wiped the blood from Jess's shoes. She washed them carefully in the bathroom and thought they might be OK. She packed them back into their tissue paper and stashed them away. Would there be hell to pay? she wondered as she shut the door of the wardrobe. In the kitchen she ate quickly, drinking the soup and mashing the tuna with borrowed mayonnaise. She scooped everything into her mouth. When she had eaten, she washed her plate in the sink. She wrote:

Dear Mr Bright, In reference to your advertisement for a Human Wretch (salary scale B for Blimey that's not much), I would like to present myself. I am quite sure I am lowly and ravaged enough for the job. A starting salary of B for Barely enough for rent and food is just what I want. I am aware that, being almost entirely witless, I should expect no more. Yours ever, Rosa Lane.

Dear Sir or Madam, I would like to ask you if you are really sure you don't want me for the job of librarian? I am really quite certain I love books – big books, as well as thrillers and the rest – more than anyone. I would dust them lovingly and talk with faltering enthusiasm to borrowers. Surely you have a place for me? Are you sure you're not tempted? A little after all? Yours eagerly, Rosa Lane.

Dear Madam, I would like to propose myself as a piano instructor at your school. I can play the piano, took a few grades, I was quite good at sight-reading. I wasn't ever going to be brilliant, you understand, however much I practised, but I was all right. The old liked to listen to me play, grandparents and the rest. My parents suffered it – my father never really liked it but my mother quite enjoyed it. It was my mother who was really musical. She had a really lovely voice. You should have heard her sing the Queen of the Night. Oh, it was really beautiful. If I listen to that music now, I weep wretchedly, I confess. But thanks to my mother, I'm good at beating time. I'm sure I could help a few children learn the basics. I would dress appropriately and never be late. I would never slam the lid on their fingers if they forgot their scales. I would not wrap their knuckles with a stick. Unlike Mrs Watson in year nine I would not tremble with ecstasy when sopranos sang. I always found it embarrassing as a child, to see her there, so surrendered and out of control. Yours, Rosa Lane.

She flicked on the television for the evening news. The friendly announcer, explaining things quietly. *Today the pound rose and the dollar fell. The Bank of England announced that interest rates would go up. Fifty people died in a car bombing in the Middle East. A whole host of people left the planet, gone we know not where, and a whole host arrived. The TEMP remained unsolved.* She changed channels and found a quiz show, a well-greased presenter with a fistful of cards. Two members of the public stood there, in their ordinary way. 'Now, Wendy and David,' said the host, smiling broadly, 'we'll have the Quick Fire question round. The Prize is waiting for

you. Fingers on the buzzers. Are you both ready?' 'Yes, Dale.'
'Yes, Dale.' 'OK, Wendy and David, let's play. Name two of
the stars of the Hollywood blockbuster *Titanic*.' Bzzzz. 'Yes,
David?' 'Kate Winslet and Leonardo DiCaprio.' 'Very good.
Next question: who is now divorced from Brad Pitt?' Bzzzz.
'Wendy, I thought you might know that one!' 'Is it Jennifer
Aniston, Dale?' 'Good! Next question: what are the two ways
in which Hume claimed impressions come to us as ideas?'
Bzzzzzz. 'Yes, Wendy?' 'Ideas of memory and ideas of imagination.' 'Good, good. What is the part of Kant's treatise which
is devoted to the necessary conditions for human sensibility
called?' Bzzzzzzzzzzzzzzzz. 'Yes, David?' 'Oh, God I know this,
I know this . . . Oh, the Transcendental Aesthetic!' 'Very good!
Staying with Kant, what did Kant establish to contest the
inescapable contradiction within any attempt to form "cosmi-
cal concepts"?' Bzzzzzzzzzzzz. 'Ah, Wendy you just got in
there first. Yes?' 'Antinomies.' 'Very good Wendy! It's neck
and neck, now. So, last question. What the hell is going on?'
Silence. 'I'll repeat the question. What the hell is going on?'
Wendy and David, hands above their buzzers, paused and
looked at one another. 'Time's up, both of you! Well, that was
a shame. Neither of you gets this week's prize, which was a
luxury break in the Temple of Truth!'

As she surveyed the small debris of the evening, the sheets of
paper she had stained with prose, the tablecloth stained with
tea, she thought she had to get out of the city. It was making
her skin crawl. She tidied everything up again, thinking of Jess
and the key in the door and the disapprobation of her stare. It
was only dignified to run. She thought of hills and trees and
then she was trying to find a number, a number she suddenly
needed. She went into her bedroom and searched her address
book. She was well into her notebooks, flicking past notes of
great age and certain irrelevance, but she still couldn't find it.
If she could just get out of the flat, she thought, if she could
just get out before Jess came home. Then she saw the number
scrawled on a piece of matchbox she had taped to a section of

her address book, a section unrelated either to Will or Judy. There was the sound of a phone ringing through the rooms of a quiet cottage, and Rosa imagined Judy and Will out walking hand in hand across the fields, or chopping wood for the fire, or planting herbs in their kitchen garden. The phone rang for a long time, and then Judy picked it up, sounding breathless and happy.

'Judy, it's Rosa,' said Rosa, waiting for feigned joy. But Judy seemed genuinely delighted to hear from her.

'Rosa! How lovely! Where are you?'

'In London,' she said. 'I was just sitting here wondering about taking a couple of days off, heading north. I thought I might come up to the Lakes. It would be lovely to see you while I'm there. I would stay in a B and B, of course, and I wondered if you had any suggestions.'

Judy started talking, her voice teeming with kindness. That was Judy all the way. Gracious, uncontrived. 'Rosa, we'd really love it if you came. And you must come and stay with us! I know, the kids are absolutely everywhere. But you get used to them after a couple of days.' She laughed slightly. Rosa joined in, weakly. 'No no,' she said. 'I'd really love to see the children. But I shouldn't impose. It's so last minute.'

'Oh, rubbish, we've masses of room. Really, I'd be horrified if you didn't stay. Promise me you'll come. When? Come as soon as you can. Come tomorrow!' Judy was open and honest, as always. She was standing in a rural kitchen, a cake to her left, a row of pots and pans to her right. Rosa could see her there, patting a child on the head, a symbol of nurture and comfort. A healthy woman, with glowing skin, bright eyes, glossy hair tumbling onto her shoulders.

'That's really kind. Could I? Would that really be OK? I'd only stay a night.' Would it? she wondered. And what would happen when she arrived? The giving of presents and the taking of tea. Walks on the fells. Children at her feet. It would only help. Certainly it would calm her, and while she was there she could apply for some more jobs, ring Liam about the furniture, explain things to Andreas. There was much she could usefully do.

'Of course. We're always doing the same things. Our house is so big we could lose you in it. Promise me you'll pack for a few days, give yourself the option.'

'Judy, that's really kind. But I do have to get back to London. I have a lot to do.'

'What is it you have to do?' asked Judy.

'Just detritus, but it's very pressing.'

'Can't you do some of it here?'

'Oh, you know, possibly. But thanks so much.'

'Rosa, come on, surely a rest would be much better? Just give yourself a break. A few nights won't make a difference, will it?'

Now, with Judy so generous and insistent, Rosa found she didn't know what to do. That was the glaring question. The dilemma of the minute! Already breezing away into nothingness, but still, she was concerned about it. She wasn't sure. She was still trying to excuse herself. 'Well. I'll do what you say. Pack for longer. But I'll probably come back. Thanks very much. How are your kids? How's Will?'

'Oh, we're all great. The kids are lovely. It's mad and complete havoc, of course. Will is great. He loves them. So you'll come tomorrow then. Stay until the weekend.' Judy was sounding firm. She had sussed Rosa out; she understood it was only nerves that were making her reluctant. 'You can work as much as you like.'

It was startling but Judy genuinely seemed to want her to come. That made Rosa so grateful that she gripped the phone and started nodding. 'I don't want to impose,' she said. But it was clear that she would. 'I'd really like to do that,' said Rosa. 'Perhaps I can help with the kids.' She could hear her voice and it was thin and tinny. She coughed and tried to deepen it. 'Thanks so much for offering, you modern-day saint,' she said, trying to throw in a joke. Judy was kind as anything, but Rosa hadn't spoken to her in a while. Thinking of it now she reckoned it must be nearly a year. Of course Judy had heard. She had heard everything. She had doubtless been informed that Rosa was crazy and sad. This made Rosa feel embarrassed, and she was thinking she really ought to decline everything, explain she had an appointment, couldn't leave the city after all. Judy was still insistent.

'Rosa,' said Judy. 'That's all great. Now, when are you coming? Do you know how to get to our house?'

So Rosa took instructions. She said she would leave London after lunch, when she had seen her father. She was willing to be persuaded, and she thought at least this would get her away from the *TEMP* and the things that perplexed her. The neon-lit shop and the dusted archways and the shaved strands of twilight. And the trains that woke her before dawn. Yet even as she thanked Judy she was wondering if silence was the last thing she needed. She nodded and wrote down directions. They parted the best of friends.

Later, when she had packed a bag and checked the trains, she knocked on the door of Andreas's flat and found he was definitely alone and quite happy to receive her. 'Rosa, darling,' he said, smiling and kissing her cheek. 'It's been a while.'

'Yes, so many hours.'

'And what, what has been happening? We didn't really talk earlier. Well, I think I talked and you were mysterious, as ever. Come in, come in. What have you been doing?'

'Nothing at all. And you?'

'Oh, I was abused by the dentist. It was truly horrible. But it's my fault, for being so scared I never go. Look,' and he opened his mouth to show her something – a new set of fillings. 'All of these are new,' he said. 'Terrible. It cost me so much money. I almost cried. Now I am just numb.'

They walked along the corridor greeting each other. 'Good,' said Andreas, apropos of nothing much. 'Good. Come in, come in,' he said again. The flat was warm, and she was aware she was sweating, out of breath. 'You ran?' he said. 'Eager to see me?'

'Yes, yes, couldn't wait,' she said, smirking at him. And it was true, she had run, because the evening was cold.

'I like my women to come panting to the door,' he said. She laughed indulgently, and he said, 'Anyway, you have perfect timing. I'm just trying to digest the terrible food I made.' They walked along the hall, which he had adorned with antiques – a grandfather clock, china figurines and the cuckoo clock on the wall. There was a Bavarian hat hanging on a peg, with a green feather in it.

'That's new,' she said.

'Yes, it's vile,' he said. 'My grandfather sent it, to remind me of my roots or something. I think I will throw it away soon.'

'So you have a grandfather?' she said.

'I have four grandparents.'

'That's amazing,' she said. 'I have none.'

'Well, that's a shame.' And he pouted at her, trying to stop her from being too serious.

They walked past the mirror which distorted their reflections, so old the glass, and into his kitchen. That was a place of solid wooden chairs and a big old table which smelt of sap. He pushed a chair out for her. There was a plate of food on the table, a book open next to it. 'I've been trying to learn my lines,' he said. 'I'm in rehearsal at the moment. I told you – I have a real job. Fortunately I hardly have any – lines that is. My best line is "Fuck you fuck you all you fucking fools, you wasted shits and fuck you all." You can imagine it's a real task getting the fucks in the right sequence.'

'Who is the playwright?' said Rosa, as she followed him admiring the contours of his legs and the strong line of his shoulders. She wanted to put her hands on him, but he was setting a place for her.

'I don't know, I've no idea. It doesn't concern me. The play is so terrible that I really don't want to know. Imagine if I met them, one day, I would have to fight them! "I'll fuck you so you cry and I'll fuck you so you want to die you bitch you bitch get down there and I'll fuck you" – there's another bit I get to say. All these beautiful lines, and just for ME!' And he slapped his chest, in mock pride. That made her laugh, quite genuinely.

'Wow, it sounds like the play really taps into the zeitgeist,' she said.

'Ah, you know German,' he said, putting a fork in her hand. 'Anyway I get paid. Really, I actually draw a cheque each week, and it's going to be running for several months. It's on south of the river in an experimental theatre, of course. I've always hated experimental theatre, but now I find they pay you to do it, so who cares? I am a convert. You should come and see it, if you want to experience something truly horrible. I'll get you some comps. Bring your friends. I am on for literally three minutes. The play goes on much longer, all will say too long. They are hoping it will run for months, though. But I can imagine we'll be playing to a house of five each night. So the more the merrier. Anyway you can imagine how pleased my mother is. She's even saying she will come over from Berlin to see it.' He smiled slightly, cracked his knuckles, and looking more closely she thought he was tired. His face was more shadowed than usual.

'Is she really pleased?' asked Rosa.

'Oh yes, she's delighted. Do you want ketchup with your melted cheese?' He had a bottle in his hand.

'I'm not sure.'

'I'd have it. Otherwise the cheese is quite monotonous.'

'OK, thanks.'

'Anyway, so you'll come to my terrible play, yes?' he said. 'You can meet my mother.'

By now she was sitting at the table, while he stood at the cooker, stirring some food in a pan. 'Yes, of course,' she said. There was a gentle pause, while he turned to the pan and pretended to sniff the air like a chef. She smiled at him. Then she said, 'So, have you been burning the wick?'

'Burning the wick?'

'You know, staying up late?'

'A little, at the bar,' he said, putting down the book again. 'I've been rehearsing all day and then working at the bar. In a few days I'll have to quit the bar. They won't keep my slot open while I do my Art.' And he laughed again. Still, it was clear that he was becoming industrious. A glimmer of success, and he started trying. Perhaps he would never be more than a bit-parter. Perhaps he would go from one minor play to another, stating the lines of bad playwrights. But he would throw himself into it, all the same.

'But you know, these bars, you can always find another terrible bar to work in. Although I am sentimental about this bar, because it's where we met.' And he patted her hand, laughing.

'That's true, how could you leave it?' she said, awkwardly, and thought *Now what?* But now he was giving her a plate of something he had cooked, which tasted of cheese and spinach and grease. 'You know, I should have cooked something better,' he said, shrugging at the mass of cheese he had created.

'It's great,' she said. 'Delicious.'

'You're lying, and you can't even do it well,' he said. He smiled. 'You are such an honest person, to see you struggling to praise my food is moving. Really, it's moving.'

'I'm not lying,' she said. They smiled at each other. That was easy enough, and then there was a pause. They brushed each other's hands, claimed it as an intimate moment. They paused again then Rosa told him she was going away. 'Tomorrow, for a few days,' she said. 'But only for a few days.' *Then I will need a place to stay. But how about it, Andreas? For a week, or so?* The problem was she hardly knew him. This banter, and the way they stuck to facts, concrete statements about family history and observable qualities, meant they never really progressed. They talked like friendly strangers, for the most part. It unnerved her. It seemed to be what he wanted. And she, perhaps she had also insisted upon this careful talk, because it allowed her to conceal her thoughts. Much of what she thought she couldn't say to him, aware that he would believe her arrogant or a fool. And what would she say? *Andreas, you're a great guy, better than I deserve. It's a failure of mine that I can't respond to your overtures of kindness. But thanks for the melted cheese.* She would hardly be saying that to him. So she put her head down to the trough and ate.

'Lucky you, to go away,' said Andreas. He took her hand and brought the fork to her mouth. Then he smiled and made to wipe her lips. She shook him off, but gently.

'Where are you going anyway?' he said, leaning back in his chair again.

'Oh, friends of mine. They have a house in the Lake District. It's very beautiful.'

'Why are you going away, when you could hang around with me and be fed with a fork?'

She laughed and said, 'I know, it's crazy.' But he seemed serious. 'Really, don't go away,' he said. 'Or come away with me in a couple of weeks. When I get paid I'll take you away.' Now he took her hand. 'You know you want to.' He looked directly at her, and this made her embarrassed. She held his gaze for a brief moment, then dropped her eyes. She was trying to think of something light to say. 'I'd love to,' she said, looking down at her plate. 'The thing is, I've been promising these friends of mine for months that I would go to see them.'

'Aren't you worried about how it looks?' he said. She looked up at him, and saw he was quite relaxed, his legs slung over the arm of a chair, his hair falling onto his fine face. He lifted a hand and seized his glass. He drank, staring at her over the brim.

'What do you mean?'

'It's looks as if you are running away because you can't control yourself with me,' he said.

'Yes, that's right,' she said. She always entered into his badinage, though she sometimes cringed a little as she did it. 'I'm hot-footing away from my powerful feelings.'

But that was close to the bone, if not the bone of their relationship – dalliance, friendship, however she was naming it – then certainly it was quite close to the raw and ragged existential bone, and Rosa stopped. She even blushed, which confused him, and he leant across the table and kissed her on the cheek. Really, Andreas was like a symbol of simplicity – dark eyes and hair, white shirt, crisp clothes. This is how it might be, he was saying, if you just relax. She dropped her fork on the plate and sat back. 'Still, I tell you, you are a little too thin,' said Andreas. 'You need much more cheese in your food.'

'It's delicious, thanks.'

'So how was your day?' he asked.

'Oh, busy,' she said.

There was much Andreas didn't know, and at present he thought she was between contracts, looking for something truly fine with a decent offer already in hand. He thought that because she had told him and he seemed to believe her. She wasn't sure why. It only made things more complicated. Instead of telling him about Brazier and the agony of the shoes, she had to summon an altogether different day, invent and galvanise. 'How's your search for the perfect job going?' he asked. He spooned her out some more food.

'Nervous energy,' she said. 'That's the thinness.'

'Yes, but you could plump up and no one would mind,' he said. 'I'd enjoy it.'

'The job hunt is fine,' she said. 'Just as usual.'

'I'm glad you came,' he said, kissing on the cheek again. 'I was having a really boring evening.'

'I wanted to see you,' she said. 'Of course, that's why I came.'

In fact I wanted to ask you. Could I come and stay? Just for a few days? The weekend and then a few days beyond. Just while I look for somewhere else and find a job? She was very hungry, so she thought she would eat a little more and then ask. When she had finished she ran her fingers across the plate and licked them. A neon light spluttered above their heads; behind the smell of soap was a background trace of detergent.

Andreas passed her a glass of wine and said, 'Better?'

'Much better,' she said, cracking him a smile. He took her hand and kissed it.

Later they were sitting in his small living room, where the furniture was old and matted with dust. There was a jaundiced collection of newspapers on an oak table. 'My cuttings,' he had explained, when she asked. A spotlight was angled from the mantelpiece, beaming at the fireplace. He had stacked a series of plants by the window, set off against thick green curtains. The effect was determinedly theatrical. There was a piano, its keys chipped at the ends. On the piano was a portrait of Andreas, in theatrical mode, lit carefully, the shadows making him more chiselled than he was. But he looked more beautiful in the flesh, she thought, turning towards his wide, solid back and the slender lines of his hips. Their talk kept drying up, like a stream in a drought, but they battled on, determined to wring out every last word they could think of. That was part of the problem, these heavy pauses they sustained. She felt them like a kick to her stomach; they made her hunch up. He was more relaxed than she was, and didn't seem to mind. He could sit cracking his knuckles, smiling at her. As if it didn't matter at all! Several times, Rosa asked Andreas about the other actors in his play. Several times he replied. It was a conspiracy between them, to pretend each time was the first. And when he talked he moved his hands, and his hands were elegant, good to watch. He had a wide jaw like a dog. This suited him and made his hair curl up at the ends. It was all delightful, this vision of youth was quite the consolation she required, and for a few moments she thought that instead of going north she would settle herself in Andreas's flat and stay there, until he noticed that she did nothing and asked her to leave.

'Can I help you with your lines?' she said.

'Which lines? Oh those. Yes, well, I have managed to commit them all to memory. It's been a long day. But you are a sort of highlight.'

'Thank you.'

Then Andreas said, carelessly, 'Are you going to stay up in the country and become a lass?'

'A lass?' she said.

'You know, a wench. These are archaic words I was definitely taught when I studied Chaucer.'

'You studied Chaucer?'

'Yes, they let me do it, even a person as idiotic as me,' said Andreas. He smiled, but she thought he was offended.

'No, no, I meant, I'm surprised, in all your international schools and so on, that they bothered with medieval English.'

He thrust out his lower lip and looked more boyish than before. 'Well, they had to teach us something. So are you?'

'Staying in the countryside? Of course not,' she said. 'My invitation is for a few days only.'

'Well, make sure you come back,' he said. And there was a subtle shift to his expression; she noticed he looked briefly embarrassed.

'So tell me something else about your play,' she said, quickly.

'Rosa, there's nothing more to tell.' He took her hand again.

'Job interview,' she said, to change the subject. He hardly knew the half of it. 'I had an interview with a company in Hoxton,' she said, dimly remembering a scenario from some weeks before. Then she really had an interview, had really worn a suit and tried to impress some kids of thirty who were wearing spotted ties and handkerchiefs in their breast pockets. They claimed to be a 'media consortium'. She claimed to be a 'top arts correspondent for a leading newspaper, enjoying a career break while I reprioritise'. They were all on the same page for a good twenty minutes and then Rosa was aware that she had fallen silent a while ago and so had they. Perhaps it was round about then that they looked her up and down and wondered why her suit was frayed and what she had done to her hand – earlier that day she had shut her hand in a door in a mistaken moment, and had really ripped it apart. Her hand was black with bruises. She couldn't do it, and after a decent interval they thanked her and said they would call her. That was a resounding lie, and she never heard from them again. The doors of their office were swing doors, like a cowboy saloon, and once she swung them open she trotted out of their particular town and never went back. She was telling this to Andreas, cutting out some of the details, and he was laughing at the image of the kids and the cowboy door. 'Kids?' he said. 'How old?' Five years older than you, she didn't say, and laughed and said, 'Kids in mind, of course.'

'Rather than kids in station, like me,' he said. That was another of their clunky bits of repartee, and she laughed and allowed him to stroke her hand. If there had been an audience she would have cared more. Still, she had to drink a jar just to get over the embarrassment of watching herself tapping her hand on her knee as he played her a song he liked. All this furniture, she thought, suggested permanence. It was clear that Andreas had affluent parents, because there was no way he could have bought all of this from his bar tips. It evoked a large parental house, rooms full of superfluous objects, shipped out to their son as he struggled in London. It was a touching idea, these comfortable generous parents. For a moment she admired the leather of the chairs and then she wondered what she was doing here, smiling and talking very loud, lying mostly. It was a good question, one she consistently failed to answer. It was solitude she craved and feared, attracted to its possibilities and then repulsed again when she glimpsed them. So she came round here and said her nothings to Andreas. She was a metic, she thought. But perhaps they were all metics, after all, waiting patiently for keys to the city.

Andreas leapt at the shelves with enthusiasm, and brought back a CD. It was traumatised guitar music, he said. 'It has a veneer of angst. Musical *Weltschmerz*. I picked it out thinking of you.' That was another joke and she laughed. *This mess we're in*, went the song. *The city sun sets over me. And I have seen the sun rise over the river . . . This mess we're in*. This sort of music was familiar to her. As a teenager she had consoled herself to the sound of countless guitar bands. Like millions of others, she sat in her room with the curtains drawn, headphones on. It irritated her mother, who thought she was wasting her time. She was indiscriminate – miserablism to the sound of a guitar was fine enough. The Smiths, The Jesus and Mary Chain, The Field Mice, The Breeders, Babes in Toyland, The Sugarcubes, The Pixies. *A dreaded sunny day so let's go where we're happy and I'll meet you at the cemetery gates. Keats and Yeats are on your side . . . they were born and then they lived and then they died. Seems so unfair, I want to cry.* She had listened to The Pixies at the age of sixteen, touting around in second-hand shops for bargain bohemian cut-offs, wearing grandad coats and black plimsolls. Andreas had been six at the time, though perhaps that didn't matter. She had always liked guitar music. But she was quite eclectic, even as a kid. Opera, classical orchestral, plainsong. *La Traviata*, Bruckner, Mozart, *Carmen*, Schoenberg, Tallis, Schubert, Cage, Glass, anything, almost anything, except jazz. *We sit in silence you look me in the eye directly* sang Thom Yorke in a falsetto. Rosa tapped her foot. She had recently stopped listening to music, because she had sold her stereo and all her CDs. Of course, this is youth, she remembered. Not so much has changed.

'I was thinking about you the other day,' said Andreas. He put his arms around her. It was a clumsy gesture, but they sustained it.

'And what were you thinking?'

'I was wondering if you would like this band I was listening to. They're called The Kills.'

'Love is a Deserter,' said Rosa promptly, thinking of the signs she had read.

'Very good. And there's another song I've been listening to, I'll play it,' said Andreas. There was a static pause while he stood and switched the CDs over. Then she heard a guitar and a voice and the lyric was 'Hey Lyla, a star's about to fall.'

'Very interesting,' said Rosa.

When the cuckoo clock rapped out midnight, Andreas moved her on to the sofa, told her to lie back and relax. 'Let's stay up really late,' said Andreas. 'You only have to travel and travelling when you're tired dulls the boredom and I have, as I said already, almost nothing to do.' He always spoke in this precise way. He was careful with English, concerned to keep himself accurate. For him it was definitely a game. The idea made her more comfortable, and she tried to relax into it, watching his back while he went to find another CD. He flicked his hair from his face, showing a fine stretch of cheekbone. His shirt was still creaseless. At 1 a.m., with empty bottles lined up on the table, she said, 'Andreas, do you believe in providence? Or in something else? Do you believe in God? Or in Osiris, Shiva, Buddha, Viracocha, Yabalon, Allah, any of the rest?' He shook his head. She wasn't sure if he meant he didn't believe in any of them or he didn't see the point of talking about it. Always he was more decisive. He stopped drinking. Batting away another enquiry, he undid his shirt. She was tired; her vision was no longer clear. She saw him as if from far away, bringing his mouth towards hers. Automatically, she received his kisses. He was moving her towards the bedroom and she allowed him to lead her. She watched him undressing, smoothing out his trousers and putting them on a chair. She allowed him to take off her clothes. She saw the smoothness of his skin, the strong contours of his thighs.

At 3 a.m. she was watching the time flashing on a radio alarm clock. Andreas was lying with his head in his arms. She turned towards him, thinking why not just say it all, when she heard the regular sound of his breathing and saw his eyes were shut. She stared at the gaps in the curtains, where the streetlights flickered across the darkness. She saw Andreas's shirt, hung neatly on his cupboard door. She fell into a doze which continually threatened to become wakefulness, coasting uneasily through the dark hours, lying half-conscious with the day breaking around her.

Get a job.
Read the The History of the Decline and Fall of the Roman
Empire.
Read History of Western Philosophy
FIND A PLACE to live
ASK ANDREAS
Read Francis Yates on Giordano Bruno
Explain everything to Andreas
Wash your clothes
Clean the kitchen.
Phone Liam and ask about the furniture.
Go to the bank and beg them for an extension – more money,
more time to pay back the rest of your debt.
Read the comedies of Shakespeare, the works of Proust, the
plays of Racine and Corneille and The Man Without
Qualities.
Read The Golden Bough, The Nag-Hammadi Gospels, The
Upanishads, The Koran, The Bible, The Tao, *the complete*
works of E. A. Wallis Budge
Read Plato, Aristotle, Confucius, Bacon, Locke, Rousseau,
Wollstonecraft, Kant, Hegel, Schopenhauer, Kierkegaard,
Nietzsche, and the rest
Unearth the TEMP
Distinguish the various philosophies of the way

WALPURGIS NIGHT

She heard the storm rattling the window when she woke. She lay on her side and stared at the room. In the distance, she could hear the humming of the fridge. Every so often the pitch rose, the fridge shuddered and there was a pause. Then it started up again. It was constant in its inconstancy, like the interrupted trilling of the birds. She heard Andreas breathing beside her. The place smelt of him, a musty smell of aftershave and warm skin. There was a high whine in the walls, sharp and penetrating. She didn't mind it. She liked the mingled sounds. Now she could hear a noise in the pipes, like the beating of a distant drum. There was a clock somewhere in the room, scraping out seconds. She heard the city opening itself up to the morning. Cars and a low murmur of lorries. An engine moving up the gears. A few drills hammering into concrete, industrial arpeggios. Now a bird sang a soprano solo. She heard a train honking through a tunnel, the noise muffled, and the grinding of wheels on tracks.

Things to pack, she thought. She went on weighing things up with her head in the consoling softness of the pillow. *A warm pair of shoes. A jumper. Your jeans. Socks and other small items. A shirt. Buy them some presents. Take a newspaper. Ask Andreas.* But she thought she would phone him from the Lakes. She would try her father first, over lunch, and then she would go away and phone Andreas with the soothing distance of a few hundred miles between them. Through the window she saw it was a tempestuous day. The night had blasted at the clouds, tearing them into vapour rags. Everything was ragged, the trees were bowed. Rain was falling in thick lines and leaves were gusting along the pavement. She turned to Andreas and kissed his head. He moved slightly and said,

'*Was?* What?' She kissed him again, and he settled. She gathered herself in the half-light, reaching for her watch, twisting it onto her wrist. There was a plant on the table, something like an orchid, deep red. Behind it she saw faint rows of books. It was too dark to see the titles on the spines. She heard someone walking along the corridor outside; she listened to their footsteps on the stairs.

Slowly, she moved into the bathroom and shut the door softly behind her. She sat on the toilet, sluicing her mouth with toothpaste at the same time. Then she flushed the toilet and splashed her face with water. Still much the same, she thought, with a glance at the mirror. She heard the loud gurgle of the pipes and wondered if that would wake him. Then she took a raincoat from the cupboard in the hall, and left a note. *Andreas, thanks so much for dinner. I've borrowed a raincoat. The oldest one you had.* She tore that up. *Andreas, my dear young man. I've gone away for a couple of days. Good luck with learning your fucks. Love, Rosa.* That wasn't quite right either. *Andreas, my dear young pup. Thanks for dinner. I'm going away for a couple of days. Rosa. Rosa X. Rosa xxx. Back soon, Rosa x.* So she took that one and folded it into her pocket. *Andreas, thanks for dinner. Sorry to go without saying goodbye – I had to catch a train. Will call you on return. Took a raincoat – the oldest you have (I hope!), R x.*

Outside she crossed the bridge and stepped under the Westway, alert to the morning clash of tyres and steel. She surrendered herself to the wind and the rain. Fumbling with the raincoat, she walked with her head bowed. HEY LYLA: A STAR'S ABOUT TO FALL; she saw the words on a lashed and rain-licked wall. She turned at a shop selling kimonos and passed on to Golborne Road. Mod's Hair Salon was already busy, and in the window a woman was going blonde. The shops had their fronts open, and their shelves were filled with ornamental tagines. The street smelt of fish and coffee. A woman passed by wearing a sealskin coat. And there was a woman walking slowly in a green jellaba. A man sat on a bench in his shop. He was selling old ceramic baths and antiquarian mirrors. He had on a ski hat and shorts, and he was holding a cigarette and a mobile phone. 'Yeah, right,' he said, 'right, yeah', as she passed him. From the upper windows of a building a round of applause broke out. Thank you, thank you all very much, thought Rosa. HEY LYLA: A STAR'S ABOUT TO FALL. With the stone turrets of the Trellick Tower above her, she went to Café O'Porto and ordered coffee and custard tarts. It lifted her mood. She found a discarded paper and rustled through it. She ate a couple of tarts and sipped her coffee. She whistled a tune and wrote: *I'd not mention a man, I'd take no account of him, if he were the richest of men, no matter if he had a huge number of good things, unless his prowess in war were beyond compare.* She paused, and then she gripped her pen again. *To the Guardians of the Laws, with my apologies for behaving so badly.* She stared around at the others: a woman feeding a custard tart to her child; a man with a hacking bronchial cough, drinking greedy gulps of coffee in between his fits. To her left was another man, this one with a tie and an edgy stare. She recognised that look, the look of a man who had worked hard already, and would keep going all day. He was the last man to leave every evening, devoted to his four feet of office space. It had made him toad-like, flabby and flattened. There was a crowd who knew the café owner, speaking Portuguese into a cloud of smoke. The toad-faced man was assessing her with a beady glare. He had pushed his chair against the window and was leaning back, surveying the room. The room, or her? She was sure he had been staring. She was so certain that she was on the verge of turning round and asking him what he wanted. *YOU! What do you want? How can I help you? Is there anything I can do?* She knew she was being absurd, at one level she was quite lucid and aware that this was mental rambling, superfluous, even preposterous. She understood that a man is allowed to stare. *Why look at me?*

she was thinking nonetheless. *I can assure you I'm as befogged as you are! From my vantage point, even with the width of idle months between my former self and this person you see before you, I still have nothing to say on the compelling subject of TEMP.* She was trying to clear her thoughts. Staring is quite common, she thought. There's nothing to stop him, no law set against those who stare. He stared at you, then he stared at the man with the distressing cough. He stared at the counter where the cakes are, at the women talking, at his newspaper. He's been staring all over the place. No doubt you are staring too, she said to herself. If she was honest she had given a good eyeing to the woman with a child. So she bowed her head and looked at her custard tart. She thought of the things she had to do. She gripped her pen and began a list.

Get a job (embrace your inner toad)
Wash your clothes
Phone Liam and ask about the furniture
Get a place to stay
Go to the bank and negotiate an extension on your overdraft
Meet your father
Explain to Andreas
Read the comedies of Shakespeare, the works of Proust, the plays of Racine and Corneille and The Man Without Qualities.
Read The Golden Bough, The Nag-Hammadi Gospels, The Upanishads, The Koran, The Bible, The Tao, *the complete works of E. A. Wallis Budge*
Read Plato, Aristotle, Confucius, Bacon, Locke, Rousseau, Wollstonecraft, Kant, Hegel, Schopenhauer, Kierkegaard, Nietzsche, and the rest
Buy Judy and Will some presents
Catch a train
Go to the Lakes
Understand the notion of participation
Be kind to their children

Stop thinking about Liam and Grace
The fifth combination?
Be bloody bold and TEMP
Retrieve the plot. Guard it well
Stop writing lists

Go to your father and beg! she wrote. *Then get out of here for a night.* Even a night, that would kick-start her conscience. She really might come back galvanised and determined to stop wasting her time. She only needed a change of scene, a simple remedy, age-old, well-practised, generally advocated. A nice dose of difference. Dr Kamen had been ragging on about holidays, taking it easy, others had said the same, Grace and Whitchurch and even the other day Jess had said it, though that had been a feint to get her out of the flat. Now, Rosa was quietly optimistic. A few gaudy fells, a few evenings spent listening to the soft sounds of the English countryside, a pub lunch, a change of mode, and she would send off applications while she was there. She would write to people who might want an amanuensis, someone roughly literate to proofread their work. She would try to find that sort of job while she was away. If not, she would seek out a good office and die quietly into it. She would learn to love the paper shredder, the coffee break, the woman with the squeaky voice who delivered sandwiches, the whirr of the lift running people up and down the building, the tea-stained kitchen, the photocopier, the round robins and office games, the squabbles over territories no one really wanted anyway, the conspicuous waste of time, the death in life! She would learn to love it all. *You! You the toad-face, over there! I'll come back with you, whenever you like. Just name the day and we'll walk hand in hand, back to the open-plan office, and I'll never ask WHAT THE TEMP again. Just tell me when.* Now she told herself to stop. There was still Madame la Braze, who hadn't called her yet. She would sort a few things out. Andreas, for one. She would certainly write to Andreas from the Lakes. Safely ensconced, far away, she would come clean. She would explain everything and ask him for a place to stay. *Oh God*, she thought, shaking her head. *Tell him you're a despairing toad. That you have dyspepsia.* As long as she kept limping round to Andreas, she would never really resolve anything. But it was absurd to call him a distraction. He was so tranquil. Whenever she thought of him she felt a stabbing sense of guilt. Guilt or lust, she couldn't quite tell. She desired him even as she sat there, and that confused her. She thought of his body – perfectly rounded buttocks, hair-downed legs, straight back, smooth skin, long nose, brown eyes – it amused her that she saw him buttocks up, first the moon-like rounds of his arse and then the rest. *Cerebral*, she thought. Now she wanted to call him. With Liam they suffered from platonic drift. By the end they were lying side by side in a sexless bed. Still, with Andreas she felt the sort of basic passion she had entirely forgotten. It recalled her youth when she was, she now saw, green in judgement but perfectly handsome in an unformed way. She wanted to go back to his flat and lie in bed with him. She wanted to touch his skin. Would that be so bad, she thought? Still she couldn't decide, so she stayed there writing in her notebook.

She turned again and caught the ragged toad-face looking towards her. Now the tables between them were starting to clear. Any moment he would say something to her; she could see him leaning forward, licking his lips. He would be stern and decisive: *Come back now! What do you think you're doing? You've been out of work for months, and what have you got to show for yourself? NOTHING! A few books read, but that will hardly help! A few walks through the city! Who do you think you are, Henry James? Samuel Johnson? Get back where you belong!* She could imagine him phrasing the order. Her last line of defence, the mother, put the child in her buggy and walked away. This made Rosa anxious, so she retreated. Banished by her inner fool, she took her tart and walked. As she left she looked over at the man and saw he was staring straight ahead. She went slowly along Golborne Road.

The wind was still up, and the street was awash with coasting litter, leaves and cardboard and plastic bags. Everyone was a swirling mass of clothes and coats, smothered in ravaged cloth, holding their umbrellas to the wind. Rosa walked with an eye on her reflection in the windows. She was another tousled ruin as she walked, hair unkempt, coat flapping. Another burst of rain and she started to walk faster. The damp stalls were selling wine and cheese. A wooden table blocked the path so she edged round it. She heard a car behind her and stepped out of the gutter. Outside the shops were boxes of brightly coloured Turkish delight, scattered with sugar. Rows of dates and figs. And in another shop they were selling halal meat, *Cash and Carry* said the sign. Now the shop owners were pulling plastic sheets over the boxes, holding up their hands against the rain. She had once bought a table in a shop round here, she thought, just one of the bits of furniture Liam was refusing to pay her for. Her reflection was bouncing alongside her, this flapping form. Everyone was sublimely indifferent to her; the man selling copies of the Koran, collar up, the woman selling baguettes and tomatoes, hood over her eyes, the man going slowly past on a bicycle, nearly beaten by the wind.

At Jess's flat, she put the key in the door and stepped into the hall. Concerned about the carpet, she scraped her feet on the mat. Once inside, she cast the raincoat onto a hook in the hall, wrung out her jumper and put it on a radiator. She undressed as she walked to the bathroom and then stepped into the shower. She poured shampoo on her hair. Things were quite simple, she thought, if you just kept yourself clean and warm. She closed her eyes and lifted her face. She flexed her thigh muscles, drawing her legs tightly together. Her skin was red now from the warmth of the water. As she watched water coursing down her body, she stood her ground. Here she was, a tall woman with wide shoulders. Her arms had always been lean. Her stomach was taut. Her legs were thin; her shins were covered in fine brown hairs. She agreed, she needed to bulk up a bit. Apart from that, she was attractive enough. She would attract men for a while, then they would deem her too old – most of them – and she would attract fewer of them. But she didn't need a horde. She didn't want an adoring mob behind her!

Later she turned off the shower and towelled herself down. She dressed quickly, putting on her jeans and sweater. She slung a few changes of clothes into a bag. She borrowed some books that might yet goad her into action. She took a notebook, an apple and some painkillers. She felt like a child, running away. In this spirit she made herself a cheese sandwich and wrapped it in paper. She took out the rubbish and slammed it into a bin outside, noticed the bins were overflowing but walked straight past them. The smell of rotten food was briefly pungent, whipped away by the wind. She was nervous as she walked down the steps. She was briefly devastated that Jess would be so pleased she had gone. She felt a low sense of melancholy about her small, rootless life. It was a shame, when you left a place and people were glad. But she was anomalous, the day was moving swiftly and a mass of people moved along the road. Above the clouds were grey, drifting across a pale sky. She was drawn into it all, the gliding shapes of cars and people.

She went to the shops, fearful of arriving empty-handed. Portobello Road was awash with people buying lunch. Crowds hung around the stalls, people holding multicoloured bags of fruit. She saw a green patch of park, gated off from the street. With her neck craned, Rosa saw the shops were full of winter cuts, big boots and long coats, clothes for dressing up in. The windows glinted in the sun, though the day was cold.

Wrapped in a thin coat, the wind gusting at her, Rosa stepped through the crowds. In the first shop she came to she bought bath salts and in the next some costly chocolates in a scenic box. She added in a couple of children's books, splashed with cheerful colours. She had a small spasm when she handed it over, her ravaged credit card. The presents looked fine; the shop assistant wrapped them in pink paper, and wrapped a ribbon round them. There was a label which Rosa filled in. *With love from Rosa.* That was because she couldn't remember the names – or ages – of Judy's children. She was quite sure they would have everything they needed. But she stacked up presents anyway, eager to show willing. At noon she saw she was late, so she ran along panting like a hound. The street was flooded with people. With the inevitable bad luck of the furious, Rosa missed the bus. It passed her as Rosa ran up to the stop, and she saw no sign of another bus, so she clenched her fists and carried on. LYLA, said the sign. A STAR REALLY WILL FALL. And soon. THE KILLS were still celebrating the launch of their single. She went along fast enough, enjoying the wind on her cheeks, admiring the dextrous way she danced around other people, but then she turned onto Kensington Park Road and the street started winding uphill, which slowed her down. She passed a brasserie with fake flaming lamps and a yellow-stoned church like a piece of textured mustard and when she was at the top, sweating and muttering under her breath, she stood for a moment and watched three buses pass her. That made her curse but she was on a downhill slope now and she picked up speed towards Notting Hill. Then the crowds destroyed her momentum, it was impossible to get round them quickly, however dextrously she danced, and she was forced to slow down, raise her hands, make offerings to angry people. Apologising for everything, she kept running. She couldn't look at the time because she knew she was late. She was sweating like a dog, but this had its advantages, she thought, at least her father would understand she had made an effort, really stubbed her toes on the kerbstones getting there.

She stood at the lights wheezing and marking time, and when they changed she passed quickly across the road, stumbling on the corner. She was gasping for breath as she ran. Antique shops in Victorian village style, and some of the buildings were older still. There was a pub garlanded in flowers. A bright blue house, she passed it swiftly, noting how clean it was. Polished windows. It was wrong to say the city was grimy. There were parts that surprised you; they were kept so clean. Here she was, avoiding a man with his hand out-stretched, and finally she found the door and pushed it open. She arrived in a breathy state of panic, thinking that she must usher on lunch and be sure to catch the train. Across the restaurant she saw her father sitting – slouched – and stood there for a moment, paralysed by guilt. She was stock still and weighted down with it. It held her, until she saw his head turn, and found him not so sad and old from a different angle.

Her father had never really liked Liam. When she called him up and explained it all, he was sanguine. He was restrained and didn't say, 'I always disliked that untrustworthy man.' That might have been the truth, but her father never said these sorts of things. He almost never said what he thought. He was an inscrutable man. It wasn't that he was dishonest; he just hated to hurt anyone's feelings by presenting them with some-thing so unwieldy as the truth. So he dissembled, constantly, and no one had really known him except Rosa's mother. Well, and Rosa knew him a little, though he rarely told her the truth either. It was an indication of how things had turned that he had been so honest recently. Rosa knew she was like him. She was ruder than her father, but she still had bouts of politeness, moments of insane performance, more stressful than an argu-ment. It was like clamping a brace onto yourself, it left you with a sense of pressure, a dull ache.

He had once taken Liam down to the pub and they had, according to Liam, talked about the history of the railway and its effects on tourism in Bristol. They had also discussed the origins of dog racing. Liam had said it was all most informative. But they were never good friends. They shook hands readily; on special occasions they extended themselves to a mutual slap on the back. They gave each other suitable books at Christmas. It never quite sparked. Liam was a prac-tised adept, good at putting people at their ease. He spilled words into pauses as if he was following instructions. Rosa's father was silent for much of the time, shy and undemonstrative, except when he disagreed really violently with someone. Still it was clear to Rosa that they didn't enjoy talking to each other. With Rosa's mother, Liam was gracious and respectfully flirtatious. That was wily, though at the time it was most likely well intentioned. Perhaps sincere. He had always kissed her mother when they met, warmly, with conviction. It seemed so at the time.

Rosa's father was tall and thin, with gaunt cheeks and large pale eyes. He had looked old for decades, perhaps because of his predisposition to overwork and smoking. One side of his family had been Flemish, some of them merchant seamen who arrived in Britain in the seventeenth century. They settled in Bristol, but little was known about them. There were odd relics: some fine pipes, a seaman's trunk which Rosa's father said his great-great-grandfather found floating in the harbour at Bristol. Rosa never believed him. The men of that famly went to sea; the women stayed on land. Neither sex had written memoirs or poems, and they had receded like the tide across the mudflats. Rosa's father tried to be active, to play up to his nautical heritage, but he was hardly robust. He swam a little, and he played occasional games of tennis. In the autumn he sometimes liked to roam through the forests along the Avon Gorge, whistling out of tune. But really he was natively sedentary: he was a historian, he taught for a while at the university, and he had his own private archive of dusty books, their pages spotted with age. The shelves of his study were layered with ancient manuscripts in rolls, file cards, folders, neat boxes, drafts of his writings. For years he had written about local history and the Arthurian legends. Once her parents had a fight and Rosa's mother told him to sell his books, his manuscripts in coils. 'A waste of a life,' she said. Then she was pale and penitent for a week. Perhaps as a result, his great work on the Round Table remained unfinished. For a while Rosa entertained a fear that it would be left for her to edit after his death. Now she thought Sarah could do it – Sarah with her scholarly air and round glasses, who taught him Spanish when he was trying to rebuild his life, as his friends had told him to – her father who took advice better than Rosa and was determined to salvage something. He met Sarah and Rosa hardly wanted to imagine the rest. Sarah was scented; she smelt of floral perfumes and she wore Omega workshop prints and sandals. That made it hard to love her. She told stories about everyday things, pleasing, convivial stories that Rosa might have liked, had her mood been better. *But why*, she thought, panting at the door, *why the hell am I thinking about Sarah?*

She was eager to see him, though she knew why he had come. The thought of him caused her a mixed sense of love and pain. Or a sense that she was causing him pain. As she said hello he stood and kissed her. He had been hopeful for a while and now he was searching and intent. It was clear that he had come to berate her. He had come there in an old pair of cords and a worn jacket, with a blue shirt that made him look paler than usual. She saw his hair was passing from grey into a more brittle whiteness. It was like fluff, or as if spring blossom had drifted onto his head. His eyes were tired, darting glances around the room. He kept fiddling with his knife. In short, her father seemed on edge. They sat under the wings of a fan, which beat a circular progress above their heads. For a while Rosa couldn't talk, and then she got her breath back and her father said:

'How are you? What are you doing at the moment?'

She had the menu in her hand. She understood his point. Because it was only in doing that you could prove your commitment to being. Being, alone, was insufficient. Being was a state of idle passivity – anyone could 'be'. To 'do' was the thing. *We do, therefore we are*. And onwards, she thought, turning to her father.

'You look tired,' he added, when she didn't reply.

'So do you.'

'Well, that's the prerogative of the nearly dead. But you're young.'

'You're not nearly dead.'

'I feel half so.'

'Half nearly dead, that doesn't sound too bad. Sounds quite far from the final snuffing out to me.'

'Who can say, my dear child, who can say,' said her father.

They smiled at each other. There was a brief pause. *Would they like wine*, asked the waiter. Oh they thought they would. A nice bottle of house wine, said her father, looking at the price list with an eyebrow raised. An order was dispatched, and the waiter departed. Then her father got straight back to the bone, gnawing on. For a few seconds she pitied him, this old man, consigned to a house which must be – no matter how much Sarah talked and splashed her skin with floral potions – steeped in the past. At least Rosa was away from all of that, those synecdochical horrors, everything in her mother's taste. She hardly visited him at all, for reasons of cowardice. He had come to London, a journey of several hours, and she pictured him sitting on the train with the paper, ruination on his weathered cheeks.

She said, 'How have you been, Dad? How's your health?'

'Oh not too bad at all. The doctor says there's not much to worry about. That's a vagueness I positively encourage. I don't want them giving me a sentence. So I see the doctor as seldom as possible, and he stays away from me. He's told me I can drink a bit, in moderation, and that's much better. Horrible when you have to eat yoga bars and dry biscuits. Quite takes the pleasure out of things,' he said. His brow creased and he was smiling very slightly. These things embarrassed him.

'That's good,' she said.

They ruffled their napkins and sipped their drinks. The restaurant was over-lit, and the roof was high above them. It made the place like an airport lounge. It was far too fashionable for her father. Simply a bad choice, thought Rosa. He would have been happy in a pub, with a pint of lager, a steak and kidney pie. He was pawing gently at the tablecloth, brushing crumbs onto the floor. He had been well, he explained. 'And how is Liam?'

'He's getting married, I told you.'

'Oh yes, when is that?'

'Friday.'

'And who's the bride to be?'

'Grace, you never met her. I told you all this, Father.'

'Yes, yes, I remember.' Of course he remembered. 'Well, and you're going to the wedding? Or staying well away?' He was trying to be jocund. She understood why he adopted this insouciant tone. That particular quagmire was nothing. He had dealt with much worse. He had been ill when her mother died, distraught and abandoned. Of course it had been bad for her, but for her father – her rage and despair were nothing compared to her father's grief. For some time he been alone, just the neighbours and a few old friends for company. He had his tennis friends and a crowd of local historians. But they could hardly fill the gaping void left by his wife. So Rosa always felt guilty when she saw him because she couldn't help him, and, still worse, she had started to worry him. For months she had been causing him pain. It was clearly unfair. She should be taking care of him. Honouring him, even.

'I'm going to stay with friends today,' said Rosa. 'There's no point discussing Liam. I'm pretty much indifferent.'

'Indifference seems unlikely in this situation,' said her father.

'That's why I qualified it with "pretty much",' said Rosa, pertly.

'Yes, I understand.'

'How is Sarah?'

'Oh, she's very well. She's redecorated the kitchen. And she likes teaching the neighbours Spanish.'

'What are you doing now, father? Are you writing things?'

'No no, not at the moment. But I have an idea. I wanted to write a history of the Avon Gorge, from the first settlers to the Suspension Bridge and then perhaps even to the present day.'

'That would be interesting,' said Rosa.

Perhaps it was something about authority. Her father never

really had any. Still, here they were, in this smoke-strewn room which Rosa had inexplicably chosen. He had come to see her, finding his way here. Probably he had printed a street map off the Internet, an X marking the spot. He had brought her an article of his to read, a piece on local shipping which had been printed in an obscure journal. He had neatly stapled the pages and put them in a plastic folder. He had stapled the pages and packed them to show her. Oh God, thought Rosa. There was no need to pity him. Her father was fine. On the brink of death, so old his hands trembled when he grasped the handle of a knife, but he was fine. It didn't work; life simply couldn't wander along if you assumed everyone was in despair. So she took the folder and said it looked enthralling.

'Thanks,' she said.

The rest was undistilled palaver. She palavered on through the menu, musing on the specials, listening to her father talk about the quality of the wine. The table next door laughed uproariously. There were two bald men in suits trading jokes and two women screaming with laughter. The women were dressed in plumage and bright colours, little heels. Virtuously, they had won the coveted plume, and now they were being fed and watered. The men had their ties in their food. Now they all laughed again, and someone to Rosa's left scraped a chair across the floor. Then a knife clattered on a plate.

'Loud in here,' she said. 'My fault. Bad choice.'

'Shall we order?' said her father.

The waiter had arrived. They ordered. They had to raise their voices and as the waiter wrote things down the women laughed again. How polite they were! Or perhaps they are simply happy, thought Rosa. The waiter said, 'What would you like?'

'Yes, the pea soup,' she said. *Pea soup, everything is fine, just a nice bowl of pea soup, a bit of conversation with your father, then you'll go and visit some friends, forget the TEMP, that word that you are investing with unjustifiable significance, as if to compensate you for your failed schemes, and you will return and go into service for Brazier, if she wants you. That's that*, she thought. *That is damn well that. Now, on with lunch!*

Another couple sat down at an empty table to Rosa's right. The man bellowed as he sat down. Now they were cornered. Trapped in a crowd of people talking loudly, all of them certain, somehow, of the justice and solidity of their speech.

'You have to grip life, or it all collapses into chaos,' said her father.

'But that's the question, isn't it?' said Rosa. 'It's a question of courage.'

'. . . Like your sweater,' said the woman to the man on the next table.

'Thanks, thanks. I did my seasonal shop.'

'Very nice.'

'Courage about what?' said her father.

'And Barry said, look, love, why not just leave your knickers here . . .' said one of the bald men at the other table. The women screamed.

'How about jobwise?' said the man with the nice sweater.

'Kind of OK. I do need to do more. I've applied for two jobs. One at CEA. The other was agency work. But I didn't get interviews in either.'

'Bad luck.'

'I need a sideways move somewhere,' said the woman.

'HA HA HA HA HA HA HA,' said the women on the next table.

'And then I said what's the fucking problem? And you know what Barry's like with ten pints down him!'

HA HA HA HA HA HA

'I wonder,' her father said, 'what is behind your . . . your . . .' Then poignant ellipsis. She was meant to fill it.

Trying to be helpful, she said, 'Father, I waste whole days in self-analysis. Don't start wasting your time too.'

'But you haven't worked for such a long time. It worries me. It must worry you. I wonder . . .' That was her father. As elliptical as anything. Always when he spoke about things that really mattered, he faltered. It was Grace's old fatal caesura, except with her father it was less a caesura than total silence. Once he slipped into a pause there was nothing on the other side. That made her talk, of nothing much, and after she had presented him with a series of small things, cast and re-cast, pearled and knitted together, she paused for a sip of wine. Then the food arrived and they raised their forks. Her father said: 'I don't know what you live on. Why don't you come home for a while?'

'Thanks, but I'm not insolvent,' lied Rosa. That was her congested lie, and now she would have to stick to it. That meant, and now she was furious with herself, that she couldn't ask him for a loan. *Failure of mission! Abort! Abort!* Once more her cravenness made her fidget. She had her hands in her lap, and she scraped her nails together. *Nothing to be said*, she thought. *Now you must sustain the illusion you have fostered.* Even though he didn't seem to believe it. 'You must be living off your friends,' he said, with a touch of scorn. He put a hand to his fringe. He had abundant curls – they softened his hard, thin face. His hands were covered in liver spots. They weren't a long-lived family. Her grandparents had faded out long before seventy. They put in respectable performances. They dragged themselves towards the mean. Then the women became demented and the men dropped dead. Her mother had seemed to be robust and vital, with her bright eyes, her clear skin. She moved gracefully and well, and at fifty she had run in a local marathon. She played tennis with friends, even when she was sixty-three. She had good legs, fine broad shoulders. Now Rosa was saying, 'I understand you're worried. But I'm quite certain it'll be all right. I'll find a way to solve it, a way to live.'

'None of us knows how to live. The quest for psychological perfection, for the right "state", for "happiness" – my dear, we never troubled ourselves with this sort of thing,' said her father. 'We just got on with it.'

'What was "it", precisely?'

147

'What do you mean?'

'This "it" with which you were getting on?'

Her father paused. 'It was a job, a wife, a family, money, work. A life.'

'Whose life?'

'One's own. The lives of one's family. Your generation drifts towards forty without putting down roots.'

'Who's that, Dad?'

'You, your friends.'

'Don't worry, they're all putting down roots.'

Oh how they are putting down roots. All implanting themselves nicely. They do it well. Very well, thought Rosa. You don't see the strain. It's apparently effortless. Liam, for instance, look at the man. An indeterminate span of months with Grace – if we believe their story three months, if we believe intuition, rumour, more like nine – and already they're going up for the legal bind, the holy blessing at the altar, till death do 'em part, and may they live long and prosper and the rest.

Tell your father. Ask him for help.

This is something you must do now. There was not much time left. The hour was slipping away. She had another course and coffee in which to marshal herself. Could she do it? That was the question hovering over Rosa as she sat there with a fork in her mouth. 'Good food,' said her father.

'I mean, perhaps, that it is only when we are aware of the grounds of fear and hope, only when we really understand the nature of the problem, that we can really judge how to behave,' said Rosa. Verbiage! Really she was thinking, *Go on! Get him to lend you money. He is your father. It won't kill him. Will it?*

'But that's too much to ask. You want to understand before you enter into things. That's quite impossible. You'll never understand,' said her father.

'Yes, yes, I know.'

Her father said quietly, 'Rosa. I don't want to put pressure on you to behave in a certain way. Equally I don't want you to throw your life away. Of course I want you to be happy. But there are sacrifices. Some things we have to do because they are necessary, not because we want to do them. This requires strength of character. You have to arm yourself.'

'I want you to understand that I have been trying to get a job,' said Rosa.

'Somehow your generation got spoilt. We must have been too eager to please.'

HA HA HA HA HA HA HA HA.

'For once I agree,' said Rosa.

'Really?' said her father.

'Not with you,' she said, nodding in the direction of the laughter.

'There's no purpose in misanthropy,' said her father. 'It's too easy to feel remote from your kind. You judge them from what they show to you, not from what they are.'

'How can I find out the difference?'

HA HA HA HA HA HA HA.

'I've always believed in patience,' said her father. 'No one is superior to anyone. It's just circumstances and luck that differentiate between people. You have to understand.'

'Dessert?' said the waiter. *A slice of tiramisu, to go with your existential crisis?* They ordered dessert. Rosa was mentally calculating the cost, wondering if her father knew he was paying. Only one more course to go and how could she supplicate? If she implored him would he help? Just a thousand, nothing more, and by the time that ran out she would certainly have a job. She would take whatever came first, Brazier or whoever else she could persuade to pay her for her time. They were silent, while Rosa struggled with her native spinelessness and her father finished the wine. All she had to do was phrase the question. Still she couldn't. She was quite chilled by the thought of it.

'And is there anything else you would like to do?' said her father.

'Alchemy? Necromancy? Automatic writing?'

'No dear, not those.'

'And Bob said shut up, darling, I'm trying to make a fucking JOKE,' added a man to her left.

HA HA HA HA HA HA.

HA HA HA HA HA HA.

'I was on a frigging roller coaster,' said the man.

'Dad perhaps I will come and stay with you some time? I won't come for ever. Just for a few days,' asked Rosa.

'Of course, I'd love you to come. You should come soon,' said her father. 'Before winter sweeps along the Gorge.'

'I'd really like to, thanks.'

He wouldn't be alive much longer, thought Rosa. And lying wouldn't hurt for a while. It wasn't fair. He had done enough already. She felt this was true – he had reared her, consoled her, supported her for many years, and he had always been kind. But was this cowardice? She had generally concealed from him her failures and small humiliations. She was his only child; of course she felt he had tried hard and she should strive to repay that. Why trouble him now with the truth? So they took their spoons and ate. *Father*, she thought. *What have you discovered, in your long life? Anything to impart? All my other relatives went quietly to the grave, without spilling any secrets. My mother simply vanished one day, leaving no clues. Do you have anything further to say?* She imagined a scene in the future, a few years hence, not long, she thought, looking over at her father's hollow cheeks, his shrivelled hands. One day she would regret her lack of resolve. So much would go unsaid. It was that sort of family. Why rattle the cage? Her father had waved off his parents without saying anything violent or unpalatable. They just talked in careful phrases, too worried about bruising each other with anything like the truth. Grandfather Don and grandmother Mary had vanished into the dark. Grandfather Don had been dying – he knew it, his wife knew it, his son knew it. Yet none of them mentioned it to the other. They all kept it quiet, fastidiously. The way you should. It drove her wild. Yet it wasn't her father's fault. His love for Rosa was so unobtrusive, so unassuming, that it had always made her crave his attention. He had been aloof, hiding in his study, at work on another book he would never finish. He was a master of inconclusive prose. Then he spent hours marking essays, his glasses on his nose. Rosa's mother was the garrulous one, and she was always talking to Rosa. Her father would spread the newspapers across the breakfast table, brew up a great cylinder of coffee, and pass the morning engrossed, answering Rosa's questions in terse sentences. 'The chairman of the Tory party, Rosa. You should know that.' 'He's the Minister for Education, a vicious man.' 'That's the Chief Whip.' She had only ever really talked to her father about politics and battles. She liked to see him animated – he had a good memory, and he talked of cause and consequence, the origins of the House of Tudor, the Restoration, the World Wars. Always she had been careful when she spoke to him. No wonder she couldn't ask him for a loan! But it was ridiculous. He had the money. He would be angry that she hadn't asked. When she was finally taken off to debtor's jail, there to rot with the shopaholic and the incontinent and plain unlucky, the much unluckier than her, he would tell her she should have asked for help. But she couldn't anyway, and that was the end of it. She simply couldn't phrase the words.

Contrite, she said, 'Delicious dessert. Really good food. This place is better than I remember it,' because her father was paying and it seemed ungrateful to complain. 'Nice chocolate sauce. Delicious.'

Her father said: 'We are meant to be industrious. And our industry should make us happy.'

HA HA HA HA HA HA HA said everyone together. The whole restaurant was laughing. It was only Rosa and her father who were sitting pensively at their small table.

Later Rosa allowed her father to pay for her lunch. He had known all along, and only grumbled briefly. Embarrassed, she said she would buy him lunch next time. They stood outside the door of the restaurant, and he eyed her bags. 'Off on holiday?' he said, arching his brows and, Rosa imagined, thinking of the money he had just spent.

'No, I told you, I have to go to see a friend. Just for a couple of nights. I'll apply for jobs while I'm away. Then I'll be back and busy, don't you worry,' she said. 'But, Dad, are you sure you're OK? I never really asked.'

Her father's face was pale in the sunlight. But his eyes were still bright blue. He fixed her with them and said:

'I told you Rosa, my days are very structured. I read a lot. Most importantly, I feel I have improved in some things since September. My Spanish is slightly better, even with my ancient brain. My bridge is much improved. I am fitter, if more deaf.'

He was like a character in Gogol, his jacket almost worn through at the sleeves. He was carrying folded papers in a shabby satchel. Now he was talking about the virtues of planning, about how important it was to plan a life.

'You have to have a scheme,' he said.

'I do,' she said. 'Rather, I am in the process of developing one.'

'Well, there's the telephone,' he said. 'Give me a call soon. Don't leave it another month.'

'Of course,' she said. 'Of course I won't.'

They stood in silence for a while. Then he said, 'Nothing is more important than happiness. Nothing is worth being unhappy about.'

A bus went past. The wind blew in their faces. Her father's faded jacket flapped at the corners. Rosa was still thinking about the money and her unanswered question. She had it phrased. *I wondered, could you lend me a small amount of money? I'll pay you back almost immediately. Just to tide me over for a few weeks.* Instead she said: 'I understand that. But there's the theory and the practice. It's hard for the two to coalesce.'

Coalesce? she thought.

He turned to go, and she said, 'Father?'

'Yes, Rosa?' He turned back towards her, holding his satchel with both hands. That was the moment! Just a hundred or so, though she knew that made little difference. Still she stood there, trying to say something. A thousand, and I will have a job by the end of the month! Just a thousand! He was expectant, troubled, waiting for a confession. He had come for lunch, hoping to rally her spirits. His story about having a friend to see – she wasn't sure she believed it. Her father didn't really have any friends. He had paid for a ticket, a lunch, the trip had cost him a couple of hundred. She had his stapled article in the pocket of her coat. She thought of him sitting on the train, holding a book to his face, his legs under a plastic table. If she divulged all, he would go home sad. She had caused him pain already. Now to ask him for money!

'Have a good journey home. Thanks so much again for lunch,' she said.

'My pleasure,' he said, and walked away quickly, not turning back.

She said goodbye to his retreating form and headed towards Notting Hill. She was thinking of him going to the station, his jacket flapping in the wind. She imagined him holding out his ticket to the guard, his face blank. It was clear she had no sense of proportion. But she was crying hot tears as she walked along. She was moving as fast as she could, rubbing her face. It was nearly too late, she was suddenly aware just how late it was. With her head down, she walked on. Her train was leaving soon, so she turned the corner and found a bus. It was a fine bus, which took her past the park, where she saw the trees in their autumn severity, thin and sinewy, and underneath she saw the lower lines of bushes and the meandering silver string of the river. With her nose against the glass, she noticed joggers on the path below, and the straight-backed forms of cyclists, turning circles with their feet. There was a queue of cars at Hyde Park Corner, jammed up at the lights, waiting. The traffic shifted slowly. The bus turned left at Marble Arch, and moved up towards Marylebone.

Hunched into her coat, she tried to stay calm. It was absurd to be so mournful about her father, who was a grown man with a lover and a sense of a benevolent deity to console him. Her father was religious, she thought. He had found his church and locked the door behind him. It was how he coped, in the end, with the death of his wife. His belief rendered things palatable, perhaps. When he went home, he thought of God and a celestial palace. He went to church on Sundays with Sarah on his arm. This should make her pity him less. It was of little importance if he was right or wrong. What matter if he boiled off into oblivion, so long as he was happy while he lived? He was right in that. Of course it didn't matter, and the only thing to do was keep your head up, keep on going. Jung said that for psychotherapeutic purposes it was best if a person believed that death was not the end. For the sake of mental well-being, it was the most relaxing state to be in. You would-n't know until it was too late either way, so why not chance it? Still she couldn't. And she thought of Tolstoy with his life cri-sis, at fifty or so he suddenly wondered what the point of it all was, and she had always thought he had left it late, but there he was trembling under the sentence, horribly frightened, in such torment he thought he would hang himself, and he resolved it by thinking himself into faith. He looked out at the peasants tilling the fields and worshipping a just God, and he rendered himself religious. *Rendered himself, through a willed process of reasoning – it seemed impossible!*

Even so, she was fortunate. It was a slick trade-off, from the former certainties of religion, to a better state of finitude. Instead of a cloudless eternity, the prospect of an afterlife, in this age you got the consolation prize – death as the unspoken secret of life, immanent but ignored, suffering as something that happened to other people, life to be lived free of the awareness of death, like being a dog or a cat. Free and igno-rant. Then suffering came as a shock, and death as something incongruous, having nothing to do with life. Perhaps it was better like that. She had read about Zeno and she understood the argument though it hardly helped. If you were rational about it, death didn't happen to the individual because it was at the point of death that the individual ceased to be. At death, one's subjectivity ceased. You were no longer yourself. This was all well and good, thought Rosa, quite coherent philosophically but no damn consolation for the snuffing out of me! Me of all people! she thought. This made her grip her bag in a spasm of fear, and then she turned to a man near her who was shuffling his feet and wondered how he was bearing up under the knowledge, this irrefutable knowledge that he would be nothing, one day, or at best something else entirely. Then there were days when she thought it was absurd to mind so much. There was nothing of interest about her – why not feel far more scandalised by the death of Shakespeare, or the death of Socrates – murdered by Athens – or the death of Mozart with his works unfinished? With Rosa, the world would only lose another drone, supplied with her set of interests and anxieties. For her grief, her self-mourning, she was a fool. It had sent her off in a great hurry, trying to find something she was too unreasonable to identify. She was chasing over the hills, following the weft, thinking *I lost it last time, but just one more try, I'm sure I'll find it* – stamping over ruins and then it would vanish and she would be thinking some miniature thought, something diced about Liam, or her concerns would shift to the rent, or she would notice her neighbour – and here she glanced to one side and found her neighbour was a gun-faced man of forty-five, baked in body odour. She moved away from him, she didn't want his energies flowing into hers; she didn't want to catch a trace of his aura or id, or any other categorisable aspect of him that might be coming her way.

On this bus full of people casting sharp glances at each other, she was thinking of Socrates, who said that it was foolish to fear death, because there was no knowing if death was a better state than life. That was sensible enough, in the abstract, but there were absolutes. In the here and now death – the deaths of others – robbed you of love. While you were living it robbed you; who could say what happened later. A couple of decades ago she had been a teenager, loved by both her parents, by her remaining grandparents. She had been young and mostly oblivious, and she had passed the days driving through the Avon countryside with her friends in borrowed cars. They went off drinking cider; they went to caves in the cliffs where the boys smoked pot. They were impetuous and lucky. There was nothing illustrious about her youth. She didn't really read and she wasn't talking ancient Greek at the age of six. She was bred on teenage magazines and TV; it was only later she started leafing through Plato with a guilty conscience, trying to please someone or impress herself, she wasn't sure. Of course we were barbarous, thought Rosa, but it didn't matter. That was our undeveloped state. Now we have no excuses for our barbarity. Then we could say – hand on heart – that we were truly witless. Pure in our lack of wit. We drove out with boys in the back of the car, thrilled by their closeness, the proximity to sex they represented. Peer pressure was mighty and terrible. Despotic youth, thought Rosa, smiling to herself.

And now she was thinking of grandmother Lily, who never really recovered from the death of her husband. Grandfather Tom went modestly, in his prime. It had become his custom to spend the days after his retirement working under the car, for no real reason other than his liking for spanners and grease. He emerged around teatime smelling of sweat, wiping his hands on a rag. In the evenings he liked to go to the working men's club. He played bowls, watched Tom and Jerry cartoons, wrote comic verse, smoked with friends. One day he had observed the usual ritual, wiped a rag around the back of the car, polished it and washed his hands and he was sipping tea in the kitchen when it started to rain. Grandmother Lily ran outside to bring the washing in, calling to her husband to help. He failed to follow her; exasperated, she dragged the basket in, preparing to remonstrate, and found he had collapsed. He recovered a little in hospital, waking to say that he had fulfilled all his ambitions; he had no complaints, he said, and then he had another heart attack and died. But grandmother Lily preserved a quite unSocratic view of things. She wasted slowly, grew thin and blotched. And there was grandmother Mary, tall and graceful, with her hair newly permed. She was the direct antithesis of grandmother Lily: she was always smart and cheerful; she went out regularly for a shampoo and set. She had ten outfits that she wore in strict rotation. A pleated skirt or two, a cashmere jumper. Much of it in pink and blue. Then she had a pair of blue trousers, long and wide-legged. Her clothes were forties in style. She had fixed her taste as a young woman, and had never faltered. She liked watching snooker – she called it *snukker* – and reading crime novels. Rosa always thought it was incongruous: her delicate, kindly grandmother, holding a book with a bloody corpse on the cover. She had a drawer full of multicoloured pencils. They had belonged to grandfather Don, who had been an engineer. She was devout, a quiet member of the church. Dear grandmother Mary, who never worked in her life. She knitted jumpers and made Victoria sponges. She helped with a thousand village fetes. Early in her marriage she took in girls – fallen women, pregnant at sixteen, cast out by their families. It was a gentle life, spent in small villages, dealing with people who knew her well. Virtuous, in its way. When Rosa thought of grandmother Mary she saw her in the living room of her house surrounded by ancestral china, in repose.

Grandmother Mary believed that things were orchestrated by a benevolent deity. Still she died alone, stricken by dementia. She never questioned the God that sent her mad, but Rosa wondered how she might have understood it, had she still been capable of rational enquiry. Because the self was memory and memory defined the self, and at the last grandmother Mary had no memory at all. She would be a fugitive eternal being, unable to find anyone she recalled in the celestial wash of souls, or confusing those she found, mixing up her father and her husband, uncertain of her friends. Though there might be an essence, and Rosa had hoped this was what grandmother Mary had thought, on those few days when she was lucid enough to understand what was happening to her. There might still be a kernel of the self, untouched by disease, preserving the original personality of the creature. *This might have been what Socrates meant*, thought Rosa, *when he talked of the self. Something untouched by all the things of life. Untouched even by memory and the shifting pattern of concerns that define the individual. An eternal spark, divorced from everything ephemeral.*

She shook her head hard, and forced herself to focus. Now the bus was stuck behind a ritual file of cars, hemmed in on all sides. Gathering her bags around her, her hold all weighed down with a pair of Jess's walking boots and now these presents in their plastic wrappers, Rosa stared at the street, at the flecks of brown and black on the buildings, flecks of great age, at the columns of a church, the glass sheen of an office block. The street was a mingled frieze of shine and drab. It was mottled, but she liked it. She stared around at the other passengers. She watched a pair of boys slapping each other warmly around the head. There was a man with an immense nose reading a paper, apparently absorbed in it. Each nostril a work of art. Truly unusual. That was a characterful face, she thought. The bus was taking its time, shuddering along Euston Road, the glass shaking. Not far from here, thought Rosa, Mary Wollstonecraft wrote her works, birthed her children, and expired. *Rousseau declares that a woman should be made a coquettish slave in order to render her a more alluring object of desire, a sweeter companion to man, whenever he chooses to relax himself. What nonsense!* Still the wind was gusting down the streets. Everything outside the bus was controlled by the force of the wind; on one side of the road people were hunched against it, on the other they were gusted onwards. The bus came to a sudden halt, and everyone jerked forwards. For a moment their faces showed confusion and injured pride. For a brief instant, they knew the whole thing was unnatural and absurd, being on this bus in this road jammed with traffic, being jolted around as the bus trembled on its sluggish course. They understood, briefly, all of them, that it was crazy, that wherever they were trying to go it didn't really matter, and really they should have just stayed in the savannah swamps firing arrows at the fauna. That would have been better than sitting it out on this rattling clattering bus with a mounting feeling of nausea and this underlying sense of perplexity, this semi-suppressed question of why the hell? But then she looked around again and they were all rustling newspapers, and she was no longer sure if that was what they had been thinking at all.

The buildings were stained black and brown. She liked their weathered faces. At the junction of Tottenham Court Road everything stopped again, and Rosa stared up at the blank windows of the high-rise offices. But the sky was deep dark, clad in clouds, dynamic ether, even as Rosa festered in the bus. Rosa could see the grimy face of Euston Square station, with the dome of UCL just visible round the corner. She wondered if she should beg the driver to let her off. She sat up straight and looked at her watch. She sang quietly to herself: *Would you like to swing on a star? And be better off than you are? Or would you rather be a Pig? Yeah yeah, tell 'em 'bout the pig.* She stared around, stared at the traffic stuck to the heels of the bus, remembered her bags and subsided. She was tense for a few minutes, then the bus started its shuddering progress again. It started, moved quickly, stopped as quickly again. There was a fierce sound of horns outside. And now she could hear the King's Cross backing track of diggers and drills, the shuddering scrape of metal on concrete, and she saw clouds of dust dispersing.

When the bus came to a halt outside Euston, Rosa was staring up at the sky. Then she stood. Pulling her bags along, she moved towards the exit. It is almost too late, she thought, as she saw the glass doors of Euston Station. She passed the police with their guns, and arrived at a big clock telling her the time. If you were ever so slightly out of synch these clocks and the people beneath them quite confused you. You weren't sure what might happen but you were fearful all the same. She was uncertain on the forecourt and then, with minutes to go, she remembered the drill. Thinking only of the task at hand, she rushed for a ticket, fumbling with her purse, dropping her credit card, stuffing it into the machine again, seeing the price and cursing faintly, receiving a delayed then spewed out ticket, running for the platform. She was trying to keep her thoughts clean and practical. She saw a train and ran towards it. But her hurry was superfluous; the train was delayed. Everyone was queuing at the doors. A man in uniform was holding a whistle, ready to blow. Was it a race? thought Rosa. They were all poised for the off. She saw some ruddy, fat families, and kids smiling, and a host of the elderly. Daytime travellers from London. A few business types in suits, men and women, holding their phones and palms and computer cases. Most of that crowd filed off to first class, while Rosa set her bags down on the floor and waited with the rest. The atmosphere was good-tempered. Everyone fidgeted and raised their eyes to each other. There was a strict sense of protocol – you had to be stoical and expectant. The train stood on the platform and the clock ticked past the hour. 'Not too bad,' said one old man when the carriage doors opened, and the clock said they were fifteen minutes late.

Things to do, Tuesday

Find a place to stay – call Andreas
Get a job
Phone Liam and ask about the furniture.
Call the bank and beg them for an extension – more money, more time to pay back the rest of your debt.
Phone your father and apologise
Read the comedies of Shakespeare, the works of Proust, the plays of Racine and Corneille and The Man Without Qualities.

Read The Golden Bough, The Nag-Hammadi Gospels, The
Upanishads, The Koran, The Bible, The Tao, *the complete
works of E. A. Wallis Budge*
*Read Plato, Aristotle, Confucius, Bacon, Locke, Rousseau,
Wollstonecraft, Kant, Hegel, Schopenhauer, Kierkegaard,
Nietzsche, and the rest*
Distinguish the various philosophies of the way
THE TEMP
Distribute presents
Be polite and grateful

When the doors opened they streamed into the carriage, in
search of the perfect seat. Within seconds, the seats were full of
people. Still, Rosa was confused and couldn't understand. She
was constantly surprised by density, the sheer quantity of
things around her. She wondered why they were heading
north, all these people with their bags and coats. Entire families, squashed in with their cases and sandwiches and piles of
crisps. Rustling away, feeding sandwiches to their young. If the
train crashed, or was blown to pieces, dynasties would be
wiped out. The children were already on the squawk, beginning their small symphony of need, trilling up the octaves.
Rosa was a solitary passenger and this detail made her rela-
tively desirable. Soon she was surrounded by the old in search
of silence. She was joined by a woman with a Bible, a head-
scarf and a stringy neck, and an ancient man who edged slowly into the seat opposite her, kicking her foot and apologising.
He apologised for so long that Rosa could see they were in
danger of having a conversation. Really what she mostly
wanted to do was sleep, but though she closed her eyes the
sound of voices kept her conscious. Everyone was arranging
plastic bags and bottles of water. There was a constant low-
level rustling of bags and food and papers. A man was guard-
ing an empty seat beside him. Earlier he had eaten a sandwich
and left cream cheese and crumbs around his mouth. In his
hand he held a piece of paper with PRODUCTION QUOTA

written on it. The rest Rosa couldn't read. His wrist was covered with threaded scars, as if he had once smashed his fist through a window. She wondered if he had done it as a child. And now he was a fat-cheeked man of fifty or so, one hand in his salted hair.

Days were passing, time's limitless express-train was speeding onwards, hurtling everyone towards their own personal tunnel. Time's TGV was breaking the sound barrier, though her real-time InterCity slugtrain was moving more slowly. She thought of a slogan for the railways in Britain, like an old slogan she had heard as a child, 'We're getting there', only more applicable to the present day: 'Our Trains are Slower than Time Itself.' Yet, having queued patiently outside the carriage, nervous and worrying about her bags, Rosa had her own little seat, and her legs fitted snugly against the ancient legs of her opposite neighbour. The train had a welcoming smell, a homely aroma of coffee and chips. The windows were clean and through the glass she saw the girders of the station. 'Welcome, ladies and gentlemen,' said an automated voice. 'Please remember that you are required to travel with a valid ticket. This train will call at Luton, Birmingham International, Birmingham New Street, Wolverhampton, Crewe, Preston, Manchester Piccadilly, Kendal, Oxenholme and Glasgow Central. There is a buffet service selling a wide variety of sandwiches, crisps, tea, coffee, hot chocolate, cakes and biscuits. First-class accommodation is at the front of the train. We hope you enjoy your journey.'

The train eased northwards, passing under a steel canopy into the dim light of day. They passed rusted tracks, faded grass sprouting between them, and Victorian bridges reinforced with steel. PRIZE she saw painted on the brick arch of a bridge. PRIZE. And the prize was what? *TEMP TEMP TEMP* she saw, and nodded. They passed a depot made of corrugated iron. She saw the blurred front of a carriage inside. They passed metal grilles and the red steel of a bridge. Cameras and lights suspended above the tracks and an interlocking network of wires. Metal railings merged into a grey wall as the train picked up speed. Now the sloped sides of the cuttings were covered in foliage, dry shrubs. 'I'm on the train,' said a man to her left. 'Did Ed get the report done? On the way back I'll get a taxi.'

'You can't worry about it,' said another to his phone. 'Don't worry about it. It's fine.'

'Tell Ed to sort out the report. I'm back in the office tomorrow.'

Outside the clouds were heavy above the long lines of trees. There were broad-brushed green fields and rows of post-war houses with bay windows and long thin gardens. Out of town debris, business parks and warehouses and building sites with planks stacked in piles. As the train climbed to its top speed, objects outside were flung backwards before she could fully describe them to herself. ASIA'S FINEST FOODS, she saw, on the edge of a warehouse. 'The buffet car is now open' said the tannoy. 'The buffet car is selling a wide variety of sandwiches, crisps, tea, coffee, hot chocolate, cakes and biscuits as well as an assortment of narcotics and bandages, soma, hemlock, and gold, pure gold.' She kicked off her shoes and slept, head on the window, arms on the table, and woke with a start to discover that the train was running even later. Something had failed, some rusty old signal, but she found she accepted it all, every minute tacked onto the journey, she reclined into it, watching the green and grey of Britain pass outside the window. The view was made up of contrasts: the soft moss on the bridges, the variegated textures of trees and fields and the primary colours of the stations. As they moved slowly through one station she saw FOOD TO GO in orange neon and turned her head away.

She put her hand above her eyes and stared out at fleeting buildings, factories and clouds of smoke and the compressed shapes of city centres. There was a thick smell of hops for a while, and then a sweet coil of sugar as they passed another factory. She saw rows of cars, parked at a station, but the train passed through with a shudder. BLUE written on a bridge, and something else she couldn't read. The train moved through stretching ranks of suburbs, past the shabby backs of interwar houses, walls covered with peeling plaster, brickwork crumbling. Sand and gravel, litter at the side of the tracks, mingled with weeds. Then there were places so steeped in tranquillity that she envied their occupants: long low fields, pale lakes and careful gardens. In places the tracks cut a furrow through the land, and the train barely lifted its head above the fields. Then she only saw the outline of trees against the sky.

When the train slid into Birmingham New Street, the carriage partly emptied. The old man opposite edged slowly out of his seat, hitting her feet and smiling apologetically. She nodded goodbye. With a bank of vacant seats around her, Rosa found she could read in peace. She read slowly through the leftover newspapers, noting the by-lines of her former colleagues, and felt no sense of regret at all. She liked the fact they were all still there, working hard, advancing every day. At least poor old Peter hadn't been let down by everyone else. She was glad about that, Peter with his worried way of looking and his tempered charisma. It was all too far away now, as the train moved through an old brick tunnel into a flush of countryside. The last suburbs receded, and the crumbling warehouses and chimneys gave way to fields. She saw rubbish and dust at the edges of the tracks. Beyond was a garden and she saw a child running on the lawn. As the train drew northwards there were long grey-backed ridges, sprawling under the sky. Then she smiled. Years and years, she thought, feeling a retrospective urge coming on. The train was taking her through the secondary scenery of her childhood, the provincial towns with their flyovers and whitewashed shopping centres and the long lines of the hills. She remembered their family journeys to the north. She travelled with her parents on the train. Oh lovely, the past, she thought, sinking idly into thoughts of when she was a child, and her family had gone on holiday to the Lakes, year after year. Those were comforting memories, purely happy, though she felt a jolt as she summoned them. They had rented the same cottage almost every time, near Lake Windermere, in the grounds of a farmhouse. Rosa's mother grew up in the Lakes, near Barrow, and when grandmother Lily and grandfather Tom were still alive they used to come to visit. She was thinking about these summers, and she remembered the cottage they rented: slate slabs, a large fireplace with a bread oven, window seats in the bedrooms. The doors had latches, exotic to a child. The farmhouse was larger and more terrifying than the cottage, and the old professor who lived there said the cellar was haunted. It was a friendly ghost, he added, but after that Rosa could hardly bring herself to cross in front of the big house, and she only played in the small garden of the cottage. She wondered if the old professor was still there, still anywhere this side of silence. But he had been ancient when she was a child. He must be long vanished, he and his wife. Still, she thought she would find out what had happened to him while she was there. She wondered why she had never written to him. That would have been a gesture, kind at least. *Dear Professor, I wanted to let you know that I was there, years ago, at your house. I was small and I remember the woods seemed like immeasurable forests. Your orchards were abundant with apples and – I confess! – I sometimes ate the windfalls. I remember the smell of wet ferns, and the ferns stuck to my legs as I went down to the lake to swim. In the mornings I woke to the sound of birds in the trees. When we arrived the cottage was often cold, and yet you had always left wood for a fire. My parents would light it and I would sit there looking at the flames. I remember placing my hands on the big cold stones of the walls, the slate stones. One night I slept in a tent in the garden. I remember my father had to stay there with me because I was so small. When it rained we played Monopoly. My mother always won. It drove my father mad. I don't know why I never wrote before.* She should write to him while she was there! But then she thought she wouldn't after all. There would be the need to add, *Recently, my mother died.*

Very abrupt, no pain. It was absurd, but it had stopped her writing to so many people: old friends from school, teachers, kids she had grown up with. *Dear Mrs Morton, Thanks for teaching me about Hamlet. It helped me greatly when my mother died.* Yet it hadn't in the end.

Rosa thought that her mother had been an elegant and frugal woman, and it was a shame she couldn't ask her advice. It would have been nice to be able to talk to her. Rosa had been idle and had never asked enough questions. Her mother – and now Rosa felt despair and yearning like a kick in the stomach. It was impossible to accept. And yet she had to. It had to be. Still, she despised it and wanted to cry out loud, protest. It was iniquitous! If she was undisciplined, it started, and she hated the way it made her feel, abandoned and unkempt. She remembered a tall woman, almost as tall as her daughter, with bobbed brown hair, vivacious and outspoken. Rosa's mother had so many friends that when she died the church was heaving with mourners and some had to stand outside and listen to the service. Everyone was shocked, absurdly. 'It was so sudden.' 'At least she didn't suffer' – dozens said that, and it was perhaps true, though Rosa was surprised by their certainty. Still, they took Rosa's hand at the door, and said, 'I'm so sorry. Look after your father, and yourself, dear Rosa', and she smiled and thanked them for coming.

Bristol was hazy under a misty winter, which Rosa later remembered as pale and frigid. Her father was faint-hearted in the service. He couldn't speak, so after the vicar ('Oh Lord, we come here today to celebrate the life of Harriet Lane, loving wife and mother, who died recently after a short illness' – a very short and despicable illness, a shock to the head, a haemorrhage which swept her out before she could say goodbye – 'Oh Lord, thank you for smashing up Harriet Lane, so impressively . . .') Rosa had to address the church. That was the worst of it, looking out at a sea of sympathetic faces, wanting to cast herself on the coffin and scream. The Ancients had it better. You could ululate as much as you liked. Wailing was positively expected, scrabbling in the sand quite allowed. The modern British funeral was all wrong, Rosa decided, as she said a few terse words and tried to imagine she was talking about a remote acquaintance. She read a poem, Larkin's 'For Sidney Bechet', which had been one of her mother's favourites. For a while she wanted to fall into a faint, she had never really noticed how long that poem was, but it coursed on, verse after verse and Rosa's voice breaking with every word. *On me your voice falls as they say love should/ Like an enormous yes.* That messed the congregation up; they all started snivelling and rubbing their eyes. She kept on with it, though she saw her father had his head in his hands. *My crescent City/ Is where your speech alone is understood/ And greeted as the natural noise of good/ Scattering long-haired grief and scored pity.* She got to the end, bitterly and with a sense of mounting disbelief. The poem didn't reflect her mood at all. She didn't find anything natural or good at the time; she found her grief quite bewildering and devastating. Not only had she produced a dreadful reading but, more importantly, she had committed perjury over her mother's coffin. She dropped the book on the floor as she walked back to her seat. When the music started playing her father had to be helped from the church. She was angry with him at the time, thinking he was weak.

Of course the dead faded away. It was impossible to mourn them all the time. The memories dissolved, slowly. But if she thought about it she became aware just how furious and abandoned she felt. She was sure her mother would have helped her. 'The matter, Rosa? Explain to me?' 'Not sure, mother.' 'Well, write it down, call me up again when you want to talk. Let's think of an action plan. Lots of love.' Their conversations would have been pertinent, to the point. It was her father who was irresolute. Her mother was always brisk and quick-witted. The family home was shabby and comfortable. The kitchen was sparsely furnished with old-fashioned appliances, things her parents bought when they first married and never replaced. The cooker was a monument to an earlier era of domestic technology. The furniture was always second-hand, bought from adverts in newspapers, never fashionable or expensive. It wasn't that her family was poor, though her parents had irregular jobs. Rosa's mother with her shop in Clifton Village, selling jewellery and scarves. It never boomed, but it brought in enough. Her father worked hard on his works of local history. He was always engaged on a new project, working in his study for hours, and eventually a book was published, something about the Victorians in Bristol. He bought up dozens of copies and gave them all to his friends. That made Rosa cringe in her chair, because she remembered mocking him, talking with her friends about him and his free books. Suggesting they have a competition, first prize a copy of his book, second prize two copies, and her teenage friends snorting in the garden, hands to their faces. She had no idea at all; she was ignorant of everything that was important. In their home in Redland, a crumbling Victorian town house, Rosa remembered her mother and father preparing food, and it seemed now she thought about it that there had always been something steaming on the cooker, some pot of stew or soup. She saw her father standing over it, adding vegetables and talking to her mother in a soft voice, her mother pushing back her hair, leaning over him to stir the soup again. Hardly aware at the time, Rosa now knew that her parents had been happy.

Now she was sitting rigidly in her seat. Her mouth was trembling. She rested her arms on the table and put her head in her arms, feigning sleep. Certainly it would be a terrible thing to shatter the tranquillity of the carriage. No one would thank her, and the old Bible reader would be quite perplexed. Rosa lifted her head and cast a glance towards her, and still the woman was engrossed in the Holy Book. Her mother had always fallen silent as they approached the Lakes. Well, of course, thought Rosa, no reason to assume you have a monopoly on retrogression. Possible that the entire carriage is musing on years long vanished, the freefall of the seasons. Though the woman with the Bible and the knitting couldn't be, thought Rosa. She would be praising the Lord, and the child eating crisps would be thinking about crisps, and the small hunched man by the door who was tapping his stick on the floor – it was impossible to know what he was thinking about! Perhaps he was reciting an Upanishad, *in the beginning this universe was but the Self in the form of a man. He looked around and saw nothing but himself. Thereupon his first shout was, 'It is I!' whereupon the concept 'I' arose.* Perhaps he was thinking something she couldn't imagine, something so rich and holy she would never think it (or something so perverse and disgusting, she thought, glancing across at the man again).

Really, she had nothing to complain about. For hundreds of years – time uncharted – her ancestors were anonymous hordes, busy with the practical conditions of survival. They tilled fields; they went down mines. Some of them went to sea. Then in the twentieth century there was a subtle shift. At fifteen grandmother Lily left school and started work. She was one of seven children; two died in infancy. She went to work in a shop, a miniature revolution. At the age of thirty she married Thomas Marswick, a carpenter. Rosa remembered her grandmother as a tired old woman with a round face and tightly set hair, wearing an apron, distributing sweets. Her idea of leisure was to talk over the wall to the next-door neighbour, Jackie, about other neighbours who had recently died. Rosa's grandmother loved disasters, and in response to polite social questions she would release a volley of despair, deaths, cheated expectations. This attraction to the mournful overtook her progressively, and she fell into depression after the death of her husband, sliding through the house in her slippers, muttering about adversity. According to family legend, she had hidden all her money around the house, and most of it was never found after her death. She had a pair of false teeth which she kept in a mug by the bed. She accepted the structures of society, the random distribution of wealth, accepted it all and died quietly.

For many years after, grandmother Lily was preserved in a few tattered photograph albums. She had been young in the

1930s, and there were bleached black and white shots of her on day trips to Windermere, smiling at the camera, wearing her smartest clothes. Grandfather Tom stood by her, in a group of young couples, soon to be married. There were photos of her laughing at an outrageous friend, hovering at the edges of a dozen groups, petite, her hair carefully curled. Sitting astride a donkey on the beach, waving at the camera; singing on stage, dressed in stage finery, feathers and furs; bent double at the sight of a vast turkey, which her husband had just won in a Christmas tombola. Her parents, Rosa's great-grandparents, whose names she didn't know, lived in a small cottage in the village of Cartmel, which Rosa always remembered as a verdant garden bathed in a rosy dusk. If she went, she thought, what would she find? Nothing changed like the landscapes of childhood; it was scale that changed, the simple fact of individual growth. Former vistas, vast plains, were compressed into simple playing fields and modest gardens. The aspect shifted but there was much in the mind that changed.

As they passed through Preston station she was thinking of grey-stained streets, and the old grey slate of her grandparents' house. She was remembering the excitement she felt as a child on these trips north. For no real reason at all, Rosa had once had a vivid childhood dream that her grandfather Tom had turned into a camel. Worse still, because he died when she was six this camel version of the man became entwined with her early memories of him setting her on his back and crawling on all fours around the room. She had a few other fading visual memories of her grandfather: a large man, she thought, though all adults were large to a child, with ears that moved when he chewed. A man with a shining pate and a long pointed nose. To her his features were gargantuan, outlandish, though in photographs she saw he had been handsome enough.

The arrival was a series of snatched kisses, embarrassed expressions of affection, with grandmother Lily supreme in the kitchen, rattling cutlery, telling her mother – who pulled faces – what to do. Her father was feted, given a cigar. Grandfather Tom took Rosa into the living room, where there was an ornamental brass dog with a poker resting on its back, superfluous by the electric fire. He dressed her in his braces. He took her out and sat her on swings and there was a photograph of Rosa at four, her eyes glassy from the flash, clutching a terrified tiger cub, with her grandfather smiling beside her. It had been taken at a circus, under a Big Top when, after all the people juggling plates and women in leotards hurling themselves from high platforms, the ringmaster had taken the tiger cub into the crowd. You could hold the cub and pose for a photo. Grandfather Tom thought it seemed like a good idea, and called the ringmaster over. But when the ringmaster arrived, a fat man sweating under his greasepaint, Rosa had shrunk more from him than from the frightened animal, which looked like a soft toy, compressed into the fat man's armpit. The ringmaster had been dismissed, but as the cub disappeared across the other side of the ring, Rosa had begun to cry. It was an early sense of a moment in time forever lost, demoted from memory to mere possibility. Of course she thought nothing like that at all, she just saw the tiger cub vanishing away from her and wailed. Her grandfather asked her what was the matter, reassured her that the cub had gone, that it wouldn't bite her anyway, offered her ice creams and other small bribes, but she held her head in her hands and sobbed. He knew anyway, and just as the cub was about to disappear backstage he leapt from his seat and ran across the sawdust, to ask the trainer to bring the cub back to Rosa's seat. So they took a photo of her and her grandfather bought it. Now the trainer, the cub and her grandfather were all dead, thought Rosa. Perhaps not the trainer. He might still be clinging on. But definitely the cub! The cub had been dead for years.

Grandfather Tom wrote comical verse in his spare time, after he had injured his knee, which ended his career in amateur football. He never published anything, but Rosa's mother's desk at home was crammed with folders of his writings, immaculately drafted and redrafted, poems for friends. He had written until the end, making neat copies of even his swiftest doggerel, storing them away. For years, Rosa thought he might have been an unsung genius of modern letters, and had prepared to campaign for his reputation, but after her mother died she read all his poems again. They made her cry, but she understood they would never be published. They were loving, funny poems, but nothing more. *To my dearest Rosa/ Whose mother really chos-a/ tricky name to rhyme/ I've tried it time and time/ but can't get my old brain/ To find a good refrain./ It's hard to tell your daughter/ She really didn't ough-ta/ Call her daughter Rosa/ Because the name would pos-a/ Such a rich conundrum/ To Rosa's old and humdrum/ Very adoring grandpapa/ When he tried to write to her!!* That was one she remembered. It was definitely not Swift. But it wasn't bad for a man who left school at fourteen. His collected poems, his life's work neatly copied into a school notebook, was inscribed Thomas Marswick, Barrow, 1975.

She had been lucky with her family. They had been kind and loving, these long-dead people. It was odd she thought about her grandparents so seldom. Only as the train ran north did she really consider them. It took a jolt, a change of location, for her brain to grind backwards. Of course she had hardly known them at all. It was just a dim sense of familial recognition, a twitch of the genes, but it made her shift sadly in her seat. They would have been appalled by her, she understood. They would certainly have told her to calm herself. Grandfather Tom had been a clever man, but he was pragmatic. He had a wife and a daughter, a group of good friends, he played sport at the weekends. He divided up his time – work and play, everything in its place, a time for fooling around and a time for getting your head down, earning some money. His daughter had done well, and he expected things to progress from there. Rosa's parents expected her to better them, as they had bettered their parents. That was how they thought it went, they assumed – onwards and upwards with every generation. And if not upwards, then at least an effort, in honour of those who had tried before you. They were all trying to tell her this, her father and the ghosts of her family. You had to live. You had to try your best. There was nothing else for it. But at this she felt rebellious again and kicked them all off, these kind-eyed ancestors of hers.

And now Rosa watched the sun sink towards the hills. The day was drawing on. The closeness of the evening made her tired, and she closed her eyes. When she opened them again she had gripped her pen, and she wrote:

God exists eternally, as pure thought, happiness, completeness. The sensible world, on the contrary, is imperfect but it has life, desire, imperfect thought. All things are in a greater or lesser degree aware of God, and are moved to admiration and love of God. So the sensible world aspires towards the perfection which is God. God is the cause of all activity.

Now she stopped. If you understood God as an ideal, as something thought, part of the human longing for perfection, perfection unattainable but possible to imagine, to feel a sense of, then perhaps she understood. The mind was impersonal and therefore divine. The body was personal and therefore mortal. *Dream the dream the dream the dream . . .* Yet she – like the rest of the race – possessed a mind that felt its finitude as unnatural, though really it was the most natural thing of all. That was the problem. Her mind felt the disappearance of her mother to be incomprehensible, whereas in reality it was inevitable. It seemed a crazy way for a species to think. It didn't help with morale. Why, she wondered, had the species not evolved with an inbuilt acceptance of death – not the sort of acceptance that would cause people to die without a struggle, but a sort of inbuilt sense of death as the natural end of life? Why did the mind – *the mind, or your mind*, she thought? – return constantly to the very element of life which made it so unhappy? Especially when it sapped your will, stopped you from achieving anything? If you were so preoccupied with this immutable fact, so very concerned about it you could hardly participate, then what was the good of that?

Had she been more self-disciplined, altogether more Zen, she might have understood that age was an arbitrary marker, that growing old hardly mattered, because one could die any day. Would she not have apprehended the absurdity of human time? What about *durée*, she tried to remember, what about inner time? She could only perceive this relentless linear motion, this surging wave that was carrying her ever onwards. She should become more magnanimous, she thought. It was impractical to think so keenly about herself. Her hands were sweating, and there was a strong smell of coffee around her. It made her think about buying a cup, but she stayed in her seat, holding onto the table. For ten years, she had a simple means of self-definition. She was a journalist. It lent a confident ring to her voice. 'Rosa Lane, calling from the Daily Rag, could you give me a few moments of your time.' Through the years, Rosa's voice had dropped, becoming more deep and jovial, trustworthy and efficient. 'Hi, I'm Rosa, this is my partner, Liam. Yes, I'm a journalist. Liam is a political lobbyist.' Subtext: *We're a pretty savvy couple, and you'd better know it.* If something failed, if something went briefly awry, they could bask in the regard of the other – until the last stages at least, when there was no basking and mutual regard had been extinguished. Prior to that, she had delivered her lines well, with assurance, self-importance coursing from her larynx. 'Hi, Rosa Lane here, I'm a veritable goddess of the media. Hey, listen to me! And I have a fine relationship as well, no doubt I'm on the way to something called a happy life.' *I hardly thought about this stuff at all*, she thought. It was true she was sounding more hesitant. She had become afraid of striking up casual conversation with her neighbours. What do you do? they might say. Well, that was a question! What did you say? *I do nothing, or nothing worth revealing anyway. I bow before the unrevealed secrets of TEMP. I am, professionally speaking, a despairing toad. Yet there are many things I intend to do! Even today, I fully intend to find a place to stay. Then I will phone Liam and ask about the furniture. I will call the bank and beg them for an extension – that's Mr Sharkbreath, you see, he's been quite cruel recently and I'm not very pleased with him. I assure you, it's quite terrible what he did. He loaned me a load of money, and then he asked for it back, the callous varmint. I fully intend, after dealing with Sharkbreath, telling him exact-ly what I think, to read the comedies of Shakespeare, distin-guish the various philosophies of the way, read* History of Western Philosophy, *Proust, Cervantes, Racine, the Ancient philosophers and the works of the major religions and a few more peripheral and the rest, find the TEMP – my own person-al TEMP, you'll have to find yours yourself – whatever that is, I don't suppose you know either.*

So she kept her head down.

Outside the sun was fading. The conductor appeared, a large gruff man, and she handed over her ticket. She saw peo-ple cycling along a path set back from the train tracks, a fam-ily out for an evening ride. It was cold and the children were wearing hats and scarves, smiling brightly. The whole family was smiling, frozen in happiness. She thought of a song; she was trying to remember the words, some eternal pop: *Video killed the radio star . . . In my mind and in my car . . .* Something she remembered singing when she was a child, picked up from her parents' radio. That betrayed them – in those days, her parents were young and they even listened to the charts. The song struck her as funny and she longed to mouth the words. She noticed her hands were still sweating; they had created a sticky film on the table. Anyway the table was covered with empty crisp packets, grains of salt, an apple core, a few plastic cups full of cold dregs. The carriage had been converted, over a few hours, into a place of dust and debris. But she liked the refractions of light, the elegiac end of the day. She saw sheep grazing in fields, and a motorway receding out of view. There were deep red ferns on the hills, and the dwindling sun had stained the sky. When she arrived she would send her father a postcard. Loving, low-key. *Daddy, gone to the Lakes. Remember, we went there all the time when I was child. Of course you remember. The stone cottage with the thatched roof and the wheelbarrow and the water barrel. At dusk bats flew from the rafters, zig-zagging across the garden. Thanks for taking me swimming in the lake in the mornings. I never appreciated it at the time, but there you were, on holiday, a couple of weeks off work, dragging your middle-aged bones out of bed at dawn to take your small daughter to swim. Love Rosa.*

Then she saw a series of hills emerging to the west, deep curves of rock and moss. She saw a cold pink band on the horizon. The train was nearly at Lancaster. There were steep slopes and small grey cottages scattered across them. A road winding through the fields. Tribes of sheep and cows, standing in the sketchy grass. She settled against the window, staring at the broad shanks of the hills. Now she slapped her pen down and thought of the view and the sky and the wandering flecks of cloud and the low light of the evening. The country was shadowed in dusk.

At a small country station she stepped down from the train. The air was clear and she could see the shadows of hills, silhouetted against the lights of distant towns. She found a taxi which drove her to Ulpha, through the rugged valleys of the southern Lake District. The roads wound over the backs of the hills, and the traffic streamed past on the other side. In the last light she saw a lake glittering between the mountains. That must be Coniston, she thought, as the road twisted up the gradient. There was a grey ferry moving slowly across the water. The car rounded the corners, picking up speed, and at the edges of the roads were dry stone walls, fields stretching beyond them. A few weeks ago, the driver had said, the fields had been covered with frost, but recently there had been a thaw. Rosa saw a quiet row of houses by the road, and in the distance she saw lights on blackening water.

The driver seemed like a friendly man, though after a few rounds of quick fire question and answer they fell into silence. In the seeping darkness the trees on the slopes were purple, their branches bare. And then there were rows of evergreens, leaves fluttering in the wind. She wound down the window though the air was cold, because she wanted to look at the trees. They drove through moorland, moss ground covered with dark hillocks. There were sheep lying on the rocks. Now the car went over a cattle grid and started to move slowly up a slope. There was a large slate building to the left, set back from the road. Ulpha was barely a village at all, a few houses with smoke pouring from their chimneys and a church. It seemed deserted when Rosa arrived; everything was so quiet. There was a light drizzle falling.

As she left the taxi, she wasn't angry with anyone. She walked to a drive which looked promising, and as if it led to Will and Judy's house. The ground was wet; mud coated her shoes as she walked. At the end of the drive she stood for a moment, breathing the cold air and listening to the sound of the River Duddon flowing swiftly. Her family had never stayed in this part of the Lakes. But her grandparents had lived near-by, and the air was thick with memories, as she glanced over at a cluster of slate cottages, set against russet fells. Already she was quite cold. Still she lingered in the evening air, puffing on her hands. On the muddy drive, the trees formed a canopy above her. The sky between the trees was serene, dotted with stars. She saw a bank of cloud hanging over the valley. She could hear a Land Rover in the distance, moving slowly over the cattle grid. Its lights swung around a corner, shining through a hedge. Then the sound of the engine receded.

Judy and Will's house was a large farmhouse made of slate. Ivy creeping around the windows. When Rosa had walked up the drive she found a sign by a gate, saying 'ULF'S FARM'. There was a low hedge, and over the hedge Rosa saw a garden, a large tree, a swing dangling from a branch. The gate creaked loudly as she pushed it open, and the curtains twitched in a first-floor window. She waded through the puddles on the path, and knocked briskly on the door. There was a scramble of children and dogs and adults and the door opened. Among the array of images, features, hands coming towards her, she distinguished Will, beaming broadly, half of his face covered in a ginger beard and his hair, also ginger, standing up in patchy clumps. Judy was looming behind, plumper than before, ruddy-cheeked. Still the same long blonde hair, gathered today in a wide plait. A big radiant face. Both were wearing mud-stained trousers, vast woolly jumpers and dirty wellington boots. There were dogs barking and jumping up, drooling on Rosa's hands as she tried to pat them.

Judy grappled through the dogs and seized Rosa in a hug. Then she thrust her dramatically away and said: 'My God, Rosa, you look so thin.'

Will, who was kissing Rosa on each cheek, rustling his beard against her skin, stood back too and eyed her silently. There was a slight pause, then Rosa shrugged.

'Yes yes, I lost some weight, by accident rather than hunger strike,' she said, trying to make a joke of it. She was suddenly aware how tired she was. Now she felt dizzy, and put a hand on the wall. She had forgotten to eat on the train. She had forgotten even to drink; she had sat in the carriage sniffing the smell of coffee and hadn't drunk a drop. This abstinence was clearly having an impact on her hosts. Judy was staring at Rosa as if something awful had just happened, as if Rosa was actually naked, or covered in dung. Well, of course spiritually I am, thought Rosa, but is it now so obvious? Judy looked at Will. Will looked back at Judy. All you've heard is true, Rosa wanted to say. It's me! The one they call crazy and sad. I've come here precisely for those reasons. Would I really lug myself all the way up here, in the middle of October, having failed to come and see you in the years you've been up here, if I was anything else? A crise, evidently! A minor crise! What were they expecting of her anyway, she wondered? They all stood around, and while they stood Rosa glanced up the hall. There were coats and hats hanging on pegs. There was a dog bouncing around by Rosa's knees, a small yappy dog, Rosa couldn't think what breed it was. And there were two larger dogs, something like collies with pointed faces, barking by the door. The animals were all fine, shaking their coats, while the humans were standing stock still, poised on the brink of gaucheness.

Striving to wrench things back, seeing as she was still in the porch and already the mood had shifted, Rosa turned to Judy and said: 'Well you look wonderful.'

'I'm so sorry,' said Judy, blushing slightly, or was it just her ruddy glow, Rosa thought. 'I didn't mean to be rude. It's lovely to see you. Come in, come in.'

A few things came to mind. Rosa, tall and thin, dressed in old jeans and a grey felt coat. Overburdened with bags and another sort of weight, failing to understand how frothy and ephemeral things are. Judy, large, rotund moreover, happy, dressed in mud-stained clothes. She and Will were both pretty splendid. That was quite the word for them, the rough and ready pair of them, standing in their practical garb. Eyeing her. Friendly, but inquisitive. Definitely observant. She could imagine them, later, mulling her over. 'Terrible, she looks terrible.' 'Oh, quite terrible.' 'Oh, terrible.' 'Poor her.' 'Poor poor her.' Or perhaps they were insincere, and later they would string her up with the thick cord of their condemnation. 'Presumptuous as anything.' 'Fancy coming up here.' 'Desperate.' 'You're so right, darling. Desperate.' But she thought they were sincere after all. Now there was a subtle transition. Will gave Rosa a hug. 'I think you look great,' he said. 'We'll feed you up.'

That made her baulk a bit, but she was glad they were so rust-coloured, mud-coated, glowing. They looked like a different breed, that breed of country people who walk all day in fields or ride around on horses. She admired them for the girth and firmness of their legs, the strength in their arms. Their bodies were tested daily. They were fit, happy, fecund; they had birthed several children. Rosa could hear a couple of them crying in the bowels of the house. Will glanced towards the door. He put a long arm round Rosa, his hand flat like a spatula on her back, and guided her along a whitewashed hall. 'Have I disturbed you in the middle of something?' Rosa asked.

Judy laughed, boisterously. 'Rosa, we're always in the middle of something. But come in, come in, it's wonderful you came.'

It was bonhomie, simple and reviving. They had all recovered from the opening, and now Rosa was being bonhomied along the hall and into the living room. There they stood for a moment, while Rosa felt the warmth of the room. There were lots of red cushions and red curtains and an orange sofa and some bright red rugs. The walls were decked with paintings and photographs of the children, of Judy and Will, of Lakeland landscapes. The mantelpiece was a domestic shrine, scattered with homemade birthday cards, big numbers painted on the front. HAPPY BIRTHDAY BABY BOY! YOU ARE THREE!!!!! TWO TODAY WHAT A BIG GIRL! There were photos of christenings and baptisms, 'in the village church,' said Will, as she stared at them. There were pot plants everywhere. The dogs each had a cushion. Even the dogs had a sense of purpose, thought Rosa. It made her smile. There was the small brown mutt busy gnawing a plastic cat and the big white mutt eating a discarded shoe, and the other one sniffing something, all of them devoted to a specific end. There was a fire burning in the grate.

'Would you like tea?' said Will, as Judy sat on the sofa, arranging herself on several cushions, emanating joy.

'Do you have coffee?' asked Rosa. She sank into the beckoning folds of a large red armchair. Her head was pounding and her lips were dry. Despite the warmth of the room, she was nervous. That creeping sense of being anticipated, she thought, of discussions having preceded you. It was inelegant and she tried to stop it. She was trying to appear relaxed, resting her hand on the table.

Will was a robust man. He looked as if he spent his days chopping wood. He was shaking his head, flexing the muscles of his neck. 'I'm afraid we don't. Judy gave up coffee when she was having the babies, and I did too, for support. So now we just don't keep it. But tea? We have some rooibos and some camomile. Probably some Earl Grey somewhere.'

'Earl Grey would be lovely,' Rosa said with a tight smile. And she was thinking they were a pair of super saintly swine. Even coffee banished! They would live a thousand years. There was a wail from upstairs, a baby's cry. For a heavy woman, Judy was swift to move. She sprang up, saying, 'So sorry, Rosa, I'll have to get this. The other two are fine; Samuel and Leila are lovely. But Eliza has been very tricky. Very ill at ease. We're worried it's because she's the third. She's had so much less attention than the others had. My mother says it can make them very relaxed, they don't feel the nervous eye of the parent upon them. But poor Eliza is struggling.'

'Can I help at all?' asked Rosa, knowing that she couldn't.

Judy smiled, 'Oh no, of course not. I'd love you to meet them a little later, when they've had their baths and the nanny has gone. But I'll just go and see what she's up to,' as the wail reached a crescendo.

'Of course, of course, you must go,' she said.

Judy disappeared. Will had gone away. Rosa found a pile of magazines on the sofa, furniture magazines, gardening magazines, magazines about childcare. Guides to the Lakes. *Country Life. House and Garden*. Already she was aware of it. It seeped from the sofas, coursed across the dog baskets, flickered at the grate. There was an overwhelming sense of goodness to the house. Altruism, understanding and love. It swept you in, deposited you by a raging fire and a few handsome dogs. Rosa patted them each on the head. 'Good dog,' she said. 'Good good, steeped in goodness, little dog dog.' She ambled round, looking at the big plush curtains, read some cards set out on the bookshelves, loving notes from friends – 'Thanks so much for a gorgeous stay. So lovely to meet the fabulous Eliza, and to see those sweeties Sam and Leila again. Love to all of you'; 'Congratulations, my dear friends, on the birth of your third! Hope you're all doing very well. All my love . . .' They were doing the right thing, making a life for themselves. Three children, it was a towering achievement. And the place was a work of art, with the vivid upholstery and the fire spitting in the hearth and the neatly varnished window-frames. Everything was immaculate.

When Will returned, with a tea set on a tray, she was humbled and grateful. Now she looked at him carefully, he did look older. Perhaps his hair was thinning on top. Flecks of grey in it, anyway. Nothing too blatant, a subtle shift towards midlife. He had a few lines around his eyes. His hair had grown long at the sides. He had taken off his muddy wellingtons and his jacket, and was wearing shabby blue jeans and loafers and a green V-necked sweater. He put the tray down on a solid oak table. 'Do you take milk?' asked Will and Rosa nodded. She did. 'Just a spot, thanks so much.' *A spot*, she thought? Serving out tea from a silver tea service, Will looked incongruous. He had a furrowed brow, and sharp blue eyes. He looked like an overgrown choirboy with a holiday penchant for rugby. It was a curious combination. Judy obviously liked it. His children, judging from the photographs scattered around the room, were all as stocky as him. He would breed a tribe of prop-forwards who would never be ill.

He was staring at her, thinking of something to say. Determined to practise virtue in all its forms, Rosa reeled off pleasantries. She was digging in her store of remembered questions. It was a while since she had been so stubborn and polite. She said, 'Well, you have a lovely house. How do you find it living here? Do you like it? How do you find the region? How did you find the house?'

'Rosa,' said Will, uncurling his big legs and setting his feet firmly on the floor. 'I love it. We live in total bliss. You should try it.'

'Any time, Will. Any time you feel like a house-trade, your

lovely farmhouse for a room with a view of the train tracks, just let me know,' she smiled.

Will smiled back. 'Sounds great. Just what we need, an away-break in the city slums.'

'How old are your children? What are they like? Are you planning more?' asked Rosa.

Will rattled off their ages. Rosa nodded profoundly and failed to commit any of them to memory. Meanwhile Will was explaining that they wanted more children. Another one at least. Maybe two. 'It's genuinely miraculous. You hear everyone talking about it, and you can't possibly understand it, but then you produce this being, and after a few weeks you can't imagine that they never existed before. It's extraordinary. I can't recommend it enough. It's so much work, of course. The work is insane. We farm some of it out. We have a nanny who lives a few doors away. She must be about to leave now. But she's here most of the day. That's a great bonus. And we have people from the village who help. But you know, we never sleep. One of them sleeps through the night, the other wakes up; Eliza goes mad at dawn, you know, it's crazy. But still, it's extraordinary how much I love them all.'

He was still smiling, beaming with wonder. When people talked about their children Rosa smiled and looked intent, but it seemed to her as if they alluded to something hermetic. Still she nodded, batted a few more questions towards him, about the neighbours and the sense of community, a few more platitudes, a compliment on the tea which was making her long for a hit of coffee.

He was grateful she was making the effort. Later, she knew, he would be just as polite to her. 'Oh, they're wonderful,' he said. He meant the neighbours, she thought. Rosa was nodding with conviction. Now, as Will said: 'Yes, the neighbours, really great. Some of them are incomers too. It's such a quiet valley, the Duddon Valley, where we are. By summer there are fewer tourists than elsewhere. And we've helped a bit with local events. It's sublime' – as Will continued, Rosa felt her expression was becoming fixed, like a mask. 'Sublime,' she said. 'How lovely.' She nodded and smiled again. She couldn't drop the smile for fear of losing it altogether. Will, she thought, I am quite sure that you are dear to the gods. They have poured blessings on your head. There was a pause and Rosa was hunting for something else to say when Will puckered his brow and said, 'Rosa, I'm very sorry about everything that's happened. About the death of your mother. And I couldn't believe it when I heard about you and Liam. Neither of us could believe it.' His expression was open; he looked like he meant it.

'Well, thanks,' she said.

'We just wanted you to know that.'

'Good of you,' said Rosa. 'But really, it's fine. No need for sympathy. I was knocked back for a while, but now I'm fine.'

'I have to say, you look a little strained,' said Will. He was leaning towards her, he seemed to be thinking about putting a hand on her arm. But he didn't. 'You look like you haven't been having the best time of it recently.'

But that was a funny thing to say. *Who ever had a best time? How did you get a best time? Tell me where to go for a best time*, she thought, *and I'll be out of here in a flash*. But she stopped herself again. *Discipline*, she thought. *Gratitude*.

'Oh that's because of a lot of other things,' said Rosa. 'Other stuff. You know, existential.'

'No, really, you look very worn.'

He was sipping his health tea and looking pensive. He seemed to find it painful, personally painful, that Rosa was so mashed. She was sure he was a good man. She certainly had them both pegged as good people. Their mantelpiece displayed it, all those shots of community functions and smiling small children. They were virtuous and productive. She had known them for years. She had met them – she could barely remember when she had met them. A long time ago, it must have been through mutual friends. A party, in the days when life was a pattern of parties and everyone thought they were unique and possibly immortal. In those days no one thought much about the essential unknowability of things in themselves, *an sich* and the rest. They hardly cared a jot if space and time were merely intuitions, and they hardly considered the *ens realissimmum*. If they thought about it, they talked it through over a beer, but in a detached way, as if it didn't directly concern them. Mostly they drank and fell in love. They trusted the physical world, invested heavily in it. Judy and Will met during that period. She had known Judy first, yes, she remembered a few coffees with Judy early on, and she remembered something about Judy and Will meeting and becoming so compelled and excited by each other that Judy cried. Was that real? Or a disturbed echo of something else? She had always thought of them with affection, though distantly, people she semi-knew but liked. When they lived in London she and Liam had them round for dinner a few times a year. That was cosy, and then they met at parties, in large groups. It was the closeness of their scrutiny that was freaking her out. But if you lugged bags of unwashed breeches around the country, pursued by rapacious bank sharks, you had to accept it. Still she thought it was strange he wanted to question her so closely. For all he knew, she was truly mad. He was lucky she still had some of the carapace stuck to her.

'It's very kind of you to bother about it, but I really don't much care what I look like,' said Rosa, trying to shrug him off.

'It's not that I care what you look like,' said Will. 'I'm only concerned if this outer layer hints at any turmoil within.' When he said turmoil, he stuttered. As if he hardly remembered the word. As if he was saying, *Poor Rosa, I am not fluent in your dialect of crazy-mad*. Really he was quite at ease. He folded his hands in his lap and waited.

Briskly, she said, 'Really, Will, I'm fine. I've just got a job, well at least, a good prospect of a job, after a period which I just devoted to nothing at all.'

'We were all surprised when you just walked out of your career. We had you pegged as the first female editor of the paper!' He was laughing.

'Best thing I ever did,' said Rosa, fiercely. First female editor? How little they had known her. But she didn't want to offend him. There was an uncomfortable pause, and then Will said, again: 'I just think you look, sort of, fried. Frazzed. Done for. I don't know how else to express it.'

God freedom and immortality, thought Rosa, looking at Will. The problem was, she didn't believe in any of them. *What do you think Will about the categorical imperative? Does it concern you at all?* Well, he acted well enough, and if Will's life became a general natural law, she wouldn't complain. Will was looking at her in a kindly way, expecting an answer. She wasn't sure what to say, so she gazed across the room, glancing at the careful arrangements of lamps, rugs, country furniture in mahogany, books, magazines, papers, toys, the flowers in the vases and the paintings – a view of Coniston Water, a view of Skiddaw, now she looked. With an effort, she said: 'Oh, I'm not that serious at all. Not serious enough to be any of those things.'

After Will's opening, there was the re-emergence of Judy, who lifted her reddish neck, threw back her hair (released for the evening, flying around her face like a force of nature) and said, 'Oh Rosa! It's so nice to see you!' Then the children appeared, and they were dazzling and exhausting. It was impossible to imagine spending more than a couple of hours with them, as Samuel kept shouting and slapping his hand on Judy's knee, and talked a lot of child nonsense and tried to kick Leila who played with boxes except when she was crying because Samuel had kicked her, and Eliza the baby dribbled and sometimes cried. Rosa played with them and sometimes over the sounds of the children they tried to talk. Then Will started to cook, and Rosa said she would help Judy put the children to bed. In the process, she read Samuel a story about a boy who saw snow for the first time, which Samuel knew by heart already. Then Judy reappeared to kiss him goodnight and turn off the light. When the children were settled Judy told Rosa about the mothers' group in the village, and how

Will thought it was unfair there wasn't a fathers' group and had proposed establishing one, but there were only a few couples with young children anyway. Most of the villagers were older, though they had all been welcoming and kind. There followed some stories about tractors and power cuts and the exchange of bacon and eggs and lifts to the playgroup. Then Judy said, 'Of course you'd find the people I deal with deadly dull. If I wasn't such an earth mother I would too, and there's a side of me that knows I've completely lost my analytical faculties. If I ever had any! It's amazing how it takes you. The first time you find the dugs and lactation thing actually quite bizarre, but the next time it doesn't even seem odd any more. Do you want them?'

Rosa made a noise that sounded like benign coyness, and Judy laughed. 'All about the right time, right place, of course?' she said. And Rosa nodded again, smiling broadly, aware she wasn't giving Judy much in return for all her generosity and charm.

'Now, I want to show you your room, Rosa,' said Judy. They passed along whitewashed corridors into a room with scruffy sofas arranged around an old slate fireplace, and piles of toys and books. 'Where we really live,' laughed Judy, and then into a room which had a long wooden table and a sculpture of an anguished naked woman in the corner. 'Will made it,' said Judy, and they stood in front of it for a few minutes while Rosa exclaimed in delight. 'It's me, when we were trying to get pregnant for the first time. Don't I look depressed!'

'Mmm,' said Rosa, leaning on the sound like a crutch.

'A month later I found out, but when he modelled it, I really thought it would never happen.' Judy turned, her eyes sparkling, and Rosa thought for a moment she was crying, but then Judy emitted another expansive laugh, and said, 'Ridiculous! Quite neurotic. Chance would be a fine thing, to stop now!' And you are, thought Rosa, like a conveyer belt, pounding out the human race. Forging it. They passed into Will's study, which was crammed with careful clutter, books piled on books, a computer with Post-it notes stuck round the screen, a leather armchair, a battered sofa with the stuffing spilling out, and a sculpture which seemed to represent a man drowning in mud. Rosa admired it, knowing it was another one of Will's. Was this Will when Judy was failing to conceive, Rosa wondered? It was pretty good, when she looked more closely. Will was a modest Renaissance type, working a farm and loving his wife and kids and cooking and occasionally fashioning something from stone. He was far from talentless! And the house was charming. Every room, Judy was telling her, had been completely restored. Much of it Will and his sister had done together. The bedrooms were cluttered with children's clothes and toys, and Judy and Will's marital bed was a bright orange fertility symbol.

Rosa was reeling from the colours and scents and the general vibrancy, and her repetitions of 'lovely' were echoing along the corridor as they passed into another room, spartan and nearly empty. As Rosa admired the frilly farmhouse curtains and the pristine whitewash of the walls Judy turned and said: 'Rosa, this is a complete secret, for the moment, because I'm not quite at three months, but it's so wonderful to see you and I really want you to know – I'm pregnant again!'

Rosa was genuinely startled. A fine tally. Four children. And Judy barely thirty-five.

'But that's really it,' said Judy. 'I really can't do any more.'

'Hardly surprised,' said Rosa, and it was the first truthful thing she had said for an hour. 'Hardly surprised at all.'

And Judy laughed and patted her on the arm. 'Literally, Rosa, I will go mad if I do another!' Now Judy turned her head and walked again, drawing her along another corridor, past the sleeping brood – Judy with a finger raised to her lips – and then they passed into a cold wing of the house, where the wind seemed to rattle at the shutters.

'We're still renovating this part,' said Judy. 'But we've done this guest room', and she pushed open a latched door to reveal another immaculate whitewashed room, with an iron bed and a handsome iron fireplace, and an assortment of Lakeland prints on the walls. There were green jalousies across the windows. Judy walked across the room and flung them open.

'You can't see it,' she said, gesturing into the blackness, 'but this room has the most beautiful view of the lot. Tomorrow you'll see. The fells are a brilliant red, and the sound of water you can hear, that's the most gorgeous ghyll thundering down the slope, you'll be able to see that too tomorrow. It's exquisite. I wanted Will and I to use this room, but it's too far away from all the children. You'll be very glad of that when Eliza starts bawling at 4 a.m. Which she will, I assure you.'

Rosa put down her suitcase in the corner. There was a long mirror and a hat stand. There were some books on the windowsill. *Sons and Lovers*, Rosa noted. The complete works of Wordsworth. John le Carré. Some P.G. Wodehouse. They were educated but not showy. They didn't stack up piles of Kant and Kierkegaard. There were fresh flowers in a vase on the bedside table, beautiful red and white flowers, she had no idea what they were. It was too much for Rosa. Feeling suddenly ashamed, she said, 'Judy. I shouldn't have come. You're so busy with the children. And you put flowers in a vase. It's so kind of you. But I really shouldn't stay.'

Judy paused and turned, as if this was the frank admission she had been waiting for. She was stern and definite. Her face was puce, but her hands were steady. 'Rosa. I won't hear anything of the sort. You're to stay as long as you like. I think it's just dreadful, what's happened. You have my utmost sympathy. I don't know what happened between you and Liam, but I know there are always two sides to such things.'

'Sometimes three sides,' said Rosa. 'When you're in a triangle.' She smiled, hoping by that to lighten the mood, but Judy was like a policeman, holding up her hand. 'Rosa, I don't want to get into it,' she said. That was slightly bemusing, but it hardly mattered. 'It's wonderful to have you here' – and Rosa murmured something in response. 'Come on, let's go to dinner,' said Judy. And she turned them both around and sailed them back along the corridors, past the portraits of Judy and Will painted by Will and the watercolours by an unknown hand, the latches making solid, comfortable sounds as they opened the doors. In the bright living room, where the fire was crackling and candles had been lit, Will had a fistful of plates and on the table stood a casserole dish.

They patched an evening together. By the sheer force of Judy and Will's goodness, they found some phrases and turned them out. Rosa was quite consumed by the strain of it, pawing at her food, striving to stay away from the truth. Judy and Will talked in a rich slew of adjectives – words like delightful, gorgeous, beautiful, special, wonderful and extraordinary. Rosa founded the repetition uplifting. It was like watching someone carefully remaking the universe, spilling shafts of light across the shadows, turning grey to yellow and black to gold. Rosa, lacking necessary words, tried out 'lovely' a dozen times, but couldn't quite get her tongue around it. It wasn't that Judy and Will lacked imaginative range, thought Rosa. It was just that the place repeated certain qualities. As in the city Rosa found her brain consumed by recurring thoughts of grime and grey and surprising beauty and moments of being and litter and menace and noise and insistent bass-beat and wide-eyed crackhead and insalubrious shanty town and sprawling chaos, so they talked about the fells and the silence and the freshness of the air and the beauty of the view and how much it revived them. Then they were bawdy for a while, and Judy told tales of cracked nipples, and the slow recovery of her body from childbirth, and how tired she was because Leila and Eliza never slept, and Will smiled at his wife, and kissed her hand. There was an established pattern. Judy emanated a worthiness that made Rosa feel still more acutely the isolation of her self-centredness, her overdeveloped ego. Her fear of subsuming her own desires and impulses. Her ambitions, unfounded as they were. Her lack of realism! Her squeamishness and moral cowardice. Her committed procrastination. Rosa thought that friendship was a curious thing. She really had little in common

with Will and Judy. Yet they listened to her, committed themselves to a tumbling series of questions. In response, she really
bored on. Stimulated by food and wine, she was mighty, boring and terrible. They raised their eyebrows and diagnosed her.
Clearly a nervous breakdown, said Will. Not surprising in the
circumstances.

'I think I merely opened the doors of perception,' said Rosa.
That was after a jar or so of wine. Doors of perception! The
words only came with drunkenness. Otherwise it was quite
impossible to say them. They made her think of Blake with his
naked tea parties, visions of souls dancing in trees, the rest.
Jim Morrison in a kaftan with a chiselled chest. 'Everything
was obscured before. I wasn't looking carefully at things.
Without the death – you know – my mother, death death, I
would have lived on for a few more years, quite content, in a
dream. You understand.'

'Rosa, you were under too much strain. You know, the
death of a parent, it's very hard. And your relationship was
ending. There was a lot going on for you. And people are busy,
they don't have time,' said Judy. 'You should have come to see
us sooner. Grace and Liam, we saw them not so long ago,
when was it? They came to stay, it must have been a few weeks
ago. Liam is a good person, Rosa, you mustn't forget that.
And Grace is very compelling. We understand their attraction.'

'Oh, he is good, yes, of course,' said Rosa. This made her
angry, but she kept feeding herself wine.

'Really, he is a fragile man,' said Judy.

'I've never thought of him like that,' said Rosa. 'But I've
been wrong about a lot of things.'

'Of course it's hard to say – but we understand some of what
he's been saying. What they've both been saying,' said Judy.

'You know, you were both at fault. Or rather, perhaps,
there's no one to blame. The relationship had clearly decayed,'
said Will. 'That's not to say his timing was sensitive.'

'Decayed?'

'They say you were depressive, overbearing, self-obsessed,'

said Will. He was so naturally congenial that he smiled as he said it.

'Not really depressive, not then. But the others, of course,' said Rosa. 'I would have to confess to the others.'

'Liam says you were wild for a long time, and he was too afraid to end it,' said Judy. 'He says you tired him, he couldn't keep supporting you emotionally, and eventually he couldn't cope. He felt he was only an emotional crutch to you, nothing more.'

'No doubt I said a lot of foolish things.'

'Perhaps you're being too hard on them. Your relationship has clearly declined, you're angry and frustrated, you explain to Grace how demoralised you are, how much you want to get out, and you tell her over and over and Liam is there – and of course Liam is attractive, intelligent – who would blame her?' said Judy. 'I mean, you can blame her, but can you be sure you wouldn't have done the same?'

'I don't know what I would have done,' said Rosa. 'I haven't been in a similar situation. I can't possibly guess.'

'They were in love. It sounds like a grand passion! And that's hard to resist,' said Judy, and Rosa detected a trace of autobiography in her voice.

'Grace says you hit her once at a party, a few weeks back,' said Will. 'She had a cut eye. I remember that – it was still bruised when they came here.' He was looking carefully at her now, monitoring her response. Did they think she was putting on a front? Did they assume she was about to lose control, release a screaming fit, a violent outburst? She had raged, of course, but internally, to the walls of Jess's living room, to the self-assembly furniture. She had never really raged to anyone. Perhaps occasionally she had emitted something, but it was mere metonym. Anything she expressed was more like a personal code.

'My jacket hit her, when I put it on to leave. I was in a hurry, I wanted to leave so she would stop talking to me,' said Rosa. 'I think that must be what she means. I seem to remember the zip caught her. I was being clumsy; I was desperate to get out of the room. She was hounding me at a party. You know she can be sanctimonious.'

They stayed silent.

She knew what Will was talking about. She remembered it clearly; her memories were cut glass, quite polished. In a flat on Elgin Crescent – one of those generic places of stripped pine floorboards and big mirrors, the proprietor a proper denizen, more so than most – Rosa had seen Grace moving slowly, wearing black. She hadn't wanted to go to the party, this con-gregation of the righteous in a crowded room, but Jess had insisted and Rosa had followed orders. The flat was packed with the young and wealthy, picking at vol-au-vents and sip-ping wine, leaning their satin-clad limbs against fine antique furniture, and the place was too small for Rosa to hide. By the time she sighted Grace, there were only a few metres between them. Grace nodded, and came towards her, seeming to falter though that had to be an act – or who knows, perhaps she was nervous as anything, it was hard to tell and Rosa had long stopped thinking she had any grasp on the thoughts of others. Rosa gritted her teeth, waiting, drinking wine in gulps to steel herself.

Grace arrived, holding a glass of sherry, her beauty as strik-ing as ever, her voice soft and her eyes cold. She was wearing a tense black dress, and it worked well on her hips. She had a slung motion to her walk, as if she was carrying something on her head. She delivered her opening line in a low tone, as if they were plotting someone's downfall. She was saying *con-nive with me* and for a moment Rosa bent towards her. 'Rosa,' she said, a hand on her arm. 'Rosa, I'm so glad to see you. I left you messages. I thought you were wasting your energy in rage and it pained me to think that.'

And Rosa said, 'Grace, there's no point us discussing any-thing.' She was aiming for lofty indifference, a look of distaste, but she was slightly drunk and couldn't control her mouth. Grace, pushing back her hair, said, 'I want you to know that I struggled with my feelings,' as if she had been swept towards Liam by forces beyond her control, and perhaps it was so, perhaps she had been overwhelmed, thought Rosa. 'I struggled not because I thought my feelings were wrong but because I was concerned you weren't yet ready, you couldn't move on. I knew it was right, but I was aware you would find it difficult to understand. But months went by, and you were so angry, and finally I felt sorry for Liam.' Grace's mouth – small, rather too small somehow, thought Rosa, though she'd never really noticed it – was pursed in contrition. 'But you must understand that for much of our friendship I just thought of Liam as your partner. I never thought of him in that way, the other way, I mean.'

'As "not-my-partner", you mean,' said Rosa.

'Exactly,' said Grace. 'I don't want you to think I was biding my time, waiting for a chance.' She struck this resoundingly, quite certain of herself.

Rosa smiled in embarrassment and took a slug of wine. She wasn't sure why she had ever liked Grace. After a gap of a few months, Grace sounded like a zealot. Why the hell did I like Grace? she wondered. Why did I even invite her round for all those dinners? It turns out she's contrived. Was she always so contrived? Grace was performing one of her old gestures, which Rosa had previously thought was quite charming, her head cocked to one side, a hand on her hip. Rosa couldn't help it. She thought Grace looked funny. She began to laugh.

Grace pushed back her hair again, and licked her lips. She smiled a little. 'Rosa, there's no need for that. It's very simple, wonderfully simple if you'll just accept it. Our arms are open to you. We both love you, of course, as much as ever. If you could return to us, then you would find we could celebrate the friendship and closeness – all the elements you needed from Liam and myself – without the drag of a failing relationship. I know it sounds unpalatable to you, but if you think you could try that would make me very happy. Liam too, I'm sure. We miss you.'

Rosa found it hysterically funny. She was laughing, sipping wine. Then she started hiccoughing. Grace stood and stared, in apparent confusion.

'Rosa, what's wrong? We love you, and there's nothing funny about that,' said Grace.

There was Grace, dashing towards the winning tape, and Rosa, Rosa had trapped her spikes in the sand and fallen off the track. Rosa had thoroughly flunked the race. She had the element of surprise on her side, though. She had the inappropriateness of her response. She couldn't quite control herself. Grace wasn't sure whether this was the moment to walk away, shaking her head at the wreck that was now Rosa, or to stay and stare in bemusement. She stayed and stared. Hoping to drag out the scene, thought Rosa. Grace never backed off. She was usually victorious. It was Rosa who was dredging around for something to say, trying to wipe her mouth with her frock.

'Rosa, come on, calm down,' said Grace.

'You're like a large coiled snake,' said Rosa. 'And Liam is your rat. I mean, he is your nourishment, your perfect complement. You look better than ever, on your diet of perfect fodder.' She watched Grace winding along with another phrase, a few more maxims for free living, deconstructions of stifling mores and the rest. Grace, sighing, suggested that Rosa sit down and have a glass of water. Then she supplied a staccato performance of sympathy and something else, something more mysterious and uncertain, a trace of condescension, that was what it felt like, as if Grace was approaching Rosa from a long way above her, drifting cloudlike over her mortal mess. Rosa didn't sit and when water was found she refused to drink it. Grace was still there with her open gaze and her hands cupped around her glass.

'Rosa, I'm sorry you've taken it all like this,' she said. 'I understand, things have been terrible for you. But you must see that I care, I care passionately about our friendship. I'm so sorry about the way it happened. But you spent months telling me you felt restless and bored. And I went to see him to say how sorry I was, and things just happened.'

'You went to see him?' said Rosa, very calmly now, regaining gravitas, apart from her occasional hiccoughs.

'Yes, yes, of course, as a friend.' Grace's eyes had narrowed again. She took an elegant sip of sherry.

'But you never told me,' said Rosa. 'When was that?'

'I'm not going to get into this,' said Grace, holding up a hand. 'It won't help us at all. You should understand that.' She smiled again. Her hair was lustrous with health, and her skin shone. That despite her fags and booze, thought Rosa. She was plain lucky, and her face would be beautiful for years yet. Decades, perhaps. Her cheekbones were fine. Lovely shoulders she had, and the dress set them off well. All that made Rosa nod at the inevitable. Of course, some slide – slide into a slump, slump down and drop and the rest – and some ascend. Of course, she was thinking, nodding and smirking.

'Roughly,' said Rosa. 'A week before he ended it all? Months before?'

'Come on, Rosa,' said Grace. 'I understand that you feel betrayed but this is ultimately an erroneous feeling, a mistake in emphasis. It's very straightforward. Your behaviour is textbook. You're looking for people to blame for the mess you're in. Liam and I seem to be likely culprits. But you know yourself the truth is more complex.'

'Well thanks for letting me know,' said Rosa. 'Thanks so much for assuring me of the complexity of truth.' Briefly she despised the pair of them. She definitely despised the party. This glass of cheap wine she was holding in her hand, she wanted to throw it to the floor and stamp on it. *Childish*, she thought. *Truly childish*.

'Rosa,' said Grace, trying to put her hand on Rosa's arm, but Rosa flicked her away. 'What can I say? How can I make things better?'

'There is really nothing to say. And now I'd like you to stop talking to me.'

Now Grace – looking resolute, really determined to settle it – drank down her sherry. She set down the glass and put both her hands on Rosa's arm. That was uncomfortable and Rosa moved away.

'Rosa, come on. Don't you think you're being unreasonable? What, you didn't want Liam, so no one is ever allowed to have him?'

'Have him?' said Rosa. The script was terrible. She wanted to shoot the writer. Who has produced these gutter-slinging phrases, she wondered? Were they really having this conversation? Was it really they, and not two women at some other party somewhere else entirely? She gathered herself together, she set down the glass of wine which had made her head ache and said 'Grace, I don't want to talk to you any more. As this room is too small for me to get as far away from you as I want to, I'm going home.'

'Why don't I walk with you to the tube?' said Grace, with an open gesture that indicated she really thought that might be a good idea, a quick walk together would clear the air, sort everything out, Rosa's jangling nerves and her failure to accept the justice of the case before her.

'No,' said Rosa, firmly. She grabbed her coat, whipping Grace on the cheek with it as she pulled it from under someone's haunches. Well, it served her right for being so small, thought Rosa. She was overcome by an urge to slap her. But instead, like a slack coward, she slunk down the steps to the street.

Grace had always been a great talker. She liked to discuss everything in depth. She found the mistakes of others mostly funny, and she never really minded if people disliked her. Rosa could imagine how entertaining she had made that encounter, how much she had trimmed and tailored it. 'Really,' she said to Judy and Will, 'she's completely exaggerating. It's a trait of hers. It can be really amusing. It makes her anecdotes larger than life. But you can't rely on her at all. The truth is not her main concern.'

'But you must have cared,' said Will. 'You must have been devastated by their relationship.'

'No, no, that's not it at all,' she said. That sent them nodding away, looking as if they knew her well. Ever she was tempted. She was feeling a rising urge; she wanted to fling the plates across the table, scream at them, tell them it was they who were mad! Surrounded by darkness on every side, rolling coursing night and still they were sanguine! They had to be crazy. Napkin at her mouth, forkful of peas in her hand, she wanted to warn them. Vapour, she was thinking. Yes, she added, that would clarify it. Just say that. Judy and Will, all is vapour. That would surely convince them. So she stayed silent.

'You're upset they lied,' said Judy, with parched understatement. 'That they hid it from you. But perhaps they were afraid. They saw that you were distraught. You were grieving. They didn't want to make things worse for you. Of course, they cared about you. But they were in love. It's very hard, isn't it?'

'They've been indiscreet,' said Will.

And they sat there nodding for a while. Silence settled over the table. There were candles burning in silver candlesticks. The tablecloth was white. Still, Rosa couldn't finish her food, though it was delicious. She caught them glancing at each other. Halfway through the main course she had been diagnosed. It was impossible to tell if they believed her or not, and anyway it hardly mattered. Will kept massaging more food towards her and Rosa thanked him voraciously, with abandon. It was a wonderful meal, a big pile of lamb and vegetables, which Rosa knew was bound to have come from their farm, or someone else's farm nearby, and she tried to eat. She didn't have their appetite, but this hardly troubled her. The effort of the table was palpable. After a silence which pulsed around them, becoming acute and uncomfortable, they all started throwing each other bits of information about mutual friends, observations on the state of the nation, sprawling anecdotes. Will and Judy were delicate and practical, ladling food at her, smiling broadly when she told a joke, because now she felt obliged to be jovial, to show them just how rational she was. They both spent a lot of time patting her arm. It bemused her, the arm patting. It began to put her off. Will was patting her arm during the main course, offering her more. Judy patted her, and she couldn't understand why. Was it an idiom? Did they pat everyone who came, or was she being treated to an intensity of pats, a concentration of reassuring gestures? Were they trying to put her at her ease? Did she seem so ragged to them? Quickly she tried to smile. She said, 'So really, how are you both?' She was trying for conviviality. She had her teeth gritted, her fists clenched. *Conviviality or death!* she thought. *Pour encourager les autres.*

'You know how we are,' said Judy. 'But tell us more about what you're doing now, Rosa.' There she was, preparing for the pat, and Rosa said, quickly, 'Well, I have a new boyfriend.' That was to salvage her pride. It didn't quite work even as she said it, but she was tired of them looking so lovingly towards her.

'You do?' said Judy, quite beaming with pride. 'You do? Rosa!' and she delivered another pat, but this time it lingered in enquiry. 'Tell me, tell me everything!'

'He's called Andreas. He's German. Hilariously, he's twenty-five. He's an actor.'

'Twenty-five! Well, how about that!' said Judy. Will was smiling in an avuncular way.

'A real whipper-snapper,' he said.

She laughed through her drunkenness and said, 'Oh yes, he's great. So young and vital and optimistic. He's currently in a West End play.' That sounded nervous, so she stopped.

'What's his name?' said Will.

'Will, you heard, he's called Andreas. Rosa told us,' said Judy, in a mock admonitory tone.

'No, no, his full name.'

'Oh, he's not famous,' said Rosa.

'Go on, tell us. Or is it one of those liaisons where you don't

199

know each other's full names. Each time you play a different part? Meet in disguise?' said Judy, smiling broadly. Rosa was glad that she was entertaining them. 'Oh, no, he's called Andreas Beck. But you won't find him on the credits of a film. Not yet.'

'But soon, soon,' said Judy. 'I can picture him – is he very handsome? Blond? Gorgeous and slightly cruel blue eyes?'

'No,' said Rosa. 'He's not like that at all.'

'Judy, you're not being very serious. This is, after all, the new love of Rosa's life,' said Will, and now Rosa felt her arm once more caressed by a benevolent hand.

'Rosa,' said Judy, 'I'm so sorry. I really am being disgraceful. Of course, I'm trivialising it. I'm so sorry. I'm just thrilled for you.'

'It's fine,' said Rosa. 'I understand the spirit of your questions. He's not blond or blue-eyed. But I suppose you would say he is handsome. I find him so.' That sounded pompous, so she said, 'Anyway, most people at twenty-five have that lustre of youth.'

'God, twenty-five, I can hardly remember it. Do you find he keeps saying worrying things about never having heard of The Cure, or never having watched *Withnail and I*, or that sort of thing?' said Judy.

'He claimed for a while only to listen to jazz.'

'Jazz, oh he's that sort of kid,' said Will, knowingly. 'You know, arty.'

'Well, actors, they're a pretty arty bunch,' said Rosa.

'I think he sounds lovely,' said Judy, though Rosa had hardly described him at all.

She nodded at the kindness. 'Will and Judy,' she said, because she really was drunk now. 'I want you both to know that my attraction to Andreas is not quite merely physical, as I imagine you are both assuming.' She saw them denying it with short sharp nods of their heads, but she continued anyway. 'Yes, he is a marvellous lover. Really, a virtuoso. But you don't want to know that, I imagine. Anyway, that's not it. It's something else, something about his naivety – well, that's unfair, perhaps patronising, but essentially he represents the unthinkingness of youth, its lack of suffering, its blissful ignorance of the worst elements of life, the way in which the young live naturally, natively, they are happy in their young bodies and live without a sense of easeful death coming to snuff them out, or some of them do, perhaps it's that. I've analysed it enough, and it may be nothing more than the fact that I like his musky smell and the touch of his hands. But I think it's the aforementioned . . . well, whatever I was saying. He is free of foreboding. Foolishly, of course, but I'm not going to shatter his idyll. It'll get shattered anyway.'

'What you mean is, he offers escapism,' said Will.

There was a brief silence, while Rosa absorbed the crashing veracity of this remark.

'Well, he sounds great,' said Judy. 'In the circumstances, I think whatever works for you is a good thing.'

'Thanks,' said Rosa. Now she was embarrassed she had brought up the subject anyway. She felt guilty and as if she had sold Andreas into slavery, or prostitution. Certainly she had been disloyal. 'Anyway, that's enough about that. How the hell are you?' she asked again, determined to change the subject. She clinked her glass awkwardly at theirs, trying to toast them, but she clinked it too hard and there was a profound crack. One of the glasses broke. Wine gushed onto the table-cloth and there followed a flurry of apologies and reassurances. They all raised their voices to assert their benevolence. Rosa was really yelling her contrition, and Judy and Will were shouting back their lack of concern. 'Old glasses, very cheap,' said Judy loudly, and Rosa said, 'God, I'm so sorry. I'm such a fool', and Will was bellowing, 'It had to happen soon enough. Got them from a garage.' But of course they hadn't. After that ruckus, after the wine had been mopped up and Judy had found another glass and filled it, Rosa said, again, 'I'm so sorry. So, tell me how you really are.'

'Oh us, us,' said Judy, touching Will's hand. 'We're just fine.'

'Well, you certainly seem to be,' said Rosa.

'More lamb?' said Will. Will with his thick hair and his look of health. A shank of meat at his elbow. As he handed some more lamb onto her plate, ladling vegetables after, Rosa was trying to formulate a thought, but discovered she was too drunk to finish it. There was no doubt that Will was hard-working. But he was blessed with fortune, all the same. His mother and father had bought this farmhouse for him, a fantasy playground, a breeding-ground. He had obliged them with a lovely brood; he was a worthy addition to the family line. She was happy for them, of course she was ecstatic, agog with delight, but something lurked beneath it. She was thinking of grandfather Tom, who had lived and died not far from here. At fourteen, his father told him to get a trade. He obeyed; the rest was compromise, happy enough, but hardly the dream. He always said he was fortunate to have been born in such a beautiful place – not Barrow itself, but the country-side around. He went walking in the hills at the weekend. He had never travelled the world; he had never gone far from home. He worked long days, brought home money for his family, played sport, walked a little and he had written comic poems. That wasn't a bad effort, thought Rosa, as she accept-ed another spoonful of vegetables. She shrugged it off and tried to think lovingly about her hosts. Nothing more than this, she thought. From now on, nothing else, just kind thoughts.

She said, 'I have this Platonic phrase in my head, is it Platonic? It runs something like if one person desires another, or loves them passionately, they would not desire them or love them passionately or as a friend unless they somehow belonged to their beloved either in their soul or in some char-acteristic, habit, or aspect of their soul. Where's that from?'

'What are you saying, Rosa?' said Judy.

'But this food is staggeringly lovely. Thanks very much.'

'Perhaps it's true, what you say,' said Will.

Suddenly, there was a scream from upstairs, and Judy

instantly leapt up and left the room.

'That we are beholden to those we love, and accept their claims on us,' said Will.

'*Santé*,' said Rosa.

'You should try a bit more,' said Will. He was smiling again, in that ready way he had. It was easy for him to be convivial.

'Should try a bit more to do what?' said Rosa. The remark seemed to apply to a spectrum of things.

'No, no, try a bit more of the lamb shank. Try it, it's excellent,' said Will, tipping it onto her plate. Rosa was like a plotter in a melodrama presented with the simple goodness of the heroine. She was there in her cape, whispering away, soliloquising madly, and Will was reaching towards her with his lily-white virtuous hands. Offering her lamb shank. She was too ashamed to say thank you. There was another pause, while Rosa racked her brain for anecdotes, witticisms, anything to entertain her host. Now they had dealt with Liam and Grace, set up their stalls, it was time to say something light and vague. Will, she was thinking, you are very good. And useful to your family. That is to be admired. Then why, she wondered, am I beginning to fear him? It was his eager line in understatement, she thought. His unceasing kindness. It affected her chemically, as if it was alkaline to her acid. I'm like a leech, she thought, that has been treated with salt. Or was it fire? She couldn't remember how the Moses you treated a leech and realised her simile had been ill-judged. So she turned to her host and forced a smile.

'So, Rosa, what's the plan?' said Will, slicing his lamb neatly and putting a piece in his mouth.

'The plan, for what?'

'Well, for the future,' said Will, with a waving gesture, as if signalling the time to come.

'Whose future?'

Will laughed. 'Yours, Rosa, your very own future. Your recovery, if you like.'

'Oh, Will, you know, it's only a very tiny crise. Nothing

major. Just a freak out. Better to have it now than in ten years, I say! We are all quashing the freak-out, do you not think? The freak-out lies coiled in the heart of being, like a worm. It's not remotely important,' said Rosa. 'If you need a farm labourer, or a spinster governess for your children, you might think of me. My values are quite sound. I believe in truth and beauty, something like that, and I am sure there is such a thing as a good person.'

He laughed and patted her on the arm. I must look desperate, thought Rosa, as she held the fork to her mouth and tried to eat something. Now she thought she should never have come. The thick stone walls, the roaring fire, the farmhouse itself were too redolent of the places she had stayed as a child. The spectre of the past was lurking in the whitewashed rooms. The stacked-up books, the board games for a rainy afternoon, the fresh-faced lovely children; it was all making her think of when she was a child herself, forlorn in these draughty stone houses, fearful of going upstairs on her own, troubled by thoughts of immaterial things, conjurings. In one Lakeland house they stayed in, not the professor's, a year when her mother wanted a change, there were big ancient portraits on the stairs, a man and a woman clad in Puritan garb, and Rosa hated them. She couldn't pass them on her own and their eyes gave her nightmares. The shadows of the rooms disturbed her, and the creaking and rattling of old timbers. Her mother was always there, holding her hand. Now, what was she afraid of? As she and Will ate, and as she moved her mouth in pleasantries about the quality of the lamb, making light phrases, she realised. It was her mother! She was in the stone walls and the smell of the rain. She was treading softly in the garden. She was a distant reflection at the window, lurking behind the silence of the evening. Gently reproaching Rosa, for being so bound to the self, bound up in her selfishness. It had been a mistake to come, she thought. 'Yes, yes, the lamb,' she said, sounding desperate. 'And what are your plans for Christmas?' she asked. Will started to reply; he was always loquacious. She could rely on a full few minutes while he talked of in-laws and the logistics of driving children round the country. The Land Rover was apparently better. There was something about presents. Yet she faded him out, sat there nodding and thinking that she just had to tussle it all down again, push it back. She wanted to drop to the floor, grovel and wallow, beg them to send her mother back, but that was hardly appropriate. It was the stone and the smell of the rain, she thought again. Better still when she had confined herself to raging about Liam. Far better. More productive and possible to endure. Will was talking about Judy's parents, and how tricky they were. Too generous, it seemed. Tendency to spoil the children. What do you do? What on earth do you do? Then there was a pause and when she looked up again she saw that Will was staring at her strangely. He had a hand in his orange hair; he looked like an attic frieze, expressing distraction. And she thought, there was the hand again, on her arm, but this time it wasn't quite patting, more stroking. He was stroking her arm and saying 'There, there, Rosa, really, it's OK.'

Judy, who had just reappeared, was there in an instant. 'Rosa, are you OK?' She put her arm round Rosa. It was odd but she seemed to have caused a scene. She had started to cry. She couldn't remember what had begun it but she was weeping into the lamb shank.

Later they went to bed, Rosa clattering along the corridor, quite ashamed even in the stew of her drunkenness. She had one hand to her head, in the other she held a pint of water. Judy had insisted. 'You might need it in the night.' She might need it when she woke, ravaged by embarrassment, that was the idea. She had developed a coursing headache, which seeped across her forehead and ebbed around her eyes. Her head was pounding and in a fleeting moment of lucidity she knew she had drunk all the wine.

Sobered by the coldness of her whitewashed room, she sat for a while staring at the floor, then she pushed open the jalousies and breathed in the night air. She could hear the sound of the ghyll spilling down the mountainside. It was a beautiful clear night. The sky was almost cloudless; the stars were brilliant in the sky. With the air bringing her round again, she knew she had behaved badly. She had started out well enough, but the wine had smashed her resolve. For a while she had perhaps convinced them, but her loss of control had done nothing for her cause. By the end they suspected her. They had been trying to help her, and that made it even worse. Whatever she might whisper, they had enough to think about already. Anyway, she had come to exploit them. She had come knowing that she could rely on them to host and understand her. She had only expected tolerance. They had once admired her, she thought, vanity seeping through her drunkenness. 'Well,' she said aloud, 'they don't now.'

She fell onto the bed. Fumbling for the covers, she managed to pull them around her. For a long time she lay there staring at the ceiling. The rich food was heavy in her stomach. Her heart ached and a lamb chop pained her colon. She thought of many things. She said out loud, 'I am grateful after all. I am grateful to all of them.' It was silent all around the cottage, and the room was steeped in it. Outside darkness stretched beyond. That made her start and shiver in the bed. Struggling against it all, these tidal waves of silence, she thought,

Go back to London
Find a place to stay, explain to Andreas
Phone Liam and ask about the furniture.
Get a job.
Sit down with Jess and apologise for everything
Go to the bank and talk to Sharkbreath.
Hoover the living room
Read the comedies of Shakespeare, the works of Proust, the plays of Racine and Corneille and The Man Without Qualities.
Read The Golden Bough, The Nag-Hammadi Gospels, The

Upanishads, The Koran, The Bible, The Tao, *the complete*
works of E. A. Wallis Budge
Read Plato, Aristotle, Confucius, Bacon, Locke, Rousseau,
Wollstonecraft, Kant, Hegel, Schopenhauer, Kierkegaard,
Nietzsche, and the rest
Understand the stranger verse of Blake.
Read The Vedas.
Write to Whitchurch and explain.
Phone Braze and beg her.
Stop writing these lists that waste your time

And she thought *TEMP.*

Grandfather Tom was dead tonight, untroubled by a sense of
failure or banished hope. He had been dead for nearly thirty
years. And then she wondered what grandfather Tom had to do
with it, and why she was clutching at the covers, terrified. *Go
to the bank and negotiate an extension on your overdraft, and
ask them if you can extend the limit on your credit card.
Hoover the living room. Re-develop the carapace. Calm your
nerves. Read Marcus Aurelius. Accept the necessary limits of
human life. Immortality quite impossible. Eternal life implausible. Wash your clothes. Call Andreas and explain. Develop an
awareness of the finer points of pragmatism. Determine
whether you will sink or aim to float. Stop bothering people.
Find a place to stay. Get a job. Stop writing these lists. Go your
own way. It's hard enough to go your own way without trying
to second-guess the others. Read* The Republic *to the end – no
dropping out. Gather names. Forget the longings of the self.
Things are considerable but not insurmountable. It's impossible
that you would ever know how the universe was made. So stop
worrying. Read* Finnegans Wake. *You've tried it before but this
time you might enjoy it. Revere great art. Find a place to stay.
Get a job. Sit down with Jess and apologise for everything. Re-
develop the carapace. Calm your nerves. Read Marcus Aurelius.
Accept the necessary limits of human life. Immortality quite*

impossible. Eternal life implausible. Call Andreas and explain. Develop an awareness of the finer points of pragmatism. Determine whether you will sink or aim to float. Stop bothering people. Find a place to stay. Get a job. Stop writing these lists. Don't wait to become perfect. Just do it now. Go your own way. It's hard enough to go your own way without trying to second-guess the others. Read The Republic *to the end – no dropping out. Gather names. Forget the longings of the self. Things are considerable but not insurmountable. Read* Finnegans Wake. *Revere great art. Honour your father. Plunge into the void, dispense with the world. Accept the thunderbolt. Avoid the bell. OR should you ring the bell? Drop the jewel and pick up the lotus. FIND THE TEMP.* Then she thought her grandfather Tom was sitting next to her, quite calmly and quietly, holding her hand. She shook off the thought, but she couldn't open her eyes. She pulled the covers around her and tried to sleep. But she imagined him again, kindly, tall with his bent nose, explaining to her that she hadn't behaved well, as he had done when she was a small girl. He wasn't angry – she had never seen him angry – but he was disappointed. She thought he was there, emanating waves of kindly reproach. *Your mother is very tired, and so we've left her to sleep. Mummy gets tired sometimes, when she's had too much of her lovely daughter.* That was how he spoke to her when she was a child. *So darling, you just be nice to your mummy, won't you? She's a lovely girl, quite my favourite in the world, after you of course. And you must understand, Rosa, you haven't time for this sort of thing. Life is sweeping you onwards. There's hardly time to look around. You must get on with it.* And she imagined – imagined, she knew, because she had her eyes shut tightly, and there was no way she was opening them, though she felt a cold wind around her, like a force gusting from the grave, but she clamped her eyelids down and huddled beneath the covers – her grandmothers behind him, and grandfather Don, and she saw them in the garden of a small suburban house, the kind of place they had worked a lifetime to buy, saying *Come on, Rosa, look at you – you! In a room, drunk and out of control!* She was hearing them as a discordant chorus, and she kept her hands down by her waist, she curled into the covers and hid herself, afraid that she would feel something, a real hand coming towards her, a real voice sounding through the silence of the room. She imagined him again, this kindly old man, her mother's father, *Please, Rosa, understand this*, a jovial, talented man, a loyal friend, a good sportsman, who worked so hard to bring up the daughter who had died so suddenly, her death predestined or merely meaningless, she would never know, never never never and then she sat up in bed and with her eyes shut, still clamped tightly shut because she was a coward and drunk and still more cowardly in her drunkenness or intoxicated with fear, she thought *TEMP must mean CONTEMPTIBLE and that means you* and now she was shouting, 'HELP! HELP! SOMEONE PLEASE HELP!' She grabbed at the covers and tore them off her. She tumbled out of the bed and found she was bent double on the floor, shaking in the cold air, crying loudly. For a while she was quite beside herself; she couldn't think at all. She was drooling and rubbing spittle across her face, trying to push back her hair, which was falling into her mouth. She said HELP HELP! again, down below the iron bed and she put her head down so sharply on her knees she bit her tongue. She came round, slowly, and realised that there was a danger Judy might come in and find her. Still, they frightened her, the cold white sheets and the stone room. And she was kneeling on the floor, speaking quickly, saying, 'Mother, I understand, I am failing to enjoy the experience of being here. After all the trouble you went to, the years you passed in my birth and nurture. I am sorry for having deviated from the path. You spent decades trying to make me happy. And now! And NOW!'

'And now!' she cried, and stood up suddenly. 'It has gone too far!' She had let things slide. And now Rosa said, 'It has gone too far!' again. There was a thick feeling in her head, as if she couldn't think fast enough. Agitation, rich in her veins. Her body was busy breaking down proteins, filling her cells with oxygen, her heart was busy pumping blood round her body. 'To what end?' she cried. 'Why?' She pushed the lamp off the table, grabbed Judy's collection of classics and hurled them on the floor, stamped and shouted and it was only when she hurt her foot that she came to her senses. Then she sat down and looked at the mess she had made.

Hiccoughing loudly, and aware that she was far from heroic, she turned on all the lights. With the lights on she felt less afraid. She lay down on the bed, dragged the covers around her. Then drunkenness overtook her, and she fell into a snorting dreamless sleep.

She woke before dawn, coughing. Her head ached and she thought she would be sick. For a while she lay with her face above the floorboards, unable to move, hanging there like a warning to others. She had certainly lost her poise. She was blushing as she fished for her watch and reeled it in. Dragging herself up, she lay on her back. Once she had her watch in her hand, she saw it was 6 a.m. She tumbled out of the duvet and, finding she was still in her clothes, was glad she had saved a little time. At the window she stared into the darkness. When she pushed up the sash the stillness soothed her. She could hear the vibrant songs of birds in the hedgerows, the wind tousling the leaves. The sound of the ghyll, sweet and clear. When her nausea had passed, she packed up the few objects she had used. The goggles and walking boots hadn't quite been necessary, but she had at least been prepared. She tidied the bed. She folded the sheet carefully over the duvet, as if that would save her. She drank the water down. The fresh flowers in the vase made her want to crawl to Judy and Will and beg their forgiveness. But going quietly seemed the only thing to do. Anyway, she couldn't face the tight politeness of the closing scene, the benign protestations. They would drive her to the station and she would talk hopelessly on the platform, promising to write, then she would spend the journey rephrasing everything, muttering into her scarf, disturbing her neighbours. She saw the sky was growing lighter. Soon dawn would break. So she picked up the books and stacked them on the shelf. She tidied up the lamp. Then she crept out of the room, dragging her bag, trying not to scuff the walls. She moved slowly along the corridor. A creak in the timbers made her heart flutter, but after a few seconds with her face pressed against the wall, no one came.

She still had time and now she drew herself through the house and moved softly down the stairs. She arrived in the living room, sweating with the strain of moving so quietly. Her bag was heavy and hastily packed. Bits of it bulged as she walked. She left the presents she had forgotten to give them the previous evening, the chocolates, books and bath salts tied up with string. She stacked them in a pile on the living room table. She thought she should leave a note. So she stood there with her pen above the paper, thinking what to write. *Dear Judy and Will, Thanks so much for your unstinting, humbling hospitality. I've had a lovely time. The sort of evening I haven't had in ages. You have shamed me with your generosity. You are wonderful parents, and I admire you. You use your time so well. Your children are beautiful. Your idyll, this community you have created, makes me feel ashamed and as if I have been wasting my time. All is Vapour. Thanks so much again, Rosa.* She stopped. She took the piece of paper and folded it into her pocket. Then she wrote: *Dear Will and Judy. Thanks so much. I remembered in the middle of the night – oh horror! HORROR! I promised – ages ago – to meet someone today. I'm so sorry to have left without seeing you. These presents are no return for your great kindness. It made a huge difference, to see you here, so happy and tranquil. I'll remember it with great fondness. I'm sorry about the small scene – I was merely drunk, nothing more – and wish you so much luck with the next baby. You have a wonderful set-up here. Fucking vapour. Thanks so much again. Love, Rosa.*

So she tore that up. *Dear Judy and Will, Thanks so much. I*

remembered in the night – I have a meeting in London. I'm so
sorry to leave without seeing you – I didn't want to wake you.
The presents are small return for your kindness and warmth.
Good luck with the new arrival. Thanks so much again. Love,
Rosa.

And now she thought she heard a sound, so, abandoning the note on top of the presents, she turned. She was still for a moment, trying to listen. Furtive in the fresh dawn, she tiptoed past the table. Passing through the kitchen she felt sick again. She twisted herself out of the door, trying to keep everything as quiet as she could. Now the sky was grey. There was mist on the hills; white trails were falling across the trees. Her feet crunched on frost. A layer of ice had formed on the mud. She walked quickly down the drive, through the mist. At the road she stood and looked back at the farm. A light was on upstairs. Any minute now, she thought, a search party might issue from the solid walls – Will with a torch, flashing a light towards her. She stumbled and started to run. She wasn't sure where she was running, but as she went, fumbling with her bag, she saw the sky growing paler. The stars were receding into the clear dawn. Ahead she could see the misty valley, mist-draped fells, the ghyll tumbling down the rocks. She could hear the river and the sound of it made her run faster. She heard a door slam behind her, and thought it must be Will. Trembling with shame, imagining him finding her there with her bag scuffed with mud, she thought she had to hide. Like a fugitive, she dived off the road and ran down the bank of the river. Her heart was beating unsteadily and the nausea had returned. She dropped her bag into long wet grass and soaked her feet. Now she thought she heard soft enquiring footsteps on the gravel, but she couldn't raise her head to look. Shivering, she huddled by the river, wondering who it was.

As she waited by the river, she found she was questioning the Romantic assumption that nature was reviving to the soul. It was possible for a particularly dark and miserable soul to resist even the consolations of a perfect view. She thought of

Wordsworth walking the fells. He had gone up – was it Helvellyn? – on his seventieth birthday, limber and bold-hearted. That was a fine man! Hwaer cwom Wordsworth, she thought. Whither Wordsworth. She snorted quietly and held her head. It felt swollen. Swollen with booze, she thought, her capillaries quite flooded with the stuff. The light seeped across the sky. Later, she dragged herself along the bank and threw up. That felt cathartic, so she walked upstream and washed her face. She stood and gripped her bag. Looking at the slender shapes of the winter trees, Rosa understood perfectly well that the scenery was ancient and she was very small. She was adequate to the task of perceiving the beauty around her, the lovely contours of the hills, the cold glinting waters. She saw no one when she raised her head above the bank, so she started to walk slowly. She found the road, no longer mist-clad, and followed it down the valley. She kept low on the ground, hoping they couldn't see her, and when she lost sight of the farmhouse she began to breathe more easily. Through the gaps in the trees Rosa saw the sky, and then the sky looked like a lake, with the shapes of the hills spread around its shores. Then it started raining, and she turned sharply down the hill towards Broughton, passing a few houses with their curtains drawn. The rain slapped her face, and she held up her hands as she ran; through sheets of rain she could see the valley, grey and wind-blown. She stumbled slightly and brushed against the damp hedges, feeling the branches on her face. She watched the trees moving in the wind. The rain cooled her head, and made her feel better. The sheep were standing on the hills, sheltering under trees. Their funny faces turned towards her. In front of an audience of sheep she went over a cattle grid and slipped on the metal.

Then she felt a low boom of thunder across the valley, she could feel the vibrations under her feet and deep in her stomach. The sky flared, and thunder rolled around the valley, drawing echoes from the rocks. The rain was falling in thick white lines, more like flowing milk than water. She heard a gate slamming in the wind, and the thunder and the rain. The valley was drenched by the downpour, and now she could smell the bracken. Brackish, she thought, and she noticed the interwoven smells of grass and trees and the taste of dampness in the air. Another flash of lightning, followed by a round ricochet of thunder, and the trees shuddered under the wind and the fresh force of the rain. Now the rain sounded like a river in full flood. Above she saw a chastened sky, and the deep green colours of the leaves, the stained trunks of the trees.

Drenched and weighted down by her clothes, Rosa ran. She was revived by the forces around her, the wind blasting against her, volleys of thunder resounding deep within her. The sky flashed again. She saw a line of oaks bowing and shaking their leaves. Rain hissed at her feet, falling as steam. She darted around a puddle, brushed a wet hedge, lifted her bag higher on her back, heard the all-shaking thunder burst around the valley again, felt the rage of the wind and said, 'Crack Nature's moulds!' Dense shards of rain. White steam and a cold sky. She moved through mud and newly created streams of water. She skidded at a corner and fell against a trunk to steady herself. Ingrateful man, she thought. Everything was monochrome, the trees and low houses dark against the blank sky. She turned onto a road where the cars lashed her with water.

Another throb of thunder, and the rain slapped her face and arms. When a woman in a car wound down her window and shouted out, 'Do you need a lift?' she tried to speak and found her lips were rigid with cold.

'Thank you,' she managed to say, shaking her head. She stepped aside as the woman drove off. The thunder was rich and raw; she was a sounding block, nothing more than another surface for the thunder to echo from. She saw the dusty sides of the rocks, doused to blackness by torrents of water, and she saw a flock of birds hanging in the air, sweeping a course across the furrowed mass of clouds. Then she felt a sense of great joy, of something glorious and ancient beneath everything. She was beginning to say, 'But this is the sublime', and then she said, 'You have to be quite determined, not to become ridiculous.' She shook her head and walked on.

She arrived in the village of Broughton as the clocks chimed 10 a.m.. She had lost a lot of time, hiding by the river and walking in the rain. She hadn't noticed how far the morning had advanced. Now the rain was easing off. Her clothes were wet; her bag was heavy on her back. The local baker was just opening her shop, and Rosa briefly explained her predicament – terrible mess – she had come to borrow a friend's house, forgot to bring the key, no one had it, would have to go back home to get it, have invited friends for the weekend, can't break in, tragic start to a holiday. Never mind, she said, stoical in response to polite sympathy. Yes, it was a bit of a fuss but it would be fine in the end. The baker – a woman called Sue with perfect teeth and a thick Lancashire accent – called a taxi. Rosa waited in the shop, sipping coffee. She found herself writing in her notebook, though the pages were greasy with rainwater.

Will and Judy, I am more sorry than I can ever say. Words cannot express how sorry I am. They are inadequate to the task, or I can't turn them so they would phrase a fifth of my feelings. Had I but words enough and time, I would verse you a verse – oh yes, such a verse, they would write about it for years to come – but my coat is soaked and my head is full of something – it feels like putty. I am quite aware I drank all the wine. But I don't want you wasting any time thinking about me. Really, there's no need. I am only sorry I lost my dignity. My bearings I lost long ago. Yours ever, Rosa.

Then she shivered violently and moved closer to the fire. She wrote:

Get a grip on yourself now. This is descending faster than you can winch it up. Your brain isn't working fast enough. You need to be quick-witted. Contain yourself. No one is impressed

by you, and Jess is furious. This wouldn't bother you if you had
managed things well for yourself. But you haven't, that much
is blindingly apparent. Now you have to:

Go back to London.
Find a place to stay
Explain to Andreas
Get a job
Match your words with actions
Get Liam to sell the furniture
Wash your clothes
Sit down with Jess and apologise for everything
Go to the bank and talk to Sharkbreath
Read variously
Detach yourself from illusion altogether
Scale the wall
Traverse the threshold
Find the TEMP

Then the taxi came.

RETURN

She woke again before dawn and stood by the window, staring out at the shadows. The dawn was later by the day; the year was drawing to an end. A coarse wind had ruined the trees; leaves gusted along the pavement. It was Thursday and she had wasted too many days. All through the previous day she had fleeced the clock of minutes, bartering them down. On the journey home, she had found herself thinking of the things she had to do. At Manchester she thought *furniture from Liam find a place to stay get a job* and as the train eased through the suburbs of Birmingham she thought *explain everything to Andreas* but by Luton she was thinking *leave the country* and that insistent thought – escape/retreat – brought her to the outskirts of London. There she watched the city seep towards her. The train ran through rising districts of concrete and steel. All around was incessant motion; she was moving against the current, heading towards the centre while the commuters were going back to the suburbs and their well-earned homes. She saw banks of glass reflecting the sunset. At King's Cross the crowds moved beneath a giant display. Details changed, platforms were announced; the process was continuous. After she had waited in the tube, dimly aware of her reflection swimming in the darkness, she walked from Ladbroke Grove to the flat. The living room was dark and quiet.

Now she stayed in her room until Jess went out to work. She heard the assertive slam of the door and breathed more easily. When she rose and walked through the flat, she found a note on the table in Jess's handwriting. *Dear Rosa, Hope you had a good trip. Let me know if you need any help with the move. Jess.* That was definitely a reminder, tactful in the circumstances, but firm enough. The day felt different. She heard a humming in the distance. It was necessary to be resolute. As she sat at the window she tried to think what to do. She crossed her legs and noted the fleeting progress of the street. As she sat there a car was revving up the scale, from gear to gear. A man stubbed his toe and hopped a step. He glanced up, his mouth rounded in a whistle. A woman walked below, holding a bag of shopping. Rosa pushed up the window and stuck her head out to breathe the air. The sky had been tousled in the night and now she saw the ragged folds of the clouds. And the street, this noisy, random street she knew so well.

She went into the bathroom and found it had been cleaned. Purged by Jess. She was an eternal swab, always dousing something, tidying something else. She opened the cabinet – its newly wiped mirror gleaming smartly – where she found a stash of painkillers. She took a couple, bending her head to the tap and scooping water into her mouth. She remembered a few cursory things, and then she remembered she had to get the furniture money from Liam. That was a certain goal, and one she was sure she could achieve. She thought it mattered for reasons beyond the fiscal – though it mattered for reasons entirely related to the fiscal too. She washed her face and blew soap bubbles at the mirror. When the bathroom was steamed over, furred up, she dried herself and walked back into the living room. In a fit of fleeting courage she dialled up Mrs Brazier, that iron bar of a woman. La Braze answered the phone in a strident voice, suggestive of self-love. That made Rosa nervous, and her hands were trembling as she said, 'This is Rosa Lane. I came for an interview the other day.'

'Ah yes, Rosa Lane.' The voice was businesslike.

'I just wondered if you had made a decision yet. Not wanting to overstep the mark,' she said.

Fortunately Frau Braze was quick and to the point. She was sorry but she didn't want Rosa after all. 'I'm afraid the children didn't like you,' she said. 'I thought you were fairly suitable.' But her little darlings, the pashmina-touting infants, hadn't wanted Rosa. Balanced in the scales, she had been judged unworthy by children!

'Well, I understand,' said Rosa. 'I understand. Of course, it wouldn't work, if the children didn't like me. Thanks for letting me know.' She kept her voice quite firm and relaxed. Just before she hung up she thought of saying, 'I could try, I could try to make them like me,' but stopped herself in time. *Please ask your infant bastards to give me another chance!* she thought, but instead she said, 'Goodbye, Mrs Brazier. So nice to have met you.'

'Yah, herum,' said Brazier.

Then she put the phone down. She was aiming for stoicism as she snagged it on the cradle. And now the children hadn't liked her. The mini-Brazes had seen straight through her. They knew she didn't care a hoot about them, couldn't care less if they lived or died so long as she got money in her hand each month. The profundity of children, she wanted to raise a glass to them, those clever kids! Anyway, they had sniffed her out. The question of money was as pertinent as ever, quite as harsh and pressing, though she had definitely had a go at solving it. She had gone along, ripped her feet to shreds, inhaled a few pints of lung death and sat there talking in a measured way. Now she took her notebook and sat down. The birds were still singing in the silver trees. The trains still shuddered on the tracks. A car stalled on the corner and was answered by a choir of horns. A cacophony of rage. Outside, the denizens of *TEMP* were waiting. Then the car revved up again, revved away, and the horns abated. She had to think more clearly. She had the interest to pay, she had to service her overdraft or watch as everything came crashing down on her. So she wrote a pared down list. Economy, she was thinking. The basics. These small things you can do!

Things to do, Thursday

Find a place to stay
Phone Liam and ask him to sell the furniture
Phone Kersti
Explain to Andreas
Get a job
Find the way to the truth that is concealed
Unlock the casket
Unearth the TEMP

She looked at it admiringly for a moment. It was certainly succinct, expressive mainly of the essentials. She really had to find
a place to stay. She phoned Whitchurch and found she wasn't
in her office. Then she tried Jess, who was in a meeting. She
was tapping her fingers and then she found she was dialling
Andreas's number. She wasn't sure what she would say to him
if he picked up the phone. Calmly and at a moderato pace, she
would unfurl it all. *Nothing sensational. The starting point is
a place to sleep. I have options, of course. Of course I have
options!* And the rest, the whole rest and nothing but the rest.
Much in her approach was foolish, that was plain to her.
Andreas was genuinely relaxed. *Of course he is. It's only you
with your tone of melodrama, trying to sweep the boy into a
farce of your own devising. He doesn't much mind! Things
should be easy, if you just accept Andreas as a nice kid with a
big heart and a surprisingly consistent way of being. That's all.
No need for further talk.* Yet she couldn't stop it. It was absurd
to be so reticent, when the man even liked her. But he liked her
because he hardly knew her. That was far from the point, she
thought. Why would he care, if she was slightly in debt?
Everyone was in debt. The entire world was in debt, whole
countries, economies, why, the whole thing could collapse
tomorrow. If she was lucky, it would. Her debt would be
wiped out in an instant. Wishing for a global recession was
unkind, hardly fair to those who worked so hard amassing

money. But anything, thought Rosa – a lightning bolt, a fire in the vaults, the banks destroyed. A collective realisation that money was meaningless! It was a blank wall.

She thought all of this, while the phone rang into empty space and then Andreas's voice said, 'Hi there, leave me a message. If it's work then call my agent on –' She was clandestine and didn't leave a message. She dialled another number. A few rings, and she had conjured the voice of Kersti, though it was peremptory this morning, rich in reluctance.

'Yes,' said Kersti. 'Yes, Rosa, don't you know it's Thursday?'

'And Thursday is?'

'The worst day, after Monday. Full of disorganised fools who should have called me earlier in the week.'

'But I did call you earlier.'

'Not you, Rosa. I can never complain about you failing to call me.'

'You sound a bit spun out.'

'You know, Rosa, it was strange, yesterday the birds were singing, the sky was blue, I felt a great sense of joy and couldn't work out why. And now I realise, it was because I hadn't heard the word furniture for the whole day.'

'I went away for a night,' said Rosa.

'Sounds nice,' said Kersti.

'Though perhaps you mean undeserved?'

'I mean I really don't have time to talk. Yes I've phoned Liam. Yes the guy's busy. Yes he's getting married tomorrow. He says, and I understand his point, can't it wait? He appreciates you want to sort it out. But it's a load of mouldy old furniture. He's not going to sell it, so you have to come to an arrangement. He thinks a thousand is probably too much. So he says when he's finished with the wedding chaos he'll talk to you.'

'Oh yes, I'd forgotten,' said Rosa. 'I'd forgotten the wedding was tomorrow.' But those words sluiced down the phone, saturated with improbability.

'OK, Rosa, I'll call you if there's anything to say. So you're not going to the wedding, I assume?'

'No, not,' said Rosa.

'Well, speak to you later.'

'Sorry. Thanks for everything. Goodbye.'

Rosa put down the phone. Now she was gritting her teeth, feeling a sturdy sense of her impotence. Her moods were shifting from one extreme to another. She had returned with a sense that she must progress somehow, that she had finally plumbed the depths and formed a resolution – desperate, tenuous, but a resolution all the same – to reach, if not the surface, then a point less deep than the depths. But the waves were strong and she couldn't break the water. She was struggling with this heaviness, weight of water, something was pulling her down even as she struggled. *At the surface you'll breathe better.* She stood by the radiator and thought how fine it was to be inside on a day like this, casting a glance at the window which was slurred with rain. Bent trees beyond, a dancing row. Green and grey, the slick sky flooded with clouds. She had failed to have breakfast, so she ate a bowl of cornflakes and drank one more cup of tea. The stuff keeps you happy, she thought as she drank. She rang Liam at work. He wasn't there. 'He's gone to a meeting,' said a secretary. She was determined and so she left a message asking him to sell the furniture. The secretary said, 'What?' and Rosa said, 'The furniture. F-U-R-N-I-T-U-R-E. Tell him thanks. From Rosa.' Still she was sounding reasonable, even as she dictated the sentences. She couldn't quite explain about her cash-flow crisis. It was definitely none of his business, and she hardly thought he would reach into his pockets. Would he? Sudden hope, and then she thought it was impossible. Call up Liam and ask for money! It would never happen. Better call up Grace and – and she wondered – could she? – but that was a poor idea. She had to come up with something much better than that.

So she called her father. She heard the phone ringing through the rooms of his large house, and she imagined him setting down a piece of work, a Spanish translation or something in the garden, or apologising to his bridge partner and rising from the table.

'Father,' she said, when he answered.

'Rosa, my dear. How are you?'

'Thanks very much for lunch the other day.'

'That's fine. It was good to see you.'

'I wondered if I could ask something?'

'Yes, of course. I'm just here with some friends, and we have to go to play tennis now. Will it take long?'

'I'm not sure. Depends.'

'On what?'

'On your response.'

'I see. Well, now you've whetted my appetite, come on, be quick now. Bernard will be round any minute and I have to feed the dog before I go.'

'How is the dog, Dad?'

'The dog is very well. Is that what you wanted to ask?'

'No. You know it isn't.' She laughed, but there were days – today one of them – when her father's jocularity seemed like nerves. *Keep cracking the gags, Dad, that's just fine. That'll steel you nicely against the inevitable.*

'The thing is' – her father was clearing his throat impatiently and so she said, 'I wondered' and cleared her throat back at him. That made her think of their shared genes; she could sense them working away in her reluctance to come clean.

'Rosa, come along, dear,' he said, kindly but briskly.

'OK, Dad. Well,' she said.

Then there was a pause, while Rosa experienced a brief moment of illumination, a glowing, flushed with dawn colours realisation that there was something else stopping her tongue, something more than native cowardice. Her father was a crumbling column, succumbing to the elements; she wouldn't rely on him any more. *And finally, at the age of thirty-five, deep in the forest, profoundly lost in the thicket, you decide that your father isn't the man with the answer to the riddle of the Sphinx or your cash-flow crisis, or any other problem. And that*, she thought, with a nod to Dr Kamen, *could be a step forward.* She saw that it wasn't a question of genes or any such thing, but that coming clean to her father was not part of the process. She had hardly helped him at all, this bereaved and antique father of hers, and this was one thing she could do. She could keep it all quiet, omit to tell him any of it. That was something she could do for him. This made her feel much better, though it hardly helped her. She was uncertain if this was her best conspicuous rationalisation yet, as she said, 'I just wanted to say how good it was to see you, and how glad I am you are happy with Sarah.'

'Well, thank you, Rosa.' He sounded hesitant, as if he suspected something else might be coming. Then she heard a bell in the background. 'That's Bernard,' he said.

That's the bell, Sharkbreath is coming! 'OK, Dad. But thanks again. And you know, I understand what you were saying.'

'OK, good,' he said, and rang off uncertainly.

Her brow was damp. She put her head down to the clammy tip of the phone. A monotone confirmed that her father had gone. Of course, she thought. He has to play tennis and prepare his body for dispersal. Really there's no point expecting him to dole out money. He doesn't have much, and what he has, well, he needs. Of course he does! He needs it to bribe the ferryman, all the rest. She hovered by the phone for a moment, thinking of calling him back and leaving a message. *Daddy dear, the dough is all yours. You enjoy it, you old cricket. Splash out, buy Sarah a new wig. Thanks so much, Daddy. Thanks.* Instead she called Kersti again, risking her thundering wrath. This time Kersti was out. 'Would you like to leave a message?' *Tell her the guardians of the laws are angry. Tell her I have failed to unlock the secrets of TEMP. That a star is about to fall. The Kills are abroad. Tell her I still believe in the possibility of perfection and I wonder if she feels the same.* 'No, no message,' said Rosa. 'I'll try again later.'

Rosa put down the phone. Again she was smiling. Her moods were shifting from one extreme to another. There was this lurking sense of despair and as if her own personal eschaton was nigh but she was trying to ignore it, quash it at least. Then the phone rang again and Rosa, hoping it was Andreas, said, *'Jawohl?'*

'Hello, can I speak to Rosa Lane?'

'Yes, speaking,' she said.

'Martin White here, from the *Daily Post*,' said a happy elegant voice.

'Hello,' said Rosa uncertainly. *Well, this is a surprise*, she thought. She sat on the folding table and nearly slid off it, steadied herself and said 'Hello' again. *Encore*, she thought.

'Good idea, your idea for the piece. Good idea. Nice sound to your style. Good enough. A little manic, perhaps you could tone it down. Just send it in, a little calmer,' he said.

'You really liked it?' said Rosa.

'Yes, yes, quite a good idea. Elective destitution. Good. A bit odd, just what the readers like,' said Martin White. 'Not really your largest demographic, I mean I can't imagine there are so many of them, but I like the bit about blaming the baby boomers. Good idea. Give it a go. Send it to me whenever you can. About 600 words. Sorry not to give you more. You know, in plain English for the general reader. OK?'

'Thanks, thanks very much,' said Rosa.

She put the phone down and, because this was the best news she had had in ages and the first sniff of money for a long while, she cried. She wasn't sure why she started gushing like a sap. It was an over-reaction. As she stopped crying she felt a sense of great joy, but then she wiped her eyes and realised that Martin White's intervention, which had seemed so fortuitous just a few seconds earlier, so much like manna from heaven, didn't really solve her immediate problem. Even if he took her article, she wouldn't get the money for weeks. And, anyway, wasn't it precisely her inability to write that was the problem? And now she thought she was saved, because someone had asked her to be a journalist again! 'Shog,' she said aloud. 'Bloody shog!'

She started to write *Dear Mrs Brazier, I wondered if you might need an interim tutor, before the real one gets started. Just for a few days? Just to get some money in my pocket . . .* But she stopped. These letters won't help at all, she thought. No more letters, and no more lists – she had a thousand things she thought she ought to do, but she was trying to keep herself disciplined, and she thought, *You must simply make these calls. Find a solution. You've run out of time.* Now she sat up straight. She saw the room in blurred vision, red dots danced before her eyes. She sliced the air with her arms. It was not too late; there was time. She picked up the phone and rang Whitchurch. There was no answer. She tried Jess at work. It switched to voicemail and Rosa lacked the barefaced ludicrousness to leave a message. She tried Andreas, but the man was still absent. *Useless!* she thought. *Not there at all when you need a favour, a small spot of pedestrian salvation!* She tried Kersti one more time, but Kersti had gone away. 'She won't be back in today,' said Kersti's secretary. 'Not at all today?' 'Not at all.' That was firm, and Rosa left no message. She called Whitchurch again. It was incredible; no one was at their desk. They had all bunked off, gone to walk through the dampness of the crowds and sluice themselves in rainwater. It was just downright unlucky, but today they were perpetually out to lunch, in meetings, the rest. She thought of Liam and Grace preparing for their wedding. Grace with her wedding dress stashed away somewhere. Her trousseau at the ready. Their honeymoon planned, somewhere flashy. Hoping the weather would be fine.

She walked to the fridge and looked in it for a few minutes. At the bottom of the fridge she found a bar of chocolate, which she ate. She ran her hands under the tap in the kitchen. Then she poured herself a bowl of cereal and used up the last of the milk. She imagined Jess shaking the container in fury, noting the absence of her chocolate, counting her cornflakes at

228

midnight. That was probably why she had stopped the deal. Too many small pilferings. She was thinking again about the thousand pounds. The unceasing quandary of the furniture. *As you have pilfered so others pilfer from you*, she thought. Galvanised by all the sugar she had eaten, she called Liam again and found him at his desk. Of everyone, all the other shirkers, he was there. It was strange, and Liam seemed to be finding it so. He seemed stone cold and mystified. Really they hadn't talked for months and as she spoke Rosa found her voice was trembling. Her hands were shaking; her entire body was in nervous motion. She was gripping the phone, as if that could steady her. She didn't quite know how to start, so she said:

'Liam, how are you?'

'Very well, how are you?'

'Good. Anyway. I just wanted to ask, have to rush, but can you please sell the furniture? I'm just short of liquid funds at present. I'm moving flat, it's costing a load. Could really do with the money. If you can't sell then perhaps you could just pay me my half?'

Liam was civil, if a little tense. His voice sounded dry. But he still had his melodic alto range. Liam had a light, soft voice. You didn't notice how gentle it was until you heard him on the phone. He had the slightest trace of a Yorkshire accent. 'The furniture?' he said. 'God, that friend of yours, Kersti.'

'Yes?'

'She calls me all the time about the furniture. It's like a joke. Could you ask her to stop?'

'I'm not responsible for Kersti's actions,' she said. Which was wrong, considering the hours she spent begging Kersti to call him.

'Look, you'll get your share when I sell the furniture. Or when I get back from the honeymoon. I said this to Kersti. I don't know what else to suggest. I agree we should give you some money, but a grand is a lot. I haven't been able to think about it. I've had a few other things to think about.'

'Yes, yes, of course. Your guilty conscience.'

'Rosa, I will have to go if you start on,' said Liam. She could tell he was trying to be stern with her. It was covering up. A psychic paint job if she ever saw one.

'No time to discuss. I just need the money. Really, Liam, it would really help. What about an advance? A payment plan. What about I rent you the furniture?' said Rosa.

'Hardly likely.' She could imagine him slapping the phone cord on his desk, shrugging round at his colleagues. My ex, you know, freaking out before the wedding, quite the worst time. Then she remembered someone had told her – as if she cared! – that he had recently gained an office of his own. Well, that sounded nice. She imagined him with a framed picture of Grace on his desk, a picture of his mother, a pencil sharpener and some really good pens.

'Come on, Liam, just a grand or so.'

'A grand! For that bunch of junk! Get a grip!'

'The sofa, easily, and the rest. The bed!'

'I really can't see it,' he said. Now he sounded as if he was smiling.

'Then Grace will have to buy me out.'

'Buy your share of some old furniture she hates? Rosa, come now,' he said. She thought he was trying to josh her, be jovial. He had recovered from his surprise, and now he was thinking the best way was fake conviviality. He wanted her to see the humour in it, but as far as Rosa was concerned there was nothing funny about it at all. Had he known how serious she was he might have pitied her, and this was the last thing she needed, Liam offering her consolation. *Years and years, and you end up fighting over scraps*, she thought.

Hearing his voice made her sad, and angry, and she tried to keep it back. That effort failed. She heard herself saying, 'But don't you think she ought to? Don't you think it would be decent? Both of you sitting there, on the sofa I picked, the bed I even built, putting your cups on the table I found on Golborne Road, don't you ever think – is this fair? I don't want to have to call you at all. It's plain humiliating, to have to call you up. For a grand! Come on, it's nothing to you!' And really, it wasn't much, when she thought of what he earned. It was a figure she had once commanded herself, though now it seemed like the most decadent wad of cash, superfluous to requirements. 'It would cost me far more to buy the furniture again. In fact, why don't you give me the furniture? I'll sell it and pay you your share. OK? So tell me, when will it arrive?' She was trying to sound exasperated, but she couldn't keep the latent whine out of her voice.

'Arrive where, Rosa? Where is it you're dossing this time?' And now he sneered a little. She imagined him, tidy suit, tidy hair, sitting in a tidy box-like room, surrounded by papers. Polishing his pens. Did Grace buy his ties, she wondered? It was the sort of thing she might do. With irony of course, smirking prettily as she handed them over. But she would buy them all the same.

'When can you bring it round? Saturday? Sunday?'

'Rosa, could it possibly wait a couple of weeks?' said Liam.

Now he wanted to goad her, so she said, 'Liam, let's be rational. You have everything you want and really I just want to get away. I just want to leave the country.'

'Really? Going on holiday?' He sounded amused. 'Sorry, Rosa, I really have to go. I'll talk to Grace. She's busy today, as you can imagine. But we'll discuss it when everything is calmer.'

'It's not the money that's important, it's the symbolism, the symbolism is what matters!' she said, aware that she was now shouting, but hardly bothering to control it.

'A symbolic thousand, or a real thousand?'

'It's my money, you know it is!' she said. There was a silence on the other end, then Liam, in a voice that betrayed a hint of superiority, said, 'Rosa, no one wants you to die in a ditch.' She was thinking that he was spoilt. He had always been indulged. Women had always rushed to indulge him. She blamed her sex, and she blamed him for lapping it all up, all this lust-based praise. 'Just sell the furniture,' she said. 'Or hand it over.' Then she put down the phone.

And she remembered her and Liam outside a country pub on her thirtieth birthday. The day was brilliant, the air shimmered with heat. There was Liam with his hand above his eyes. The garden of the pub wound around with ivy and wisteria. She could still remember how much they had been in love. They were incessant in it, quite steeped in it. Forlorn, she thought that five – nearly six – years was a long time, but all experience was only that, experience in the end. The conversation had lacked a conclusion. He hadn't committed himself, so she couldn't quite tick the item off her list. She took a pen, finding her hands were oozing sweat, and wrote: *Call Liam back and check whether he said yes or no.*

She shrugged it off, and went to the bank one more time, to try to talk to Sharkbreath. Stepping out of the flat she moved quickly along, locked in her thoughts. She passed the billboard on her left. *Yes, yes, here come the tears*, she thought. At the roundabout, there were cars turning the usual slow circle, the shops were sketched in their fading paints and the air was thick with petrol. Phiz had lived here, said the sign, many years ago, and now Phiz was nowhere to be seen, and Rosa passed along Ladbroke Grove with the hammer and thump of the Westway dawning above her and the sun shining through thick trailing clouds. Skeletal trees, tops to the sky. The pile of rubble and the metal grilles. A factory to her right, industrial twine around the walls. Equal People, she saw, and the celestial stairs. *TEMP.*

Much was the same at the bank, the same neon flickering lights above her, and the same acrylic carpeting that gave her a mild electric shock as she entered. The walls were touting helpful mantras: ARE YOU THINKING ABOUT YOUR PENSION PLAN? DO YOU WANT A BETTER DEAL ON YOUR MORTGAGE? DO YOU KNOW THE WAY TO THE CROCK OF CRAP? A quick enquiry at the desk returned the information – unfortunate, if a relief all the same – that Sharkbreath wasn't there. Instead she got another lowly zipper-mouth, not Mandy but another one called Jude. 'Mr Rivers isn't here today,' she said, and her zipper was fastened. No smile at all.

'Where is he?' said Rosa.

'He's gone to a management programme meeting,' said Jude.

'A what?'

Jude shrugged and tossed her hair. She had a low hairline, and her fringe cuffed her eyes. She had tucked her face into a frown.

'I wonder, could I possibly see someone else?' asked Rosa, reasonably enough she thought, but Jude frowned some more.

'What's it concerning?' asked Jude, clicking her pen.

'About my overdraft. I just need to talk about my debt.'

'If you wait a while we might just about be able to get you in to see Justin.'

'Who is Justin?'

'He's the deputy to our overdraft repayment advisor.'

It was a remark ripe for satire, but Rosa had lost her mettle. 'How long will he be?'

'Let's have a look, well, we have Mr Brick who is due in now and then Mrs Watson and so he could see you in half an hour?'

It made her nervous, but she said, 'Yes, thanks, half an hour.' She took a seat and, defying anyone to question her, picked up the *Financial Times* and waited.

Get a job
Phone Liam and ask him to sell the furniture
Unearth the TEMP
Speak to Andreas
Article for Martin White
Find the way to the truth that is concealed

Then she found she was shaking her head. *Get a job. Go to see Liam. Andreas. Simply you must act. JUST ACT!* She was trembling as she waited, wondering if the bank might finally grant her a reprieve. But Justin was nothing more than a thin-bearded official, younger than her by many years. He had other appointments scheduled; he hadn't much time. At first this made him efficient. He slammed the door behind her, shook her hand quickly, and sat her down. He had her details on the screen in an instant. He spun his chair and said, 'And what is it you wanted to discuss?' He was wearing a grey suit that was too short in the legs and shiny black shoes. He had lank hair, tendrils of it falling over his ears, and a faceful of compelling moles.

Frankly, without any introductory flannel, no sort of prolegomena at all, to begin with the beginning and not to exceed the bounds of your patience, well, really to start, to render the inchoate accessible and splendid, well, Justin, if I may call you by your first name? I come in fear and trembling to ask you in your munificence if you could help me. She swallowed hard and said, 'I'm trying hard to get a job, to pay off my debts, but this mounting interest saps my resolve. I realise it really ought to have the opposite effect, it should really give me a sense of urgency, but I find it makes me feel the whole thing is impossible.'

Justin stared at her for a moment, then said, 'What exactly can I help you with?'

Lucidity! she thought. *The Grail, the crock of celestial energy! The human divine!* 'Justin,' she said, leaning forward. 'I've banked here for years. Most of that time I wasn't in debt. It's only in the last few months that I've been racking it upwards. The credit card was the first thing – the credit card I couldn't pay off, and the interest on that is pretty dirty, and then there is the overdraft. Initially Mr Shark – Mr Rivers – was quite happy about the overdraft, because I have been such a solvent customer for so many years, but then I racked that up too. Now there's no more overdraft, and this haemorrhaging credit card. I have work, but I won't earn enough to pay off the debt for a while. So I wondered if we could come to an agreement. If we could stop the interest from rising at such a startling level each month. I don't want more debt to wallow in, not much more anyway, just for the interest to stop going up.'

Justin shrugged. 'We have to service the debt. You know the rules when you take a credit card.' He looked at the screen again. She wondered, did it have a special note to bank staff? *This woman has been cast out. Do not give her mercy. Ignore everything she says. Sharkbreath will deal with her.* Of course he saw it all on the computer, her history of former solvency and recent fraud. She had been promising she would soon have a job for months. She imagined it looked bad on his side of the screen. Still she pressed on.

'Yes, but do you think you could possibly reduce the interest on one or the other, or just stop the interest altogether? Or extend my overdraft so I could pay off my credit card? You know, I've been with this bank for years, and while I understand the rules, I wondered if you could possibly cut me some slack?'

'I can't authorise anything,' said Justin, who had clearly not been listening to much of what she said. 'I see that Mr Rivers has been corresponding with you about this. I suggest you talk to him.' He was friendly enough, but he raised his hands towards his sparsely bearded chin and said, 'There's nothing I can do.'

'I've tried to talk to Mr Rivers. He's simply never here! It's quite impossible,' said Rosa. She was gripping the table, holding on as if that would help.

'Mr Rivers is of course here regularly; he just happens not to be here today. But I can make you an appointment with him,' said Justin. 'Perhaps next Monday?'

We can do you a stripping of the self on Tuesday, a moment of epiphany on Wednesday, a spot of time on Thursday, but Monday – Monday we have to see Sharkbreath.

'Well, fine, next Monday. Fine,' she said, weakly. 'Good, count me in for Monday.'

Justin rustled through his papers and gave her a piece of card.

'These are the contact details for our debt management counsellor,' he said. 'I suggest you talk to her. Or to Mr Rivers. Try him first thing on Monday.' He nodded her away, and started typing on his computer as she said goodbye.

She grabbed her coat and a scarf and left the building. When she was on the street she ran along panting like a hound. The bus passed as Rosa ran up to the stop, and she saw the road behind was clogged, so she clenched her fists and carried on. LYLA, said the sign. A STAR REALLY WILL FALL. And soon. THE KILLS were still celebrating the launch of their single. Looking up at the sky, she walked along the street where everything moved too slowly and the cars got wedged in queues, and the buses shambled through it all, creaking and groaning. She was passing a herd of diggers breaking up the road, and a grey house with a view of the shattered street. She was passing the late-night shop and the funeral parlour and the cars were queuing at the lights but now there was a sense of elegy to it all because she knew she was leaving soon. The departure made her mark time. Nearly three months since she had come here. She shook her head. Celestial Stairs. Equal People. Pink and blue houses. Sketchy cab company. Handsome trees. Demoralised fast food restaurant. Crumbling high rise. Factory wasteland. Metal grilles. Pile of rubble. And the billboard and HERE COME THE TEARS. Her head ached, and she wondered why she was going back to Jess's flat. *To do what?* she thought. She stopped on the street, uncertain, panic making her guts churn. If she went back, what would she do? Make calls, stare at the street, commit resolutions to paper. *It was better to stay outside*, she thought. And she thought she should go to see Andreas. *No conceivable reason why not*, she thought. *He told you not to go away. He could be pleased to see you. Go and ask him.* She gritted her teeth, clenched her fists. It was of course necessary. A simple question, and then she would earn, she hoped, a reprieve. She was bold and if not resolute then at least she was moving again, cutting away from Ladbroke Grove, turning onto quieter streets. How well she knew these shadow-brushed streets, her refuge in the evenings. She told them off, one by one – Chesterton Road, Oxford Gardens, Cambridge Gardens. On a corner she passed two lovers, kissing and holding hands. Then she saw a woman standing at her front door, waving at a friend who was walking away. A man parked a car, laboriously, tugging it backwards and forwards. It had been raining and there were still puddles on the roads. The cars splashed through them, dispersing water. Rosa said, 'You've really been handling things badly,' quietly, keeping her face behind her scarf. Then she said, 'No more fooling around. You have to find a place to stay. You have to get a job. In the short term, you have to get that money from Liam. You don't want it? Of course you don't. You don't want anything! But I insist you go and get it. You'll have to be very calm and quite purposeful, and there's no point trying to scuff your shoes like that, dragging them along in such a childish way, because that won't make any difference at all. You're just slowing yourself down – of course you want to miss out again! I insist you turn up there, prepared to give it your all. Otherwise, what will you do? Do you have a plan B? There's no fairy godmother preparing to save you. No one will help you! You have exceeded the proper bounds of debt. That's the brutal truth of it . . .' and now she dropped her voice, because she was passing a woman and some children. They all walked up the steps of a house, and disappeared inside. 'They won't help you either,' she said. 'No point staring over at them. You understand the situation, don't you?' A taxi went past her, and to her left was a large church. Her limbs were heavy. If she could just sit down, if there was just a bench she could sit on, she thought. A quick rest and then she would go and sort everything out. She would do everything she had to, happily, after a pause on a bench. 'No way,' she said. 'Come on, no tricks. It's too late. Remember?'

She moved slowly, looking everyone up and down. At the corner she saw a preacher with his hands full of papers. But she didn't want to listen to him and she kept on walking. She turned onto Blagrove Road and walked under the Westway. A STAR IS GOING TO FALL. Of course, the shudder of trains, the rumble of cars. She heard the skaters in their fenced-off compound. A sign said MUGGERS BEWARE. She wondered at that and moved on. Opposite were the yellow bricks of a complex of flats. The skate kids had helmets on, and when they fell they laughed. Where the Westway seemed to curve above her, spinning its sides like a bowl on a potter's wheel, she crossed the bridge. The underside of the Westway was still eloquent. She saw *TEMP* and something next to it, something she hadn't seen before, *SOPH*. *SOPH*, marvellous, she thought. She had failed to understand the *TEMP* and now they had slung her another clue. That made her shiver. *SOPH*. *SOPH*. *SOPH? Sophisticated. Sophistry. Sophos*. It might be wisdom. Of course, she was lacking in it. They all were, wasn't that the point? *TEMP* for SOPHOS – it was certainly time for wisdom. Sometime soon, she hoped. She simply couldn't carry on in this state of foolishness for ever. And now she wondered why she was thinking about these words that some drunken man had scrawled and perhaps fallen to his death before finishing them. Abbreviated, that was all. Perhaps they meant very little in the end.

TEMP and *SOPH* she thought, moving on. Now a woman passed by holding an umbrella. She heard the clatter of the trains, the staccato thud of wheels on the track. She saw the rusted underbellies of the carriages and watched as they swung past her, moving out of sight. The motion soothed her; she thought of boarding a train and sleeping until she arrived – wherever, at the terminus, somewhere far away, waking to a still sky. As she walked she remembered a journey she had once made on a night train through France, and how she had seen the moon obscured by clouds, and listened to the breath of a stranger in the bunk beneath her, a polite woman who had asked her which bunk she preferred. Through the night the train accelerated and slowed again, the scream of the brakes disturbed the woman below, and her breathing changed. There was a clash of wheels on metal, and a sound of low speech and laughter, and Rosa had thought the voices sounded like people she knew. Some of them were English travellers. She remembered lying on her side so she could stare through the window. Waiting at the stations for the grinding of the wheels to start again. She saw lights in rows whipped backwards as the train moved faster. The train roaring at the oncoming blackness, emitting a low groan as it sank into a tunnel.

She had always had a passion for travel, for the steady progress of a train along a track, or better still the dream-stupor of a long-haul flight, the dimness of the cabin lights as the plane surfed on the air and blackness stretched away, the hum of the engines as the plane descended, moving towards land portioned into patterns of fields, sliced by roads. She was thinking that she must really get away, travel somewhere and start again, take a trip to mark her resolution, draw a line under this period of her life. *You must get out of this square mile*, she thought, *you must change your mode.* That was surely a good thing to do. As soon as she got her hands on a bit of money, that bit of money Liam owed her, she would take a trip elsewhere, try to start again. She walked onto the footbridge. She saw the pale sun. It looked like a theatre prop, it was so plain and perfect. Everything was still and yet as she walked she – who wandered around London all the time – felt afraid. She began to pick her feet up faster, slapping them down and trying to hurry. Her hair was blown about by the wind and she heard footsteps behind her; they rang out clearly. Rosa kept her eyes firmly on the street beyond the bridge and thought it wasn't far now, just twenty metres or so and she would be on the other side. She kept looking up at the sun, like a beacon beckoning her on. The noise of footsteps coming closer made her heart beat faster. There was someone behind her, someone she couldn't quite turn round to look at because she felt something might happen. Someone was right behind her, snuffling and grunting. She was almost at the end of the bridge, she could see Tavistock Crescent in front of her, and the snuffling was getting louder and now she thought she could hear words, a low murmur. She became quite rigid and superstitious, thinking she couldn't turn round, so she quickened her step, and the steps behind her seemed to follow. She could hear them, ringing out on the bridge. And in the background, distant now, she could hear cars and trains, rattling and grumbling, and now on the arches she saw *TEMP* in the guttering, sprayed uncertainly, this *TEMP* had almost faded. A wrong turn? she thought. She saw houses silhouetted against the sky. She heard her breath quicken, and found her hands were drenched in sweat. Her skin was prickling with fear. She was trying to walk faster but her legs were stiff and heavy. She said 'Hello?' in a tentative voice. She turned suddenly, saw a man dragging his heels in the leaves. He was walking towards her. It startled her, and for a moment she couldn't get her breath. When she looked at his face she saw a bloated jaw, eyes set close together. A toad-face, certainly, she thought. The same one as before? Or another one? The bridge was empty and beyond that was the quiet road. He was staring straight ahead, not seeing her at all, intent on following a straight line across the bridge. Feeling foolish she quickened her step and walked on. Behind he was still grunting to himself, muttering words she couldn't hear. She craned her head round again and saw him staring at her, nodding his head. That was enough for her, and she turned on her heels and started to run.

A train slammed under the bridge and for a few steps she could hear nothing but the thud of wheels on tracks. She half expected to feel a hand on her shoulder, and that made her shiver and pick up speed. She kept running, determined to get to the end of the bridge. She had an idea that she would be safe then, optimistic and plainly irrelevant though it was. She was so convinced about this that when she came to the end of the bridge she breathed more easily. But she was still afraid and she kept walking until she had rounded a corner and stepped into a broad and populated street. Then she turned her head and saw there was no sign of him behind her. She only saw the trees bowing in the wind and the pale sun.

She knocked on Andreas's door, preparing for an awkward pause, but he wasn't there at all. As she waited she saw a mother and child in the playground behind her. 'Good, darling! Good!' She smiled at the mother, but the mother was busy with her child. As Andreas was nowhere to be found, she felt in her pockets for a pen and paper and left him a note.

Dear Andreas, Hope you've had a good couple of days. Me, it's been bliss. The gyre, whirled in the gyre, something like that. Anyway, psychological onanism aside, may I have a bed for a few nights? I promise not to linger. All was black and entombed but now – but now . . .? Speak to you soon, Rosa.

She tore that up.

Andreas, hope you're well. Just dropped round. You're rehearsing, most likely; give me a call when you can. Wanted to ask you something. Love, Rosa.

She stuffed that through the door, as a compromise solution, and then she decided to go to Kensington Gardens and sit there until she came up with a plan. And if she failed then Kensington Gardens was a better place than most to abandon hope. Keeping an eye on the crowds, she walked slowly. Hordes of people were drifting in and out of organic food shops, designer boutiques. She darted round a family group, the mother with her hand on the shoulders of her children, staring into the window of a health food shop. She was walking towards Bayswater, muttering into her collar, saying, 'These are the things you have to do. They're all extremely simple. A fool could do them. This means you are worse than a fool. Your phobia of the telephone, your inability to ask for help, are quite pitiful. As if you can afford to be so reluctant! It's quite simple, what you must do, and do now, today,

241

before another night falls. Ask Andreas for a place to stay. Ask Liam to sell the furniture. Now!' Muttering along Bayswater she turned into Palace Green and stared like a child at the high houses with their electronic gates. A few were embassies, flying flags, and the rest were the anonymous homes of the wealthy. 'But don't start on that theme again,' she said. 'No point in craving luxury. Merely desire something better than debt.'

At Kensington Gardens the light was trickling through the branches of the trees, and even the dullest objects, benches, bits of bollard, had a halo around them. She crossed a wide lawn with the palace at her back. She walked around the perimeter of the lake, eyeing the white water. She was walking towards the sculpture of a man leaning backwards on a horse. When she came closer she saw it was called *Physical Energy*, and someone had written above that, *Human Imagination*. She heard the slurred whisper of wind in the grass. It really was an ending, she thought, with Liam walking down the aisle and her overdraft so seriously gone. There was a definite sense of culmination to the day. A phase was passing, in her own unique and miniscule life. She stared across the park, at the lines of oaks and trees with their branches pruned into stumps. The solid trunks, matted with moss, made her happy for no reason at all, except that they were old and grained with age. It's the irregularity of the trees that makes the park so beautiful, she thought. If they were standing in rows it wouldn't be as fine. That decided, she walked along a thin path, and found herself at a crossroads. The signs said: *Peter Pan. Italian Fountains. Serpentine Gallery. Queen's Temple. Flower Walk.* The signpost made her smile, with its careful options for pleasure, and she crossed the road and stood above the river, looking over a pavilion with white columns and the slung ring of the memorial fountain. In the background, above the buildings of the centre, she could see the London Eye. There was a Labrador running along the path, and behind it ran – more slowly – a batch of aged joggers. They went past her on sinewy legs. She heard distant sirens and the background hum of traffic, planes whining in the clouds.

It was getting late already, and she couldn't think where the day had gone. Her panic had propelled it forward, this sense of culmination. The park was almost empty. She passed a flock of geese, and some grebes – the word came to her, though she wasn't sure what they were – with white faces. For quite some time she sat on a bench, staring at a blank page, pen in hand. The ducks were dipping their heads in the water, spinning slowly around. *Temp for Soph*, she thought again, and wondered if that was what it meant. Or was it *TEMP of SOPH*? Then *TEMP* wasn't time, it was temple. *TEMPLE OF SOPHOS*, she thought. *TEMPLE OF WISDOM*? All this running around and it was under the bridge, in the folds of the Westway, all along! The entrance to the meaning of things – she only had to find it. She only had to furnish herself with a few of the basics, and then the sign was there. Displayed vividly, hardly a cryptic clue at all! She was trying to convince herself, but something didn't work. She couldn't think clearly at all; her thoughts couldn't alight on a single theme. Always there was the sense of the day drawing on. *While you wait for Andreas to get home, write this article for Martin White. At least do that, do that now.* So she stayed there with her pen and paper and after an hour she had made the startling discovery that she couldn't write the article. The same old problem. She sat there, livid with frustration and then she wrote: *I suppose I thought I should understand things better. I spent my time explaining things to other people. It seemed ridiculous, to trot out other people's ideas while having none of my own, no sense of things at all. And I was concerned with strings of life*, she wrote. *In the universe, there is dark matter, they have little idea what it is. Imagine! No idea at all! This substance, quite beyond us all. That troubled me and I wanted to find out more. But I've realised that if you really want to do this – really want to strip yourself down and plunge into the depths – you have to*

243

be prepared to be Diogenes, or worse. Worse than him, even!
You have to be prepared to become a real old tramp on a
bridge. And she wondered if the toad-face was Diogenes; she
wondered that while she tore up the piece of paper and scattered the pieces on the floor.

TEMP is the TEMP that means nothing at all, she thought.
SOPH means the SOPH that is Stop Oh Please Help! Stop
now! Temple of Wisdom. Something on the stones. There was
a burst of music from inside a car, and she heard the sound of
hooves on the riding track. *Now is definitely the time,* she
thought. *Surely now, you can think of something?* She sat for
a while longer, and then she wrote: *Really, it's the furniture*
that will save you. The rest you can try – Jess, Andreas, your
father, but that furniture money is the only actual claim you
have. It's a just claim, and Liam has been inexplicably reluc-
tant. It's not as if the man lacks money! Just go and see him. Be
very calm. Present a coherent petition. But the thought of that
made her palms sweat and she lost her grip on the pen. Still it
was a fine day. She looked across at the taut shapes of the trees
and the water glinting like hammered steel. In the distance she
saw the Albert memorial, newly repainted, bright with gilt. A
man stood and stretched. He had been slumped on a bench,
reading a paper. Now he shook out his jacket and slung it over
his shoulder. He had a small face, his features packed close
together. He looked happy enough. Really it was impossible to
tell. Blurred and in the distance she saw a woman coming
along the path. As she approached, Rosa heard her shoes. She
was tapping along like a bird. The sun was shining on the windows of the houses and she stared up at the patterned blue and
white of the sky, clouds moving slowly. When she looked
again the woman was still tapping towards her. The sound
stopped Rosa's thoughts. All she could hear was this rhythmic
tapping and she noticed the woman was drawing a dog along
with her, a small black and white mongrel which was snuffling
into piles of leaves and litter. The dog snuffled under a rubbish
bin, and the woman yanked it away. Then they came along

again, each with their own sound, the dog panting and the woman murmuring to it in a low voice.

Hunched over her notebook, Rosa wrote: *there's a tendency – we all share it – to invent a false image of ourselves as an exceptional phenomenon in the world, not guilty as others are, but somehow justified in sinning because one is inherently good. Everyone else is damned and fallen but one – me, myself – is good. This is quite self-righteous, it leads to misunderstanding, not only of oneself but also of the nature of man and the cosmos. The goal is to disperse the need for such life ignorance, by reconciling the individual consciousness with the universal will. This is effected through a realisation of the true relationship of the passing phenomena of time – you, this woman, her dog – to the imperishable life that lives and dies in us all.*

Then she wrote, *Dear Rosa, This won't help you at all. Stop writing immediately, close your notebook and go and get some money.* She saw a flock of geese honking on the path, aware of the approach of the dog. The dog was moving towards them, and though the woman tugged him backwards, the geese, honking violently, vituperative with panic, lifted themselves into the air and flew across the water. They settled on the other side. Governed by instinct alone, she thought. Their own imperative. Doing precisely what is expected, acting in accordance with their conditioning. When Tolstoy watched the peasants, and found faith, it was something like that he saw. He understood it as faith, but it was an assessment of the real bounds of life, of life lived without comforts, or illusions, rather than in the pampered reality-denying rooms of St Petersburg society. Because these peasants lived this life lacking in artifice, or the degree of artifice enjoyed by a Russian aristocrat, Tolstoy assumed that faith must be a natural condition of life. She saw his logic, though she couldn't follow it. She felt there must be a way of living that was germane and inevitable, some natural mode she and the rest of the toads had forgotten. The woman walked past, tapping her heels along the concrete and dragging her dog behind her. 'Come now,' she said to her dog. 'Come immediately, now.'

A rite, she thought. *A culminating rite!* And Rosa stood and walked away. She swung from optimism to foreboding as she walked, oscillating like a pendulum. Her gait was uneven as she went towards Bayswater. She passed the long lawn and saw it was scattered with a few people. They were walking on the paths, not saying much. At the road she emerged into a lingering cloud of car fumes. A bus rattled past her. A cyclist dashed past, almost hit a lorry, swerved around a car, and turned right suddenly. All the cars honked. She had hurt her back carrying her bag the previous day, and she found she was limping slightly. But the thought that Jess was eagerly awaiting her departure, that her father was worrying about her, even as he played a lento game of tennis, that Andreas was puzzling over her note, made her pick up speed. Rocking a little from side to side, hardly graceful but still going forwards. She trod steadily, engrossed in her thoughts. At Notting Hill station she found another payphone. She spent a while in the phone box, fending off all comers, the tourist with a map, the backpacker wanting a hotel, but gone were the days when countless dozens bawled each other out of phone boxes. She called Whitchurch and Kersti, but they weren't answering their phones. She called Andreas a few times, and every time it switched to his cheerful message, optimism coursing along the line. *He'll think you're mad if you call him again*, she thought. One side of her brain was trying to persuade her to desist, but she was bi-cameral with desperation, and when she had been standing there in the phone box for a good few minutes thinking about pressing the numbers again she realised she was being a fool. Now she wanted to bawl, stand in the phone box weeping like a child. She gripped the phone and dialled half of Andreas's number. She slapped down the receiver, then picked it up and dialled half of his number again. Then she stopped. She prised herself away, and walked onto the street.

She thought of a few dozen unrelated things, but through them all the idea kept coming back to her, so she walked quickly past the tube and found herself outside the block of flats she once lived in with Liam. It felt strange as she pushed through the doors. She buzzed, she slapped her hand on the buzzer, but there was no reply. In the foyer, she had a lucky break with the concierge. She had known him when she lived there, bought him a few bottles of wine. She had always stopped and talked to him. She put him in the paper once, as a vox pop. He found it hilarious. So today he smiled broadly at her, a thick-necked man, his eyes shrouded in fat. 'Sorry to hear about you and him upstairs,' he said. He gestured upwards. For a moment she thought he meant God, and she span round thinking, *What does he know?* But then she realised he meant Liam. That was kindly, so she smiled and said, 'Thanks. All completely amicable.' She smiled through the lie.

'What have you been doing? Writing stories? The usual stuff?' he said. 'Any exclusives recently?'

She laughed uproariously. 'No no, none at all,' she said. At least that was honest. He had a shining bald head and an expression of tranquillity. You'll be less tranquil later, she thought, and she smiled and laughed and went off to the lift. She pressed the button to the eleventh floor, waited while she was carried upwards. Seeing her reflection in the metal walls she wiped a smudge from her nose.

In the silence of the corridor it wasn't clear why she had come. The place wasn't as she remembered it at all. Even the corridor seemed indistinct and unknowable. With a patched carpet beneath her, a smell of dust and chemicals around her, she waited. She took out her notebook and wrote: *Tomorrow they will be married and this particular small epoch will be over. But the trials will continue thereafter. Yim yam yum. Shantih Shakti Sha sha.* She wondered briefly if she might be a prophet, and no one had noticed. She might be the emissary of a banished god. *I come to deliver unto you the true divinity,*

Shakti Yam. They wouldn't entrust such a thing to a fool like you, she thought. She stood there for a while, counting minutes, feeling really sick at heart and then she heard the grind of the lift. She saw Liam before he noticed her. She stood up, and was about to say something when she saw he was looking at her, suddenly dismayed. His expression was unstudied, quite transparent. After all these months, she could read his furrowed brow, the action of his hands, his unsmiling mouth.

'Rosa. What are you doing here? How did you get in?' said Liam, walking towards her. He was certainly horrified. Of course it was the worst time. Anyway it looked as if she had come to beg him. Retract! She suddenly thought that tonight must be the rehearsal dinner, but he hadn't dressed himself up yet and must therefore be running late. The whole thing was beginning any minute! And here he was, in jeans and a jacket, looking as if he had just come in from the shops.

He wiped his arm across his face and said, urgently, 'Rosa, what's up? What are you doing here? My God, I have to get going. What can I do for you? Come on, quickly. What is this?'

He wasn't sure what to do, no one was sure, but he was weighted down with bags and in a hurry so with a brisk sigh he opened the door. Uncertain, Rosa followed him in. He turned and said, 'God, Rosa, come on. Christ, can you go? Can we talk when all this is over? Why now? I haven't seen you for so long? What is it that can't wait? Come on, because I really haven't time.' Really, he seemed quite agitated, and that surprised her. On the phone he was always so buttoned-up, almost laconic. He wasn't looking at her; he was unpacking the bags, hurling things into cupboards, hanging his suit on the back of the door. His gestures were automatic. Clearly he was trying to work out what to do. Meanwhile, she was struck silent by the flat. The place had been transformed; the hand of Grace was on it all. The white walls had been softened to a pale red. It oozed taste, but the shade was somehow sanctimonious. There were paintings on the walls, proper art, bought from a gallery, contemporary daubs and the rest. The

West Country prints had gone. The furniture was still there, all her and Liam's mismatched articles, but now there was a lot of rustic pine and oak as well. Everything was tidy, though the place was full of colour. The flat had been recast, and now it stood in crisp antithesis to the place as she left it. This seemed significant, almost as if Grace – despite her claims to the contrary – wanted to wipe away all trace of Rosa, obliterate the past, smash it to pieces. In the kitchen, which had been painted too, the surfaces were covered with wine glasses, left over from a pre-wedding party. A half-eaten cheese stood on the hob. It looked like a flat where people had fun.

Liam took off his jacket and put it over the back of a chair.

'What are you doing here?' he said, turning to Rosa. She could see he was angry. He never liked being put under pressure. It was his controlling instinct; he felt it as an assault. 'Come on, Rosa, what is it? What do you want?'

'I apologise for intruding,' said Rosa, getting her breath back at last. 'I'm aware of course, momentous things are happening. Love and the celebration of love. Marriage. A culminating rite! In honour of the profound shift, I have one last request. Then I won't bother you at all. I'm quite spun out. Really, as I said to you on the phone, I'd like to go away. Try harder, fail better next time, the rest. So, I just want the money for the furniture. It's not much. Just a token. Look at it all, arraigned around you.' And she waved an arm at it, though seeing it now in the sallow light of a dying day she nearly saw what he meant. The sofa was wrecked, and the table was stained with grease. The bed she imagined in a similar state. They had bought it years ago. It had lasted longer than their love, of course, and she briefly considered the nature of transience, though she knew that was hardly the point. The point was how much money she could get. It was her last chance to salvage something. That sent her muttering about the need for a gesture, to close things between them. 'A final act,' she said. 'A denouement.' Meanwhile, Liam was positively pacing around, really focused on his interrupted evening and the ticking of the clock. He was thinking of Grace, of course. Perhaps he expected her any minute, and Rosa thought that would be a shame because the scene would shift and gain a different theme. Grace would add her own variety of needless talk, and then Rosa would have to leave. Even now, Liam was trying to shunt her out. 'Rosa, you can imagine that now is not the best time,' he was saying. 'But I promise we'll sort this out soon. Not today, obviously. Or tomorrow. But I'm aware it's a question you want to discuss.' He wanted to sound strict. 'I'm going to call you a taxi. It's either that or I call the police.' He was trying to look imperious, drumming his fingers on the back of a chair.

'The police?' said Rosa. 'What the hell would the police do? Put you in prison for stealing my furniture! Call them!' But that fell flat. Liam looked her up and down and said, 'Now, Rosa, don't get upset.' On further scrutiny, he looked careworn. She thought he might have put on weight. Apart from all that, his presence was quite superb. He was lovely to observe, with his careful gestures, his delicate eyes. He was standing there, uncertain amid all this elegance, but still he was a coward, that hadn't changed. He was so thin-skinned and sedentary. The man was a tent, letting just anyone pitch him and set up camp in him. Tent-like, he said, 'There's no need for a fight. We will get you your share of the furniture money. It's no big deal.'

There was a flicker in Liam's eyes which Rosa couldn't understand. For a minute or so, she waited. She eyed the bouquets on the windowsill. Deep red carnations, very fine, a bucolic cluster of them. She wondered what Grace was wearing for the wedding. She thought the bedroom must have changed too. She imagined Grace's shoes on the floor, her clothes in the wardrobe and her books by the bed. The complete diaries of Virginia Woolf – of course she would have those, and an edifying biography or two, something about Amelia Earhart or Rebecca West. Books that said she was a strong and forthright woman. The flat was familiar and yet disconcerting, like a dream. Everything had been displaced. She turned towards the sofa and said, 'Aren't you going to ask me to sit down?'

Before Liam came she had been frightened, but now she was quite calm. Liam, however, was looking incensed, even stricken with rage.

'Rosa, it's so ludicrous, you being here. It's so sad and strange. Can't you understand?' He hissed that; he couldn't restrain himself. Was it excitement or fury? It was hard to tell. 'You must get out,' he said. 'I can't even think about this now. Whatever you want. I'll give you some money. What do you need? Come on, they'll be arriving soon.'

'That's right, I must get out! GET ME OUT!' said Rosa, but now she was talking too loudly. She wondered who were 'they' and when were they coming? What did they want? Liam observed a silence, looking uncomfortable. He had his hands clasped together, and he was hunched over at the breakfast bar. More than uncomfortable, he looked agitated, as if her presence was disturbing to him. She paced towards the bookshelf, looked out over a stack of books, the combined collections of Grace and Liam, lovingly merged together. That made her fret, and so she said, lying, 'It's not a question of need. It's a question of justice.' The phrase meant nothing, and Liam shrugged. Of course he knew her well enough. He could spot her empty rhetoric as soon as she spilled it out. He said, with his hands outstretched, as if he was trying to stop her, or at least slow her down, 'Rosa, come on, let's try to get through this. Tell me what you want?'

She wasn't relaxed; there was so much to see, and she kept glancing around at the exhibits, finding a shocking display on the kitchen wall, photos of Liam and Grace together in a series of places, on European holidays, in New York, standing on the Staten Island ferry with their arms around each other, in a desert, their faces oiled with sweat. There was something appalling about it, now she confronted it. Really it was tacky, quite disgraceful! It meant nothing to them, the past. They were mutable, in love with mutability, they accepted that things moved on. *The essence of time is flux, the dissolution of the momentarily existent, and the essence of life is time.* Absolutely, she thought, that doesn't help at all. Now she felt tired and she sat down on the sofa. She stared up at the ceiling, wondering if they had painted that too. She picked up a book and tried to read the title. Nothing registered, and she set it down again.

'Come on, Rosa,' said Liam. He wasn't relaxed at all. He was holding himself very straight, preparing to act. He walked towards her, lingering above her. Really he was quite fixed on his theme, determined that Rosa should leave. He was always monologic. 'I just want a token payment. It's not much,' she said. 'It's nothing at all. Closure, you know.' And she grimaced. She could see his nerves and rage. It meant little to her, that she had the power to worry him. It was a pyrrhic victory, to turn up and convince Liam just how much he dreaded her. She saw another picture of them on the mantelpiece, Grace supreme in a little red dress and Liam in cords and a blue shirt. On that one she was wearing a sparkling ring. They were a beautiful couple, of course. They were setting such store by this small thing their wedding. It was touching how much it meant to them. *And for this reason, and for many others, they must be happy together*, thought Rosa.

Suddenly Liam turned towards her, trying to look friendly. He had gained an air of slyness. He had always been cunning, but now it was sketched on his brow. 'Rosa, please cut me some slack here,' he said softly. He was leaning towards her. 'I know you don't want to wreck my wedding. I understand. It should never have dragged on like this. I just thought what you were asking was too much, and then I didn't think the furniture was actually worth anything. But today – well, it's a good day to come! Quite the best day to get me to agree to a deal! So why don't we say I'll send you a cheque? I'll have a look at the stuff again and work it out. I'll do it before I go away on the honeymoon. OK?' He was speaking through gritted teeth. Really he wanted to bawl her out, but he was trying to coax her. He was furious, she could see just how furious he was. She wished she could have been more magnanimous. For a moment she wanted to say that she was sorry, make a pact, resolve it all. She longed to do that, to forget every slight and say she was sorry for everything. She would have blamed herself, if she could just get the words out. Still she couldn't do it. What was it, defiance or a petty sort of pride that had such a grip on her?

'Good to see you, so set up,' she said. That was the best she could do, and it sounded hollow as she said it.

'Doing fine,' said Liam, in an embarrassed way. He clenched his fist. 'So that's everything settled then. I'll put a cheque in the post. I'm sorry not to have sorted it out. Things just got hectic.' He looked at the door. That was too prompt and final, and it made her remember that the last time she was here he had been lying fluently, preparing to sling her out. Now he was doing it again, saying anything he could think of to make her leave. It was his fixed and constant aim, and this shattered her good mood, stopped her feeling contrite. He looked at the door again. 'Liam, no,' she said, and suddenly she felt a sense of aversion, a rich coursing sense of disgust about the whole furniture debate, continued conversation between Liam and her, any reference to their former flat, the rest. She understood it was undignified. Kersti had been quite right. Odd, really, that Kersti had even called him up. She thought, suddenly, that Kersti must have made a joke of her. 'Hi, Liam, had another call from poor old Rosa. Yep, still nattering about the furniture. I can't stop her. What can you do? Can you help her?' A collective conspiracy, they had been working together all along. It made her feel ashamed. *And so you should be*, she thought. More than anything she wanted to leave, but leave with an assurance, some sort of quid pro quo, rather than being pushed out again by Liam triumphant. It was childish, but she minded losing every time. It got her in the guts, made her want to spit and cry. 'I don't care, I'll take whatever you want to give me. I don't care. It has enraged me, that you've made such a fuss about this. But I'm sick of feeling so angry. Anything, a couple of quid, fifty, a hundred, anything. It's better if I never speak to you again. Really, now I don't care about the money. Just give me something, and I'll go. Anything, a token, just to demonstrate you haven't lost your sense of –' She stopped. She couldn't think what she wanted to say. Everything sounded overblown. She let the sentence drop.

It surprised her, how weary she was feeling. And Liam was standing there, uncomprehending and distracted. Of course, the wedding! He was looking creased; he had dragon skin around his mouth. His skin was worn. Had she grown used to him when they lived together, stopped really seeing him? She had never noticed how close together his eyes were. He seemed birdlike, afraid.

Then the buzzer went.

'Fuck,' said Liam. 'Fuck, that's the others. Rosa, come on, let's go. Definitely time for you to go. We'll talk more as we go.' Suddenly, he dragged her off the sofa. Then he started pulling her through the door. At first she shook him off, quite lightly, though she was confused. His touch was strange to her, redolent, of course, of long ago, but different again, like the flat. Something in the atmosphere had changed. It was the sternness of his touch that made her uneasy. All the time they had lived together, he had never touched her like that, even when everything started to slide. It felt so curious; she couldn't quite absorb it. *I am finding this a fundamentally alienating experience*, she thought, with a nod to Freud. That was the sort of cant he liked. *I feel I cannot integrate myself into this moment. I suspect I am emotionally arrested.* Was that it? And what about you, Liam, she thought? She caught a glimpse of his eyes, staring ahead. He had her arm in his hand again, and they were moving through the door. She shook him off, but he grabbed her again. 'Come on, Rosa,' he said. 'Time to go.' Now he was pulling her along the corridor. Though she was reluctant, he was stronger and of course he had the stark motivation of his

wedding, the people in the lift, his best man, his brother perhaps, all of them in smart suits, preparing their speeches. He
moved her quickly along the hall. His grip was firm and quite
detached. As they went she said, 'Liam, there's no need to be so
smug. I was being quite reasonable. That was what I said. Pay
me a token. A bit of cash, that's all. Something that makes me
hate you less. Otherwise, think of me festering away, cursing
you. It can't be what you want on your wedding day!' She
raised her voice. She was shouting randomly as she was pulled
along and every so often she would say, 'Come on, Liam, what
about the money!' 'The damn money! The fucking ducats!'

'Rosa, that's enough,' he was saying. Already he was out of
breath. 'Really, you need help.' They passed the lift, and
because his friends were in there he dragged her further to the
stairs and banged open the doors.

Rosa was pushing at his arms. 'Gold!' she was shouting.
'The fucking gold!' For a moment she was in a blind fury; not
just about the money and her sense of panic but about their
wasted life together, his betrayal of her, this rage she had been
trying to convert into something else but which had sapped
her energy and made her hopeless, a whole host of things she
had failed to manage. She was stumbling under the weight of
her anger, quite reeling with it, and that gave him a chance to
bump her down a few more steps while she shouted words,
though she was hardly noticing what she said.

'Rosa, stop being crazy,' he gasped. 'I don't have time, surely you understand? It will have to wait!' And he was shouting
now, in his frustration. He was frantic about the time. Always
he was thinking about himself. It was surely unmeasured but
she wanted to bite him. All that violence she had thought of
and never had a chance to enact, really she wanted to head-
butt and pummel him. He was dragging her faster along, trying to draw her down the stairs. He had ten flights to go; it was
looking bad. She could see that in his fixed stare and the lonely curve of his mouth. That made her think of this discarded
period of her life; she felt him as he drew her along and was

transported, though the present was jarring, and this motion was making her feel giddy again. She remembered the way he smelt in the morning, the dry taste of his mouth and the warmth of his body. Though she had hated him in recent months, she recognised that. It came over her suddenly how familiar he was, and that was despite everything, the acts he had perpetrated and his all round treachery. Now she stopped struggling. Reluctantly she understood. It was all quite pointless, and besides it was the wrong time. She felt suddenly disgusted, with Liam for refusing to pay the money, and with herself for begging for it. He was scoring a last, emphatic point, even though he had smashed her to bits already. It enraged her that she couldn't just retreat, remain aloof. So she said, quietly, 'Fine, you're right. I'll walk. I'll go.' He dropped his arms, hopeful, and she began to walk down the stairs. He was still behind her. 'I feel sorry for you. I really do,' he said. 'I feel partly responsible, of course.'

She didn't bother to respond.

'I know you were unhappy with me, but now – now you seem much worse,' he said wiping his face. His skin was shining with sweat.

'Not at all,' she said. 'Really, you have to be less of a prig.'

On the sixth floor, with a nervous glance at his watch, he said she was walking too slowly, and put his arm on hers again. She got free and walked away. Then, because she was preoccupied, she tripped and fell, hitting her jaw on the banisters. He grabbed her and steadied her again. 'Rosa, are you OK?' She pressed her hand to her mouth. Now his hand shook when he touched her. He was shaking his head at her, looking sad. 'Rosa, I'm sorry about the way things worked out,' he said. 'And now you've hurt yourself.'

'That's fine, it's nothing,' she said. She could taste blood in her mouth, and she swallowed. She really wanted to cry, but it was pure self-pity. She was standing now, dabbing at her mouth, and he was holding her arms. His face close to hers. It was an intimate moment, redolent of course. Then she found she was saying something, it quite surprised her, because it wasn't really what she had meant to say, really it hadn't been her intention to say it at all. 'Liam,' she was saying, in a choked, wheedling voice that did her no favours, 'do you have to? Maybe you don't have to after all? Of course, she's a great woman. A marvellous friend. But do you have to? It just seems unnecessary somehow. It's a step too far. You know, I'm smashed already, there's no need for another blow. I'm out for the count! On the floor, really, I'm down there, right down there, scrabbling to rise but finding this fucking wedding, this whole ritual, love-celebration, whatever you're calling it, is too much. It's only a particle, of course, a piece of chaff in the wind, and if I add it in with the meaning of things and the point, the perfect point, and my need for cash and all the *TEMP* and the rest, of course it means almost nothing. But anyway it's too much, do you understand? Tasteless, too soon, prohibitively tasteless. Just outrageous! Staggering! Like felling someone with a ton of bricks then blowing them up as well! Don't you see? Can't you see how it feels if you're quite pulverised already and then someone says, "Oh God YAH we're getting married in a big stupid wedding with white bows everywhere and cascading arrangements of flora and the bastard crazy rest?"' The whole thing was out in seconds, her drooling petition. Now she saw him so vaporised, so insubstantial and preposterous, preparing for his luxurious wedding – it should have meant nothing to her, yet somehow it unnerved her, and she was spilling garbage in a trembling voice. 'What the hell has happened to you?' she was saying. 'What the hell happened?' It was futile and she dried up with a sense that she might – any moment, and clearly ridiculous – start to cry. *Too too solid flesh*, she thought, and then she thought, *Who the hell are you kidding? The time has long gone when you could have left here amicably, with a conciliatory wave. Now you just have to sidle out of here as soon as you can.* Liam had his arms round her, as she stood there gulping and flushed with shame, and she remembered their former passion, or former conspiracy, a conspiracy of concern for each other, and now she was trying to pull herself away. She shouldn't have come, of course. She had only been appalled by the discord between them, and the sense that Liam believed he was right, about the money and everything else. 'I'll go right away,' she said, rubbing her mouth, which hurt. The atmosphere had certainly declined. It was the most awkward place she had been for a long time. She was trying not to look him in the eye. He would think she was mourning the loss of him, the death of love, but now she understood – some knot had been untied, and here they were, separate, entirely distinct, hardly understanding each other.

She was emitting some bizarre sounds, trying to say, 'Well, let's talk about the money soon,' while Liam was saying, 'Rosa, please don't come back again.' His cheeks creased. His eyes looked rheumy. She realised he was moved. That surprised her, because she knew he had other things to think about, his romance of the present and his special day. 'I will sort out the money for you, I promise. I understand you should have some. Things have gone badly, I know. I'm sorry about it.' He thought he was making a beautiful speech. That made her angry all over again, and she turned to go, shaking with mingled fury and humiliation.

As she stepped away from him she felt she should have been more serious about everything, about her lack of discipline and the bank and her job prospects and her father. Clearly her coping strategy had failed. 'Do you need a tissue?' he said, politely. She shook her head.

'I've been out of sorts,' she said. 'Seeing you just brought a few things back. It's not important. I'm glad you're happy.' All of that came out in a rush, and now she thought of his friends upstairs with their top hats and carnations, waiting for him. 'Rosa, promise me you will take action,' said Liam. 'And I promise I'll send you a cheque. I'm aware I've been remiss.' That nearly made her smile. Action! She was already busy, trying to salvage her pride.

'Even the money,' she said, aware that her voice was unreliable, her overall demeanour was letting her down. 'You're right. The money really doesn't matter,' she lied. 'If it's so important to you not to pay it, though I really don't know why, then don't pay it. You know, forget it. Forget the furniture. Take it as a wedding present. Apply whatever significance you want to it. I've other things to think about, frankly. Have a great wedding, you know, good luck.' He didn't reply. He raised a hand to her, awkwardly, as she turned away.

Things to do, Thursday – this day you have redefined the definition of a fool, scaled new heights of foolery previously unimaginable.

Get a job
Find a place to stay
Explain to Andreas
Write the article for Martin White
Plough a field with bulls of flaming breath
Slay the armed men who spring into being when you sow the field. Throw a stone in their midst, to cause them to turn face to face and attack each other.
Take the treasure and run. Legend dictates you should kill a man at this point, and throw him out. But try to escape without slaughter!
Unlock the TEMP and unearth WHAT?

As she walked away she was trying to look graceful. She went down the stairs, a hand over her mouth, passing the concierge who waved goodbye. She didn't try to speak.

Outside she stood for a moment under the shadow of the tower block. Briefly, she wondered if it was possible to expire with shame, to be felled by a sense of embarrassment and drop into the gutter. And then she wondered if it was embarrassment or disappointment, that she had seen Liam unmasked, grappling with her for nothing, money he didn't even want, tussling her downstairs to sustain his sense of righteousness. Indifference would have been the best response, scorn still better, yet she had failed to produce either. Now she was free to walk slowly through the evening streets, from Notting Hill towards Ladbroke Grove, past the white mansions with their doors locked, shutters down, windows barred tight. The day felt heavy and she tried to pick up her heels. Certainly morale had slipped. It had something to do with her failure to get money, even though this time she had come pretty close. Her conversation with Liam, until it declined into a pit of emotional cess, had been the best chance she had had in a long time. In this case alone she had a leg to stand on, she really did have a claim to some cash and she could have insisted, could have forced him to pay her. But she had given up, lost her ire – and why? Because she suddenly understood how ridiculous it was, how absurd she had been to enter into this contest, to allow him to sit there dispensing or withholding favours? All she wanted to do was forget him. She wanted to stop thinking about the money, about the scraps he was refusing her. That was all foolish enough, and she bowed her head. Leaves gusted on the pavement. She stepped around a puddle and heard a clock chiming in the distance. It was 7 p.m., and everything was almost over. She walked along watching the lights in the windows of the houses, those tall bright houses with palm trees in their gardens. When she looked into the rooms and saw their vivid normality she felt calmer. Still she found she was talking as she went, struggling to make sense of recent events. 'The whole thing! So futile. What were you thinking? That he would repent? That you would calmly discuss the wrongs you had committed, and resolve a pax?' It made her shiver. She passed a man who was coughing on the corner. A woman walked past, arm in arm with a girl who looked like her daughter. They were genetically identifiable, both with the same sling of their hips and long blonde hair. 'And now he's getting into his suit, quite relieved. Putting on his cufflinks, with a steady hand.' *Stay with Andreas for a day or so. Then find somewhere else to live. Write this article for Martin White. Visit Sharkbreath and beg him for compassion. Tell Yabalon you're not afraid. Borrow from Jess –* but there would be no talking to Jess now.

She arrived at the Westway with blisters and a bloody mouth. She walked quickly, scuffing her shoes on the street. The evening was cold and still. She hadn't eaten for a while, but she wasn't hungry at all. She felt her lip, which was slightly swollen. She wondered if one of her teeth was looser than usual; she pushed it with her tongue. At the corner of her street she sat on a crumbling wall. She was crying a little and she had sweated into her shirt. She watched the windows of the houses, imagining successive lives. Tomorrow they wouldn't be quite the same. An imperceptible change would have occurred, some small shift in their cells. She put her hand in her bag, checked she had her papers and her passport. She turned the key in the door and walked into the darkness of the stairs.

She came round; it was as if she had returned from a deep trance. She found she was sitting in Jess's flat, in the pink living room, with her face to the wall. She was confused for a moment, and she wondered whether Jess was there too. Then she remembered it was the night before Liam's wedding and that Jess was at the rehearsal dinner. She was beside herself and didn't know what to do. She must have been crying for a while, sobbing like a child or a fool, because her eyes were stinging and she had a thick headache. She allowed herself another bout of tears, but it hardly helped and she began to writhe at the sight of herself, sitting in a borrowed room crying about what? Her sense of time wasted? The whole thing was absurd, she thought, pressing her hands to her eyes. She was acting like a sap! The most sap-like she had been in months, and that made her shudder with shame. She was adrift in a small room, and she felt alone and despised this sense of solitude. She thought of the rehearsal dinner, everyone in a pool of light, smiling and shouting greetings to each other. But that was ignominious; she understood it was too predictable that she would sit there sobbing to herself while Liam and Grace got themselves hitched in a whirl of bows and satin. Even in her confusion, she despised the cliché, the sense that her life was playing itself out in so generic a fashion. She was fodder for a silly story, a basement piece in the middle of August, a missive from the world of nothing. And that made her stir herself. With her hands trembling, she wrote to Martin White. *Thanks again for the commission. I'll try to have the article with you by the end of the week.* He hadn't even set a deadline. That was fortunate, though she had to force herself to write. *You must galvanise yourself. That's really the thing.* She called Andreas, and he picked up the phone, half asleep.

'Yes,' he said, his voice muffled.

'Andreas, hi, it's Rosa,' she said.

'Rosa, dear girl, it's the middle of the night.'

'I'm very sorry. Very sorry indeed. I forgot the time,' said Rosa. And he was right, she saw it on the clock, 2 a.m. blinking a reproach at her.

'Well, tomorrow. Talk then. I have to rehearse all day. Evening. Speak evening.'

He was friendly, but exhausted. He could hardly speak. Fundamentally, he was asleep.

'OK, speak to you then,' she said.

'OK,' he said, and she thought of him dropping the phone and reclining again. He would be asleep in a second, and she counted him down, thinking of him drifting into sleep, falling, and now, Andreas was unconscious, she thought. Then she kicked the phone cord out of the socket, went to her room and whined herself to sleep.

She was woken by the buzzer. It jolted her into consciousness. She waited for Jess to take it, thinking she should stay as still and quiet as possible. She sat hunched on the bed, her chin on her knees, then the buzzer disturbed her again. There was no sign of Jess as she walked through the living room and found the intercom in the half-light. She pressed the button.

'Delivery for Rosa Lane,' said a voice. It was so unexpected that she didn't know what to do. She paused before she answered. A delivery? A book from her father? There was a danger it might be. A guide to being. Something benign and essentially unhelpful. Another of his articles, stapled in a neat folder? Or something else, some sort of punitive measure? A summons from Sharkbreath! Perhaps it was today she would be set upon by Sharkbreath's gang, toad-faces the lot of them. Still, she pushed a button and heard the door click open. She saw the messenger's head vanish inside. Then there were footsteps on the stairs, and after a while he hammered on the door. *My God*, she thought. And she felt entirely resigned, really they could take her, she didn't care any more. It's all become quite too much, she thought. Existentially, she had become supine. Besides she was half-asleep and her face was stiff from all her sterling efforts of the night before. She found a jumper on the sideboard and put it on. Then she switched on the light. Opening the door she was surprised to see a courier, wearing leathers. He had a slim envelope in his hand, which he held towards her.

'What is it?' she said.

Of course he didn't know. 'You'll find out when you read it,' he said, with a friendly nod of his head. You'll find out later, all of it, she thought. Then he went away and she heard him thumping down the stairs.

Uncertainly, she opened the envelope. There was a piece of paper, a note in Liam's writing. Written in haste, it said: *Dear Rosa, Here it is, and that really has to be all. Sorry, and love as ever, Liam.* And there was a cheque for five hundred pounds. That made her sit down suddenly on Jess's sofa. For a while she held the cheque and couldn't understand it at all. She kept looking at the cheque, then looking again at the note. She read *love as ever* again and found it was an odd thing to write. Really he had stopped loving her long ago. But he was sentimental. The cheque proved that. She hadn't turned to look at him as she walked away, but something in that final scene made him rush for his wallet. It was his guilty conscience that made him sign, or perhaps he was paying her off, bribing her not to cause any more trouble. It was for Grace's health; he saw it as an investment. Money was nothing, for that sort of thing. He wanted to cleanse himself, enter the holy state of matrimony absolved of his sins! He signed it in a hurry and sent it over, because he was late. While he was tying his cravat he asked his best man – who was that? Lorne? Or some friend of his from school? – to phone the courier. 'Bit of trouble at work,' he said, lying into his top hat. Well, it was characteristic. He wanted her tidied up, the swine. Still, he didn't want to pay what she had asked, and he couldn't resist a self-righteous flourish. *That really has to be all.* Who said so? Liam, and no doubt Grace too, if she knew about it. Both of them so reasonable, they thought, gatekeepers of the rational world. That made her angry for a while, and she thought of a dozen ways to spite him. She screwed up the cheque – but not too much – and threw it on the floor. She stood and walked to the tap, drank down a pitcher of water, dribbled most of it out because her lip was swollen and her tooth ached, said, 'The cunning cunt', and then she sat down on the sofa again. Then she bowed her head suddenly because she thought it might be compassion. She read *Sorry, and love as ever*. Sorry for what? Sorry it wasn't more? Sorry for everything? Sorry that she had made such a fool of herself, one last time? Of course things had been bad between them. She had loved him, and now the old sense of him came coursing over her; she was quite aware of Liam as she had known him and longed for him daily, and this made her want to cry out. She understood that things had become bitter. He was so closely associated with it all, her lost mother, the blankness that descended and a lot of accompanying mental debris. She had focused it on him, weighted him down with it. They had both been imperfect, hopeless. She couldn't know for certain. Then she thought if it was so easy

264

for him to do it now, why had he waited so long, why had he forced her to produce a haphazard entreaty? Once she had emerged, humiliated herself, he scrawled a cheque. The note was scribbled, too; she knew his writing well enough. He had been in a frantic hurry. For a moment she thought of the heroic gesture; she had a full-bodied, fleshed-out vision of herself marching to the church, tearing the cheque up on the steps, throwing it in with the confetti, then she picked up the cheque, smoothed it out and put it in her bag.

Indifference is the thing, she thought. It hardly mattered what she had done to get this money. It was hers, and she had achieved it. It was a scabrous small triumph, and it wasn't enough, but it was hers all the same. Liam is sorry, she thought, and then she thought, Sorry for what? Then she shook her head. As if it mattered what he was sorry for! As if it mattered at all, as he wrote the words, hardly thinking about what he was writing, and ran out of the door in his morning suit. She stood in Jess's living room, in a valedictory mood. Now it came to it, she thought she was sad to go. She had always liked the steady drift of the familiar. As she picked up her clothes she found an interwoven pattern of coffee stains on the carpet in her bedroom. That was a further shame. Now she dressed quickly. She cleaned her teeth, checking herself in the steamed-up mirror. Her eyes were baggy and she had looked better. But that would change, she thought. She wrote: *Dear Jess. Thanks again for your hospitality. I took a lettuce leaf and a bit of tea, for which my apologies. In general I have committed several crimes which will weigh against me in the final reckoning. Recently I bled liberally into your shoes. I twice used your shampoo. I ate your chocolate yesterday and I drank a glass of your orange juice. Really, I ripped through your cupboards like a locust. Yours, Rosa.* Then she smiled and ripped up the note. She wrote: *Jess, thanks very much indeed. Now I've really gone. Send me any further bills – I'll email details. Vade in pace, Rosa.* She was propelled by an urge to escape. She felt them all around her, the ambiguous hordes, bank tellers and all the rest, offering maxims, telling her what to do. She simply had to shake them off. She packed her bag – her clothes and boots and her couple of books and all her unassembled papers – in an instant, and walked through the flat. She tidied the hall, and pulled on her coat. She picked up her bag, and walked out into the daylight. She posted the keys back through the letterbox, and heard them clink onto the mat. Then she started moving along Ladbroke Grove, breathing in the fumes of the morning, dragging her bag behind her. The Westway was full of cars and the clouds were scudding above her. She raised her head to watch the cars and clouds.

At the bank they wanted the money to be deposited, used to sop up some of her debt, but she talked them into doling out cash. With the posters behind her ARE YOU MAKING THE MOST OF YOUR MONEY? ARE YOU PILING IT UP AND COUNTING IT DAILY? DO YOU DREAM OF PILES OF GOLD? she explained that she would be working again soon, and this money was required 'to supplement my business wardrobe,' she said, smirking and biting her nails. The kid sniffed, a new kid called Dave, and slapped the notes down. This meant her wallet bulged attractively, giving her a powerful if fleeting sense of security. She was leaving Sharkbreath far behind, but one day she would go and see him. She would walk in and announce triumphantly to the sceptical zipper-priestess Mandy that she had a deposit to make. She would clasp the toad-faces by the hand. Not now, but some time soon, and if not soon – Well, then she would consider it later, she thought.

In the Underground she thought of herself a few months ago, going in the opposite direction, having walked out of her job. It was nine months since the death of her mother. She marked that blankly, trying not to think beyond the facts. The months coursed on; she had lost a lot of time. The train was looping round towards Waterloo. She had missed the rush hour and the carriage was half full. A sign above her said LET US HELP YOU TO HELP YOURSELF and there was a picture of a woman smiling broadly. She wasn't sure if she was running away or regaining something. She had in mind what she wanted to do, to return to a state she had previously accepted as ordinary, a state in which she could think quietly about things. It was a long way back, she thought, recalling her desperation of the night before, her drooling incontinence and plain despair. Then, she had certainly been incapable of moderation. She had failed entirely to set aside the concerns of the self. There had been that period of blankness, when she couldn't remember what she had done at all. That frightened her a little, and she turned to stare at the man to her left, a shiny-faced man of fifty or so, wearing a shabby mac; his shoes dirty. He flicked a glance towards her, cold-eyed and indifferent, and she dropped her gaze.

Everything was going well enough, until at Waterloo she suffered a moment of indecision. She stood under the clock, watching the lines of people moving across the forecourt and she thought of going home to her father, and then she thought of leaving the country. Andreas was in her mind, too. She saw these choices like paths in a forest, and she was unsteady for a while, not sure which way to turn. She had her bag behind her, her pared-down possessions, and she felt suddenly tired and as if she could hardly stand. She wanted to lie down and sleep. She was being scuffed and buffeted by the crowds, people moving past her, constant motion, and each person who pushed past glanced back at her, as if her stasis was a crime. *The condition of everything is flux*, she thought, and then she shook her head. She thought of calling Andreas but then she remembered she had woken him, left obscure messages, hoping he would supply her with something, a bed for a few nights, another temporary solution. Anyway, it was too much to ask; he was a kind, loving man, but he wanted to act and he wanted to enjoy himself, be young, live well. She couldn't go back and lean on Andreas, assuming he even wanted to serve as a crutch. She was banged hard in the shoulder as a man rushed past her, hurrying to catch a train. He was late and he didn't turn back. She was a rock in the current, she thought. You couldn't stay here for ever. Eventually they probably winched you out, or poked you with a cattle prod. She was standing there, martyring herself to the ebb and flow, still nervous and undecided, when she saw a billboard high above her saying TEMPERANCE. That made her crane her neck and stare. It summoned something, another strand she had failed to develop. It was noon and Rosa was thinking of Liam and Grace and the whispering church. *TEMPERANCE*, she thought. *Was that the meaning of TEMP? TEMP means Temperance, that was what the taggers had been saying. And then what about SOPH?* And she thought of the vicar and the church and 'Do you?' 'I do.' 'Do you?' 'I do.' Well, that was it, rings exchanged, a kiss, the rest. They would be delighted, of course. Everyone, and she thought of Liam's mother wiping tears from her frosty cheeks. Flowers – of course there would be a lot of flowers. The altar would be decked. Garlanded the pews. She could imagine a fine bucolic row of them, chosen by Grace's mother. It would all be sublimely tasteful. Beautiful, if you liked that sort of thing. She wondered at it all, and then she stopped and thought, *But perhaps that's it. Perhaps*, she thought, *TEMP could be Temperance.* SOPH would mean Sophrosyne which meant *temperance, or moderation. Wisdom in moderation.* The right way to live – moderately, temperately – she remembered it now – it was Socratic, and came from 'Charmides', she thought. She was standing in Waterloo station as the crowd swelled around her, realising she had forgotten about Zalmoxis. *How could you have banished Zalmoxis from your mind?* she thought, Zalmoxis who said that *temperance is a great good, and if you truly have it, you are blessed.* She gripped her bag and with her swollen mouth she said, 'Sophrosyne' loudly to the air around her. 'And to you too,' said a commuter with a flushed face, as he pushed past her and descended into the scrum. That gave her another jolt, and she tried to remember what she had been thinking. *Temperance*, she thought again, but she wasn't sure. Was that it, she thought?

It was impossible to know for certain. Well, she thought, if it was *SOPH* or something else altogether, how the hell was she to know? She had been worrying away at those signs, the *TEMP* and the *SOPH*, and now she thought she would take Sophrosyne as the meaning, or decide that was what it meant today. She didn't have to know it objectively; she only had to reach a compromise, a solution that meant something to her. The debate had only ever been hers anyway; there was no one begging her to give them an answer. Civilisations were not hanging by a thread, awaiting Rosa's pronouncement on the definitive meaning of *TEMP*. She looked up at the sign again. Still she was tired, and if there had been a bed for her somewhere, she would have retreated back to it. *TEMP meaning temperance or something else altogether. SOPH meaning Sophrosyne or nothing at all. Something to her alone. A small signal.* Be moderate. Well, it was a mantra she needed well enough. Of course she should be more moderate, and she thought of the people around her colliding and smashing a way past each other, going somewhere, she didn't know where. For a brief moment as she looked across this seething tide of people going to work, wearing their smart clothes, abandoned to the immutable system of money and the city, it seemed to make a sort of sense. Moderation, of course, she thought. The world kept on going and she only had a small part to play. She saw the Ferris wheel turning slow circles beyond the hangar of the station and the crowds flowing towards a train and she stepped onto an escalator, her heart thumping in her breast. And she thought to herself, *TEMP* means you are going to take the train. SOPH means you are going to leave the city. There wasn't really anything else to do.

With a low feeling of relief, she bought a ticket for the first train that was leaving the country, and that train was going to Paris. She would have gone to Brussels or Ghent, or wherever they sent her. She didn't mind. Now her heart was thumping; her nerves were on edge. Her tooth was definitely loose, but she would see to that later. She filed along the plat-

269

form, finding her seat, arranging her bag in the luggage compartment. She was so tired she hardly noticed her surroundings, and when the train pulled out she turned to the wall and slept. She slept deeply, until she was woken as the train began to pick up speed. Stirring in her seat, she turned to the window and saw the sky was wreathed in clouds. There was a plane moving through the sky, weaving a trail of smoke that coiled and floated and then disintegrated slowly. The day had been dull earlier, but now the sun was shining faintly. Trees were moving gently in a low wind, swaying towards the tracks. It was almost winter and the hedgerows were bare. The train was moving towards the outskirts of the country, where the land met the sea. Swiftly, it was passing steel containers. She saw the shapes of hills, grey-toned, shadowed by clouds. They passed a railway junkyard full of bits of track, rubbish, piles of concrete, and a ruined engine. There was a mound of rubble by the side of the track, moss at its tip. The automated voice was telling them all that smoking was not allowed on the train. She saw lines of cars and steel fences. She had left her notebook and pen on the table, a table she was sharing with a man who was reading *Le Monde*. She took her pen in her hand. Now she saw the sea ahead, glinting in the sunshine.

With a low moan the train went into the tunnel, and the lights in the carriage became thin streams of reflected colour. There were only a few people around her. The man opposite, with his newspaper, his head buried. A family, eating sandwiches. A few lone travellers, occupied with papers and books. It was very quiet, just the low grumble of wheels on tracks, and the fizz of the air conditioning. She took her pen and wrote:

Dear Father, I have gone to France. Sorry I have been so useless in recent months. It just got too much and I couldn't shift my thoughts. You were right. I'll find somewhere to live and work and write to you soon. I might stay in France or go fur-

ther away. I might stand in a grape press, working the grapes with my juice-stained feet, or I might find something else to do. I promise I will come and see you soon. Sophrosyne. All my love, my dear last parent.

Dear Liam and Grace, There is much I am sorry about. I never appreciated either of you, while I had you around. I thought that the two worlds, divine and human, could be pictured only as distinct from one another – different as death and life, as day and night. Really, it's clear that the two kingdoms are actually one, the realm of the gods is a forgotten dimension of the world we know. Best of luck sorting it out for yourselves. Yours ever, Rosa Lane.

Dear Martin White, she wrote. *Now I really will write the article. I can feel it coming on. I'm certain I'll have it with you soon. All best wishes, Rosa Lane.*

As the train rumbled through the tunnel under the sea, she stared out of the window and thought she would call Andreas when she got to France. *Dear Andreas.* She would explain that she couldn't come to see his play. She hoped they would meet again, when she had more money and a firmer grip on herself. *Dear Andreas*, she wrote. *Sorry I woke you. Thanks for everything. I have gone away for a short while. But I will see you soon. Love, Rosa.* Now she looked out of the window again, but in the darkness all she could see was her face, hovering, neither inside nor outside the carriage. *Dear Whitchurch*, she wrote. *Thanks so much, and goodbye.* It was 3 p.m. and the service would be over. They would be at a reception in some flower-draped parlour, everyone with a glass in hand. The couple illuminated by the flash of cameras. Holding each other tightly. Well, that was done. She nodded and thought at least it was over. Her father would be in his garden, talking Spanish to Sarah. Jess would be plainly relieved, sipping champagne with the rest – Whitchurch, Lorne in an oversized suit. Liam and Grace receiving compliments. Kersti would be smiling and patting them on the back. Perhaps Liam would give her a conspiratorial nod – 'Yes, we settled it.' But she thought he would keep quiet about it all. It would hardly be his main concern. Later they would all go back to their lighted rooms, with their views of brick walls and incessant motion. Andreas would be rehearsing his play somewhere in the south, shouting lines, his face flushed in concentration. Along the Westway the cars would be moving in slow files, and the trains would be snorting into Paddington and the city would be supplying dreams to the hopeful, pace and purpose to the uncertain.

To my dear mother, she thought. *I know that you wouldn't have wanted me to get so crazy about it all. I don't yet understand, nor do I accept it. I don't accept any of it. But I am trying to find a way to resume.* She didn't want to go back to her previous lack of thought, her blitheness. She had lost that, she hoped. If she could just get back some of her tranquillity, then she would try not to slide into blitheness again. Aware of the abyss, but not staring straight down into it, that must be the best way to be. *Es muss sein*, she thought, and she grimaced and wanted to pound her fists on the window. She shuddered and thought it was a long way down, and a long way up, and all she had done was board a train. Another train, and even last time she had thought that would prove the catalyst. *I don't want this to become normality, my dear mother. It must surely be a transient state.* She was crying slightly but she thought she could keep it measured. *I really will try this time*, she wrote, though she didn't know if that meant anything. She shut her eyes again, and listened to the sounds of the carriage, the rustling of papers, the rise and fall of voices. They were all drifting in darkness, fumbling around. Perhaps that was it, after all. That was moderation, anyway. And then she thought how damn ironic that was, that you should seek obscurity and positively embrace ignorance. That you should fashion your philosophy from the acceptance of unknowability. Still she gripped her pen and wrote: *Your loving daughter*. She made a surreptitious attempt to wipe her eyes. Resolution, she thought. She had to keep herself dry and quiet. The lights beyond were blurred and she saw grey tracks through the smoked glass. She heard the sweep of automatic doors behind her. *Bienvenue en France* said a metallic voice. A cold sun was shining. *Things to do, Friday this day you are leaving the city*, she thought. *Things to do.* When the train emerged from the tunnel she saw broad fields stretching away. Now Rosa set down her notebook and stared out at the sky.